Isabelle Grey began her career as a non-fiction author and feature writer for national newspapers and magazines before turning to television, contributing episodes to numerous drama series from *Midsomer Murders* to Jimmy McGovern's *Accused*. Her first novel *Out of Sight* is also published by Quercus.

Also by Isabelle Grey

Out of Sight

the Bad Mother

ISABELLE GREY

Quercus

First published in Great Britain in year of 2013 by

Quercus
55 Baker Street
7th Floor, South Block
London W1U 8EW

A CIP catalogue record for this book is available from the British Library

PB ISBN 978 0 85738 648 9
EBOOK ISBN 978 0 85738 650 2

10 9 8 7 6 5 4 3 2

Printed and bound in Great Britain by Clays Ltd, St Ives plc

Typeset by Ellipsis Digital Limited, Glasgow

For my daughter

PROLOGUE

A neat sign fixed to the fresh white stucco of the Victorian terrace read 'Seafront B&B'. Ed Fowler glanced up at the house number over the front door, one of those modern transfers that looked like etched glass, and rang the bell. He turned for a final look out to sea. It was an idyllic summer evening and the view could not have been prettier. He hated these calls. Most missing person enquiries were quickly resolved, but as he'd left the office his inspector had reminded him of the ACPO guidelines: If in doubt, think the worst.

The guidelines meant that for the next hour he'd have to be both reassuring and suspicious. It had happened in enough cases across the country that the worried parent – or more often step-parent – who reported the kid missing turned out to be its killer. It was important to take nothing for granted.

The door was opened by a tired-looking man in his early sixties. 'Mr Parker?' asked Ed.

'No, Hugo Brooks,' the man said, clearly encouraged by

the sight of a police uniform. 'Tessa Parker is my daughter. Thank you for coming. We didn't know what else to do. We're all downstairs.'

Ed followed him to a large basement kitchen where Hugo made the rest of the introductions. 'My daughter Tessa. And Mitch's father, Sam Parker.' Ed noted that Hugo declined to identify the father of the missing boy as Tessa's husband. 'This is my wife Pamela,' finished Hugo, taking a seat at the big pine table beside a thin, colourless woman.

Ed turned to Tessa Parker; she was probably in her mid-thirties, dark brown hair cut to frame her face and direct grey eyes that contrasted with her delicate features. 'It's your son, Mitch Parker, who's gone missing?'

'We've not seen him since yesterday evening.'

'How old is he?'

'Seventeen.'

'Has he gone off like this before?'

'Never.'

'He's very reliable,' said Hugo. 'Very conscientious.'

'Do you know what his plans were when you last saw him?' Ed picked up on the guilty looks exchanged by Tessa and her presumably estranged husband. It could be that there'd been a row and the kid had run off – happened all the time – but he'd have to wait to see it proved before he could relax. Meanwhile Tessa Parker was taking just that bit too long with her reply.

'He was upset,' she said. 'A problem with his girlfriend. He ran off.'

'Then he'll probably be back any minute,' Ed suggested with deliberate optimism. 'Have you tried phoning him?'

'His phone's turned off.'

'Have you spoken to his girlfriend?'

'She left for America yesterday.'

'Is she American?'

'No, English. But her mother's working over there.'

'Could Mitch have tried to follow her? Teenagers do sometimes get crazy ideas. Have you checked to see if he's taken his passport?'

The brightness in the mother's eyes made Ed hope, too, that this one *was* just a runaway, but he could also see from the father's unease that he was burning up with shame over something. Sam Parker didn't look the type to be violent – a boyish sort of man – but Ed knew enough never to trust appearances. The grandparents seemed to be in shock, but at least they weren't the interfering type: they sat mutely together at the end of the table, watching and listening.

Ed took a closer look around. The rear windows of the half-basement were wide open, and warmth seeped out of the Aga, but it wasn't a homely room; this was a place of business, filled with stainless steel machines, labelled storage boxes and efficiently stacked bulk catering packs. On one wall was a whiteboard with names listed beside room numbers and boxes ticked to indicate choice of newspaper or vegetarian options. There were no fridge magnets, family photos, school projects or even postcards. 'What about your guests?' Ed asked. 'Are you able to give me a list of who's been staying recently?'

'Yes, of course. It's all on the computer upstairs.'

'Was Mitch particularly friendly with any of them?' Ed asked.

'No.'

'Any regulars who took an interest in him?'

'No.'

'Do you mind if I take a look around, Mrs Parker?' This was always a tricky moment, when it first dawned on families that, however genuine the police officer's concern, they might also be considered as suspects.

'No,' she said weakly. 'No, of course not.'

'I'll need to search the guests' rooms as well,' he told her.

'Most of them have gone out for dinner, I think.'

'Perhaps you could go up ahead of me and check who's there? Let them know?'

But Tessa sank into the nearest chair, and Ed watched as Sam, the husband, went to her, was about to touch her shoulder, but then rested his hand on the back of the chair instead.

'I'll go,' said Pamela, the grandmother of the missing boy.

As she slipped out of the room, Hugo also got to his feet. 'I'll show you around,' he offered.

Ed followed Hugo from room to room. Next to the kitchen was a laundry room with massive machines and wooden pulleys on which hung white sheets and pillowcases. He rather liked the dry smell, thought it evoked order and cleanliness. Next were a storeroom, a larder, and then what Hugo described as the 'snug' – a dim, cheerless little place with a battered couch and shelves of folders and box files.

Upstairs, four light and airy double guest bedrooms and an interconnecting family suite occupied the first floor, where it became clearer how the three terraced houses had been knocked into one, the space once occupied by staircases now taken up by additional bathrooms. The three front rooms looked directly out to sea, and all were decorated in misty blues and greens. All were occupied, suitcases, clothes, shoes and magazines strewn across beds and chairs. Ed searched thoroughly but as swiftly as he could, while Hugo remained each time in the doorway, answering any questions but offering no distraction. Only once, as they passed a landing window, did Hugo remark that it would be getting dark again soon.

The low-ceilinged attic flat bore no traces of bloody confrontation, and Mitch Parker's narrow room seemed typical enough for a teenager, as did his sister's. The kitchen arrangements up here were rudimentary and the family's living room, though tidy and bright, was little more than a couch, easy chair, coffee table and television. Ed never ceased to be amazed by what he learnt from people's homes. Sometimes it was squalor, with dogs all over furniture that wasn't yet paid for and kids with no sheets or blankets on their beds. Here it was as though the family had neatly squeezed itself into as small a space as possible in order for the business to thrive. All the best rooms, decked out with obvious love and care, were for visitors – the rest didn't seem important.

He completed his search on the ground floor – reception area in the wide hallway, office and guests' breakfast room – finishing in the guests' pleasant lounge. The bay window looked out to sea and the blue walls drew the last of the evening light inside. Beside the empty fireplace stood a substantial wooden doll's house. Ed went to open it but discovered that two small padlocks secured its hinged door. He turned to Hugo, who seemed to understand immediately. 'I'll go and ask Tessa for the key,' he said, and disappeared.

Ed felt rotten. He knew it was ridiculous to insist, but evidence such as murder weapons had been hidden in more bizarre places, and it was his job to check. The front of the doll's house had been painted to replicate the windowed facade of a wide Victorian terrace identical to the house in which it stood. Ed squatted on his heels to peer in through the miniature windows, and could make out a staircase with tiny spindles and a curved and winding balustrade. Three and a half rooms on each floor, one above the other, led to an empty attic. Opposite the front door a woman's coat lay over the banister; on the floor beside it sat a white vanity case small enough for a mouse.

Expecting a quaint Victorian stage set, Ed was surprised that the immaculately detailed furnishings were at once both modern and old-fashioned. He failed to understand why anyone would go to such trouble over the kind of dull, second-hand stuff his grandparents had, but though his spying gaze felt oddly intimate, he could see nothing significant or unpleasant inside. He became aware of Tessa

Parker behind him and, as he straightened up to take the tiny key from her, knew he must look as foolish as he felt.

'I found Mitch's passport,' Tessa told him. She looked dejected at the elimination of a possible explanation.

'Right. We'll circulate his details on the Police National Computer.' He forced himself not to avoid her anguished gaze. 'Juveniles are automatically assessed as Medium Risk and all cases reviewed after forty-eight hours,' he went on, desperate to offer her something to cling to. 'The vast majority are quickly resolved.'

Ed opened up the doll's house as swiftly as he could, double-checked, then gave her back the key. 'I'll leave you to lock up.'

'It belonged to my grandmother,' she told him. 'She tried to pretend that life could be kept tidy and in order like that. But it can't, can it?'

'I'm sure he'll be home soon.' Ed tried to sound reassuring, but she shook her head.

'If something terrible has happened, then it's my fault.'

'Is there anything you'd like to tell me, Mrs Parker, while there's no one else present? Anything that might help?'

She stared at him in obvious torment. 'Whatever's happened, I'm the only one to blame.'

'Why? Do you know of anyone who might have harmed your son?'

She nodded. 'Me. I'm responsible,' she said. 'I'm his mother, and I failed him. Now he's gone, and it's too late. I don't know how to bring him back.'

ONE

Four months earlier

Each snowy cotton pillowcase was the size of a postage stamp, the frilled edging almost invisible. The satin coverlet on the tiny double divan had to be nestled back *under* the pillows, never over them. The padded fabric on the scalloped bedhead – a replica, Grandma Averil had told her, of one she'd admired in a Doris Day movie – was held in place by twenty-six microscopic fabric-covered buttons. Tessa knew this because she had begun trying to count them before being taught her numbers properly at school.

The annual spring-clean of Grandma Averil's doll's house had been a special event ever since Tessa could remember. Her mother had seldom joined in, making Tessa's own initiation into the ceremony all the more special. To her knowledge, no 'people' had ever occupied the house, but nevertheless it contained a haphazard selection of their possessions. The only piece she hadn't been permitted to touch was the white vanity case in the hallway, but over the years Grandma Averil had told her the history of every piece, from the coloured plastic bathroom suite she had bought at a special fair, to the white-painted wooden cradle on its delicate rockers that she bought when she was pregnant with Pamela, years before there was a doll's house in which to put it, to the horn-handled carving knife, smaller than an old-fashioned bodkin, that had arrived anonymously in the post, presumably from a guest who had peeked in at the imaginary rooms. One of Tessa's favourite games had been to chant a list of random things that *weren't* there (a cake tin, school books, a violin), then listen as Grandma Averil patiently enumerated the reasons why their presence was unnecessary. As a small child she'd loved the despotic logic of this tiny universe, and found such arbitrary authority satisfyingly absolute.

Nothing had been added or moved for nearly four decades and never would be now. The story went that Averil had declared the doll's house complete when Tessa was born, though even as a child Tessa had accepted this compliment as a partial fiction. As she replaced the delicate cradle in its exact spot, she sighed with a mixture of satisfaction and irritation: she knew she would never abandon this duty, yet was aware that the annual dusting, washing or polishing of these rather ugly and outmoded toy furnishings contained a fetishistic element that was also tawdry and ridiculous. Her own daughter, Lauren, often begged to have the doll's house in her bedroom, and to be allowed to help look after it, but Tessa remained in two minds about passing on the questionable ritual to another generation.

Stiff from kneeling and stretching into the back of the doll's house, she rolled her neck, taking a contented look around the refurbished room. When she had inherited the bed-and-breakfast after Averil's death two years ago, she had felt no guilt about the speed with which she had immediately swept aside her grandmother's red carpets and gilt-framed mirrors, replacing them with seagrass flooring, duck-egg blue walls and squashy armchairs with loose covers in off-white linen. Tessa knew with utter certainty that despite their very different styles they had shared the same quiet passion, and that what Averil would most want was for her only grandchild to make a new generation of guests comfortable.

One thing was missing: Sam's return. When Tessa had married Sam, straight out of college and already pregnant, Averil had willingly vacated her attic flat and even declared herself content to 'retire' and hand over the day-to-day running of the B&B. It had been fun at first, but Averil never did let go of the reins, and although she bought a tiny bungalow where she washed, dressed and slept, she continued to spend all her days keeping an eye on things from her lair in the basement snug. For years Tessa and Sam had felt stifled and stir-crazy, unable either to afford a place of their own or, from enforced gratitude, to rebel. Both longed to make something of their own, so when, soon after Averil's death, an old college friend had offered Sam experience in a Michelin-starred kitchen in

London, Tessa had encouraged him to spread his wings and go. Sam was a wonderful chef, and it had been right to accept such a prestigious offer, but now that he was back in Felixham their arrangements were threatening to slip out of control and end up dangerously adrift.

The doorbell rang just as Tessa closed the doll's house door and was about to hook it shut. In the hallway she glanced at her watch – 2.15. Guests were encouraged to arrive between five and six o'clock; even those staying more than one night were not permitted to remain in the house between eleven and three. She opened the front door and made a quick assessment of the woman on the threshold: well dressed, in her mid-fifties, with stylish blonde hair, scarlet lipstick and glitzy jewellery. The woman smiled and took a step forward, already peering eagerly over Tessa's shoulder into the hallway beyond.

Like all her fellow Felixham proprietors, Tessa was vigilant about strangers on the doorstep and only ever accepted confirmed bookings or occasional recommendations from colleagues who were fully booked. She shifted sideways to block the open doorway. 'Can I help you?' she asked pleasantly.

'I'm hoping you might have a room free?' The woman spoke with a discernible Australian twang.

'I'm afraid not.'

'And tomorrow night?'

Tessa shook her head. 'It's coming up for Easter. We're fully booked. I expect everyone is.'

'Are you Tessa Parker? It gave your name on the website.'

'Yes.' Tessa waited for the woman to introduce herself, but while she continued to gaze at Tessa, she offered no name.

'Well, might I take a look at the rooms anyway, for future reference?'

The woman took another step forward, once again glancing over Tessa's shoulder. Tessa stood her ground, leaving little personal space between them. As the woman backed off, Tessa noted that her handbag was expensive and her smile professional, and decided it might be politic after all to give her a quick tour; for all Tessa knew, she might be a scout for a new holiday guide, someone it would be best not to offend.

'Come in,' she said with a welcoming smile. 'I'll fetch you a brochure.'

'Great. Thanks.'

When Tessa came back out of her office with the brochure the woman was standing motionless in the doorway to the guests' sitting room. There was something about her stance that made Tessa pause, but the woman, feeling herself observed, gave a quick smile and followed Tessa upstairs to be shown one of the bedrooms.

'So it's across three houses now?' she asked.

'Yes,' said Tessa, surprised. 'Why, have you stayed here before?'

'Oh, a lifetime ago!' The woman walked further into the room, running a hand along the back of a chair then going to look out at the view. 'The beach hasn't changed. It's just like I remember.' She turned and sank down on the window seat. 'You've done a fabulous job,' she said, her eyes on Tessa rather than the decor.

'I'm sorry that we can't accommodate you,' Tessa responded politely. 'Let me show you the breakfast room.' She moved encouragingly towards the door, but the woman continued to sit and take in her surroundings. 'All our food is organic and locally sourced,' Tessa added, taking another step backwards. This time the woman rose and followed her.

The breakfast room, in neutral creams with classic chintz curtains, was big enough for one large and four small tables with twelve matching chairs, all modern and the least ostentatious Tessa had been able to find. Although the woman's gaze travelled approvingly around the room, Tessa again had a sense that her thoughts were elsewhere. Perhaps, Tessa thought, she was remembering some family holiday here long ago and this visit was not professional after all, but merely nostalgic.

'Our email is on the brochure and the website. Do get in touch if you'd like to make a future booking.' Tessa spoke briskly, glancing deliberately at her watch.

The woman gave a deep sigh. 'Thanks, but I'm only over for a few days.' She nodded to herself, and then led the way back to the front door. There she turned and held out her hand. 'Nice to meet you, Tessa.'

Noticing her expensive fashion rings and varnished nails, Tessa shook the offered hand but avoided the slightly searching gaze. 'Goodbye. Have a safe trip home.'

Tessa closed the door with relief. She doubted the woman had truly wanted to stay here, imagining rather than she had rung the doorbell on a passing whim. Repeat business was good, but one of its hazards was that people often wanted to share their memories – of first meetings, honeymoons, long-dead parents, grown-up children. At least the woman hadn't produced photographs over which Tessa would've had to fake some interest. She remembered she hadn't shut the doll's house properly, and went to fix the little padlocks top and bottom that prevented any curious guest from rearranging its contents. With a final satisfied glance that everything was properly in order, she resumed the tasks of her busy day.

TWO

As the nearest road bridge was several miles inland, it was almost as quick for Tessa to walk to her parents' house as to drive. The next morning she set out along the footpath that led to the narrow metal bridge over the river. The sea, a distant freshness, lay to her left; she'd noticed as she left the house that the tide was on the turn. She'd lived by the coast all her life, growing up half a mile inland in her parents' Edwardian semi but always adoring Grandma Averil's seafront terrace. She had been surprised, during her few years away at college, by how much she missed the sea's constant and pervasive presence. Even indoors a quick glance out at the sky, the gulls, the wind animating garden hedges and bushes, and she could predict the colour of the water and the size and appearance of the waves. Out of doors she could tell by the smell and dampness of the air when a storm was brewing miles out to sea.

Her grandmother's attic room, in which she used occasionally to sleep as a child, now belonged to her son, and she was pretty sure that Mitch loved it as much as she had at his age. When he was a baby and she'd needed to feed him during the night, she'd loved to sit there enclosed in the darkness with him in her arms listening, even in the wildest weather, to the familiar sounds of the sea. And even now, when he was at school and she had a little time to herself, she would sometimes rest on the window seat, stare out at the mesmerising waves and clouds and allow herself to be soothed.

As she walked, Tessa's thoughts once again became occupied with the conversation she needed to have with Sam. When had they stopped truly sharing their lives? She had to admit that it was probably some time before Grandma Averil had died. In her will Averil had, with Pamela's full approbation, left everything to Tessa, and while Sam was in London Tessa had been excited to pour her energies into a complete makeover of the B&B, cherishing the house she'd always loved and finally making real all the ideas that Grandma Averil had dismissed as unnecessary. On Sam's irregular visits home it had seemed easy enough to ignore their lack of physical intimacy; after all, they'd been married fifteen years by then. Equally committed to building on their talents now they had the freedom to do so, they'd simply never questioned that each passionately supported the other's potential. And yet something had been lost.

On Sam's eventual return to Felixham, Tessa's inheritance had enabled him to secure a mortgage on an abandoned joinery in the High Street. It had always been his dream to open his own restaurant, and she wholeheartedly applauded his decision. The town centre needed a bistro-diner that would please both locals and weekenders and draw those tourists attracted by Felixham's retro chic, and the synergy of recommending his brasserie to her guests for lunches and dinner was perfect. She and Sam had even insisted to their sceptical kids that he'd rented the studio flat only to avoid getting drawn back into the day-to-day running of the B&B and to be next door to the joinery while he concentrated on its conversion. But she had been foolish to believe in the fiction they'd spun to everyone else. The brasserie was due to open in a matter of weeks, and it was time to put a stop to the pretence and get their marriage back on track.

Leaving the estuary marshes, Tessa now turned onto the lane that served the ribbon of sixties houses that fringed South Felixham, picking out her parents' driveway by the clump of pampas grass in the middle of their lawn. Hugo and Pamela had moved into the small detached house soon after Hugo's retirement. He'd worked all his life for the local brewery, ending up as a senior manager, and Tessa suspected that he still missed the company.

She spotted a pile of discarded twigs on the lawn and Pamela's grey head bobbing about behind a flowering shrub where she was cutting away dead winter wood.

'Hi, Mum,' she said, returning Pamela's preoccupied wave as she made for the front door.

Hugo responded swiftly to the chiming front-door bell. 'Hello, Tessie,' he said. 'Come on in. Got something for you to try, a new bread recipe. Used a different sort of flour this time, and . . .'

He petered out, and Tessa turned to seek the reason for his distraction. A local taxi had drawn up by their driveway and inside it Tessa could make out the blonde woman who had wanted to look around the B&B yesterday.

'Who is that?' she asked, faintly annoyed. 'What is she doing here?'

'Don't know,' said Hugo, peering short-sightedly. 'Must have the wrong house.'

But the woman paid the driver and got out of the car. She wore a smart pink tweed suit and gold earrings, and her nails were the same scarlet as yesterday. Catching sight of Tessa standing beside Hugo, she looked almost as if she might retreat. But the taxi drove off, so she settled her handbag firmly over one arm and came forward, an uncertain smile on her face.

'Hello again,' said Tessa.

'Hello,' she replied. 'I didn't expect to find you here.' The woman turned to Hugo, who stood mystified beside Tessa. 'It is Hugo, isn't it?' she asked.

'Yes,' he said. 'Do I know you?'

Pamela emerged from behind the shrubbery, staring at the woman, who smiled tentatively back. Pamela dropped her secateurs and handful of cuttings and ran forward. 'Erin!'

Hugo and Tessa both looked more sharply at the woman. '*Aunt* Erin?' Tessa asked.

Erin, abashed, nodded in confirmation. Pamela pulled

off her gardening gloves and threw her arms around her sister.

'Oh, Erin! My God, you gave me such a shock!' she cried. Tessa had never before seen her mother so elated. 'When did you get here? You never said you were coming! Why didn't you tell me?'

'Last-minute decision.'

Seized in her sister's embrace, Erin closed her eyes and held tight for a long, long moment.

Tessa kept her eyes on Hugo, who turned ashen and took a step back, unconsciously clenching and unclenching his hands. 'What *are* you doing here?' he asked as soon as the women finally let go of one another.

'Hugo, I promise you I'm not here to upset anyone,' said Erin. Tessa could see how nervous and pale she was under her suntan and glossy hair. 'I only came to . . . I had a chance to come to London on business,' she recovered herself, 'and I wanted to see Felixham again. I didn't plan on disturbing any of you. I really didn't.'

'Disturbing us?' interrupted Pamela, clearly hurt. 'Oh, Erin, don't be ridiculous! How could you think it?'

'We appreciate that, Erin,' said Hugo, his voice carrying a note of warning that Tessa did not understand.

'Seeing the old house yesterday . . .' Erin went on.

'She came to look round,' Tessa explained.

Hugo looked furious, but Erin nodded and laughed. 'I just had to see the old place again. Couldn't help myself. So I rang the bell.' She smiled apologetically at Tessa.

'But why didn't you say anything?' Tessa asked. 'You

told me you'd stayed there before. You should've introduced yourself.'

Hugo clenched his hands into fists again, and Erin looked in appeal at Pamela before she spoke. 'I wasn't sure what to say. Whether you'd know who I was.'

'Oh, Erin!' said Pamela again, reaching out to stroke her arm. Tessa could make no sense of the anguish in her mother's voice. 'When did you arrive? Why on earth didn't you tell me you wanted to come?'

Erin turned to Tessa. 'Your mother–' she shot a look at Hugo, 'has sent me lots of photos over the years, of you, and of Mitch and Lauren too, of course. And Sam – what a dish! Pamela's been wonderful about keeping me up to date.'

Hugo appeared to relent slightly. 'You'd better come in,' he said, holding open the door.

'I'll make some coffee,' said Pamela. 'I can't believe you're actually here! After all these years.'

The normally undemonstrative Pamela took hold of Erin's hand to lead her inside, leaving Tessa and Hugo on the doorstep. Tessa looked to him for an explanation but he shook his head and turned to follow them indoors. She detained him. 'Dad?' she asked. 'What's going on?'

Hugo seemed to collapse inwardly, his spare features suddenly gaunt. He gripped her shoulders. 'You know how much we love you, don't you, Tessie?'

'Of course.' Tessa was taken aback; though generous in his affection, Hugo seldom spoke about his feelings. 'But whatever's the matter? I don't understand.'

He made an effort to smile, though his grip on her shoulders tightened. 'Nothing! It's just the shock of seeing her here again after so long. I didn't expect it. I don't see why she's suddenly decided to come back.' He sighed and stroked Tessa's hair – an unaccustomed gesture. 'You'd better come in.'

THREE

When Tessa entered the kitchen she found her mother and Erin standing side by side at the worktop, a steaming kettle, open biscuit tin and plate half covered with Pamela's homemade shortbread beside them. Erin looked around guiltily, and Tessa saw that she was comforting Pamela, who was weeping, oblivious to Tessa's presence.

'I couldn't bear it,' Pamela was saying between sobs. 'It was the worst day of my life. I've never got over it, what we did to you. I'm so sorry, Erin. So sorry.'

Erin flapped her hand at Tessa, urging her back out of the kitchen. Tessa obeyed, closing the door behind her. She stood in the empty hallway, the low sun shining through the ribbed glass of the front door, muddy marks from Pamela's gardening shoes on the usually spotless oatmeal carpet. She listened to the ticking of the old-fashioned clock on the hall table. It had been presented to Hugo's father on his retirement from the brewery, where he had been a driver, as had his father before him, though her great-grandfather had taken care of horses rather than engines. She looked at the picture hanging on the wall above it, a reproduction of an Edwardian flower painting that used to hang in the guests' breakfast room at the Seafront B&B and that Pamela had salvaged from Tessa's refurbishment. Tessa had known these items all her life, but never before had she seen her mother cry like that.

She went into the lounge where she found Hugo standing at the picture window looking out onto the muted April colours of the sheltered back garden. He turned to her with a stricken expression she could not read.

'What's going on, Dad?'

He seemed unable to find words. Instead he came and wrapped his arms around her in the kind of bear hug he used to offer when she was a little girl. Letting go, he said merely: 'We'd better wait for them.'

Out of habit, Tessa plumped some cushions on the couch before she sat down. She had never met Erin before, but her long-lost aunt's clandestine visit to the B&B yesterday and her decision to turn up unannounced here today seemed to Tessa not only pointless but also mean and unfair. Although Grandma Averil used to talk about her younger daughter, and showed pride in Erin's life in Australia and her career in the travel business, Tessa had always assumed everyone was content with little more than the sending and receiving of Christmas cards. Certainly she could recollect no plans to visit, nor even any regular phone calls. But it was obvious now that the apparent placidity of these relationships had not been due to indifference. Tessa felt deeply wary of this unknown woman; the fact that Erin could provoke such strength of feeling in her normally reserved parents left her cross and resentful. She hoped her aunt would soon go back where she belonged.

Erin came in carrying a tray laden with coffee, cups and plates. 'Pamela's nipped upstairs to change out of her gardening clothes,' she told Hugo brightly, and then took charge of serving the coffee.

'So what took you to London?' Hugo asked with studied politeness when Erin had settled with her own cup. 'Have you been over before?'

'No,' she said. 'Always avoided it.' She flushed. 'I mean, most of my work is with the Far East. Hong Kong, Singapore, Thailand, rather than Europe.'

'So why now?'

'One of the airlines had a promotion. My company puts a lot of business their way. And a first-class seat makes everything so much easier!' Erin spoke with a professionally friendly manner that Tessa recognised from her own interaction with guests. The familiarity made her look at her aunt with fresh interest; maybe now that the first shock was over, they would all be their normal selves again. 'I'm not even sure if I've ever been to London before,' Erin went on. 'Strange. Somehow, being an expat, I automatically imagined I knew it well.'

They fell silent, and sat sipping their coffee until Pamela came in carrying the plate of shortbread. She had brushed her hair and put on a little powder and lipstick, though Tessa could discern faint traces of puffiness around her eyes. Hugo, too, looked closely at her as she handed around biscuits for which no one had any appetite.

Pamela took a seat on the couch beside Erin. Both sat straight-backed. They were of almost identical height, and had the same clear foreheads and wide mouths, though Erin's features seemed somehow stronger, less faded. Pamela, nine years older, was grey-haired and narrow-shouldered, but Tessa could see that they would be immediately recognisable as sisters.

As Hugo asked more inconsequential questions about Erin's flight and where she'd stayed in London, Tessa was soothed by the evident intention to smooth over the shock of her arrival. Yet she couldn't help being curious about what she'd overheard in the kitchen. 'What made you decide to go to Australia in the first place?' she asked.

The others stiffened and exchanged furtive glances. Once again Tessa was piqued by the ability of a stranger to arouse in her parents a force of emotion they had never shown towards her. No one answered, so Tessa let the question hang in the air for a moment before probing further. 'You must have been quite young?'

'Sixteen,' said Erin. 'Same age as your kids, right? What, Lauren's fourteen and Mitch seventeen?'

'Yes,' confirmed Tessa, surprised that she was so well informed.

'So young,' murmured Pamela.

'I can't believe it,' Erin went on. 'Last time I was here, you were a babe in arms. And look at you now – all grown up, kids of your own, flourishing business.'

Tessa shrugged politely, suddenly wondering if perhaps Erin had come to make trouble over Grandma Averil's will. If so, she would fight: the B&B had been left in its entirety to her because for the past decade, without the hard graft she and Sam had put in, it would not have survived. Besides, Sam's new restaurant depended on the security of her inheritance and she wasn't about to have that interfered with.

'What made you change your mind? Why have you come back now?' pressed Hugo.

'Cousin Brenda died,' Pamela answered for Erin. 'That's why, isn't it?'

Erin nodded, her expression sad as she smoothed her pink skirt over her knees. Recovering, she turned to Tessa. 'Brenda was my second cousin,' she explained, 'and a second mother too. I lived with her family when I first went to Sydney. She was wonderful to me.'

'I'm glad to hear that,' said Hugo.

'She passed away three months ago,' Erin told him, 'of breast cancer.'

'My condolences,' he said awkwardly.

'Thank you.'

'If Erin had stayed, our lives would have been very different,' said Pamela.

'She could have come back any time she wanted,' Hugo told her sharply. He turned to Erin. 'We never stopped you.'

'Mum didn't want me here,' said Erin.

'That's not true,' objected Pamela.

'She made me promise to stay away.'

'No!'

'Yes. You weren't supposed to know, but . . . She did what she thought was best.'

'We thought you might've come to her funeral,' said Hugo.

'It was too difficult, after so much time.'

Tessa observed the look of appeal Erin made to Pamela, saw Pamela nod in sympathy and reach out to press her sister's hand. She felt exasperated by these concealed under-currents. 'Will someone please tell me what's going on?' she demanded.

Pamela looked intently at Hugo, who met her gaze with stony eyes. Crestfallen, Pamela stared at the floor.

'Oh, it's nothing – the usual story,' said Erin, her Australian twang more accentuated. 'I was a delinquent teenager, and Mum couldn't cope. She'd just managed to buy the house next door and was going to knock through. It was such a big risk. If it hadn't worked out she'd have lost everything, and then who knows what would have happened to us. She couldn't afford any hint of scandal.'

Erin spoke so airily that Tessa was sure she was lying. She glanced at Hugo who was staring sightlessly out at the garden and was shocked by how wretched he looked, by the sorrowful lines in his face that, she realised with a jolt, had always been there.

'What sort of scandal?' Tessa asked.

'Oh, nineteen-seventies Felixham! Nothing anyone would

bother about in this day and age. Tell me about Mitch and Lauren. Are they doing well at school?'

Tessa ignored the question. 'What happened?' she insisted.

A sort of hush fell. Pamela gazed at Hugo and he glared back hopelessly with a faint shake of his head.

It was Erin who spoke, with a firmness that Tessa suspected was professional. 'Nothing. I was difficult, so Averil packed me off to stay for a while with the only family she had. As it turned out, I adored my cousin Brenda, discovered I'm a city girl and was only too glad to shake the dust of this place off my feet, so I stayed put.' Erin turned to Pamela, touching her arm. 'I've been fine, really. No need to worry about me. I've got a fantastic life in Sydney.'

Pamela burst into tears

'What on earth's the big mystery?' demanded Tessa, beginning to feel afraid.

Hugo sighed and sat back, defeated. He nodded to Erin. 'Tell her, if that's why you're here. Don't drag it out.'

But Erin shook her head, occupying herself in comforting Pamela.

'Tell her,' he ordered.

'There's no need,' she protested. 'Really.'

'Then why are you here?' he asked coldly.

Pamela took a deep breath, trying to control her tears, and turned to Tessa. 'Your grandmother sent Erin away soon after you were born,' she said finally. '*Because* you were born.'

'I don't understand,' said Tessa, hearing her own voice as if from very far away.

'Erin was barely sixteen,' said Pamela. 'Little more than a child herself.'

'But what has that got to do with me?'

'I had a baby,' said Erin.

Except for birdsong from the garden, the room was silent. Pamela's face softened and her shoulders dropped as if a huge burden had been lifted.

'What happened to it?' Tessa asked, already dreading the reply.

'We wanted you, Tessie!' Hugo's voice shook uncharacteristically. 'Welcomed you!'

'I knew Pamela would take good care of you because she'd always looked after me so well,' said Erin. 'Loved me.'

'But that's ridiculous! You would've told me. Why wouldn't you?' Out of habit, Tessa looked to her father for verification. Hugo's answering look of shame was terrifying. She turned back to Erin. 'You're saying that I was that baby? That you're my mother?'

Erin looked to Pamela for permission before she answered. 'Yes.'

Tessa sought wildly for some escape. 'But there's nothing on my birth certificate.'

'No,' said Hugo. 'The adoption went through just before the law was changed.' He looked accusingly at Pamela. 'When people still believed it was best to ignore the truth.'

Pamela uttered a wail of contrition. 'I took you away from her. I stole my sister's child.'

FOUR

Refusing Hugo's offer of a lift, Tessa took the footpath home through the tall reeds, grateful for some space in which to process her shock. At first she had expected Erin to leave, to offer her and her parents some private time together; but Pamela had been adamant that her little sister would not be cast out a second time, and so it was Tessa who had said she must get back to work, and had left their house feeling unfairly usurped.

Piecing together her scant knowledge of the past, Tessa tried to make some headway against her astonished sense of betrayal. All the years they must have guarded her so assiduously from any suspicion of the truth; all those conversations – innocent childish questions or remarks about family traits and resemblances – that had been steered so firmly away from difficult waters. How carefully her parents must have monitored themselves, how false so many of their words and gestures!

She knew how hard it was to defy Grandma Averil: she'd been a tyrant. From the moment Averil had decreed – as

Pamela had just explained – that the disgraced Erin was to disappear and Pamela and Hugo should pass her baby off as their own, it would have been useless to argue against her. But why, after Erin's banishment, had it remained so impossible to share the secret with the person most closely affected by it, to ignore a child's right to know who she was? Had there really been no point during the past thirty-seven years when she couldn't have been trusted with the truth?

Tessa felt bitterly disappointed that Hugo and Pamela had failed to take charge. Their lack of certainty, of *ownership*, left her exposed and defenceless. No wonder she had grown up with a sense of not fully belonging, of being kept at arm's length.

What hurt most was that Pamela's grief today had not been for the sacrifice of her family to this divisive and inhibiting secret, but remorse at stealing her sister's child. Even when Tessa left the house it had been Hugo who accompanied her to the end of the driveway, who promised to call. Pamela had hung back, giving precedence to Erin, who had laid a powdered cheek next to Tessa's and kissed her lightly goodbye.

Had either of her parents ever really wanted her? Clearly Erin, her real mother, had not. And maybe Pamela had resented having her sister's illegitimate baby foisted upon her. Perhaps even Hugo, always so decent and loyal, had had no choice but to support his wife and make the best of it. The horrible idea that maybe all these years they had merely tolerated a child who meant very little to them made her want to run away.

As she walked, she tried to let the familiar movement of clouds and water claim her attention and untangle her emotions. The tide was flowing out in earnest now, and as she approached the metal footbridge she saw how the river's central channel had narrowed to expose the mudbanks to the attention of wading birds. A wind blew in off the sea, whipping up the water rushing in the opposite direction, echoing her overwhelming sense that the elements surrounding her were dangerously in flux.

She stopped on the footbridge where her thoughts reverted to Sam: did this lack of authentic connection at the very heart of her life explain why she had always feared an emptiness at the heart of her marriage too? She realised suddenly how hungry she was to talk to him, how he was the only person in the world she wanted to tell, or who could possibly comfort her.

Tessa dialled his number on her mobile and he picked up after a couple of rings, greeting her by name. Deciding not to burden him immediately, she spoke with false optimism: 'Sam, you're never going to believe what I've just been told! Can I call in for five minutes?'

'Sure,' he agreed. 'I've been wanting to speak to you about something anyway. See you soon.'

Tessa walked on feeling a tiny bit lighter. However horrible and unsettling, perhaps Erin's revelation would help her to understand herself better, might even add an extra dimension to her existence. After all, nothing had actually been lost – Hugo and Pamela remained her mum and dad, and Sam was still her husband. But now maybe there could be room for her to grow, to gain new perspectives, to discover parts of herself that, busy with marriage and kids and remodelling the business, had become enmeshed and lost. Listening to the racket of the gulls swooping across the shallow current and fighting over whatever food was to be found, she reflected that there was, after all, a strange elation at being at the centre of such unexpected drama, an enticing sense of ever-expanding horizons. She couldn't wait to talk to Sam, to explain why things had gone wrong and persuade him to come home for a fresh start together.

She found him in the brasserie – in what was going to be the brasserie – looking more youthful than ever in a dusty boiler suit, his hair flopping over his eyes. The major structural work on remodelling the former joinery and its cobbled courtyard out front was nearing completion, and he was hoping to open in good time for the summer season. Tessa calmed herself by admiring how well the shiny slickness of the bar would eventually work against the cleaned-up brickwork and sanded wood floors before telling him about Erin and her revelation.

'Wow,' said Sam. 'How do you feel?'

'Confused. Hurt. Amazed. Don't know what to feel yet.'

'And your poor parents. Pretty tough on them, her just turning up out of the blue like that, dropping such a bombshell.'

'If she hadn't, I might never have found out.'

'No, but she could've warned you all that she was coming. Given them a chance to tell you without being bounced into it like that.'

'Maybe it had to happen this way. Though it's pretty weird to think they might never have told me otherwise. Not sure quite how I get my head round that, how to go on trusting them.'

His shrug reminded her how easily he always sidestepped confrontation, even other people's. 'So what's she like?' he asked.

'Don't know yet. She's not here for long, though.'

'Right.'

'She'd love to meet you. And the kids, obviously.'

'Really?'

'Yes! Why not?'

'Do the kids need to know?'

'Of course!'

'They've a lot going on right now, and it doesn't really affect them, does it?'

'I'm not keeping it a secret,' she declared stubbornly.

'Fair enough. But it might be an idea to make sure you've got used to the idea first and are Ok with it all.'

'I am. I think it helps make sense of stuff.'

'Like what?'

'I don't know. Like that I never one hundred per cent belonged. That I wasn't complete in some way.'

Sam shrugged. 'All kids are like that, aren't they? Go through the fantasy of imagining they're adopted. You and your mum and dad always seemed pretty tight to me.'

'I'm not saying we weren't. It's how I felt.'

'Ok.'

'And in my case, turns out that adoption isn't a fantasy.' She looked at him, hoping for more of a response.

'Sure. But it's not really adoption, is it? It's not as if your family gave you up, handed you over to strangers.'

'No. That's right.' Tessa assumed they were both inevitably recalling the same moment in their own lives: Pamela and Hugo was been delighted when she'd confessed that she'd accidentally fallen pregnant with Mitch when still at college. Even though her parents had only met Sam a couple of times, and she and Sam had not imagined a life together, Pamela and Hugo had made everything fall perfectly into place. Erin, on the other hand, had been sent packing thousands of miles away from home, only weeks after giving birth. 'No,' Tessa agreed, feeling some sympathetic kinship with the younger Erin. 'It was Erin they gave up. Not me.'

'So you're Ok with it?' Sam repeated. 'It's not going to ruin your life or anything?'

'No. I'm angry that they never told me, that I've had to live such a lie all these years, but I'm glad that's over. I think they're relieved too. And I'm sure in the end it'll explain things, open stuff up.' She took a deep breath. 'Maybe about us too.'

'Yeah?' Sam looked her warily.

'About maybe why I find it difficult to say what I want.' She moved closer, touched his arm. 'I'm sure it'll be good for us,' she said. 'Make it easier to start over.'

'Right.' He licked his lips. 'Because I've got something to tell you as well.'

'What?' She hadn't meant to snap at him, but she was tired, and had expected him to enter more fully into what all this meant for her. After all, it wasn't every day you discovered you weren't who you thought you were. But she saw the shutters come down and wanted to shake him.

'You've probably already guessed.' He gave a feeble laugh. 'I'm moving in with Nula this week.'

'Nula?'

'Nula Simmonds,' he reminded her, striving to sound patient. 'She's part of the company that did all the design work here. You've met her.'

The mist cleared: Sam had been complaining for a while about the lack of space in his one-room flat. 'But that's what I wanted to talk to you about,' she said eagerly. 'There's no need for you to go on renting, is there? Not now this place is nearly done. Come home!'

His hesitation was like a siren going off. 'You mean you really don't know?' He looked hurt, as if she were deliberately making this harder for him.

'Know what?' asked Tessa, realising that she did indeed already know what he was going to say.

'We're going to live together.'

Her distress burst out of her: 'What about us?'

'It's been almost two years since I went to London.'

'But we're still married, still a family.'

Sam licked his lips again, and then reached out to hook

her fingers into his. 'It was you who encouraged me to leave in the first place, to aim higher. I couldn't have done any of this without you.'

Tessa recognised that smile, knew he was cajoling her into doing the rest for him, but she was too shocked to speak.

He looked around at the half-finished building. 'It's time we organised our business finances properly too.'

'We can do that. Just talk to the accountant.'

He swallowed hard and let go of her hand. 'Two years is long enough for a legal separation.'

'Don't leave me!'

'You're upset about what happened today. We can discuss this another time.'

'No!' Tessa felt afraid of yet more ground shifting beneath her feet. Dazed, she struggled to stand firm. 'Is this what you want?'

Sam nodded. 'We should get a divorce.'

'What about the kids?' She didn't know what else to say to sway him, to win him back. She thought for a moment that she had never seen him so implacable, but then reconsidered: it was always by stealth that Sam got his own way in the end.

'It'll be better,' he was saying now. 'Clearer. And Nula's got a spare bedroom so they'll be able to stay with me. We thought we'd buy a sofa bed for the living room, so they don't have to share a room if they don't want to.'

'So it's all sorted?'

'Yes.'

'How do we tell them? They'll be devastated.'

'Not really. They're cool with it. They like Nula.'

'They already know?'

'That I'm moving in with her? Yes.' He hung his head, his hair dropping forwards. 'Sorry. I assumed you did too. That you'd realised.'

The hint of injury in Sam's tone reminded Tessa how conveniently he always assumed that people magically knew about matters he didn't want to deal with. How his own sense of injury enabled him to ignore the pain he was inflicting. It had been the same when he'd returned from London and didn't move back home. And, despite her misgivings at the time, she had allowed it to happen, telling herself she was being civilised and mature, just as she seemed to be doing now. Except that this time the pain was much worse.

'I don't want you to leave. I want you to come home.'

'Be happy for me, Tessa,' he warned, brushing his hair back with an impatient gesture.

His earnest brown eyes looked at her in his old pleading way, and with a sinking heart, Tessa knew she would pander to him as she always did, would creep away and lick her wounds in private. 'I am happy for you, Sam. Honestly.' She even gave him an impulsive hug and a kiss. Drawing back, she added: 'Are you sure, though, that Lauren and Mitch are Ok with this? I mean, it's a massive change. Maybe we shouldn't involve them yet? So soon?'

'It's not soon, Tessa. It's been two years. Nula's here to stay. I'm in love with her.'

Tessa felt as if he had smacked her. Reeling, she did not hear Sam's next question. 'So did they tell you the rest?' he repeated.

'What do you mean?'

'Well, who your real father is?'

FIVE

Mitch was annoyed. But then his kid sister was always annoying these days. Right now she was taking ten minutes – *ten minutes* – to make a sandwich. For herself, not him. She was so intent on how much butter to use, and cutting off every bit of crust, that she hadn't bothered to ask if he wanted one. The thought of sitting here and watching the weirdly precise way in which she'd started to eat recently was more than he could handle.

He was about to disappear upstairs when his mum came in. She looked a bit hacked off too. Mitch guessed it was because she was running late for the arrival of this evening's guests. 'Shall I make you a cup of tea?' he asked.

'In a minute. I need to talk to you both first.'

Mitch slid back into his chair as Tessa sat down at the kitchen table. This sounded serious.

'I've just spoken to your dad.'

Lauren continued nibbling around the edges of her sandwich, her gaze fixed on Tessa.

'He told me he's met someone. And as it looks like she's going to be part of your lives, I–'

'We know all about him and Nula,' interrupted Lauren.

'Yes, that's what he said.'

Mitch didn't trust the tightly casual tone of Tessa's next question: 'How long have you known?'

Lauren shrugged. 'Ages. She said we shouldn't mention it to you until he'd told you himself.'

Mitch watched his mother's mouth tighten at the corners as if she'd swallowed something bad.

'Oh,' was all she said. 'And you're all right with it?'

'Yeah, she's fun,' said Lauren, remorseless.

'Mitch?'

He nodded, wanting to murder his sister.

'Well, that's Ok then,' replied Tessa. 'So long as you're both Ok with it. That's all that matters.'

But Mitch could see that his mum wasn't at all Ok. 'Tea?' he offered once more. This time she assented, and he went to put the kettle on the Aga's hotplate, glaring at Lauren as he passed her.

'What?' she responded. Mitch hated her sometimes.

'So are you and Dad going to get divorced?' Lauren asked with false bravado, and then stuck her face back in her sandwich as if hiding from the answer.

'I think that may be what your dad wants. We'll see.'

Lauren nodded, her eyes wide, munching mechanically.

'Sorry I'm not making much sense,' said Tessa. 'I think maybe I'm still in shock about something else I found out today.' Her voice sounded shaky. 'Something that's really thrown me, actually.'

Mitch saw how easily distracted Lauren was by her eagerness for gossip.

'We had a surprise visitor,' Tessa went on. 'Grannie Pamela's sister Erin.'

Mitch frowned, trying to place the name in the family constellation. 'She lives in Australia, doesn't she?'

'That's right. She's here for a flying visit.'

'Had you met her before?' he asked.

'Turns out I have. Turns out there's a lot of stuff that Hugo and Pamela have kept from me. That no one has ever told me.'

Mitch put a mug of tea down before Tessa and brushed her arm awkwardly with his hand as he passed behind her to sit down again. 'It's not that serious between Dad and Nula,' he assured her, crossing his fingers out of sight under his chair. 'She's been helping him with the brasserie, that's all.'

'Don't be silly. I'm fine with that. Why wouldn't I be? Sam and I will always be best friends.' Mitch recognised the upbeat tone with which she addressed tiresome guests. 'I'm afraid this stuff with Erin is much bigger than that,' she went on. 'Turns out I'm not who I think I am.'

The way she announced this seemed to Mitch a bit over-the-top, more like Lauren when she wasn't getting enough attention.

'What does that mean?' he asked, sounding to himself like Grandpa Hugo, using the same tone that showed he wasn't having the wool pulled over his eyes. On the other hand, things generally got sorted out once Grandpa Hugo was involved.

'Well . . .' Tessa took a deep breath. 'Turns out Pamela's not my mother but my aunt. Erin's my real mother.'

'Awesome,' exclaimed Lauren. 'That's so cool!'

Mitch turned on his sister. 'It's not cool. It's horrible.'

'What's she like?' asked Lauren. 'When do we get to meet her?'

'Soon,' Tessa answered.

'So why didn't she bring you up?' asked Mitch.

'She was sixteen. Unmarried. In those days it was scandalous. Well, somewhere like Felixham it was, anyway. You can imagine Great-Grandma Averil's reaction!'

'Yes! Poor kid.'

Although Tessa agreed, he could see that she bristled at his sympathy for Erin. 'You never knew?' he asked her. Tessa shook her head. 'Why hadn't they told you?'

'I don't know.' She took a deep breath. 'But what it also means is that Hugo is not my biological father. He's no relation at all. Not even your grandfather, come to that.'

Mitch saw tears in his mother's eyes, and felt like he did sometimes when he stood up too fast after concentrating for hours on his games console. He felt guilty now for assuming his mother had been attention-seeking, seriously disliked the idea of Grandpa Hugo being somehow cut adrift.

'But Erin's really glamorous, isn't she?' asked Lauren. 'Grannie Pamela talks about her – says she's been all over the world, organises vacations for celebrities and stuff.'

'So what?' Mitch demanded.

'Because this is like something mega-exciting for once.'

'You're so stupid. It's awful. Can't you see that?'

Dodging his mother's outstretched arm, her surprised, grateful face, Mitch slammed out of the kitchen.

SIX

The following morning, after the night's guests had either paid their bills or gone out for the day, Tessa set out to walk back over to her parents' house. Hugo had told her on the phone that he would take Pamela out to lunch, then to a gallery perhaps – maybe the Sainsbury Centre, a favourite of hers – and leave the way clear for Erin and Tessa to talk privately for as long as they wished.

It had been strange speaking to Hugo, to this father who was suddenly not her father, not part of her at all. Sam's question the previous day had been a body-blow, and she felt foolish that the other side of the equation had not even occurred to her. All her life she had taken it for granted that half of her identity came from Hugo. She didn't know why her certainty that she was rooted in a long line of Suffolk stock should matter, but the notion that she was descended from something unknown left her unpleasantly off-balance. All her life, whenever Pamela was remote or dismissive, Hugo had been there, loving, solid and reasonable, a known entity. But, she supposed, he had not changed: it was she who was no longer the person she thought she was.

The day had started damp and shivery, and for once she wished for the proximity of a more secure element than the sea. The brownish waves covered too many contradictions, too many hidden depths. The footpath was sticky with mud, and she paused for a moment on the footbridge to stare out towards the sea. The fast-moving clouds ran low over distant, churning water, and she turned to lean on the opposite rail, to look inland at the pale reeds and sentinel bulrushes unmoving in the chilly air, and, further off into the mist, the early green of the trees on the rising land.

She had slept badly, had dreamt of Sam. But she didn't want to think about him either. Why had she been so complacent as to let herself believe that deep down he still saw them as married, been content to assume that his recent happiness was due to the brasserie taking shape? Of course, she didn't really believe what he'd said, that he was in love with Nula. She knew Sam too well. He'd be all too ready to fall for someone who made life easy for him, who shared his enthusiasms and eased his way. But how could she not have known, not even have suspected? In the same way, she supposed, that she had never glimpsed the truth about her birth. The sole reason she had missed abundant clues to both was that she was blind and stupid. Pierced by shame and sadness, she stuck her hands in her jacket pockets and headed onwards, wishing now that she had driven instead.

Turning onto the lane, she looked down at her boots, which were heavy with mud. She would have to take them off when she arrived and leave them in the porch. She didn't want to have to hop about while Erin stood waiting on the pale-coloured carpet; but if she waited to take them off before ringing the bell, then Erin would either be mystified at what she was up to or open the door and expose her before she was ready. She felt silly worrying about such vanities in the face of so significant a meeting. And yet somehow, beyond a reluctance to be here at all, she couldn't make herself believe that this meeting with her birth mother was of any great significance.

Wondering if it was shallow of her to suppose it didn't matter who'd conceived and carried her, she experienced a flare of abandonment and loss. Her usual nagging sense that she was not enough, incomplete, not good enough, fed her deepest and most secret fear: that Sam had been able to detach himself from her with so little effort because the roots of his love had never gone very deep, that despite their children there was no real bond between them. As she rang the chiming bell, that fear transmuted into blame: they had all lied to her, concluded it wasn't worth telling the truth to her, and excluded her by sharing secrets with other people. None of it was her fault and she had every right to feel angry, upset and betrayed.

When Erin opened the door, Tessa rushed into a long explanation about her muddy boots and was aware of Erin watching, clearly bemused, as she removed them. She followed Erin into the lounge, feeling childish and vulnerable in her socks. Once again she wished that this woman in her high heels and expensive business suit had stayed in Sydney.

A tray of coffee had been laid out on the side table by the window, and Erin offered to pour for Tessa before settling herself in an armchair.

'Before we start,' began Erin, 'I want to say how sorry I am that it all came tumbling out like this.'

'You must've known it would.'

'I didn't come here intending for this to happen.'

'Really?'

'Honestly, I didn't come with any plan in mind. But I just didn't expect to be so overwhelmed. I'm so sorry. It must have been one hell of a shock.'

'Yes.'

'Though I think maybe Pamela's relieved, don't you? I hadn't realised quite how guilty she still felt, even though it was so long ago.'

Tessa nodded, hurt that still no one seemed to be putting her at the heart of all this.

'Because I want you to know that I'm not the victim here,' Erin continued. 'I don't want you to be sorry for me.'

'Ok,' agreed Tessa.

'I was a bored teenager. It was a holiday romance. No offence, but nowadays I'd probably do the sensible thing and forget all about it.'

'Why didn't you?' asked Tessa, dismayed that perhaps she ought to take offence at the suggestion that she should have been aborted.

'Left it too late. Couldn't face telling my mother that I'd let her down. It wasn't so easy in those days.'

'I can imagine.' Tessa thought of Grandma Averil's lifelong determination that Tessa should succeed her in running the B&B, how despite Tessa's own unplanned pregnancy Averil had encouraged her to finish her course in Business and Hotel Management and take her final exams. After a rushed wedding she and Sam had moved into the attic flat, and overnight it seemed, and with no effort on their part, they had a home, a business and a baby.

'I couldn't even face telling Pamela,' Erin continued. 'She was so desperate by then to have a baby herself, it made it even worse.'

'Is that why you gave her yours?'

'It seemed the best thing all round. And I knew Pamela would take good care of you.' Erin paused and sipped her coffee, smiling as she looked out at the beautifully tended garden where a gleam of sun lit up the beads of moisture dripping from the wet leaves. 'It's been Pamela I've missed the most. She always looked out for me.'

'How come no one in Felixham ever found out?'

'They probably did. Pamela had been married five years by then, and suddenly, right when I emigrated, she has a baby? But who around here would be brave enough to make a comment to Averil?'

Tessa couldn't help a wry smile of agreement. 'So where was I born?' she asked. 'It says Burton upon Trent on my birth certificate.'

'That's right.'

'They always told me they were there because Hugo was on some kind of management course to do with the brewery.'

'That's true,' Erin confirmed. 'Horrible place, but perfect timing. Mum made me join them as soon as I started to show.' She shivered at the memory, looking suddenly tired and old despite her gloss and sheen. 'It was awful, the three of us cooped up like that in a rented flat. I must have been a total pain.'

As Tessa tried to imagine it, Erin seemed to read her thoughts. 'I'd never have got through it all without Pamela,' she went on. 'And Hugo – he was a saint. If we'd been able to stay there, away from Averil, maybe things would've been different.' She shook herself, as if dispelling some old grief. 'But you're Ok, aren't you?' she asked brightly. 'It all turned out Ok?'

Tessa nodded. 'How old was I when you handed me over?'

'A few weeks. I was bundled onto a plane as soon as I'd signed the papers – no time for second thoughts.'

'Would you have changed your mind? Do you regret going?' Tessa thought back to the overwhelming flood of tenderness and protectiveness she'd experienced when she'd first held each of her babies. She could not begin to imagine the panic and terror she would've felt if asked to surrender her child. 'It must have been incredibly hard.'

Erin thought for a moment. 'I think that the important thing in life is to find out what you're good at. I'm a grafter, like Averil was. Love my job. Been perfectly happy not to marry. Got my dogs, though. Look, I'll show you.' She ferreted around in her black patent handbag and took out a leather wallet, from which she drew a picture of two black Scotties. She handed it to Tessa. The dogs had been posed against an artificial backdrop, and the photograph looked to Tessa like an expensive studio shot.

'Dusty and Daisy,' Erin informed her. 'Cute, aren't they?'

'Adorable,' answered Tessa, suppressing hysterical laughter as she handed back the picture.

'They're the reason I can't change my plans and stay longer, I'm afraid. Work I could get away with, but I can't abandon my dogs. They'd never forgive me!'

'You must travel a lot.' asked Tessa. Recalling what Lauren had said about Erin being glamorous, she realised that Pamela must have encouraged Lauren to admire Erin – and done so covertly.

'Yes. Though after a while, one hotel room looks much like another. Do you have dogs?'

'No.' Tessa felt she could not begin to explain the difficulties of keeping pets in a B&B (which in any case Erin must comprehend) without laughing at the surreal turn of the conversation. She seized the main topic again: 'How long did you look after me? Or maybe they didn't let you?'

'A few days? I'm sorry, honey, but I honestly don't remember very clearly. Pamela will know.'

The impossibility of asking Pamela such intense and personal questions brought home to Tessa that she might not get a second chance to find out about the past. 'Was it you who named me?'

'No. I think Hugo chose your name.'

Tessa hugged that thought. 'And you never wanted more children? Weren't ever tempted to come and reclaim me?'

'Can you imagine how your grandmother would have dealt with that?' protested Erin, laughing. 'Not likely to happen!' She appeared to reflect before speaking more seriously. 'I guess I refused to think about having another baby. A shrink would say I was in denial. But so what? Turns out it's suited me fine.'

Tessa took a deep breath. 'What about my father?'

'Ah!' Erin gave a well-worn laugh. 'He was so good-looking. An architectural student. Older than me. Swept me off my feet.'

'Do I look anything like him?' With a sinking heart, Tessa interpreted Erin's blank look to mean that she had no idea. 'If you don't remember, it doesn't matter,' she said hastily. 'Don't make it up!'

'Let's just say he was tall, dark and handsome,' teased Erin, as if this were an old story she had told many times – to herself, if not to others. 'Well, not tall, I don't think. But the same cheekbones and dark hair as you.'

Tessa tried not to gasp at the idea of a man walking around somewhere with the same features as her.

'And a northern accent. He came from Manchester, I think,' Erin added.

'How long were you together?'

'Well, he was here on holiday. A summer romance.'

'Did you tell him you were pregnant? About me?'

Erin shook her head. 'No. My coffee's gone cold. Won't be a second.'

While Erin was in the kitchen, Tessa reflected how she'd always assumed she'd inherited her dark hair from Hugo. But plenty of people had dark hair: it was nothing extraordinary. She waited until Erin had stopped fussing over refilling her rinsed-out mug from Pamela's thermos jug. 'What was his name?'

'Roy Weaver. But look, we were kids. Well, he was a bit older – twenty-three, I think. But it's an awfully long time ago.'

'Yes,' agreed Tessa, not knowing how else to respond.

'You're not angry with me, are you?'

'For what? Revealing the big secret?'

'For having you.'

Tessa was astounded. But then Erin laughed. 'I guess I'm caught in a time warp,' she apologised. 'Last time I was here in Felixham, you'd think the bloody sky had fallen in. Everything was my fault. No one wanted to listen to me. Even now, I keep expecting Averil to walk in and start nagging at me again. She was furious. I'd done a terrible thing to my family; I was a useless, delinquent teenager, risking everything she'd worked so hard for. Coming back here makes it all seem like yesterday.'

Tessa tried to make sense of this: a minute ago Erin could barely remember what her lover had looked like, or how old her baby had been when she'd given her up, but now she could vividly recall her mother's anger.

'I should've stayed away, shouldn't I?' Erin sighed. 'All

I've ever done here is cause trouble. I don't think any of them could forgive me.'

'Not even Pamela?'

'Especially Pamela.'

'But why?' Reflecting on how undemonstrative Pamela could be, Tessa again considered the possibility that she had been landed with a baby she never wanted. 'I suppose she did what Averil told her to do,' she said. 'She must've resented getting stuck with me.'

'No.' Erin shook her head. 'The complete opposite. You were what she most longed for.' She paused. 'It's not true that she never forgave me: she never forgave *herself.* Averil put her and Hugo in an impossible position. My guess is that Pamela's never recovered from the guilt of getting what she wanted and of getting it at my expense.'

Tessa tried to make Erin's words fit with all the other elements that went to make up her idea of Pamela, and discovered that guilt did indeed slip readily into the mix.

'And now I've made it worse for her,' Erin went on. 'I didn't think it would turn out like this, or I would never have come. Whatever he thinks, I haven't done this deliberately.'

'You mean Hugo?'

'Yes. He always thought I was a nuisance.' Erin laughed. 'I probably was, too. But I promise you that I haven't done this out of spite.'

Tessa gazed across at this other mother. They had each, in different ways, been sacrificed to this peculiar family history, but in spite of this bond she had little idea of what lay beneath Erin's smooth, professionally groomed exterior.

'So how do you feel now?' Tessa risked asking. 'Now you've met me at last?' She instantly regretted her question: Erin's answer seemed too important. For a moment Erin studied her as if she might say something big. Tessa held her breath, longing for some connection to be made.

'Thrilled to bits!' Erin said at last, crinkling her nose in a gesture that Tessa imagined she used when addressing her dogs. 'You're a real poppet, an absolute doll!'

SEVEN

The SUV with the privacy glass was there again, parked on the raked gravel behind the security gates. Mitch still had almost a week of school before the Easter holidays, but he was pretty sure that private schools had shorter terms. The house's painted shutters, which for most of the year resolutely blanked the coveted windows that looked straight out to sea, had also been fastened back, so maybe it *was* possible that she was here with her father.

Mitch had only spoken to her that one time, last half-term, when she'd been walking a cute Dalmatian puppy that had taken a liking to his trainers, but she'd seemed glad to have someone to talk to. While he could scarcely believe how flawless she was, and how impossible it was to tell whether or not such perfection was the result of skilled and expensive artifice – Were her nails manicured? The blonde streaks in her honey-brown hair natural? Was the healthy golden glow of her skin genuinely from winter Caribbean sun? – he sensed and responded to something lonely and sad in her. Her voice was low and her accent a mixture of posh English and American high school movies, which would normally have had Mitch sneering in contrived contempt, but her blue eyes – *were* the lashes tinted, the way Lauren said she wanted? – had pleaded with him to like her. And so he did.

After all, it wasn't her fault that her dad was some kind of film producer who worked in Hollywood and knew lots of movie stars. Or that last year her parents had bought the prettiest house in Felixham – a town with many pretty houses, most of them owned by weekenders – and then spent ten months painstakingly recreating the exact patina the place had possessed before their builders had gutted it inside and out. It was not the renovations that turned the good people of Felixham against Charlie Crawford – everyone knew the deep abrasions to brick and wood caused by salt winds and rain – but the fact that all the work was done by 'craftsmen' from London. They came in fancy liveried vans, some with 'By Appointment' crests on their sides, and made midweek block-bookings at the local B. & Bs, including Tessa's. That income was welcome, especially in the winter, but the local builders resented these outsiders who stole their work and, in one case, even a wife, who'd run off to Essex with a specialist plasterer once the job was done. Her son, who was at school with Mitch, had reported how his dad still wondered morosely just how specialist a plasterer had to be.

Mitch stirred himself. He couldn't stand here outside the gates until she came out with the dog, which anyway she might never do. But he'd rather think about Tamsin than about the thing he knew for sure he didn't want to think about: his mum being upset over Nula. All the same, he did not want to risk looking like some demented fan. After Christmas, a rumour had swept around town that Cameron Diaz was staying at the house. Overnight, groups of strangers were literally camped outside, rather like the crowds of twitchers who would materialise out of thin air whenever a rare bird was sighted on the marshes. It was embarrassing.

But then, weeks later – *after* Mitch had got tangled up with Tamsin's Dalmatian puppy at half-term – Carol, who came in to help Tessa with the beds and cooked breakfasts, told them that Charlie Crawford's housekeeper, Sonia Beeston, had said it was true. But, Carol confided, Sonia would've been sacked if she'd uttered a word at the time because, even though the house was mostly empty, she was paid a full-time salary in return for signing a confidentiality agreement.

All of which left Mitch very much in two minds. He would rather die than have Tamsin think he was creeping up to her. (Cameron Diaz might be hot, but only girls were impressed by celebrities.) On the other hand, he was certain his first impression was right: she was lonely, a princess in a tower. Hardly surprising if no one dared be normal and friendly just because of who her mum and dad hung out with.

He made his way down to the beach, sat on a rise of shingle and passed some time throwing stones into the sea, focusing on exact aim and distance. He reckoned Tamsin was older than Lauren but definitely younger than him. Though of course it was difficult to judge, given the ineffable perfection she carried with her. He thought of Daisy Buchanan in the book they were doing for his English exam – *The Great Gatsby* – and the thing their teacher had quoted about the rich being different to us. And how Hemingway – who appealed far more to Mitch than Fitzgerald – had remarked: Yes, they have more money.

Mitch decided to think like Hemingway. Not the drinking and the *cojones*, but remembering that Tamsin was no different from him, merely another kid marooned here for Easter without even the distraction of a holiday job. If she were to spend the summer here as well, then she'd probably be unbelievably bored and isolated. And he liked her. Why not be friends?

Mitch shifted his feet amid the shingle: he knew how badly he wanted to touch her flawless skin, maybe even kiss her. He remembered the girl he'd snogged at a party over Christmas. He'd chosen her because the other boys said she was easy; he wasn't bothered about her, just wanted to know what it was like. They were in the hallway of someone's house and he pushed her back against the wallpaper. Her mouth tasted of rum and coke, a sweetness he found rather repulsive. But he put his tongue in her mouth and then a hand up her top and finally got a finger inside her bra, felt a nipple, and had the biggest hard-on ever. Yet part of him remained detached, watching himself do this to a girl he didn't particularly like, and felt ashamed. He was almost relieved when she refused to let him slide his hand inside her knickers. He absolutely did not want to feel that way with Tamsin.

But, now that he'd seen her dad's car in the driveway, he couldn't stop thinking about her.

EIGHT

Tessa chose to follow in her daughter's wake as Lauren proudly guided Erin around the B&B. Unlike Erin's earlier fleeting and anonymous visit, this time Tessa was acutely aware of how Erin, like Lauren, had grown up here – or at least in the original house. In Averil's lifetime Tessa had innovated by stealth, but, free at last to impose her own taste, she had transformed the place into a boutique seaside destination. Aware of her desire to impress, she observed carefully as Erin took in the many changes, and was childishly pleased by her praise.

Yet her pleasure was mitigated by the forced acknowledgement that while she'd been immersed in the intricacies of a hip new website, brochures and costings for designer bathrooms, and Sam had been working fearsome hours in a London kitchen, their marriage had begun quietly to unravel. How stupid she'd been to tell herself that many marriages went through such arid patches, to cling to the mistaken hope that shared business interests were sufficient, that romance would return in its own good time, that in fact they were being brave and realistic to take the long view. Nula had brutally given the lie to all that.

They finished their tour in the guests' sitting room where Erin, instantly comprehending the clever compromises and attention to detail, complimented Tessa on her sense of style and imagination. Tessa also saw Erin's gaze drawn to the doll's house, though she said nothing, instead entertaining Lauren with stories about how awful the place had been when she was Lauren's age, never mind the visitors who used to stay there! When she was little, Erin recounted, the self-contained attic flat didn't exist. When Averil first began to take in guests, they had to give up the nicer bedrooms. Erin and Pamela had shared the box room while Averil slept on a divan in the basement snug. They had no other living room, and had always to be on their best behaviour while pretending to be blind and deaf to whatever the guests got up to.

Lauren pulled a face: 'That's still the same,' she complained. 'And Mum's always working.'

'I'm here though,' Tessa protested. 'You never come home to an empty house like some of your friends.'

'You should get a dog, honey,' said Erin. 'They're great company. I'll show you a picture of mine later.'

'Yeah!' Lauren looked to her mother for encouragement. But Tessa's thoughts were elsewhere, observing the doll's house through new eyes, no longer as a charmed talisman, but as a relic consecrated and set apart when Erin went away. The coat left over the banisters and little white vanity case in the hallway took on a new resonance.

Erin and Pamela's father Stanley had made the replica of their single seafront home before it became a B&B as a present for Pamela when Averil was expecting Erin. The joke, according to Grandma Averil, had been that after Erin's birth, nine-year-old Pamela preferred to play with the baby, and it was Averil herself who'd fallen in love with the imaginary rooms. After Stanley's sudden and premature death three years later, his terrified young widow had thrown herself into turning the real property – her only asset – into a viable business. As she'd set her sights on purchasing and extending into first one and then another of the neighbouring properties, the doll's house had continued to occupy the same hallowed place in the guests' sitting room. All her life Tessa had watched Averil offer her heart to the endless stream of guests who sustained the family, and realised now that it had been for them that she had sacrificed her daughter – and granddaughter. Even in old age, whenever the doorbell rang Averil had sprung to life like an actor in the spotlight, and as time went on, ensuring the guests' comfort had seemed to provide her with all the expression of love she needed.

Erin followed Tessa's gaze and finally went to peer in at the little rooms.

'Shall I fetch the key?' Tessa asked.

'No,' said Erin. 'What happened to the dolls?' she asked, straightening up again.

'There aren't any,' answered Tessa, surprised.

'I'm sure there used to be. One for each member of the family.' Erin shrugged. 'Well, I think it's just fabulous what you've done here,' she continued, turning away. 'I'm going to tell my friends back home, and make sure it gets on all the secret hideaway websites. The Aussies would love this! A real English home-from-home.'

Erin went on to question Tessa about occupancy and margins and the differences between the UK and Australian star-rating systems. Lauren, bored and excluded, trailed off to the kitchen downstairs. Tessa hoped she wouldn't start snacking before supper. A second later Tessa heard Mitch come in, and was disappointed when he headed straight upstairs. But Erin, explaining the advantages of a new booking system linked to a smartphone app, didn't seem to twig that the energetic footsteps signalled the presence of the grandson she had yet to meet.

Tessa had been hurt by the way Erin had greeted Lauren earlier, judging it to be thin and insignificant for someone finally offered the chance to take up her rightful role as mother and grandmother. On the other hand it was clear how much she regretted upsetting everyone, so perhaps this relaxed manner was her way of smoothing things over, of demonstrating that she had no wish to elbow Pamela aside. Tessa found herself once again studying Erin's flawless make-up – the carefully applied face powder, the glossy lipstick – for some clue to her birth mother's deeper feelings.

'I reckon you're not so different to me.'

Tessa's thoughts swam back into focus.

'You love your work, right?' Erin's eyes shone. And this place, I can see that it's all down to you.'

Erin's insight was accurate, if uncomfortable: Tessa knew that, like Averil, she had become addicted to the glow of satisfaction she felt each time a guest departed full of happy compliments. 'It's great to watch people unwind,' she admitted. 'To hear them say how relaxed and different they feel, even after only a couple of nights. I do love knowing I had a hand in that.'

'Sure! You should be really proud of what you've accomplished. And that's what's so great, isn't it? So fulfilling? Knowing you made everything perfect all by yourself.'

Seeing herself through Erin's eyes, Tessa felt a snake-like temptation to shed a cumbersome skin that was snagging, even painful, and emerge untrammelled and smooth like her. Tessa smiled at her mother. 'It means a lot that you're proud of me. I'm glad you came and told the truth.'

Erin looked confused, but then her face cleared. 'Sure!' she exclaimed. 'The facts of life, right?'

The doorbell rang, heralding the arrival of the first of the night's guests, a young couple in their mid-twenties. Erin said she could find her own way down to the kitchen as Tessa went to let them in. After chatting about their journey from London and showing them to their room, Tessa went up to knock on Mitch's door. He was sitting in the window seat, gazing out at the darkening sky. He had grown almost too tall to fit in the narrow space, and there was something coltish about his long limbs, clear grey eyes and straight brown hair. He turned his head to her, his thoughts clearly elsewhere, and she felt all her tension melt away as her heart swelled with love for him. Forgetting her irritation that he had not come unbidden to greet Erin, she saw the sweet, hopeful boy he had always been.

'Supper?' she asked. 'Come and meet the new granny?'

He nodded, and though his expression remained serious, followed her dutifully downstairs.

They found Lauren at the kitchen table with one hand splayed out in front of her as Erin painted each nail the same vivid colour as her own. Their two heads were almost touching yet Tessa could observe no special likeness between the two generations.

Erin put the brush back in the bottle of varnish and got up, holding out her arms: 'You must be Mitch!'

Tessa watched as her son cautiously accepted his grandmother's embrace, and reflected with a pang of sadness how strange it now felt to have assumed for so long that Mitch, fine-featured and straight-backed, would take after Hugo.

'My, you're tall,' Erin exclaimed. 'And so good-looking. Bet you have all the girls running after you!'

Lauren grimaced. 'It's your turn to lay the table,' she told her brother bossily. 'We haven't done the other hand yet.'

Tessa set about clearing away the day's accumulation of clutter, pleased for once that Lauren had turned on the radio to some upbeat pop music, glad she'd thought earlier to buy a big bunch of daffodils to help brighten up the room.

Lauren held up her painted nails for Tessa to admire. 'Chanel!' she exclaimed. 'Lotus Rouge.'

'It's lovely. But remember to take it off for school tomorrow.' Tessa was rewarded by a scowl.

Once more bent over Lauren's hand to paint the last nail, Erin appeared not to hear. 'There!' she said, replacing the glistening brush in the bottle and fanning her own fingers out beside Lauren's. 'Now we're twins!'

Lauren wiggled her fingers delightedly, but Tessa also noticed her daughter's wistful look as, screwing on the cap, Erin slipped the bottle back into the capacious handbag beside her. Lauren ought not to expect presents, but Tessa was certain that Pamela, in Erin's position, would have gifted it without a second thought. She and Pamela had not spoken since the bombshell had been dropped two days ago: it was never Pamela's way to have things out, and neither knew what to say. With a pang Tessa perceived that the contrast between the 'old' mother who wrapped herself up so tight, always holding something back, and the patina of ease offered by this other, newer mother, was not as marked as she'd first thought: both hid their real selves. Was she the same? Was that why Sam had been able to slide away so effortlessly?

Erin twisted in her chair to address Mitch, who was taking his time at the cutlery drawer. 'So you're what, in your last year of school?'

'One more to go.'

'And then what? University?'

'If I do Ok in the exams.'

'Of course you will!'

Tessa watched Mitch cringe. If his mother had dismissed his adolescent self-doubt as airily as that, he'd have snarled at her that he was too old to believe in magic.

'What do you want to study?'

'Maybe law.'

'Good for you,' said Erin. She smiled at Mitch, but asked no further questions. Instead she turned to Tessa. 'So where's the gorgeous Sam?'

Tessa was aware how her children's gazes swivelled instantly to her face. 'Didn't Pamela tell you?' she asked carefully. 'Sam and I live separately.'

'She never breathed a word,' Erin assured her.

Tessa knew she'd been every bit as guilty as Pamela in clinging to the fiction that her marriage was intact. Worse, her determination not to face the truth would have made it impossible for Sam to explain why he'd left, even if he'd wanted to. She sighed, thinking that soon she'd have to admit the whole truth to Pamela and Hugo.

Lauren leaned in towards her grandmother. 'So what's Australia like?'

'You should come visit,' said Erin, content to let the thornier subject drop. 'Find out for yourselves.'

Tessa felt a glow of pleasure that, however curtailed their own relationship might be, Erin did at least want to welcome her children.

'Awesome! Can we stay with you?' asked Lauren.

'Hey,' Mitch reprimanded, giving her a slight push as

he laid a place setting in front of her. 'That's rude. You don't just invite yourself.'

But Erin was unperturbed. 'Oh, you wouldn't want to stay with me. My apartment's way too small. But I can recommend some really cool places near the beach. Much more fun.' She shifted her enormous handbag to the floor, making room for Mitch to set out knives and forks.

'Is that where you live?' Lauren asked. 'Near the beach?'

'No. I'm right in the city. You guys wouldn't like that so much.'

'Could we do surfing?'

'I guess so. Some of the hotels do water sports.' She turned to Tessa. 'I can probably work you a nice discount on a package.'

Tessa could tell that Erin meant her offer hospitably enough, but hurt and deflated, couldn't help endorsing Mitch's expression of faint contempt. Not sharing their disappointment, Lauren turned to Tessa: 'Oh, Mum, can we?'

'We'll see.' Tessa smiled stiffly. 'Some day, perhaps.' And she watched how easily Erin let this subject drop too.

NINE

Pamela stood in the driveway and waved farewell. Hugo had insisted on driving Erin to Heathrow, and Erin had told Pamela gently not to accompany them, that it was easier for her to go into work mode and not have to say goodbye amid the bustle of the airport. Watching Hugo's car disappear along the lane, Pamela wondered what they would talk about on the journey.

She went back indoors, remembering her last parting with her sister all those years ago. Standing for a moment in the quiet hallway, she allowed herself a brief glimpse back into the torment she had felt, sitting in that rented flat in Burton upon Trent, Tessa almost weightless in her arms, feeding her a bottle of warmed formula even though the air still seemed to bear traces of the heady smell of her teenage sister's milky breasts. She had bent down to kiss the downy little head and promised herself that every kiss she ever bestowed would be on behalf of Erin, never herself. What she had not known then, but knew now, was how tainted and unworthy she would feel every time the growing child kissed her.

Yet despite the brevity of Erin's whirlwind stay, and the sadness of seeing her leave again, in many ways Pamela felt lighter than she had in years. The past three nights, she and Erin had sat up long after Hugo had gone to bed, catching up on everything in each other's lives that could not be said on the phone, and cramming in decades of unspoken words. It was as if they were back in the cramped bedroom they had once shared in the B&B. Reaching out to hold her sister's hand, Pamela was well aware that there were still things left unsaid, unasked, and she hoped that she had not done wrong by leaving them unresolved, but she had not wanted to spoil the joy of having Erin back beside her.

She had been nine when Erin was born, twelve when their father died, and, as their mother fought to establish a business that would ensure their financial survival, it had been she who had volunteered to take care of her little sister. She would delay her homework until Erin had been put to bed so she could play with her, had taken her onto the beach each summer with a bucket and spade, held her hand when she started primary school, and dried her tears when the other girls wouldn't let her join in their skipping games. Erin was eleven when Pamela married Hugo, and Pamela had occasionally persuaded their mother to allow Erin to spend weekends with them; the girl had much preferred a night on their couch to the chores, errands and constant press of strangers at home in the B&B.

Barely five years on, it had been Hugo who first guessed that Erin was pregnant. Pamela was devastated that she'd failed to notice how withdrawn the teenager had become, to question her preference for loose smocks. And she would never forget Erin's terror when left with no choice but to confess to Averil, or hearing through the closed door Averil's fury and disgust as the incoherent explanations and excuses poured out. Even after Erin had joined them in Burton upon Trent, Averil had made excuses not to visit until the baby was a couple of weeks old, and had barely looked at her grandchild until she'd received word from Brenda that Erin had arrived in Sydney.

Shivering at the unbearable recollection of her own cowardice at not standing up for Erin, at remaining silent as Averil imperiously arranged their futures, Pamela went to fetch the Hoover. She started in the spare room where Erin had slept, throwing open the windows and stripping the bed. She heaped the linen in the hallway, adding Erin's towels from the bathroom, ready for the washing machine. Pulling on yellow household gloves, she squirted cleaning cream around the bath, ran the taps and began to wipe around the tub, trying to efface the memory of Averil's refusal to let Erin speak, and the shame of her own silence in the face of Erin's distress.

The doorbell chimed as she started on the basin. Still in her yellow gloves, she went reluctantly to see who it was.

'Hi, Mum,' said Tessa. 'Thought I'd come and see how you are.'

'Busy,' answered Pamela, still in thrall to her memories. She kissed Tessa's cheek and headed back upstairs, leaving Tessa to follow. Tessa came to stand in the bathroom doorway, watching as she wiped down the basin.

'Are you glad she's gone?' Tessa asked, as Pamela scrubbed at a stubborn bit of limescale.

Pamela lowered her head. 'No.' She turned on the tap to rinse the bowl.

'Can you stop doing that? Come and talk to me?'

Stricken with competing emotions, Pamela didn't know what to say or do.

'What did she want?' asked Tessa. 'She didn't seem that bothered last night about saying goodbye to me or the kids. I don't understand why she finally came now, after all this time.'

Pamela put down the sponge, stripped off her gloves and laid them over the edge of the basin, then sat on the side of the bath. 'Cousin Brenda made her promise that she would. Apparently she'd tried to get Erin to come before, but . . .'

'But what?'

Pamela leaned sideways to straighten the bottles of shampoo and conditioner beside the bath taps.

'Mum, talk to me, please!'

'Erin didn't want to reopen old wounds.'

'Didn't she want to see me?'

'She didn't want to interfere.'

'But this Brenda thought she should?'

'Cousin Brenda was dying.'

'I still don't understand.'

'Apparently Brenda knew how much Erin regretted not making her peace with Averil before she died.' Pamela thought back to their late-night conversation. 'Erin told me that Brenda had asked her how she thought *you'd* feel if you discovered that your real mother had died and never come to see you, never given you the chance to meet her.'

'So her solution was to turn up on my doorstep but not tell me who she was? That doesn't make sense!'

'You're *our* child. Well, hardly a child. But Erin didn't want to destroy that. That's why she turned up here the next day, to explain what she'd done.'

Tessa nodded. 'She wasn't expecting to find me here as well.'

'No,' agreed Pamela. 'She wanted me to know she'd been so that if you ever asked about her, you'd know your mother *had* come to see you.' The words felt strange in her mouth: no matter how riven with guilt she'd been whenever she'd used the word *mother* to refer to herself, it was alien to say the truth out loud.

'But why *would* I ask about her?' pressed Tessa, reminding Pamela of what she had been like as an argumentative teenager. 'Why would anyone enquire into a secret they never even knew existed?'

The previous night Erin had revealed that although Averil had written her a weekly letter full of local news, she had never once referred to the birth or adoption. And when, in the early years, Erin had begged her to come out to Sydney to see her, Averil had simply ignored her request. Pamela knew, without Erin having to say it, that she had been no more forthcoming herself. 'It's my fault,' she told Tessa now. 'I should have ignored my mother and taken you out to Australia years ago, when you were small. I should have told the truth.'

'Why didn't you?'

'I knew what Averil would say. I wasn't able to defy her.'

'And now?' persisted Tessa.

'We all tried to do what was best,' said Pamela. 'I'm not saying we got it right, but we tried. Erin was little more than a child herself, and Averil had so much on her shoulders after our father died. We tried to arrange things as best we could.'

'Why didn't Erin stay longer? Did she really have to get home for her dogs?'

Pamela's heart bled for the pain in her daughter's voice. She had begged Erin to stay on, to remain as long as she liked; but Erin had said that it was all too much, that she'd made a new life for herself, and returning to Felixham had turned her into a child again, expecting Averil to come in at any moment and disapprove of her. Pamela had understood perfectly. 'Maybe we'll all go out soon to visit her,' she suggested.

'Erin didn't come back because she wanted to see me, did she? Not really. She only came because of a deathbed promise. And to see you,' Tessa added.

Pamela thought for a long while, hearing the echoes of Erin's confession and tearful pleas for understanding all those years ago, of Averil's harsh rejection of Erin's story, of her own horrified but frozen silence. When she glanced up she found Tessa watching her, a deep frown on her face. 'I don't think that's true,' said Pamela carefully. 'But it was complicated. What happened was a catastrophe for her. And if anyone got it wrong, it was me.'

'You mean you didn't want me either.'

Pamela felt her lips close tight in the familiar rictus of secrecy. She hated it, resented it, yet felt helpless to overcome it.

'You didn't, did you?' asked Tessa, upset.

'That's not true!' The words burst out and Pamela reached for Tessa's hand, but Tessa whipped it away childishly behind her back. Pamela strove to explain: 'Every time I held you in my arms, every time you hugged me or snuggled up to me, it was like a knife in my heart because of Erin.'

'You used to push me away.'

Pamela stood up. 'You were hers. It wasn't fair for me to have everything while she had nothing.'

'But look at her!' cried Tessa angrily. 'She's fine. She's perfectly all right. She never wanted me anyway! Why didn't you all just get rid of me, abandon me in a phone box or on the church steps?'

Pamela took her yellow gloves from the basin and watched her hands shake as she smoothed them flat. 'Let's have a coffee,' she said, herding Tessa out of the bathroom. 'Go and sit in the lounge while I make it. I won't be long.'

To her relief, Tessa did as she was told. Pamela slipped into the kitchen, closing the door softly. She opened the fridge and poured a little orange juice into a glass, aware that the tremor in her hand was more pronounced. Reaching into a cupboard she drew out the bottle of gin she kept hidden behind the bags of flour and poured a handsome measure into the juice.

By the time the kettle had boiled, the alcohol had done its job and she felt calm and empty. She made the coffee, put everything on a tray and took it through to where Tessa waited in the lounge.

'No family is perfect,' she said with a glassy smile as she handed her daughter a steaming mug. 'Every parent makes mistakes, but we try to do our best.'

TEN

Later in the week, Tessa returned from the farm shop laden with the staples of the organic cooked breakfasts she advertised on her website. Upset by the owner's cheerful assumption that she'd surely be familiar with every detail of the contract to supply Sam's brasserie, she was irritated to find Hugo in her basement kitchen helpfully checking a loose washer at the sink. His retirement had more or less coincided with Sam's departure to London, when Hugo had possessed himself of a set of keys 'just in case', then striven to give Tessa the impression that, with time on his hands, it was a kindness to let him potter about and find odd jobs. Even though she knew he had plenty of more attractive occupations to keep him busy she played along, pretending to an exasperation she sometimes actually felt – as she did now.

'Hi, Dad,' she greeted him. The look of delight on his face puzzled her for a moment, until she realised it was in response to the word 'Dad'.

He came to kiss her cheek, grasping her shoulders. 'How are you?' he asked.

'Fine.' She kept hold of the carrier bags, rebuffing his attempt to take them from her.

'We thought we'd let you alone, allow a bit of time for things to sink in. But maybe now you'd like to talk?'

'Not really.'

'Especially when . . . Mitch told me about you and Sam,' Hugo explained gently.

'Right.' She opened the door of the big fridge ready to put away the meat, relieved that she didn't have to find the words herself.

'I'm so sorry, Tessie. It can't be easy.'

'No.' Tessa began filling the fridge, moving things around to make room to put the fresh produce at the back.

'If you want advice over the legal stuff, I know a couple of good people. Divorce lawyers,' he added unnecessarily. 'I'm sure you'll want to be fair, but equally you don't want to–'

'Leave it, Dad, please!' Flushed with anger and distress, she buried her face in the carrier bags.

'Ok. Sorry. But you're not on your own, Tessie. We'll get past this together, I promise.'

'Same old cosy pretence, you mean?'

'No. Let's start afresh, shall we?'

Tessa nodded, not able to meet his eyes. Hugo leaned down to pick up an escaping tomato that had rolled out of its bag. 'So what did you make of Erin?' he asked. 'How did the two of you get on?'

'Fine, I suppose. I mean, maybe if I'd known all my life that my real mother was out there somewhere . . .' Taking the tomato from him, she saw him wince and continued unwillingly. 'If I'd always known I was adopted, then perhaps meeting her now would be different. But – I really don't care.'

Tessa's shameful fear was that Erin hadn't bothered to stay longer or offer more because, like everyone else, she'd found her daughter such a disappointment. And her heart clenched tight at unbidden thoughts of Lauren and Mitch accepting Nula's welcome, of them finding what they needed elsewhere. She banged the fridge door shut with more force than she intended. 'I don't know how to feel, frankly.' She turned to face Hugo squarely. 'What should I feel? What do you feel?'

He returned her gaze steadily. 'You've every right to be angry with us.'

'Would you ever have told me?'

'I'm sorry you found out like this.'

'Would you have told me otherwise?'

'Probably not,' Hugo conceded. 'Not after all this time.'

'Why not?' The question burst from Tessa, though she shrank from the answer.

'Because, to me, you were always my daughter.' He cleared his throat. 'Right from the second you were placed in my arms.'

Embarrassed, they both looked away, but Tessa stored away each precious word to take out later when she could fully appreciate them.

'And I think Pamela was afraid that if you knew the truth, you'd never forgive her. But that's no excuse,' he added. 'We should have told you years ago.'

Glancing around her utilitarian kitchen, a new thought struck Tessa: 'I thought Grandma Averil left this place to me because I'd earned it. But that wasn't the reason, was it? This is Erin's inheritance. That's why she wanted me to have it; not because I'm me, but because I'm Erin's daughter and Grandma Averil felt guilty for what she'd done.'

'Perhaps,' Hugo admitted with a sigh.

Her grandmother's legacy was this well-run, sterile machine: despite the perpetual warmth of the overworked Aga, Tessa always felt reproached by the discipline and efficiency of her kitchen, by her failure to create a proper home.

'I take full responsibility for keeping you in the dark,' Hugo went on. 'When the subterfuge began, I suppose I never believed it could remain secret. But it did, and then the right moment never came, and we put it off. And besides, I always felt it was Pamela's secret, not mine.'

She was suddenly buffeted by images of Sam making a new home elsewhere, and her mind seized on an ugly new suspicion – that she had been more blind than she dared admit, that perhaps Sam loving Nula had gone on for far longer than she'd assumed. What if they'd been seeing each other in London? Or even before?

'But in a way, you're right,' Hugo continued. 'Maybe it does make no difference.' He cleared his throat again, straightening his shoulders the way he did when determined to say what had to be said, however difficult. 'I love you,' he uttered. 'Nothing changes that.'

'You don't keep secrets from people you love!' cried Tessa, thinking of how Sam had not loved her, and failing to notice how Hugo caved inwards, away from her scorching words. 'It's selfish. Cowardly.'

'You're right,' he agreed. 'We lied to you. That was wrong. We didn't think it through to the end.'

'Well, that's your problem!' she replied. 'You created this mess.'

It seemed to take a big effort just for Hugo to remain there, staunch in his refusal to evade her bitterness. 'I'm sorry. And I want you to know that, in my heart, I always have been and always will be your father.'

He stood there waiting. Part of her longed to run to him: what kept her still was a little voice deep inside that feared his pity. Finally Hugo nodded, as if accepting her decision.

'Try and be kind to your mother.' His face, until then pale with worry, flushed. 'To Pamela,' he amended. 'She's not as strong as you think.'

'Why is it up to me to make everyone feel better?'

'It's not. I'm not saying that. Please, Tessie.'

She ignored his appeal. 'I don't care. It's not my mess, and I don't want to deal with it. I want to be left alone.'

'Very well.' Hugo headed for the door, pausing to touch her shoulder softly as he passed. Although Tessa understood that he was obeying her, that she would have protested if he hadn't, she also felt cheated. Part of her needed him to fight harder for her.

She stood listening to his slow steps ascend the stairs, then noticed a dirty mug and cereal bowl on the table, left there no doubt by Lauren. It was a relief to sweep them up and clatter them into the sink, exclaiming aloud: 'Do I have to do everything around here?'

She turned on the tap and the pipes juddered before water spurted out, its force ricocheting off the bowl and spattering the front of her clothes. Tessa almost burst into tears. Hugo was right: the tap needed a new washer. Everything was so unfair.

Realising she had to focus on something to calm herself down, Tessa tidied the kitchen and went up to the ground floor, where she plumped the cushions in the guests' sitting room. She looked into the breakfast room, but Carol had already cleared and straightened the tables, so she continued to the office where there was always plenty of paperwork to catch up on. At the desk, her fingers hesitated over the keyboard, lured by the promise of a missing piece of puzzle. How could she be expected to be her best self, or to see what was really going on around her, when all her life she had not known who she was? She needed to transform this mess into something positive. Something important was lacking from her life, something that would make her feel whole again, and though she had no wish to upset Hugo of all people, she could not afford to let herself be ambushed again by ignorance. A half-formed decision took on the momentum of inevitability. She opened Google, typed the name Roy Weaver and pressed Enter. A random list appeared. She searched again, adding 'architect' after his name. The new list was equally random. She added 'Manchester', then 'Manchester University'. Nothing gelled. It was too common a name. She would have to think around this, work out how to track him down.

She disowned the unsettling ripple of recognition that possessing a secret of her own would be exciting.

ELEVEN

School had broken up for the Easter holidays. Mitch sat in his window seat, deciding how to spend his day. He expected that, as usual, his mates would gather on the green to exchange banter and the occasional cigarette while lounging against the black Napoleonic canons that faced out to sea. Mitch would usually be happy enough to join in the youthful attempt to project a dangerous rural machismo, except that today he was apprehensive lest Tamsin walk past, observe their posturing, and judge them pathetic.

On the other hand, she might not even be in Felixham. In which case, why rot alone indoors? He could go over and see his dad, but he felt constrained about that too. Mitch liked Nula, she was no stress, and he was pleased for Sam. Although Mitch sometimes wished his dad would just grow up a bit, Sam was far more cheerful these days, far more *normal*. When he'd first come back from London he'd been so *stagey*, as if he were acting the part of a dad rather than just hanging out like he used to when he still lived at home. Mitch had never figured out why Sam had left home in the first place: it wasn't as though he and Tessa had shouted and fought, like he'd heard friends talk about their parents, and they'd gone on being just as friendly as they had before. Though Mitch knew that couldn't last, not now Nula was around.

Nothing could take away the sick feeling he had every time he crossed the line from one parent to the other. If anything, the fact that Mum now knew about Nula made it worse, because he could no longer kid himself she wouldn't mind. And the way she pretended not to be upset only proved that she minded *a lot*.

He ought to cycle over to pay his grandparents a visit. Grannie Pamela always did lots of baking to celebrate the start of every school holiday, and she was probably expecting him. But every time he thought about what Tessa had said about Hugo not being his real grandfather any more, everything felt wrong and he didn't want to deal with it.

He'd drawn up his revision timetable and sorted out all the books he needed to prepare for next term's exams, but it still stressed him out to sit in his room and look at the pile of work he'd have to do. Maybe he'd just go for a spin on his bike. He didn't have to stop and hang out with his mates. But he might go around by Tamsin's house. In which case, he'd clean his teeth before he set out, and maybe wear different jeans.

Twenty minutes later, after a fierce burst of speed along the main road and back to burn off his restlessness, Mitch rounded the corner of the narrow street that led towards Tamsin's house. He leant back in the saddle, steering the bike nonchalantly with one hand. When he saw her standing there, waiting for the Dalmatian puppy to finish peeing against a fence post, he put his other hand back on the bar to correct a potentially fatal wobble. She looked up, saw him, and smiled. He drew to a halt beside her.

'Hi.' He hoped she'd assume his breathlessness was due to physical exertion.

'Hi, Mitch.'

Ecstatic that she remembered his name, he smiled back, and was repaid by an answering look of relief. He remembered his vow to be Hemingway, not Fitzgerald, to behave as if her glamorous background were of no importance. 'Have you broken up already, then?'

'Yes. Thank goodness!'

'So? You here for the holidays?'

'Yes. The whole time. I was going to go see my mum, but she can't have me.'

'Your folks not together?'

'They are – it's just she's on a project in LA.' Tamsin shrugged, the ends of her straight honey-coloured hair brushing her collarbones.

'Sorry. Mine are splitting up,' Mitch told her. 'Pretended for ages it wasn't happening, but now they are. Really sucks.'

She looked at him anxiously. 'Mine aren't splitting up. Mum was offered work she really wanted, and it's taking longer than expected, that's all.'

'You must miss her.' Mitch corrected his blunder and was relieved to see her smile return.

'Dad's organised a nanny for when he's not here,' she said. 'Can you believe it? I suppose it's better than being all by myself, but, I mean . . .' She sighed and made an exaggerated pout, then parodied herself in a singsong voice. 'Whatever!'

They laughed together, and Mitch bent down to stroke the dog, scratching him behind the ears in a way that made the animal pull at the lead and jump up at him.

'Down, Blanco!'

'Not called him Pongo, then?'

'Not quite. Blanco!' She pulled again sharply on the lead. 'He's supposed to have been to training classes.'

'Probably wants off the leash.'

Tamsin agreed. 'I've got a special whistle to call him back. And he does obey. But I don't know where to go. Come next month, he won't be allowed on the beach any more.'

'Walking on sand and shingle isn't much fun anyway. I can show you some good walks, if you like.' Mitch had spoken without thinking, and now cursed himself for blushing. But her face opened joyfully.

'Oh, would you? That would be so fun.' She looked up at Mitch clear-eyed, then, succumbing to shyness herself, also bent over to pat the dog. 'You'd like that, Blanco, wouldn't you?'

'We could go now, if you like.'

'I can't.'

His heart fell: she was just being polite.

'Dad has plans. But I'm free tomorrow.'

'Any time you like!'

She smiled. 'Mid-morning? Come to the house. Over there.' She pointed, and Mitch pretended the information was new to him. 'Press the buzzer on the gate, and I'll let you in.'

'Ok. Tomorrow then. Bye, Tamsin.'

'Bye, Mitch.'

As Mitch rode away without a care in the world, he speculated that very probably his real grandfather was a racing driver or a fighter pilot.

TWELVE

Tessa was taken by surprise when the doorbell rang. She looked at her watch: 5.30 already. She left the leather-bound Visitor books spread out on the floor, and, wiping away the film of dust on her hands, went to greet the first of the evening's guests. Declan Mills was a regular. A buyer for a chain of American-owned organic supermarkets, he came from London on a monthly visit to local farmers. Felixham was slightly out of his way, but he claimed to love the chance to be so close to the sea, explaining that he used to come to the area as a kid on family holidays and enjoyed coming back.

It was when Declan had emailed to make this booking that the idea of the Visitor books had first occurred to Tessa: what if Erin had met Roy Weaver because he'd been a guest? Averil had always been proud of how many people returned for a second or third visit, if not annually. It had been the subject of heated discussion once Tessa and Sam had notionally taken over, when Averil objected to some of their changes on the grounds that her regulars wouldn't like it. It had been difficult making the point that Averil's regulars were literally a dying breed. Nevertheless, Averil's pride meant she had treasured the Visitor books, the gilt-edged pages signed, often with added comments, by every guest. For years they had gathered dust on a shelf in the snug, and it had taken Tessa a while to locate the volume she wanted.

Tessa had been born in June 1975, and she had already skimmed through all the entries from the previous summer, but without success. As she went to open the door, the thought took shape that Roy Weaver, like Declan Mills, might have come to Felixham because it was familiar from earlier family holidays. Erin had said she thought Roy was twenty-three that summer: perhaps there was a chance, however faint, that if she searched further back, she would come across the names and old address of her paternal grandparents.

Declan, a stocky man with neat, graceful movements, greeted her with his usual kiss on the cheek.

'It's your same room,' she told him.

'I know the way,' he smiled, picking up his bag. 'And I've a nice bottle of wine, if you'd join me for a drink later?'

This had become a pleasant arrangement between them. When the season allowed, Declan liked to walk over to South Felixham for a pub supper, getting back before dark, then relax with a drink and the local paper. Since Tessa did not have an alcohol licence, he often brought with him some interesting bottle recommended by his supermarket's wine buyer. While most of the other guests usually chose to watch television in their own rooms, Declan was happy to include anyone who preferred to spend their evening more sociably.

After settling the other guests – a well-to-do couple searching for a second home to buy in the area – Tessa ate supper in the kitchen alone. Only a few weeks ago she would have appreciated some quiet time to herself, but Mitch and Lauren were with Sam, who now had room for them to stay over, and the effort of not thinking about her kids making themselves at home with Nula made her restless and irritable. But neither did she want to give in to the temptation to spend the evening leafing further back through the Visitor books: she must not let the search for her father, for this mysterious untapped potentiality, become an obsession. So she was glad of Declan's promise of company. In the two years or more he had been a guest, she had got to know him reasonably well. He was fluent and well-informed, a shrewd listener with a sharp sense of humour. He wore a wedding ring, and, although he never directly mentioned his wife, he stayed on the right side of flirtatious – enough to be flattering, but not so much that Tessa felt pressured.

That evening she brushed her hair and put on fresh lipstick before joining him in the guests' sitting room with two glasses and a bowl of olives. She was glad to find him alone.

'An organic Pinot Noir from Napa Valley,' Declan announced, pouring her a full glass.

'Thanks. Good health.'

They clinked glasses and sat back. 'It's pigs tomorrow,' he laughed. 'Belly pork. One celebrity chef, and we can't sell enough of it.'

'To pigs, then!' Tessa raised her glass again.

'When does Sam open his new place? Soon, isn't it?'

'Next month.'

'All on schedule?'

'I think so.'

'So what's going to be on his opening menu?'

'Oh – I'm not sure yet.'

'Tell me to shut up if I'm trespassing, but you don't sound as enthusiastic as you used to be.' He gave her a disarming grin.

'No. Well, we've agreed on a divorce.'

Declan raised an eyebrow, and she shrugged.

'I did wonder,' he observed. 'You Ok with that?'

'Fine. But I'm trying to take more of a back seat. Let him get on with things, you know?'

Declan nodded. 'Funny business, divorce. Having to train oneself out of old habits. Then all of a sudden it's done, and you've moved on.'

'You were married before? I didn't know.'

'Why would you? Only lasted a year or two. Met at uni, a bit like you and Sam. Except no kids. Don't suppose I'd even recognise her now.'

'You wouldn't know how to go about finding people you've lost touch with?' hazarded Tessa, seizing the moment.

'One that got away?' He sounded amused.

'No. Nothing romantic.' She hesitated, unsure how much she wanted to say. But there was no one else she could talk to, and Declan would be gone in the morning: by the time she saw him again, she could tell him she'd decided to forget all about it.

'What then?' he prompted.

She took a deep breath. 'My father. My biological father.'

'Wow.' Declan reached for the bottle and refilled their glasses. 'This sounds like a story.'

'Yes, and no. Turns out I was adopted by my aunt. But I know almost nothing about the man who fathered me, and I'd like to find out.'

'Get yourself a PI.'

'What's that?'

'Private Investigator. Expensive, but that way you'll know every available route's been tried.'

'Sounds a bit shady!'

Declan laughed. 'I know what you mean. Tell you what, I could ask the Head of Security at work, if you like. He's an ex-cop with very good contacts. At least he'd have some idea of what's possible.'

'Let me think about it.'

'Sure.' He helped himself to an olive.

'But thanks.' She looked across at him, appreciating that he stuck to practicalities and did not pry too far into her emotions; but, at the same time, she needed to talk. As she tried to decide how far to trust him, he met her look with a frank and pleasant smile.

'What happens in Felixham stays in Felixham.' He crossed himself with a mocking look up to heaven. 'Regard me as your confessor, if you like.'

Tessa laughed, relaxing back into her armchair. 'In one way, there's nothing to tell. The aunt who is in fact my mother has gone back to Australia, and I don't particularly care if I never see her again. I'm not being harsh. There was nothing there. No connection.'

'Think it will be any different if you find your daddy?'

'Yes.'

'That's asking a lot.'

'But he's half my DNA. I mean, my mother's my aunt, my aunt's my mother – same difference, really. But his half I know nothing about. That's half of me.'

'What if he's not that keen on some long-lost daughter turning up on his doorstep, upsetting whatever family he's got now? It'd certainly freak me out!' Declan leant forward, pressing his point. 'For all you know, he could be a priest or a politician, or – I dunno – he might have realised he's gay!'

Tessa listened in stubborn silence.

'Did he know about you at the time?' asked Declan in a more serious tone.

'No.'

'Then he might not want to know about you now either.' He leant across and laid his hand on hers. Tessa was taken aback: he had not touched her deliberately like this before. 'Men don't think about paternity the same way a woman would,' he went on. 'Excuse my French, but it's just a fuck.

What happens after is nothing to do with us guys.' He squeezed her hand and let go. 'I'd hate to see you disappointed, that's all.'

'You're probably right.' Tessa was almost relieved. 'And I'm over-romanticising the whole thing. I've this fantasy that by finding my other half I'd be finding part of myself that's lost. But it's rubbish really.'

'No, it's not,' said Declan. 'We all think like that. Think there's a key to everything.' He leant over to pour more wine. 'I was brought up a Catholic. Was told that God has a plan for me. Even when you stop believing, you still keep asking, What's the plan? No one wants to believe there isn't one.'

Tessa laughed. 'So I'm not looking for my father, I'm searching for my place in some great cosmic design?'

'Yeah! Seriously, we all want an explanation, a cause, some meaning. Nothing wrong with wanting to explore who you are.'

Tessa was waylaid by the thought that she'd usually be listening out by now for Lauren and Mitch coming home from Sam's, ten minutes' walk away. But they were at Nula's flat. Was Nula kissing Lauren goodnight? Would Nula smile at Mitch in the morning when he came tousle-headed into the kitchen in search of orange juice?

'Look,' Declan interrupted her distress. 'If it's important to you to find your daddy, don't let me talk you out of it.'

'I can't imagine going through the rest of my life without at least trying to find out who he is. Even if we never meet.'

Declan nodded. 'You may not want me involved, but if you'd like to give me whatever information you've got on him, I can ask this guy at work the best way to track someone down. Up to you. Just say the word.'

'Actually,' decided Tessa, 'that would be great. Thank you.'

THIRTEEN

Mitch was sick of revision. But to stand any chance of applying successfully to a good university he had to do well in every exam, which meant allocating a precise amount of time to each different subject. Never before had he been so aware of time passing. Each day of the holidays that he spent indoors with his books and his computer was one day less to spend with Tamsin. Once term started and she returned to her boarding school, especially if her dad wanted weekends in London, he might not see her at all until half-term. That thought made it impossible to concentrate on European nationalism in the nineteenth century.

Seeing Tamsin was already difficult enough. He never brought friends home unless he could help it; the B&B was too public, too hard to explain to people who lived in normal homes. Besides, he knew his mum would refuse to let him take a girl up to his bedroom, and there wasn't anywhere else to hang out without Lauren sticking around, and she'd embarrass him by going on about which celebrities Tamsin had met. But Tamsin wasn't wholly comfortable in her own house either. Which was kind of strange, because everything in it had been designed to be just the way you'd want it. Lights dimmed, sound systems followed you from room to room, shutters adjusted to the movement of the sun, the sofas were huge and soft, the TV was the biggest plasma screen you could imagine, and the fridge was glass-fronted like in a supermarket – you didn't even have to open the door to see what you fancied to eat.

Mitch had now been introduced to Charlie Crawford who, glued to his iPhone, had merely raised a hand and turned away. Mitch had also met Quinn, the improbably named nanny, who, as Tamsin said, didn't seem to have caught on to the fact that she was no longer in La-La Land. Quinn's one skill seemed to be making fruit smoothies, which were, he had to admit, delicious. All the same, he could see it wasn't much fun for Tamsin spending so much time with only Quinn for company, especially as she'd told him how much she missed her mum and wanted her to come home, even though she knew the work she'd been asked to do researching costumes for a film was a fantastic opportunity.

Their best times were out walking Blanco, following the marshland and coastal paths. Tamsin had been anxious the first time she let the dog off the lead, and didn't let him go far before blowing on the special high-frequency whistle the dog-trainer had given them. But Blanco responded immediately, and after that they'd relaxed and let him bound ahead. She worried they'd get lost among the tall reeds, but Mitch reassured her how familiar he was with the various landmarks in sight along the higher ground, how he'd spent his childhood exploring the paths and waterways. Without thinking, he'd named an unusual warbler as it darted out of sight, and she'd been genuinely interested, even asking him to identify some other birds. She was so easy to be with, he almost forgot she was a girl – except that she was unlike any other human creature he had ever seen. He could look at her forever.

He couldn't remember how it had happened, but during their second walk they'd ended up holding hands. And before he left her, he had kissed her. Just lips to lips, but hers were soft and warm and, close up, her skin and hair smelled like heaven. After that, slowly, every day, they'd touched a bit more. Faces, then arms, then his hands on her waist, hers on his shoulders. Everything was all the more precious for being chaste, for being a way of getting to know one another, the same as the long conversations in which they took turns to tell about their family, friends, school, likes, dislikes and dreams. There was nothing about her he didn't want to know.

He knew Lauren was onto him. She'd even tried to follow him once, and he'd had to threaten to tell Tessa how the day Lauren took off school with 'food poisoning' had been due to drinking half a bottle of Bailey's at a friend's house the previous night. He knew he was being mean, that Lauren missed hanging out with him and that she wasn't as happy as she made out about Nula being around all the time. He could see that she always had her hand in a bag of crisps or the biscuit tin because she was bored and lonely, but he couldn't help her. Being with Tamsin was like being on a different planet, and there simply wasn't room to think about Lauren as well.

He closed his history file: European nationalism in the nineteenth century could wait. He picked up his phone and sent Tamsin a text asking if Blanco fancied a walk. He'd worry about his exams later.

FOURTEEN

Declan's email was infuriating. *Hi Tessa*, he'd written. *I think I may have some information for you about Roy Weaver. But you may not like it. I thought about not telling you, but it's your decision. What would you like me to do? Regards, Declan xx.*

Tessa got up from the desk, went down to the basement and started to take a load of washing out of the machine, giving herself time to consider her reaction. The kids were out and there would be no guests in the house until later. She hung the pillowcases on the pulley maid, tightened the rope to raise it back to the ceiling, and pushed the towels into the dryer to make them soft and fluffy, all the while allowing a decision to form itself in her mind.

She returned to the computer, and typed her reply: *Hi Declan, Thanks for your help. Whatever it is, I'd like to know. Best wishes, Tessa.* She pressed Send, and sat back. Whatever she had set in motion, her action recognised the impossibility of wondering for the rest of her life what Declan had found out. Good or bad – and it clearly wasn't unadulterated good – she had to know.

The computer pinged, and she was taken by surprise to see that Declan had replied straight away. Her mouth went dry and her fingers trembled as she opened his email. It contained three links. She clicked on the first one, and read the brief newspaper report. The second was another short report, dated about eight months after the first. The third, from a different newspaper, was slightly longer, and, with an accompanying grainy black-and-white photograph, reported the conviction for murder at Manchester Crown Court of Roy Weaver, forty-eight, a design consultant from Chester.

Tessa stared at the face in an indistinct newspaper photograph taken twelve or more years earlier. The phone on the desk rang and, automatically, she picked it up. 'Seafront B&B.'

'Are you Ok?' It was Declan. 'I had to call. I feel terrible, being the one to tell you.'

'How do you know it's him?'

'Geoff – he's Head of Security for the whole UK operation – says he cross-checked everything.'

'You're absolutely certain?'

'I wouldn't have sent it otherwise. Born in Manchester in 1951. Studied architecture there. Turns up in the 1981 census in Salford as a college lecturer. Unmarried.'

'He killed a woman.'

'Newspaper says she was a girlfriend. Most murders are domestic. Could've been a crime of passion, a one-off.'

Tessa stared at the screen, not knowing what to say.

'Geoff says if you want to hire a researcher, you should be able to get more detail on the trial.'

'Ok.'

'I think he pulled a few strings to get this far.'

'Tell him I'm grateful. But it's a shock.'

'I'm so sorry, Tessa.'

'Don't be. Better to know.'

'I guess. Look, I have to run. I'm at work, but my mobile number's on the email, in case you want to talk later.'

'Thanks, Declan.'

'Ok, then. If you're sure you're all right, I'll say goodbye.'

'Bye.'

Tessa hung up. Somehow the idea of Declan, a man she hardly knew, having this knowledge about her seemed worse than possessing it herself. Women in Greek myths were always punished for their curiosity: well, now it had happened to her.

She tried googling some of the details in the brief newspaper reports, but could find nothing more online; had there been, she was sure Declan's security expert would have provided it. Unless Erin was mistaken, or there was another Roy Weaver of the same age who had also studied architecture in Manchester, then the man in the indistinguishable photo was almost certainly her father. She wondered if Erin knew that he was in prison, but dismissed the idea. There were no lurid headlines to win syndication of the story in Australia, so why should she have found out? Tessa's fleeting regret that the story of summer romance had been tarnished gave way to curiosity: what on earth could have happened to the handsome young architectural student for him to end up convicted of murder?

Tessa stared again at the photo on the screen, willing it to reveal more. Embodied in this face was a new genetic blueprint, a whole new story about who she was and where she came from. Not only her, but also her kids; this one man gave them all new grandparents and great-grandparents and great-great-grandparents. Yet all she knew about him were the stark words of the crime reports, stubbornly reminding her that she was left with only one bare fact: she was the daughter of a criminal.

She looked at her watch. Hugo and Pamela were due for lunch. After their last meeting Hugo had taken Tessa at her word and left her alone, but the Easter holidays would soon end and Mitch and Lauren wanted to see their grandparents before school began again. Hugo had his key – they would let themselves in – so she closed Declan's email and went downstairs to lay the table.

As she carried out the familiar tasks, she attempted to scan her reaction. Overall, elation at having identified Roy Weaver outweighed the – what? She wasn't yet sure how she felt about his crime: disappointment, revulsion, distaste, fear, pity? The random images that came to mind – a lifeless body on the floor, bloodstains, a penitent or defiant man being led away in handcuffs – seemed overly dramatic, the stuff of movies. Surely, when all was said and done, he was still an ordinary man?

Tessa heard the front door open and close, and then descending footsteps. Pamela followed Hugo into the kitchen. Tessa knew her refusal to acknowledge Pamela's hesitation was childish, but she felt justified. Any reminder of the obduracy with which Pamela and Hugo had held out against telling her the truth unleashed an unmanageable rush of grief and anger. It was up to them, not her, to make amends.

Once Mitch and Lauren drifted in Tessa was able to withdraw from much of the conversation and to observe her 'social parents' – a term she had learned from an adoption website she'd consulted – from her new perspective. They were no longer her mum and dad but adults who kept secrets, and she was not their daughter but a child they had lied to and misled. She wondered how much their shared secrets had formed the two of them, how far it was the dread of exposure that had left them so uptight and reserved, and how different they and their marriage might otherwise have been.

Observing Pamela unobtrusively move the carton of ice cream out of reach before Lauren could help herself to an extra portion, Tessa was struck by how much of her mother's constant vigilance must stem from having always to navigate around the hidden rock of the adoption. But she continued to resist any pull towards sympathy for them: they had chosen to nurture their secret and she had been left helpless, out of the loop, forced to be ignorant against her will. They had not cared what happened to her.

As Mitch and Lauren got up from the table, Tessa remembered something she wanted to tell her daughter. 'I ordered that film you wanted,' she said. 'The DVD came in today's post. I'll watch it with you tonight, if you like.'

'Seen it already,' replied Lauren as she gave Hugo a hug. 'Nula had it. It's fun though. You should see it,' she added, turning to kiss Pamela.

Tessa couldn't miss the sympathy in the look Pamela directed at her over Lauren's shoulder. As soon as the kids disappeared upstairs, Tessa got up and began to clear the table. Her hands shook as she stacked the dishwasher. Hugo came up behind her, handing her more dirty plates. 'All right?'

She looked into his kind, open face. He had aged since he retired, although it was only since Erin's appearance that she had noticed. It gave her pause for thought: she didn't really wish to hurt either one of them. She shook her head. 'Fine,' she said. 'Just tired.'

'You ought to talk to Lauren about how she's putting on weight, you know,' said Pamela. 'It's probably only getting into the wrong habits, but all the same you want to nip it in the bud.'

'It's just puppy fat,' responded Tessa.

'It may be as simple as not putting so much fattening food in front of her.'

'I've got enough on my mind right now.'

'I could make you a big batch of fruit salad if you like,' persisted Pamela.

'I don't need you to tell me how to bring up my daughter!'

'Hey,' soothed Hugo. 'Let's not start a fight over it.'

'You have no idea!' Tessa slammed the dishwasher shut, rattling the crockery inside.

'Then sit down and talk to us,' he replied.

Tessa looked from one to the other: Pamela apprehensive and miserable, Hugo tense but determined to be reasonable. She could not help experiencing a defiant satisfaction that for the first time in her life she possessed knowledge that they did not, that the tables had been turned. 'I've found my father,' she announced.

She regretted her brusqueness immediately. Hugo dropped heavily onto the nearest chair, his mouth falling open in shock, and Pamela went to stand behind him, placing a comforting hand on his shoulder. She met Tessa's eyes, a look of panic in her own. 'Tell us, then. Who is he?'

Tessa sat down across the table from them, sorry now for dragging them into it. 'Erin told me a few facts about him, and I'm pretty certain it's the right man.'

'What did Erin tell you?' asked Pamela anxiously.

'Not much, but enough to track him down.' Tessa took a deep breath. 'He's in prison for murder.'

'Oh no!' It was Pamela who reacted first, her hand across her mouth. She gripped Hugo's shoulder, supporting herself as she sank into the seat beside him. 'What kind of murder?'

'He killed his partner twelve years ago. That's all I know.'

'His partner? A woman?'

'I can show you the press reports, if you like. They're

pretty basic. They didn't give any details so it can't have been a very sensational crime.'

'But you'll stay away from him, now that you know?' pleaded Pamela.

Tessa nodded. Seeing her paternity through their anxious eyes made her feel contaminated and dirty, made her want to repel the connection, unmake it, return to when Declan's email had never existed.

'If only Erin had stopped to think before coming back here,' began Hugo, as if following Tessa's own line of thought. 'She's no idea what she's started.'

'She's paid her own price,' said Pamela quietly. 'None of this was Erin's fault. If you have to blame someone blame my mother – blame Averil. Blame me.'

'You haven't told Mitch and Lauren about this, have you?' asked Hugo.

'No. Not yet. Though I don't want any more secrets either.'

'You're not going to contact him!' pleaded Pamela. 'There's no need. You owe him nothing.'

'I haven't thought it through yet.'

'You're nothing to do with him,' Pamela insisted. 'You have a father.' She reached out for Hugo's hand, but he squeezed hers briefly and let go.

'Tessa's right, no more secrets,' he said, his voice dull.

'I'm sorry,' said Tessa. 'I'm not doing this to hurt you. But I do have to find out. I have a right to know who I really am.'

'Of course you do. But . . .' Hugo gathered himself

together. 'You deserve better, that's all. What can there possibly be of you in this man?'

'What if he has other children?' asked Tessa. 'What if I have other relatives, or grandparents still alive?'

'Be careful, darling. Tell her to be careful, Hugo!' begged Pamela. 'She listens to you.'

Hugo shook his head. 'We can't stand in her way. Not if she has other family out there.'

Pamela looked as though she wanted to argue, but said nothing more.

'I won't say anything to Lauren and Mitch until I've decided what I want to do,' offered Tessa.

'No,' agreed Hugo, lifting himself to his feet.

'It'll be Ok,' she said, though she knew it was a futile refrain.

Hugo nodded. 'You know where we are, if you want us.'

'Ok,' repeated Tessa.

She watched the two of them pause for a moment in the doorway and thought they all might as well be a thousand miles apart, three barren little atolls dotted across a vast ocean. Whatever the magic essence was which made people into a family was no longer here between them. Right this second, if she could be granted a single wish, it would be for these two people to be once again, uncomplicatedly, her parents. But that was no longer possible.

FIFTEEN

Sam stood with his arm draped around Nula's waist as she attended to the stir-fry on the stove. She laughed at something he said and he pushed his face against her long wavy hair, kissing her head. Mitch tried to look away, but it was difficult in Nula's tiny kitchen.

Lauren was peering into one of the kitchen cupboards as if memorising its contents. Standing on tiptoe, she reached in to pull a jar out from the back, examined the label, then turned to put it down beside her place at the table. 'Do you have any ketchup?' she asked.

'In the fridge.'

She added ketchup to the collection of dressings and sauces fanned out around her knife and fork and then sat down, waiting for supper to be ready. Mitch could see that she had given no thought either to what anyone else might want, or to how little room there was on the table for superfluous jars and bottles, but nor did she notice when he shook his head at her. He would like to have felt more affectionate towards his sister, but sometimes he couldn't be bothered.

Sam spooned rice from the steamer into a mould, levelled off the top and upended it deftly onto a plate, leaving a neat mound around which, taking the wok out of Nula's hands, he arranged the ingredients from the stir-fry. As Nula handed each plate to the table she gave Sam a little grin, though Mitch could see that he didn't grasp the reason for her admiration, so used was he to serving food with this kind of perfection.

'Looks great, Dad.' Mitch realised he was hungry, and dug in. Sam's rice was perfect, but Nula's stir-fry was gelatinous and Mitch couldn't entirely blame Lauren for smothering it with ketchup – though she could do so with more tact. He chose not to examine the various reasons why his dad tolerated Nula's culinary lapses (and expected them to do likewise), nor why Sam might find Nula's casual failures more beguiling than Tessa's tidy achievements. 'Thanks, Nula,' Mitch added, struggling not to be unfair: it wasn't their fault he didn't want to be here, that he'd rather be with Tamsin.

'So, how's the revision?' asked Sam.

'I'm sticking to my timetable. Can't say how much is going in though.'

'It's important to take breaks,' said Nula. 'Get some oxygen to the brain.'

'Mitch is always sneaking off somewhere,' said Lauren. 'Won't tell me where.'

'He doesn't have to,' Sam pointed out.

'I wanna know what you're being so mysterious about,' complained Lauren.

With all three of them looking at him – Sam and Nula with amusement, Lauren with stubborn resentment – Mitch was tempted to tell them. The holidays would soon be over anyhow. But the fear of how it would be once Tamsin was out of reach at boarding school for weeks on end was too terrible, and he wasn't sure he could bear to share that misery with anyone.

'I think he's got a girlfriend,' announced Lauren. 'That's why he won't say where he goes.'

'Good,' said Nula. 'Any boys in your life, Lauren?'

Mitch smiled to himself. But Lauren refused to take the hint. 'It's Tamsin Crawford, isn't it?' she crowed. 'I saw you together.'

Mitch blushed and glared at Lauren in fury.

'Really?' asked Sam in surprise. 'You don't have to tell us,' he added quickly, as Nula laid a hand on his arm. 'None of our business.'

'It's not fair,' protested Lauren. 'You get to go inside her house, and you won't even tell me what it's like. I won't tell anyone. Promise!'

Mitch didn't believe her. 'It's just a house.' He knew as he spoke that it wasn't wholly true. He felt different around 'Captain Gorgeous', as Tamsin teasingly called her father. Being subjected to Charlie Crawford's full-on charm was an extraordinary experience. He could quite see why Quinn was totally under the spell of it. And it was exciting to listen to Charlie on the phone making decisions – bang

bang bang – do this, cancel that, tell so-and-so to change it around and get back to me. It didn't bother Mitch if Charlie's attention was permanently elsewhere, if after their first few encounters Charlie just looked through him as though either Mitch were not quite present or Charlie himself was elsewhere, but Mitch despised him for treating his daughter that way.

He looked at his own father. Sam was making the brasserie happen: he was a fantastic chef and was in the process of transforming a ramshackle building into a shiny new restaurant. Mitch respected him for that, but also saw how it took every ounce of ingenuity and energy Sam possessed. And once or twice he had witnessed Sam's despair when he worried about money or doubted his ability to see it all through on time. Captain Gorgeous never lost his nerve. He was on the phone to LA juggling multi-million dollar budgets, approving special effects and car crashes and night shoots in rain forests with temperamental stars and their huge retinues, while Sam could only just cope with the responsibility of opening one small restaurant in Felixham.

'Charlie Crawford's not much of a dad,' he told Lauren. 'He's often only there at weekends, and then he's usually working.'

'So who stays in the house with the daughter during the week?' asked Sam in a deliberately casual tone.

'Her name's Tamsin,' supplied Lauren.

'The nanny, Quinn, is there. She's American,' he added, in case they thought Quinn was a man.

'How old is Tamsin?'

'Nearly sixteen.' Mitch could sense parental alarm beneath his dad's questions and smiled, glad to have Sam's qualities as a good parent confirmed: 'Don't worry, Dad. We're not running wild.'

'So has she met, like, *everyone* in Hollywood?' asked Lauren.

'Sure,' replied Mitch. 'Same as you've met everyone in Felixham. It's not something she goes on about.' Now his casual tone was fake; this was an answer he had anticipated and rehearsed, because it would feel so disloyal to Tamsin to admit how thrilled he'd been the first time she'd mentioned a few starry names. But he'd been aware of her discomfort, of how awkward it was for her to show that while this wasn't stuff she got excited about, she didn't judge you for being in awe. Once she began to trust him, she'd explained how sometimes people at school or wherever could be nasty, as if she was being patronising or making out like she was cooler than she really was. With some people, she said, she could never win. The regret in her voice made Mitch recall his first impression of her as lonely, and knew he would do anything – *anything* – to protect her.

'You'd be welcome to invite Tamsin over for supper,' offered Nula, oblivious to the impossibility of squeezing another person around the kitchen table, and Sam signalled his agreement.

'Wicked!' said Lauren, her eyes shining.

'Thanks,' said Mitch. He felt mean, not committing

himself; it wasn't as if he intended to cut Lauren out, but she was a kid, she didn't understand.

All the same, since being with Tamsin Mitch had begun to cherish an active sense of what it would take to be a man, and now he asked himself how the kind of man he wanted to be would treat an annoying younger sister. He looked at his dad, trying to see him as Nula did: he was good-looking, easy-going, reasonably generous, but also weak, afraid of confrontation, keen on the line of least resistance. Sam would let Lauren take advantage of his lazy good nature whereas Charlie, so bold and dizzyingly ambitious, was a bit of a shit who would probably crush a kid like Lauren without a second thought. Mitch knew exactly the kind of man he wanted to be: Hugo would find a way to make Lauren feel better about herself without giving in to her. But whenever Mitch tried to get his head around how Hugo wasn't actually related to him any more, his brain seized up and he had to think about something else.

SIXTEEN

Tessa dropped Lauren and her friend Evie at the station in time for the train to Norwich. The girls had insisted they were old enough to spend the day there shopping on their own, and Evie's mother would pick them up on their return. They had chatted excitedly together in the back of the car as they planned their trajectory, and Tessa watched indulgently as they now disappeared through the ticket barrier clutching one another tightly by the arm. She had given Lauren money for lunch and emergencies, and hoped their adventure would not disappoint them.

She reversed the car, ready to head home, then, idling the engine, sat for a little longer, acknowledging her own desire for escape. Mitch was fine by himself, and she could always call him later. Tonight's guests weren't due to arrive until six, and Carol had already given her a hand making up the rooms. She put the car in gear and turned out of the station car park in the opposite direction, away from Felixham.

As she drove, she thought of Lauren the previous night remonstrating as she'd once again gone over the 'rules' that would safeguard a young girl in the city: 'Mum, I'm not a kid any more!' It was true. Her children were growing up and no longer wanted or needed her in the old way. True, too, that it was hard to let go, but there was also a measure of relief in being, as she felt now, off the hook. She took the slip road onto a dual carriageway, accelerating to pull out ahead of a lorry in the inside lane. It felt good to speed away from Felixham, to escape the tangle of old loyalties and new emotions. She wished she'd brought some CDs so she could play some of the music she and Sam used to listen to at college – Oasis, maybe or Nirvana. Maybe she should go shopping for some new clothes, get a different haircut? She wanted to remember how it felt to be young and without responsibility, to remember who she used to be.

When had life started to happen so fast that she forgot who she was? To begin with it had felt like contentment, part of being with Sam and of becoming a mother, of growing up and accepting herself. But maybe, without even realising, she had crossed some invisible line and lost sight of 'Tessa'. One more year and Mitch would be leaving for university; whatever course Lauren followed, she wouldn't be far behind. Whether or not Sam stayed with Nula, he'd be forever occupied with the brasserie. Tessa would be alone. But it struck her that the countryside through which she was driving was abundant with signs of spring – green rows sprouting in the arable fields, young leaves on trees, white blossom in the hedgerows. Erin's revelation had been, if nothing else, a wake-up call.

She stopped for petrol and to look at the map. There was no particular reason to drive so far except that the name, and images from some TV news programme, had stuck in her mind, and now she was determined to see it through. As she followed the route she'd outlined, the landscape became flatter and more featureless, the small villages further apart, huddled low under the spreading skies. She passed numerous waterways, the banks piled up with brown earth and rotting vegetation. After miles of nothing but wide fenland, she saw a sign ahead to HMP Whitemoor. Soon afterwards the prison loomed up ahead of her, the two-tone brick walls dominating a car park planted with young trees. A separate low building off to one side looked like a modern health centre or library. Except for the razor wire atop the wire-mesh fences, the whole place could almost have been built as an out-of-town shopping centre.

Tessa parked facing the high walls and switched off the engine. Although the facade of the prison was virtually unbroken, the sense of being under surveillance made her reluctant to get out of the car. Now she was here, she could not avoid questioning why she had driven so far. She had no idea which prison Roy Weaver was in, and had no reason at all to suppose he'd be here. She had already researched how to find him, and had learned that she was only allowed to know his location if he gave his permission. She supposed her reason for being here was to test out if she wanted to take that next step; whether she could imagine herself entering such a place, could tolerate the idea of having a father who belonged here.

There was no one to talk to. No one could help her decide. She could drive away and no one need know she had ever come. Or she could stay and accept the challenge. She stared at the barricades, at the huge, fort-like entrance, at the flat, empty landscape that stretched away to the horizon. She was not being overly dramatic: this isolated stronghold was designed to incarcerate dangerous men. Behind the massive walls lived rapists, terrorists, child-murderers. It was not a place to enter lightly.

Yet she felt a frisson of excitement. She knew she ought to disown it, but could not. There was a malign glamour, an almost sexual charge, attached to the idea of such moral and physical extremity. It gave her a heady sense of power. Tessa thought back to when she had first asked Erin about her father, drinking coffee together and looking out at Pamela's sheltered garden. How naive she had been to assume her journey would be uncomplicated, its outcome inevitably positive. Suddenly she did not necessarily want it to be so simple. No explorer setting out into unknown terrain truly wished for a tame or uneventful experience. She too wanted to be free to develop in new and unexpected directions, to be tested, and survive, as an individual alone in an unknowable world. She knew for certain that she would not turn her back on whatever experience lay ahead. The murderer who was locked up somewhere in a prison like this was her *father*. Truth was truth. It had no obligation to be benign. It might be terrible. But she would end up stronger for not turning away.

Her mobile pinged, interrupting her thoughts, and she lifted it out of her bag: a text message from Lauren, reporting that she hadn't yet been robbed or murdered. Tessa's stomach turned over. She opened the car window to let in some air, texting back a smiley face. She felt ill. What nonsense was she selling herself? What was she doing here? How could she envisage allowing any possible contamination between a prison inmate and her teenage daughter? She watched as a group of officers came out of the gaol and walked towards her. Some were women, but a couple of the men had shaven heads. All wore sturdy black boots, and as their black anoraks flapped open she could see their thick leather belts. Their solidarity as they moved past the car, their show of strength, betrayed the realities of their working day. Prison life was not romantic, it was tough.

She tried to imagine how she would feel if Hugo were beyond those walls, a Hugo she had never met. Whatever he had done, she would have no choice but to refuse to believe that he ought to be shunned or forgotten. Roy Weaver had come into her life, his existence forcing upon her a realm of experience she had never asked for and did not wish to accept. She could choose to drive away and never look back. She knew that was the best thing, the right thing, to do. But it was impossible to unlearn the fact of his existence. This other father had entered her life, and she had to find a place for him.

Tessa sat in her car as the officers drove away and the area became quiet again. She was here because somewhere behind a similar wall was part of who she was. Part of her children too, and *their* children. To spend the rest of her life in ignorance was unthinkable. Some of the exhilaration she had felt while driving kicked back in. Her ambitions had never been world-shattering, but she was no coward, and she had to be prepared to take this thing on, wherever it led.

By the time she reached home, Tessa's decision to start the process of making contact had taken on an inevitability that made it seem natural and right. Mitch was out, and she had an hour or so to herself. Ignoring everything else on her desk, she immediately went online to find the official website through which she could request information about which prison Roy Weaver was in. It was, she had already learnt, up to him to consent to the disclosure of his whereabouts. She hesitated over the question on the form asking her to give the reasons for her enquiry. Unknown relative? Long-lost daughter? Daughter he never knew he had? It felt unreal, mad, the kind of avowal that no one could take at face value. But what else could she say? The form felt intimidating, as if she were entering a quasi-judicial hinterland where any mistake might slide her helplessly closer to this parallel punitive world.

She got up from her desk. This was a bad idea. She circled the small room, trying to decide. Should she go ahead? If she did, what could she put down on the form other than the truth as she knew it? She was struck by sudden doubt: other than Erin's rosy-tinted account, she had no proof that this man had ever been Erin's lover, let alone that he was in fact her father. What if it was all complete nonsense, some lie Erin had for some reason concocted to tell her mother and now come to believe?

Yet all the time she knew that she would send the form, would declare that she believed Roy Weaver to be her biological father, and that the reason for her enquiry was to discover the truth.

Although the official website warned her a reply might take weeks, when the phone rang around six o'clock Tessa irrationally hoped it might already be a response, and so it took her a moment or two to realise it was Evie's mother, asking if Tessa had heard from the girls. They had not come off the prearranged train, and Evie was not answering her phone. Recovering from the first plummeting drop into fear, Tessa called Lauren, her heart hammering in her chest as she waited to hear her daughter's voice. Lauren answered after a couple of rings and explained sheepishly how Evie had left her phone in the changing room at a clothes shop, and by going back to look for it they had missed their train; the phone could not be found and Evie, by then in a state, could not remember her mother's mobile number, stored on the lost phone. Lauren had idiotically delayed calling Tessa in the hope of avoiding a telling-off, but they were now safely on a later train.

Her hands shaking with relief, Tessa called Evie's mother to explain and recognised the same edge of terror in the other woman's voice. She sank into the nearest chair, unable to believe her own wilful stupidity. The very thing she most feared – that some predatory, violent man would harm her precious daughter – she had herself conjured into their lives.

SEVENTEEN

Pamela found Hugo in what he called his den, originally the inadequate third bedroom. It had a view across the front garden to the river marshes that pleased him, and in it he had recreated a semblance of the office he had vacated at the brewery. She wasn't quite sure how he passed his time in here – reading crime novels he borrowed from the library, she suspected – but guessed he liked the bit of structure spending an hour or two at his desk gave his day when they had no other plans.

He moved a box file off the old kitchen chair for her and she sat down, folding her hands in her lap.

'Time to talk?' he asked.

She nodded. She never found it as easy as he did to put things into words; there always seemed to be an unwelcome finality in doing so, and once something had been said it could not be taken back. Better to say nothing, or very little, than to risk saying the wrong thing. Even though the secret was now out and there was no reason to hold back, old habits died hard.

'What are we going to do?' she asked in reply.

'Nothing.' He smiled sadly. 'What can we do?'

'Stop her seeing this man!'

'How?'

Pamela stared at him in mute appeal, and he reached out to pat her hands. 'There's nothing we can do, my love. At least, so far as we know, he's not aware of her existence.'

'But what if he is? Or she does decide to contact him?'

'She may not. But whatever she decides, we have no right to stop her.'

'What if he's dangerous?'

'Then we do our best to protect her. As we've always done,' he added.

'No! We mustn't let this happen. You must talk to her, Hugo. Stop her.'

Hugo gave a bitter laugh. 'All those years I did nothing because you and your mother insisted that was the way it had to be. And now you want me to act!'

'I'm afraid we're being punished,' she said.

Hugo withdrew his hand. 'For what?'

'Everything.' Pamela wished she'd had a bit more Dutch courage before she'd come upstairs. 'She was never ours,' she said. 'I've dreaded this day ever since we took her.'

Hugo pushed his chair back, his mouth set in a hard line. 'Stop it, Pamela! If you want to think like that, you should never have agreed to take Tessa in the first place. It's no good to anyone, this endless guilt and regret.'

'Will Tessa ever forgive us?'

'We should have told her. I always said that. But what's done is done. She knows we love her, and that's all that counts.'

Pamela shook her head, rubbing her hands around in her lap. 'But this man . . .'

'Her father.'

'We know nothing about him.'

'What does Erin say?'

'I haven't been able to get hold of her. She must be off on a trip. She hasn't been answering her phone.'

'Well, she obviously gave Tessa enough information to track him down. And if he is Tessa's father, then we just have to focus on that, not on his conviction. He's doing his time.'

'*You're* her father. It's not fair on you!'

'We have to leave Tessa free,' said Hugo. He took hold of his wife's hands again, trying to contain their restless movements, but she pulled against him, releasing herself from his grasp. 'We believed before we were doing the right thing. We can't interfere again.'

'And what if this man has done terrible things before? Other crimes?'

'Then that's the way it is.'

'What if she can be hurt by what he's done?'

Hugo shrugged. 'We'll just have to hope that if she does contact him, he'll feel as any father would.'

Pamela felt a surge of rage against Hugo's reasonableness. Fearing her own anger, she stood up. 'Ok. But I worry about you too.'

'It's not about what we want any more.' He managed a weary smile, not meeting her eyes. 'It never should have been.'

She bent to kiss his cheek and went downstairs to the kitchen in search of something to deaden her apprehension.

Later, she once again dialled Erin's number in Sydney and once again got her answering machine. This time she left a message: 'Erin, it's me. I have news. Tessa has found Roy Weaver.' Pamela paused for so long that the device automatically cut her off. She rang back before her mouth became too dry to speak. 'Please call me back, Erin darling. Talk to me. This time I'll hear whatever you want to tell me. I will listen to what you want to say. I promise.'

EIGHTEEN

The reply from the Prison Service arrived in early May. It supplied the name of the establishment, HMP Wayleigh Heath, and Roy Weaver's prison number, LH5238. Over the previous few weeks Tessa had almost persuaded herself that Roy Weaver would not reply. After all, it was preposterous to expect him to entertain her claim nearly four decades after an event he must surely have forgotten. Indeed, she'd rather hoped not to hear back so that she could quietly let the whole subject drop, while telling herself she'd done all she could. Yet, as she read the sparse information, she was taken aback by the intensity of her relief. Her father had opened the way for them to meet. He did want to know her! Until that moment, holding this document in her hands, she had not honestly considered how she would react if he had refused, and could now admit how painful a rejection would have been. She had been naive not to believe that the instinctive need to know one's paternity would overpower any argument against bringing this dubious man into her life.

In the grip of this emotion Tessa drew a sheet of the B&B's headed paper towards her, and picked up a pen. It seemed far too formal to send a printed letter. She hesitated over the wisdom of giving him her address before reassuring herself that he was behind bars – she and her family were perfectly safe. What should she call him – Roy or Mr Weaver? *Dear Roy*, she wrote. *You will already know why I want to contact you. I have reason to believe you might be my biological father.* She paused: did 'biological' sound too cold? Or did it convey sanity and realism? She let it stand. *My mother, who now lives in Australia, is Erin Girling. She has told me that you met one another in Felixham when you were on holiday there in the summer of 1974, and that you are my father.* Tessa broke off to consider how she might lay her hands on a photograph of Erin in 1974, to jog Roy's memory, then realised she would have to ask Pamela, and decided it could wait. She also brushed aside the rapid calculation that Erin, then only a year or so older than Lauren, had not in fact turned sixteen until the very end of August. She thought for a while, pondering what more she could add. *I have very little information, so if this is not you, then I apologise for writing. If you agree that my mother is correct, then I hope we can correspond further.* She signed off, *With best wishes*, folded the sheet into an envelope and copied out the address provided.

She locked the letter from the Prison Service into a filing cabinet and decided to take her own letter to the post immediately, so that neither Mitch nor Lauren could stumble across it and be curious about the significance of the address. She slipped out of the house and into spring sunshine dancing off the sea. White horses raced into shore and small white clouds scudded across a blue sky. Beneath the promenade a man was repainting a beach hut the colour of lemon sherbet. She posted her letter in the red box set in the wall by one of the many flights of steps that led down to the beach, and walked on along the front. She was not yet ready to go back to work, and there were some errands she could run in town. The preoccupation of the morning had blinded her to the outside world, but she also felt vividly alive, sensing some possibility of completion, of comfort and self-explanation, that lay waiting over the horizon. The world had only to keep turning in order to bring it to her: it was as natural as the tides.

Roy Weaver replied by return of post. *Dear Tessa*, he wrote on lined prison notepaper. The envelope was ordinary, cheap and anonymous, but the letter it contained bore his name and prison number in preprinted spaces in the top corner. *I don't know what to say! I do remember that long-ago summer in Felixham, and a lovely girl I was half in love with, so I suppose it is entirely possible that what your mother tells you is true. I have sadly remained childless, so the idea that you might be my daughter is thrilling – though goodness knows, I don't deserve it. I enclose a Visiting Order. If you would care to come and see me, then ring and book a visit on any day that suits you. Warmest regards, Roy Weaver.*

Tessa placed the letter down on her desk, aware that her hand was shaking. She took a deep breath, trying to identify what she felt. There was relief from uncertainty: Erin's account of her conception was true – it had been a youthful holiday romance – and she had found her father. There was some excitement about the unknown, about having to rise to this challenge. And there was dread.

She picked up the letter again. The handwriting was distinctive, each letter clear and well-formed, the words precisely spaced and the date written in Roman numerals. She liked the apparent fastidiousness, telling herself it signalled an articulate, educated man. She noted how gracefully Roy Weaver acknowledged his offence – describing himself as undeserving – and the considerate way he suggested she might like to visit, leaving it easy for her to decline or postpone. She tried to imagine him as he must have been when he and Erin had met, the same as every generation of young men that she had watched come and go each summer, and to picture him promenading arm-in-arm with the admiring girl from the seafront boarding house, the sun shining as they went off in search of a grassy hollow at the edge of the marshes where they could be alone and private together. Unless she decided otherwise, this was the only part of his life that need concern her. And, she reminded herself, the decision was entirely hers. This thought gave her confidence: however much she could wish for a less uncomfortable father figure, Roy Weaver's predicament unquestionably put her in control.

She did, however, freely acknowledge how disappointed she was to discover she had no siblings. She realised how she'd seen a meeting with Roy Weaver as a chance to relive her childhood, to retrieve an alternative identity as someone else's child, as a member of a different clan. She'd enjoyed falling asleep recently already semi-dreaming about the amazing bond that would exist between herself and a younger sister, or adventures she might share with a gang of brothers. She'd hoped to be introduced to a version of herself she had never known, to slip into a new constellation, another galaxy, another solar system. It was a compelling notion, and she let go of it now with regret. But, recalling Declan's harsh realism, at least Roy would be free to welcome her into his life without fear of awkward complications with an existing family. And she consoled herself that his childlessness would allow their relationship to take centre stage.

As Tessa began to compose various possible replies in her mind, feeling her way into what action she might take, she was interrupted by the office door opening. It was Carol, with a brightly patterned make-up bag in her hands. 'The guests in number four left this behind,' she announced.

Pushing Roy's letter out of sight under some other papers on her desk, Tessa took it from her. 'Thanks. No doubt they'll realise once they get home again.'

Tessa reached over to put it on top of the filing cabinet, then glanced at her computer screen, hoping that Carol wouldn't want to stay and chat.

'Got a bit more time to yourself now the kids are back at school,' Carol observed from the doorway.

'Yes. A lot to catch up on though.'

'I saw Mitch made friends with Tamsin Crawford in the holidays,' Carol went on. 'They walk the Crawfords' spotty dog together.'

'Really?'

'Did you not know?'

Tessa caught a glint of satisfaction in Carol's eye and laughed. 'Mitch is seventeen. I don't keep tabs on him any more!'

'Have you met Mr Crawford?'

'No, not yet.'

'You know I'm friends with Sonia Beeston, who works for him?'

'Of course.'

'He's a generous employer, but she says there's all sorts goes on at the house.' Carol paused significantly. 'Drugs and stuff.'

'Well, I doubt the dog's involved,' Tessa observed lightly.

'Cocaine, apparently,' Carol persisted. 'Sonia says they don't even bother trying to hide it.'

'Mitch and I have talked about drugs,' said Tessa firmly. 'He's very sensible.'

Carol nodded. 'All the same, you know what those people are like. If anything happens, a man like Mr Crawford won't rush to blame himself.'

'Thanks, Carol.' Tessa tried to hide her irritation. Carol had watched Mitch and Lauren grow up and was undoubtedly fond of them, but all the same Tessa didn't want to sanction Sonia's gossip against her employer in case Carol reciprocated by running to Sonia with tales of her own. 'I appreciate your concern.' She turned back to her desk. 'Call me if you want a hand turning the mattress in number three.'

Carol pursed her lips but accepted her dismissal. Relieved, Tessa waited until she heard her ascending footsteps before withdrawing Roy's letter from its concealment. She looked again at the neat architectural handwriting, her *father's* handwriting, a father thrilled to meet his daughter for the first time. Of course she would go! Ready for a life outside the petty, gossipy confines of Felixham, she dialled the number printed on the Visiting Order.

NINETEEN

HMP Wayleigh Heath was, like Whitemoor, a modern prison, set in an equally featureless stretch of countryside. Tessa parked and looked around. She'd been too flustered to ask for information when she'd phoned to book the visit, and was now unsure where she was supposed to go. The high concrete walls dominated the view, but off to one side was a single-storey building with large windows, all the woodwork painted red, green and blue like the forced cheerfulness of a primary school. Noticing an elderly couple leave their car and walk towards it, she decided to follow.

Inside was one large room with fixed rows of chairs. No one looked up when Tessa entered. Most of those already seated were young women, some keeping watch on a small play area where three or four toddlers eyed each other warily; the older people waited silently, as if both resigned and disappointed at having to be here. Tessa joined a small queue behind the couple from the car park in front of a desk where a man in a short-sleeved white uniform shirt sat before a computer terminal.

When it was her turn, the officer took her Visiting Order and asked for some ID, taking meticulous note of the details of her driver's licence. 'Do you want some tokens?' he asked.

'Tokens? I'm sorry. I've not been before.'

He looked at her without curiosity. 'You can't take money in, but you can exchange cash for tokens to buy tea and biscuits. You can take in reading glasses, tissues and essential medication. Everything else goes in a locker.' He nodded towards the back wall, where she now noticed rows of grey metal doors.

'I brought some photographs. Can I take those?'

She started to take the envelope out of her bag, but he looked at her wearily. 'You can hand them in.'

'Will I get them back?'

'Ask the prisoner to return them on your next visit.'

'Ok.'

'You want to hand them in?'

Tessa thought quickly. She had told no one about having written to Roy, let alone visiting him, so had been forced to dissemble when asking Pamela for photos of Erin as a girl. Since Averil had never owned a camera, Pamela had only been able to produce half a dozen snaps, half of those annual school photos, and Tessa wasn't ready to part with them. But equally she had to be sure that Roy remembered Erin, that he *was* her father. Impulsively, she handed the envelope over, signed where the officer asked her to, and exchanged a few coins for some bent cardboard tokens. The officer wrote a number on her VO and gave it back to her, then looked past her to the next person in the queue.

'Sorry, but what do I do now?'

'Wait for your number to be called.' He was already reaching past her for another set of paperwork.

Tessa moved aside and found herself an unoccupied seat beside a restless little boy who was evidently with his grandmother. She felt bad about parting so recklessly with the photos. It had been terrible deceiving Pamela, especially when she'd seemed so pleased by Tessa's interest in Erin. But Tessa had bolstered herself with the idea that she needed a little longer to explore the sensation of living with withheld knowledge, to taste the corrosive power offered by the possession of a secret and to match their silences with her own. She fortified herself now with the idea that Pamela and Hugo must have felt similarly empowered by not telling *her* the truth. If her secret was creating a rift between them, then it was they who must find a way to mend it.

The little boy kept kicking his chair, jolting hers, but she didn't like to move elsewhere. In an attempt to distract herself, she took a proper look around. The walls were festooned with posters and welfare notices about help with drugs, alcohol, debt and housing, or other legal advice, many repeated in different languages. Covertly observing her fellow visitors, Tessa was guiltily aware of her great good fortune in being decently nourished and provided for. She chose not to think about what would have become of her if Hugo and Pamela had abandoned her to the Care system; the endless possibilities of the other adoptive parents and families she might have had were dizzying and pushed her sense of disloyalty to disquieting levels.

Beside her, the boy set his sights on the play area and struggled to free himself from his grandmother's grip. Catching Tessa's eye, the grandmother winked then turned to the boy. 'If you don't do as you're told,' she said, 'that nice officer over there will take you away and lock you up with a great big key.'

The boy subsided immediately. Avoiding further eye contact with the grandmother Tessa made her way to the toilets, remembering that she wanted to freshen her lipstick before locking away her bag.

On every cubicle door and over the mirror and hand-dryers were more notices, this time about domestic violence and the penalties for smuggling drugs into the prison. Tessa dug in her bag for a comb. She'd had her hair cut the week before and it fell into neat layers, framing her face. She applied lipstick, then stared at herself in the mirror, examining her bone structure, the colour of her eyes, the shape of her mouth: would the man she was about to meet look anything like this? She was horribly nervous. She had lain awake the night before, rehearsing what to say, fearful that, once they met Roy Weaver would dismiss her story or think her stupid. Even if he did accept that he was her father, she was unsure what more she really wanted from him. She looked again at her face, but the endless notices about drugs and violence reflected in the mirror bore down on her like the special effects in some old Hollywood film where the actor fears they are going mad. This was not her world, she did not belong here, yet she remained certain that she had to meet this man. What would her father think of her? Would he like her? To want a prison inmate to be proud of her was ridiculous and yet mattered desperately to her.

The door opened and a young woman with a fierce, pinched face, her thin bare legs mottled as if with cold but wearing little but a skimpy vest and a short skirt, slid into a cubicle and bolted the door. Tessa pulled herself together and went out. She locked away her bag and went back to her seat, relieved when a moment later the little boy and his grandmother had their number called and left to go across to the prison. Visits had begun at two o'clock, and although she had arrived ten minutes or so before, it now dawned on her how many other people ahead of her were still waiting. There were some tattered magazines and a discarded tabloid on a side table, and she despised herself for not wanting to touch them. She took a deep breath, resolving to imagine that she was at an airport waiting to be called for a holiday flight.

It was another forty minutes before her number was called. She followed the elderly couple the hundred yards or so across to an open door beside the massive main gate. Inside was a hive of activity as jackets, shoes and baby equipment were passed through an X-ray machine. Tessa took her turn walking through the metal detector and stood with her arms obediently outspread as an officer passed a wand around her body. She then took her place on a small plinth while a female officer patted her down, checking inside the waistband of her jeans and the neckline of her sweater before asking her to open her mouth and squinting inside. Tessa put her shoes back on and, following the example of the elderly couple, held out her hand to be stamped with a fluorescent dye. Her group was then marshalled into a transparent holding pen; the door behind them swooshed shut electronically and, watching themselves in the surveillance monitor bolted high in one corner, they waited until the door in front was opened to allow access to the secure area of the prison.

So far, Tessa told herself, it had all been as courteously impersonal as her experiences of airport security; but now, escorted by two officers with thick key chains attached to their belts, and pausing frequently for grilled gates to be opened and refastened, she began to feel as if she were being led deep into the heart of some mythical kingdom, as if all this security were designed as much to keep out the ordinary world as to contain those inside. Seldom claustrophobic, she felt the reality of incarceration press in upon her.

The visits room was like a huge warehouse, with numbered tables fixed to the floor. There was a colourful play area, a tea counter set into the wall, and a raised platform from which several seated officers kept watch. The elderly couple headed joyfully towards a middle-aged man wearing a fluorescent tabard, who got to his feet to greet them. Glancing above him, Tessa noticed that small cameras suspended from the ceiling were trained on each table. She looked around. There were several tables at which similarly dressed men sat waiting, and, although she had stared at the computer image of the grainy newspaper photo of Roy Weaver from twelve years ago, she wasn't certain she'd be able to pick him out. She turned to the officers seated above her.

'I'm here to see Roy Weaver. I've not met him before.'

An officer pointed. 'That's him.'

If the officer was curious, he did not show it. Tessa looked in the direction he indicated and saw a slight, distinguished-looking older man with a full head of short grey hair sitting alone at a table. He wore his tabard over a striped grey shirt and tidy jeans. She walked over to him, and he glanced up. His expression changed so rapidly to one of interest and welcome that she did not quite catch what his face had revealed before, although some odd quality about it registered with her. Then he was on his feet, arms by his side. She moved closer, holding out her hand. He hesitated before taking it, his smile seeming to indicate his appreciation of the gesture.

'Tessa?'

'Yes. Hello.'

'You'd better call me Roy, at least until we get to know one another properly.'

As he released her hand and sat down, she realised that although from a distance he looked of average male height, he was in fact slightly shorter than her. Tessa took the chair across from him.

'You've not been inside a prison before?' He was regarding her openly. His eyes were grey, she noticed, like her own, and his skin was pale, as if deprived of sunlight. Despite his scrutiny he seemed relaxed and confident, and it was she who was nervous.

'No.'

'It is what you expected?'

'I don't know. Probably.' She glanced over to a door that she assumed must lead to the accommodation blocks, where a pleasant-looking female officer, middle-aged but with striking red hair, was exchanging a joke with the prisoner she had just let through. 'I guess it's more ordinary than I expected.'

'Yes, all pretty mundane, unless someone kicks off. But most people here have longish sentences. They tend to settle down and get on with it. It's the kids in for a few months who cause trouble, but we don't usually get many of them.'

'Right.' She looked around again. Most people at other tables were intent on their visits, leaning inwards, studying each other's faces; some of the young couples stared awkwardly past one another, fiddling with hair or a child on their knee as they got used to being with each other again. She looked back at Roy, met his steady gaze, and blushed. 'Do you get many visitors?' she asked.

'A few.' He leant forward. 'So, Felixham thirty-eight years ago. And now here you are!'

'Yes!'

'So why not before?' His question was the one she'd been hoping to avoid, or at least delay, not ready yet to expose the secrets of her upbringing; but she had an answer prepared.

'My mother went to live in Australia. Her latest visit made me think it was time to know more about myself.'

'Erin Girling, you said in your letter.'

Tessa nodded. 'Do you remember her?'

'I remember a girl one summer.' A certain wariness beneath his light facade made her heart go out to him; how terrible it must be to be branded forever by one's crime.

'I handed in some photos for you,' she said. 'Of Erin around that time.'

He nodded. 'Good. Of you too, I hope, as a little girl?'

'Oh, no, I didn't think of that. Sorry.'

'So what's your story been, all these years,' he went on, 'about how you came to be?'

'That the two of you had a holiday romance.'

'A romance.' He sat back. 'That's right.'

'You're from Manchester?'

'Near there. And she says I'm your father? No other proof?'

'No.'

'She must've kept pretty close tabs on me for you to find me now?'

'Not really.' His close regard made Tessa wretched; she did not want to begin with lies, but neither was she confident of disclosing truths she had not yet fully absorbed herself. 'She was very young. She said you were older, studying architecture. I think you made quite an impression.'

'A good impression, I hope?' He smiled ironically.

'Yes.'

'That's nice. So what else do you know about me?'

'Nothing,' she admitted.

'Erin said no more about our romance, then?'

Tessa shook her head. Roy nodded as if amused and sat back. 'But you're still in Felixham?'

'Yes.' Tessa was relieved that he seemed to have accepted her scant evidence of his paternity. 'I inherited my grandmother's boarding house. I run it now as an upmarket B&B.'

'Which grandmother?'

'Erin's mother.' Once again, Tessa felt in danger of giving away more information than she wanted to. 'So now you can tell me all about my other grandparents,' she said brightly. 'Do I come from a big family?'

'My parents passed away some time ago.' Roy looked away, blanking further enquiry. But Tessa persisted.

'You wrote that you don't have more children, but do I have any uncles or aunts? Cousins maybe?'

'Hey, slow down! Let's take one thing at a time. Get to know one another before we bring anyone else into the mix.'

Tessa felt admonished, as if she had acted clumsily. 'Yes, of course. Sorry.'

'How about a cup of tea? I'm not permitted to fetch it, but if you'd like some, and have any tokens . . .'

'I do, yes. Of course. What would you like?'

'I feel bad asking you.'

'Don't be silly. It's only a cup of tea.'

'But I can never repay you.' He smiled wryly. 'One of the many ways they find in here to belittle you. Each small twist of the knife adds up.'

Not knowing how to respond, Tessa looked at him in concern.

He laughed. 'Don't take any notice of me! That's what prison does. Makes you oversensitive. I'd love a cup of tea! They do good Dundee cake too. See if you can get me a slice with cherries in it!'

Tessa went gladly. She stood at the counter while the pleasant WRVS lady refilled a gigantic brown teapot that looked as if it had done service during the Blitz, and found that she was trembling. She would have loved to know what people like this nice woman, nodding at her in friendly anonymity, really thought of people like her who came to visit serious criminals. She wanted to blurt out that she wasn't like the others; this was a momentous first meeting with her father.

'Sugar?'

Not knowing the answer, Tessa hesitated.

'I'll put some in the spoon for you.'

In front of Tessa was a tray of chocolate bars, biscuits and pre-packaged slices of cake, and she selected one slab of cake with two pieces of cherry in it. She didn't want anything for herself, but then worried that Roy might feel self-conscious eating on his own, so she chose a pack of custard creams. She exchanged the cardboard tokens, loaded the mugs of strong tea onto a little tray and, thanking the WRVS lady, carried everything carefully back to the table. She felt conspicuous as some of the inmates, marked out by their fluorescent tabards, automatically eyed up a passing female, and was grateful that Roy tactfully did not scrutinise her approach.

'This is very kind, thank you.' He reached courteously to take his tea and cake from the tray, and she noticed how he spent a moment aligning them to his satisfaction. His precision showed an attention to detail that she admired: it was how she liked things to be too.

'You were an architect?' she asked.

'My degree was architecture. I lectured for a while, then had my own consultancy. Drawing up plans for loft conversions, that sort of thing.'

Tessa nodded, then took a deep breath: she still had some difficult questions to ask. 'So what happened?'

Roy raised his eyebrows in mock surprise. 'Well, the birds and the bees. You know!'

'Oh, no. I meant . . .' She knew she was blushing again, and lowered her head. 'I actually meant, how come you're here?'

When he did not answer, she looked up and found him staring at her sternly, waiting until she met his gaze. 'It's not considered polite to ask that kind of question in here,' he said.

Tessa was disappointed. 'Sorry. I didn't realise.'

'I know what I am. But I was found guilty and I'm paying the price. The rest is in the past.'

'But—'

He held up a hand to silence her. Surprised by the authority of the gesture, she obeyed. 'It was a tragedy for all concerned,' he instructed her. 'A very traumatic event. Besides, I have too much respect for the dead to be able to talk easily about what happened. Believe it or not, I still grieve for the woman I lost that day. My sentence is that I have to live with what I did.'

She was touched by his dignity. 'At some point I'd like to know though,' she told him. 'To try and understand.'

'Very well,' agreed Roy. He sat back, arms folded, observing her.

She waited, but he did not move. She was reminded of how she had occasionally to resist when strangers stood on her threshold demanding a room, of how it felt to stand firm. 'One day?' she prompted.

He gave the merest nod, still studying her face. 'You have my eyes,' he said, unfolding his arms and smiling at her. 'Do you have children?' He must have seen in her face that she did, and did not wait for a reply. 'Do they take after you?'

'My son does.'

'How old are they?'

Tessa felt compromised discussing her children in this place, but could not refuse to answer. 'Fourteen and seventeen.'

Roy nodded. 'And when's your birthday? Must be soon?'

She laughed that he had already calculated forwards from his summer stay in Felixham. 'Yes. In June.'

His face softened. 'My daughter's birthday. I'm sixty-one,

and that's the first time in my life I've been able to say those words.' He whistled in quiet astonishment. 'That's quite something!' He leant forward, stretching out his hand, but as swiftly withdrew it. Touched by his delicacy, Tessa placed her own hand palm up on the table. He hesitated, then laid his hand on hers, as if in blessing. They smiled into one another's eyes. 'My daughter,' he breathed.

Half breathless with elation, Tessa was nevertheless half tempted to mock the mawkishness of this performance.

'Thank you for coming here to see me,' he went on. 'It can't have been easy.'

A bell rang, making Tessa jump. She followed Roy's glance up at a big wall clock: it was almost half past four, the end of visiting time. She was ambushed by an unexpected sense of loss and looked at him, stricken.

He nodded sympathetically. 'If you'd like another VO, let me know. I only get four a month, so I won't send one unless I know you'd want to use it.'

She opened her mouth to reply, but again he held up a hand. 'Don't say now that you'll come. You may feel differently once you get outside.' He paused, as if struggling to suppress his own emotion. 'Rejection is hard to bear in here.' He gave a brave smile. 'Prison gives you time to think. Too much time.' He got up, pushing his chair in neatly and standing behind it. 'If you do decide to return, better that you arrive earlier, so you can be among the first to be brought across. As I say, I only get four visits a month, so time is precious.'

'Oh, yes. I'm so sorry about that. I didn't know.'

He waved her apology aside, and continued kindly: 'Go now before the rush, or you'll get kettled on the way out.'

He kept his hands by his sides. Impulsively, Tessa held out hers and he took it, covering it briefly, before letting go and moving back to stand behind his chair again. She noticed that several other men were also now standing at attention like Roy – a vivid reminder of the restrictions the inmates lived under. Not wanting to shame him by registering her perception, she smiled briskly, felt automatically for her bag before remembering it was locked away in the Visitors' Centre, and took a step away. 'Goodbye, then.'

'Goodbye, Tessa,' he replied, pulling back his shoulders and standing upright as she walked away.

TWENTY

Mitch heard his mother's voice below, thanking Carol for staying late. He felt bad about Lauren. He'd seen her sitting by herself on the bus home from school, munching her way through two packets of crisps, one after another, then heading straight for the fridge when she got home. He'd known for some time that things weren't right with her, but had turned a blind eye, hoping someone else would notice and do something so he wouldn't have to get involved. Besides, even if he did try to talk to her she'd probably just get furious and tell him to leave her alone. He knew girls could be peculiar about food, becoming anorexic or bingeing and throwing up, and hoped it wasn't as serious as that. It was Tessa who needed to step in, not him.

It was precisely because Mitch understood some of the reasons why Lauren might be unhappy that he wanted to keep his distance. There just wasn't enough room in his life right now for anyone else, and he needed to stay in the bubble of his own concerns. His exams were about to start, and it was hard enough trying to focus on any proper revision when all he could think about was Tamsin. He couldn't wait to see her again at half-term. Although they were keeping in touch online and through daily phone calls he still worried she'd forget him. And today she had texted again to say that it was looking increasingly likely that her mother would want her to fly out to Los Angeles for half-term. Mitch didn't think he could last out until July. And with Charlie Crawford's mercurial lifestyle, there was no certainty that he would even get to see her then. He was sick of being at the mercy of adults and their pointless whims.

He heard Tessa's footsteps heading up to the attic. He waited, hoping she'd go and check on Lauren, notice all the chocolate wrappers in her wastepaper basket, get things sorted out. He didn't understand how it could be so obvious to him why his sister was being such a pain while her freaky eating remained apparently invisible to both parents.

He heard his mother's exasperated voice across the hall. 'Lauren! You said you'd tidy up! Your room's a tip!'

Mitch's heart sank as he heard Lauren remonstrate in her whiniest voice. He had no interest in making out the words, and pressed play on his iPod to drown out the argument. The first track was halfway through when he heard the bathroom door slam. He knew this was designed to infuriate Tessa. It had been drummed into both of them since birth that guests were never to be disturbed, and they had long ago learnt to argue and fight in hushed tones.

He couldn't wait to get out of here. In the autumn, if he got good results, he could start looking seriously at which courses and universities to apply for. The dream of escape was enticing. It was no fun feeling responsible for everyone. Hugo and Pamela had gone into retreat since Erin's visit, and things were different with Sam since he'd moved in with Nula. Mitch worried that maybe it was somehow his fault, because he was so preoccupied with Tamsin, but however hard he tried to keep the flood of emotion under control, he couldn't stop how he felt about her. And if he didn't direct what energy he had left at his exams, he'd never ever get out of here.

There was a tap at his door and Tessa looked in. 'Supper?'

Mitch nodded, hoping she'd come in and chat, but she gave a tight smile and went off downstairs, leaving his door ajar. Out of habit, he checked that his appearance was respectable enough to encounter a guest on the stairs, and went out onto the landing. The bathroom door was still closed, and he hesitated, considering what best to do. He went up close to the door. 'Lauren?' he called softly.

'Go away.'

'Mum says supper's ready. Why don't you come down with me?'

There was silence, so he waited. He heard the sound of a tap running, then the toilet flushing, but Lauren did not appear. Disappointed, he made his way down alone to the kitchen.

'Hey, Mum,' he greeted her. Tessa turned from throwing open the windows as wide as they would go. He thought she looked unusually pale and tired. 'Anything I can do?' he asked.

'Thanks, love. Just move the bake to the top oven so the top crisps up a bit. Don't know about you, but I'm starving!'

As Mitch concentrated on sliding the dish out of the bottom oven and onto a shelf above, taking care not to burn his wrists on the metal, he was aware of his mother watching him, studying him as if she wanted to draw him or something. As he hooked the Aga door closed and flicked back his hair, she laughed. 'So like your dad.'

Lauren entered the kitchen and went straight to the fridge to begin what Mitch now recognised as her ritual of building a semicircular barricade of bottles and jars around her place at table. He had noticed that although she seldom added any of the condiments to her plate, they had to be set out in the same precise order and position every time. What drove him mad was not so much the fact that she did it at every meal – he half expected her to start surrounding her breakfast cereal with chutney, mayo and ketchup – but the intensity with which she focused on placing them just so.

Tessa placed salad on the table and Mitch laid out the plates as she took the hot pasta out of the oven. It smelt delicious, and used to be one of Lauren's favourite meals. But sure enough, half-hidden behind her wall of jars, Mitch could see her start to separate each individual piece of penne, scrape off the sauce and clinging vegetables, and then halve it before putting it in her mouth. He stared at Tessa, willing her to see, but she merely smiled at him again.

'Ready for your first paper? English Lit, isn't it?'

'Yeah. The Great American Novel.'

'You'll be fine with that, won't you?'

Mitch sighed. He had read all the books, and enjoyed them, but that didn't guarantee that the questions would be straightforward. 'Sure.'

'Good. Once they start, you'll get in the swing of things and the adrenalin will carry you through. We ought to celebrate when you've finished. What would you like to do?'

Mitch could see Lauren's head drooping lower behind her barricade, and guessed she felt left out.

'Maybe we could all go off for a day somewhere at half-term?' Tessa suggested, looking at Mitch.

'No!' Mitch spoke without thinking, but half-term was sacred to Tamsin. Lauren raised her head to glare at him. He knew he had turned red, and tried to recover himself. Desperate to get Tessa to pay attention to Lauren, to notice what was going on, he asked his sister to pass the ketchup, and instantly saw his mistake as her expression turned to panic.

'Don't worry,' he said quickly. But Tessa reached out automatically and lifted the plastic bottle out of its place.

'No!' Lauren made a grab for the bottle.

'Don't be silly!' said Tessa, passing it to Mitch.

Mitch didn't want any, but squeezed some onto the side of his plate before reaching over to put the bottle back carefully into position. He noticed Tessa lick a finger to rub away a funny mark on the back of her hand.

'Honestly, Lauren,' she chided. 'I hope you're going to put all those away again.'

Lauren made an inarticulate noise of protest.

Tessa shook her head. 'I had to do it yesterday. And the day before.'

'I forgot.'

'That's what you always say. It's not asking much, especially when you're the only one with nothing else to worry about.'

'I'll do it!'

'You don't know how lucky you are – no exams, no business to run . . .'

'I said I'll do it!'

'Once the brasserie opens, your dad won't have time to chase you about stuff either.'

'Ok!' Lauren hunched over her plate and, using her knife to scrape the small pile of discarded sauce and vegetables onto her fork, crammed as much as she could into her mouth. In two more mouthfuls she had swallowed the lot.

Tessa looked away. 'I suppose Nula lets you get away with those kind of table manners,' she said. 'But it's not how I brought you up to behave.'

Lauren ran out of the room, leaving Mitch to feel as if the walls of the only civilisation he had ever known were crumbling around him. The rubble was falling onto his shoulders, a crushing weight, and he had no idea how to stop it.

TWENTY-ONE

Pamela was trimming back the forsythia that grew beside the front porch, and had left the door open so she would hear if the phone rang. She was still waiting for Erin to respond to the messages she had left about Roy Weaver, and hoped she might call while Hugo was out. She'd never made any secret of how often she spoke to her sister, but when he picked up the phone he seldom greeted Erin with more than a brief hello, and Pamela always felt their chat was constrained by his presence.

She heard the first ring and darted indoors. She recognised Erin's voice immediately. 'You're there!' she cried.

'Yes, been in Hong Kong for a while. Rather good fun, actually.'

'Did you not get my messages?'

There was a slight pause. 'Sure.'

'And my email?' Pamela had sent Erin the link to the article about Roy Weaver's trial.

'Yes.'

Pamela couldn't believe that her sister could sound so casual. 'Did you recognise him?' she asked. 'Is it him?'

'Oh, I couldn't be certain. All too long ago.' Erin paused again. 'How did Tessa find him? Did you know about him?' Pamela thought she heard a note of rebuke in her sister's voice.

'No,' Pamela assured her. 'I knew nothing about him. I simply never dreamt she'd try to find him.'

'And that's all you know? The stuff you sent me?'

'Yes. Do you remember him?' Pamela held her breath, waiting for Erin, ten thousand miles away, to respond. She looked out of the open front door into the soft May sunshine. 'Erin, I'm sorry we've never spoken about the past before,' she said.

'Don't be.'

'But he's killed someone.'

'There was a guy in the advertising agency we work with,' said Erin at last. 'I used to have lunch with him regularly. Never heard him utter an angry word. Then one day he killed his wife. Turned himself in and is doing six years for manslaughter. I heard they're even going to give him his job back when he gets out.'

'You really think that's all this is?' Surely Erin must know that, with Averil dead and gone, she could tell her sister anything she wanted?

But Pamela could almost hear Erin's shrug. 'Why not?'

Pamela wanted so much to believe her, but something caught in her chest, preventing her from breathing freely. 'Why don't you come back? So we can talk properly.'

'Tessa's not planning on meeting him, is she?'

'No! I don't think so. I don't know.'

'So it's Ok then.'

'She wants to know you too. She asked for pictures of you the other day. She wants to know her mother. Please come back, just for a while.'

Pamela waited expectantly, but then heard the careful distancing in Erin's voice. 'I've thought of her all these years as your child – yours and Hugo's. It's better this way.'

Pamela stared at her spring garden, the tall clump of pampas grass so symbolic of domestic security. 'I don't know what to do!' she cried, as much to the docile scene before her as to Erin, so far away in an apartment she had never visited.

'Let's speak again soon, Pamela,' said Erin in a managerial tone. 'I've had a long trip. I'm all tuckered out. Let's speak another time.'

Pamela could only agree and hang up. She ought to feel relieved. There was no reason why Roy Weaver's crime should not be similar to that of Erin's colleague in the advertising agency, no reason not to believe the account Erin had given Tessa a few weeks ago of a summer romance. But Pamela couldn't go back to pruning shrubs or dividing up the thick clumps of Michaelmas daises in the border and pretend that the world was a safe place.

She headed for the kitchen. Hugo would be home soon, but she dared not discuss her fears even with him. Should she have pressed Erin for an answer, or was this one secret that must go on being kept forever? Opening the cupboard and lifting down the comforting bottle, she told herself that perhaps her nagging doubts were groundless after all, and merely the residue of her years of guilt at Erin's expulsion.

TWENTY-TWO

When Sam rang, Tessa felt a rush of joy. They used to speak most days, but once Nula's presence had been openly acknowledged, Tessa had been forced to accept how abruptly their relationship had atrophied. Even the brasserie, which she had regarded as a joint venture, something she co-owned, part of a shared life, would be officially signed away in the divorce settlement. The other day she had driven past and seen the new nautical blue-and-white sign – *Sam's Place* – positioned over the entrance to the courtyard. She knew it had been designed by the firm Nula worked for because Sam had shown her the drawings some time ago and she'd approved of the jaunty lettering, knowing it would attract the right kind of clientele; but now it seemed to take on the power of a *No Entry* sign, denying any last claim she might have to belong beside him.

Everyone else took Sam's unavailability for granted, leaving her no one to whom she could admit the sense of loneliness that lodged in her chest like a block of ice.

She recalled an expression she'd heard of a theatre 'going dark', and considered that the sadness of a cold, deserted space once filled with passion and applause perfectly described how her heart felt now.

Yet Sam's voice on the phone, asking if he could pop round, sounded unchanged, and Tessa invited him gladly. Although he'd said he'd come right after lunch, she made a fresh batch of the lemon biscuits he liked and had the kettle ready on the Aga. It still felt strange for him to ring the bell to be let in, but he had insisted on relinquishing his key. He followed her down to the kitchen, showing his usual perceptive interest in business, and sat himself familiarly at the table while she made coffee. Tessa smiled fondly as he absent-mindedly helped himself to the biscuits.

'I'm a bit concerned about Hugo,' Sam announced, once she'd sat down beside him.

'You still see him?' Tessa was surprised, and a little put out.

'We meet for a jar now and then.' He had the grace to look sheepish. 'He told me some rigmarole about a guy in prison.'

'My father,' replied Tessa firmly, trying to repudiate her bitter disappointment that Sam's primary concern was not for her.

In the few days since the prison visit, Tessa told herself it had been right to establish her true identity and meet the man who sired her, but she had decided to leave well alone. If there had been a wider family for her to meet then she might have felt differently, but it was unnecessary to pursue a relationship with a man in gaol, a man who did not belong in her life, nor she in his.

'Oh, come on!' Sam laughed. 'Even if your biological father had turned out to be some Nobel prize-winning brain surgeon, what does it matter? Hugo's your dad.'

'Except he's not. And Pamela's not my mother.'

'But that doesn't mean you ought to get in contact with some psychopath or whatever.'

'I have a right to pursue this if I want.'

'Can you honestly say you learnt a whole lot about yourself from meeting Erin?' asked Sam. He picked up another biscuit, waving it around as he spoke. 'Plus there's the kids to consider.'

'Roy Weaver is their grandfather,' Tessa informed him, recalling how she and Roy had looked at each other and known immediately she was his flesh and blood. While he had remarked on the colour of her eyes, she had seen similar shaped hands, a familiar upward fleck at the corner of his left eyebrow, the same cheekbones. It came back to her vividly how unexpectedly visceral and even joyful her sense of their genetic bond had been. 'Eventually they might want to know who he is.'

'What, even if he's some serial killer?'

'He killed a girlfriend, not a stranger.'

'I don't think you should tell Lauren and Mitch anything about him.'

'It's not your decision. It's nothing to do with you.'

'They're my kids too. And Hugo agrees.'

'Well, he's not been bothered enough to discuss it with

me,' Tessa responded. 'Nor did I see you asking my permission before you dragged Nula into the kids' lives!'

Sam said nothing, and Tessa knew well that his refusal to engage masked a stubbornness she could never penetrate; knew too that to hear him defend Nula would destroy her. She leant closer. 'It's about me, Sam,' she pleaded. 'You can't imagine what it's like, discovering this kind of stuff. And I feel very alone with it.' She wished he'd touch her, at least take her hand; if he did, she'd tell him everything. The need for concealment was unwelcome and made her queasy. She did not want her connection with her father to be shady or devious. She longed to describe her hopes, doubts and fears, and to ask Sam's advice about how to separate the idea of Roy Weaver the murderer from Roy Weaver her father.

But although Sam nodded sympathetically he sat back, maintaining his separateness, so she said nothing.

'Sorry,' he offered. 'Anyway, as I say, it's Hugo I'm bothered about. He's pretty cut up about this whole business.'

'Well, maybe he should be.'

'Look, Tessa, the point is he blames himself. For everything.'

'Did he ask you to speak to me?'

'No.' Sam paused. 'But I hoped maybe you'd listen if it was me.' He gave his trademark upward glance from under the hair that fell across his forehead, but Tessa was too hurt to be manipulated by the old charm. Besides, that all belonged to Nula now.

'Hugo's big regret is that he didn't stand up to your

grandmother right from the start. I told him it wasn't his fault. Pamela didn't want him to, and Averil was a bulldozer. And now he believes that what he wants shouldn't matter.'

Tessa rose from the table, busying herself with topping up the half-full milk jug. As she went to replace the plastic container the cap fell on the floor, and she swiped at it viciously before becoming aware that Sam was watching her.

'I know it's complicated,' he said, 'but remember this has been difficult for your parents too. Especially about not having children of their own, and never being able to reveal that or talk about how it felt. Hugo didn't quite say it, but my guess is that it was hard.'

'I don't count, you mean?'

'Now you're being silly. Not being *able* to father a child – that's tough for a man.'

This brought Tessa up short. Hugo and Pamela's childlessness hadn't yet occurred to her as part of the equation; like the rest of the world, she hadn't seen them as childless because they had her. The idea of them not having a child of their own turned them into quite different people.

Sam got to his feet. 'Anyway, I'd better get back.'

'Wait and see the kids. They should be home in a minute.'

Sam shook his head. 'Better not. Less confusing for them.'

Tessa felt the contents of her stomach curdle. But then Sam hung his head, lingering uncertainly, and she felt a stirring of hope. 'Actually,' he said, 'I need a word about

Lauren. You must have noticed how she's putting on weight?'

'She's fourteen. It's when all girls fill out.'

'Nula thinks she's comfort-eating. That we should keep an eye on it.'

Betrayed, Tessa spoke with more exasperation than she intended. 'You're her father. What do *you* think?'

'Maybe if we could agree some ground rules about what she eats between meals?' Sam suggested evasively. 'It's difficult when we say no, but then she argues that you're perfectly happy to let her have biscuits and crisps and stuff.'

Tessa was affronted that Nula should dare to criticise her parenting, an offence compounded by the uncomfortable realisation that Lauren *had* become extremely picky about her food and *was* putting on weight – though Tessa couldn't believe it was anything serious. 'Fine,' she said. 'I'll deal with it.'

As she expected, Sam failed to respond. 'We ought to talk about Mitch too,' she told him. 'About his future.'

'Sure.'

'Once his exams are over, he has to decide which universities to apply for.'

'I know,' he said, as if unfairly accused. 'I'll be on it as soon as I'm a bit less busy. You're coming to the opening, right?'

'Yes, I expect so.'

'Great. See you then.' Relieved, Sam escaped to the stairs, leaving Tessa to follow him with the familiar sensation of being left holding all his concerns as well as her own.

At the front door he turned. 'So what are you going to do about this guy in prison?' He kept his tone patient and neutral.

'I don't know,' she said.

'But you won't involve Mitch and Lauren?'

The image of the prison walls rose up in front of her. She remembered how shaky she'd felt hitting the open road after her visit, how the claustrophobia she'd experienced following the officer back out through the bowels of the place had clutched at her, as if it were only by sheer luck that she had managed to escape. At that moment she'd wished never to return to such a malign, inhibiting space.

Sam waited for her answer.

'No, I won't tell the kids yet.' She watched him accept her agreement. It left him free to leave, to slide away and go back to Nula. She raised her chin. 'But if my father wants to see me, then I have every right to go.'

TWENTY-THREE

Roy's letter arrived two days later. *Dear Tessa*, he wrote in his fine italic. *Thank you for coming to see me – it must have taken courage. Meeting you has left me in no doubt that you are indeed my daughter. You may not be aware*, he continued, *that all letters are liable to be read by prison staff, so I may not write as freely as I might wish. Such is my life. So I hope you will understand that my inability to describe adequately my unfamiliar sensations is not from lack of feeling.* He signed himself *Your real Dad.*

Tessa was taken by surprise at the sharpness of her sense of rebuff: this brief note, barely a single sheet, made no mention of a second visit, nor did it enclose a VO. Had she disappointed him? Was he politely indicating that he did not wish to see her again? After all, he had made a point of telling her how few visits he was allowed. Why should she assume that he'd want to waste them on her?

At several intervals during the rest of the day she took Roy's letter out of the locked drawer and reread it, balancing the poignancy of *Your real Dad* against his apparent indifference. In the end she arrived at the conclusion that his slightly stilted words in fact revealed consideration for her, his tact in placing no pressure on her, and perhaps, she thought with a pang, his own desire to avoid rejection. She, after all, had a full life to lead; he had nothing.

The following morning, after the guests – all keen walkers anxious not to waste the best of the day – had paid their bills and departed and Carol was busy with the laundry downstairs, Tessa sat down to draft her response. She had not yet fully decided if she was ready to go back to the prison, but it would be discourteous not to reply. She wasn't sure what to say. She tried to imagine how she would feel if she had first encountered her biological father in different surroundings. Yet it was his very ordinariness – quietly spoken, polite, confident – that made it so hard to comprehend that he had violently taken a woman's life or to glean insight into how he lived with such terrible knowledge of himself. She would be a fool to ignore the reality of his crime, and at some point he would have to account properly to her for what he had done, but she should avoid judging him too hastily: she must be patient and take time to get to know him.

She could not remember when she had last written such a personal letter and realised she had forgotten what it was like to compose and direct her thoughts in this way. To begin with her sentences were stiff and self-conscious, but gradually she started almost to write to herself, to enjoy the one-sided conversation in her head.

Reaching for a third sheet of paper, she paused to ask herself how wise it was to open herself to him in this way, then reprimanded herself: if she wasn't prepared to go to her father with a clear and loving heart, then she might as well not go at all.

Roy's reply came on a day when Declan was booked in for his next monthly trip to the county, and Tessa awaited his arrival with jittery anticipation, glad of someone to whom she could speak freely. Roy's letter, although brief, was warm and encouraging. He told her how wonderful it had been to receive hers, that he had indeed feared she would not want to continue their relationship, explained that his daily routine did not lend itself to eloquence but that he would attempt to describe his own emotions: *The only way I can say it*, he wrote, *is to ask whether you believe in love at first sight? It's that moment of recognition, isn't it? Something beyond the rational. Makes me rather shy!* Yet he still made no mention of a second visit.

'So you've met him already?' asked Declan in astonishment, as they settled in the guests' sitting room after dinner. 'You sure as hell don't hang about!'

'You're the only person I've told.'

Declan had brought his customary bottle of red wine, and now raised his glass to her. 'I'm honoured.'

'I don't want the kids to know.'

'I understand. So what's he like?'

Knowing the question was bound to arise, Tessa had given some previous thought to her answer. 'Normal. Pleasant. A bit cagey, but that must be a reaction to what he's done. I mean, something so extreme, it must change him, mustn't it? Though obviously I don't understand enough to tell in what way.'

'So what happened? What exactly did he do?'

'He's not told me yet.'

'There'll be other ways to find out more. Geoff – the Head of Security at work – could probably get hold of the original court records or whatever if you wanted them.'

Tessa shook her head. 'I'll wait to hear Roy's side of the story first.'

'You won't want any unpleasant surprises.' Declan gave her a straight look. 'If he starts telling you she tripped and fell on the carving knife, or her head just snapped off in his hand, m'lud, you want to ask yourself why he's still locked up.'

Tessa felt rather offended by his levity. 'He didn't mention when he'd be released.'

'No.' Declan appraised her over the rim of his glass. 'A life sentence for an average bog-standard murderer is usually about thirteen years. How long has he been in?'

'Twelve. This is my father, Declan. Whatever he is, may also be me.'

'Did you like him?'

'We had a much stronger sense of connection than I expected. Really uncanny how we just looked at one another and knew we were related.'

He nodded. 'I've a second cousin who looks like he ought to be my twin. We don't have much else in common though,' he said with a laugh. 'Do you trust him?'

'He's watchful. Careful of his dignity. To be honest, I was just relieved he wasn't some scary monster!'

'It's been a lot to take in, I imagine.'

'Yes. Does it make you feel different about me?' Tessa asked boldly.

She could see he was taken aback. 'In what way?'

'Now you know I'm the daughter of a murderer.'

'It's hardly a Cromwell Road scenario, now is it? Even if he were as evil as Fred West, he had zero influence on you growing up.'

'Do you believe in evil?' She was curious to hear his answer.

'Original sin? No. No way. Why? Do you?'

'I certainly don't think Roy is evil. In fact, given the situation, he's far more vulnerable than me.'

'What I do think,' said Declan, 'is that when people are bad, they generally stay that way.'

'He said prison had given him time to think.'

'So he's seen the error of his ways?' Declan's tone was mocking.

'People change.'

He smiled, relaxing further back into his armchair. 'You are different,' he observed. 'This has brought you out of yourself. I approve.'

He raised his glass to her again, and she responded gratefully, rather enjoying the novelty of being of such legitimate and intriguing interest to someone else.

'It's like I've embarked on a journey,' she admitted, recalling the thought she'd had sitting in the car outside

HMP Whitemoor, that there was a glamour attached to life at the edge – that by entering a prison, she had survived a test.

'It's been fascinating,' she went on. 'In one way prison is just a tedious box-ticking exercise, but it's also the banality of life there that holds the lid on. I mean, if you think of what all those men have done, all the violence, jealousy, greed, revenge, somehow it makes all this . . .' Tessa waved a hand around her cherished blue walls, seagrass flooring and linen covers, at Averil's doll's house standing like a reliquary in its corner, 'it makes all this just a desperate attempt to cower away from that reality.'

'But this is what's healthy, surely? Who wants a reality of murder and mayhem? I'm Irish, remember. My people have had plenty, and there's nothing alluring about it, I can tell you. This . . .' he waved his hand in turn at the peaceful room. 'This is normality and security. Even your toy house there,' he added, following her gaze. 'It's good. This is what people fight for.'

Tessa smiled, feeling an unaccustomed wisdom. 'But the very reason you appreciate this is because you realise how precarious it all is. I've lived by the sea all my life. The most terrible storms can blow up out of nowhere.'

Declan leaned forward for the bottle and refilled her glass, smiling up at her cheekily. 'You never used to talk like this.'

'No.' She took a drink of her wine, holding his gaze, enjoying the effects of her newfound confidence, that fleeting sense of power she'd experienced several times since Erin had first dropped her bombshell. 'I'm losing my fear of secrets, I think. What's the point of life if we don't share the stuff that's real, that matters?'

'Agreed.' Declan raised himself from his chair and came to sit beside her on the couch, leaning back against the arm, a decent space still between them. This was not what Tessa had intended by her confession, but she lulled her nerves. It was a long time since her body had made its own independent response to a man; too long since any man had looked to her for such a response. But she was determined to remain open and relaxed, to stay on the edge.

'So what did the two of you chat about, you and your daddy?' Declan asked, with facetious emphasis.

'We didn't have a lot of time. I hadn't realised how long it would take to get past all the security. I guess we were just sizing one another up.'

'Will you go again?'

'We're writing to each other. Maybe that's enough for now.'

He nodded. 'And if he weren't in prison?'

She smiled. 'That's what I keep asking myself. I don't know. What do you think?'

'In a funny kind of way, maybe it's easier for you this way. If he were out and about, he'd not be much more than someone you'd meet for a drink. Someone who sooner or later you'd be introducing to the other folk in your life. Just an ordinary guy.' He looked at her astutely. 'Not this mythical beast locked away from everyone.'

Despite his smile, Tessa felt exposed, even a little humiliated.

'Don't get me wrong,' he went on. 'This is a huge thing for you. I get that. But in the end it's about you, not about him.'

Tessa was reassured by his irresistible sincerity. 'Thanks, Declan. If not for you, I'd never even have found him.'

'No. Well, don't make me live to regret that! Finish the bottle?' He held it up.

'No,' Tessa decided. 'Not tonight, thanks.'

He reached out to stroke her bare arm with one finger. She could sense him willing her to meet his gaze. 'Not tonight?' he echoed teasingly. She moved her arm away, but he caught her hand and carried it to his lips.

'Mitch and Lauren are asleep upstairs,' she protested.

'Can't tempt you? We could be very quiet.' His eyes danced. 'No strings.' When she did not recoil, he leaned a little closer. 'Final answer?'

'Final answer!' She attempted a shaky laugh, the sharpness of her body's disappointment taking her breath away. He got to his feet and pulled her up by her hand.

'Maybe next time they'll be at Sam's?' He looked down at her suggestively, his lips not far away.

'Maybe. But now I'm going to tidy up and put the lights out,' she added firmly.

He nodded and let go of her hand.

'See you in the morning, Declan. And thanks,' she added. 'Really.'

'No problem. Sweet dreams.' He gave her a friendly smile and left the room.

Tessa wrapped her arms around her body and grinned foolishly to herself, invigorated by his admiration and elated by this further proof that she was slowly uncovering her lost self.

TWENTY-FOUR

It had become an annual custom, before the full onslaught of the summer season, for the proprietors of Felixham guesthouses and B&Bs to meet for lunch away from town to compare notes and streamline the system they had of passing on bookings when one of them had to turn away guests. Tessa usually enjoyed the event, although she knew that some of her colleagues, especially those who remembered the Seafront B&B in her grandmother's day, disapproved of her refurbishment. One was jealous of her prices, while another made no secret of his opinion that her style was pretentious, unlike his own establishment's home-from-home cosiness. Tessa took the view that there was plenty of room in the market for all tastes.

This year's lunch was to be held in Orford, where those who could spare the time could make a day of it, and some friends had offered Tessa a lift because they knew she'd be coming on her own. She put on a final touch of lipstick then went to check on Mitch, who, now that his exams had finally begun, was allowed to stay home from school to revise. For the past week he'd moped about the house, dark shadows under his eyes, stooped like an old man. The only time he perked up was when his mobile rang.

She found him lying on his bed, reading from a big lever-arch file. When he looked up, his face was a picture of misery. 'My brain won't take in any more,' he told her. 'I'm going to fail the lot.'

'Go for a little walk,' she advised. 'Or a bike ride. Try and distract yourself, even if only for ten minutes.'

'It won't help.'

'It's important to take a break. Are none of your friends around?'

'No. We've all got different papers on different days.'

As he sat up, he seemed to Tessa to have grown suddenly longer and thinner. Even his bare feet seemed spectrally elongated. 'Are you eating enough? Bananas are good energy food.'

'Not hungry. I'm never going to get the grades I need.'

She sighed, experiencing a mixture of sympathy and exasperation. He saw, and hung his head, his soft hair flopping. Abashed, she reached into her handbag and pulled out some cash. 'Tell you what,' she strove to speak more kindly, 'go and get a haircut. Here.'

He came to take the money, giving her an ambivalent look that made her feel cheap. She reached up to smooth back his hair, kissing his exposed forehead. 'No good sitting exams if you can't see out.'

Mitch nodded. 'Ok. Thanks.'

'I have to go. Bobbi's coming to pick me up.'

Mitch followed her, lingering in his doorway, fingering the paintwork on the door-jamb, obviously making up his mind about something. 'Are Grandpa Hugo and Grannie Pamela coming over again soon?'

'There's been a lot going on,' countered Tessa.

'Only we never seem to see them.'

Tessa sighed. 'It's been difficult, this stuff about my being adopted.'

'But you're not adopted,' he protested. 'They're your family. It was Erin who left home, not you.'

'Yes, but it's also complicated. We're taking a little time to adjust, that's all.'

'Family is family,' he said doggedly. 'Finding a second mother doesn't mean you lose your first.'

Tessa was touched by the earnestness with which he spoke, as if he were willing her to understand something more behind his words. He had always possessed such a sweet nature, and she was sorry for her impatience. 'You're right,' she said, smiling at him. 'Family is family.'

He nodded as if something had been settled between them, and disappeared back into his room.

Twenty or more familiar faces were gathered in the private dining room of one of the pubs in Orford. Tessa found it hard being expected to act as ambassador for Sam's brasserie, which was a sufficient novelty to be a major topic of conversation. Although most people already seemed to know that Sam and Nula were living together, they still pumped Tessa for information, asking if he would be offering an introductory commission to those who sent guests his way. Several assumed Tessa would join in the general praise for the design and decor, most of which was due to Nula's firm, and directed rather too sharp-eyed remarks at her about the lucky combination of talents. And so, tired after all the chat and two glasses of wine, she found it dispiriting to travel home again with Bobbi and her husband, sitting in the back of their car like a child behind the grown-ups.

Entering Felixham, Tessa steeled herself as the car approached the brasserie.

'Oh, look,' cried Bobbi. 'There's Sam!' Bobbi waved as the car sailed past, but Sam did not notice. He was hand-in-hand with Nula, laughing and almost dancing with her. She too was laughing, her head tilted back so her long wavy hair swung loose and free. Tessa shrank into herself, feeling flimsy and transparent, invisible to the husband she had lived with for seventeen years.

Bobbi twisted around to speak to Tessa. 'When does he open?' Not waiting for an answer, she turned back to her husband, who was driving. 'We must go for lunch. We should book right away, or we'll never get a table.'

Five minutes later Tessa waved them off and went indoors. The house was silent. Mitch must have gone out as she suggested, Lauren was at school, and it would be an hour or two before the first guests rang the bell. There was no one waiting to ask her about her day, and she was struck by how, immersed in her own small-town world, she had seldom looked outside the family-run business to find friends of her own. The place seemed suddenly cavernous, too big for her yet offering no shelter.

Picking up the post, she went into the office. She could not bear to go upstairs to the bedroom she had once shared with Sam. She longed to believe that there could still somehow be life and love in their marriage if she could only explain how they could be different together now that she was beginning to know her real self; that, if only he could face the difficulty of telling Nula, he could prevent the waste of all their years together, put a stop to the final break-up of the family they had created. But she knew this was make-believe. She had witnessed the truth right there on the street beneath Nula's jaunty blue-and-white signage.

Although Tessa had remained invisible behind the car window, she'd been close enough to witness the happiness shining in Sam's face, to watch the unhindered way he laughed. She did not think she had seen him so carefree since they'd been at college. Had he even been like that then? She felt like an outcast, discarded by a marriage that had not worked because she had failed to grasp this one small subtle thing which, dancing hand-in-hand in the street with Sam, Nula appeared so abundantly to have mastered. Tessa's sense of failure left her neutered and diminished. The final shreds of renewed confidence she had enjoyed for a few days after Declan's flirtation faded away: that sort of urge, however vital, was not the subtle, precious intimacy she had just – cruelly, obscenely – witnessed between Nula and Sam.

Tessa wondered now if maybe she should have accepted Declan's invitation after all. Even with 'no strings', sex might have offered some sense of connection, some evidence that she was still desirable. But the image she conjured up of herself in bed with Declan merely threw into greater relief the absence of what she'd been forced to witness between Sam and Nula. How had she failed to realise how sterile and unlovable Sam had found her all these years? He had taken the line of least resistance, as he always did, to escape from her, but his betrayal there in the street could not have been more public. The recognition of her loss was terrible, a grief that made her want to cry out in fury and lament.

She sat down at her desk, staring at the lifeless screen. The pile of post caught her eye, the corner of a now-familiar handwritten envelope sticking out. Seizing Roy's letter, she read it twice, dug out one of the picture postcards of Felixham that she stored away for guests, and wrote simply: *Please may I come and see you again?*

TWENTY-FIVE

Tessa arrived at HMP Wayleigh Heath a good hour before visits began and was among the first to book in, and to hand in her unsealed envelope containing a few photographs of herself as a child. She had brought a book to read, a promising-looking paperback left behind by a guest. Knowing now what to expect, she was able to look around more confidently and, when called across to the prison, to take in more of her surroundings. This time she had an impression of being on a ship, a spick-and-span naval vessel maintaining a constant discipline that heightened the awareness of how they were all alone, far from land, ever vigilant to the threat of violent mutiny. The sounds of the prison, too, reminded her of being on board a boat, where the constant background noise of metal striking against metal was reflected back off the hard surfaces of deck or water, with no soft edges to absorb its clarity. Like the sea, it was an environment that would not lightly forgive mistakes.

Arriving in the visits room, she saw Roy watching out for her. He stood up, waiting as she walked towards him.

'I'm glad you're on time,' he said, smiling. 'Means we'll have longer together.'

Tessa felt obscurely deflated. She had taken pains to dress nicely, had paid Carol extra to cover for her absence, and it had been a long, rather tiresome, drive.

'You look stressed,' Roy observed. 'A bit of a trek from Felixham?'

Instantly guilty at her oversensitivity, and certain his welcome couldn't have been intended as an admonishment, Tessa tried to imagine how difficult it must become to empathise with the everyday realities of life outside. It was, after all, extraordinary that apart perhaps from a journey in a closed van from one establishment to another, Roy had not set foot outside these walls in twelve years. The comparison with her own life put his limited existence into full perspective, like a tiny dot at the wrong end of a telescope. And besides, Roy *had* asked about her journey. 'I'm fine,' she smiled. 'An easy drive.'

As they sat down, she realised that, distracted, she had not offered Roy her hand or other physical greeting. But now the opportunity had passed, and she experienced a second pang of guilt. 'Thank you for the VO,' she said. 'I hope I'm not depriving anyone else of a visit.'

Roy smiled and shook his head.

'I brought some more photos, by the way,' she told him. 'Of me as a child, like you asked.'

'Good girl. I want to catch up on those years I missed. Bring me as many as you can,' he laughed. 'I want at least one of you at every possible age. Of Mitch and Lauren too.

So I don't miss out completely on my grandchildren growing up.'

'Of course.' Compromised by her ambivalence about associating her children with this place, Tessa turned the tables. 'I don't suppose you have any of yourself?'

Roy shook his head. 'My mother died soon after I was sent down. So far as I know, nothing was kept.'

'How terrible. Did they let you go to the funeral?'

'I chose not to.'

'I'm sorry.'

'Let's look forward, not back.' He gave a rueful smile. 'I want to know everything about you. Is that corny?'

'No. I want the same.'

'Good. So, start at the beginning.' He sat back in the pose of a good listener.

Tessa realised that even if she hedged the topic now, the time would come when she would have to tell him about Erin not being in any real sense her mother. Why had she not considered this in the car coming here, when she had been busily imagining the conversations they might have? Unable to work out quite why she was so reluctant to reveal the secrets of her childhood, she glanced at Roy's face, hoping to glean something from his expression; instead she saw something familiar, like a glimpse of herself caught while passing a hallway mirror: he was not a stranger. She relaxed. 'Did you ever meet my grandmother?' she asked. 'Erin's mother.'

'Not that I remember.'

'She made Erin give me up. Erin was only sixteen,

remember, and Felixham in the mid-seventies was hardly at the cutting edge of the sexual revolution.'

'Suppose not.' Roy retained his expression of concern.

'Did you recognise Erin?' she asked. 'In the photographs?'

'Of course. I remember she'd failed a music exam, and her mother was cross with her. Tell her that I liked seeing the photos, won't you? And that I remember her fondly. Don't forget, now.'

'I won't.'

'Good.' He seemed pleased. 'So what happened to you?'

'My aunt adopted me. Pamela. I don't know if you ever met her? She was quite a bit older, and already married.'

'Well, I suppose an aunt's the next best thing to your own mother. Three cheers for Pamela.'

Tessa was touched by his evident relief at her fate.

'But Erin was still around?' he asked. 'While you were growing up?'

'Not really. She made a new life for herself with cousins in Australia.' Tessa guessed from the way Roy studied her face that he expected more, but refrained from asking. 'We're not terribly close, to be honest,' she told him. 'So I don't miss her.'

'And do you have siblings? Half-siblings?'

'No.' Tessa felt protective of what she now knew to be her parents' inability to mourn their childlessness because of the cuckoo planted in their nest. She chose to ignore how they might view her presence here, a reward for the accident of another man's fertility. 'No siblings,' she said with genuine regret. 'Just me.'

'And your father?' Roy asked lightly.

'Hugo. A lovely man. He's been a good dad.'

'So what does he think about you being here?'

'I've told my parents all about you.' Tessa heard the pitch of her voice rise under the pressure of his scrutiny, and she licked her lips nervously. She did not want to risk wounding him by admitting that they had no idea she was here, and would be horrified if they did.

But Roy accepted her answer. 'I want to know where your talents lie,' he went on. 'Music? Art? Science?'

The swift change of subject made Tessa think that perhaps her praise of Hugo had pained him. 'Art, I guess. Well, interior decoration.'

He nodded. 'You wrote that you love designing rooms. Ever think of being an architect?'

'No, never occurred to me.'

'Pity we didn't meet earlier. I would've encouraged you. I bet you'd be good at anything you set your sights on.'

Tessa felt bathed by the warmth of his smile. 'Not so sure about that.'

'You should be! You mustn't let people value you at less than you're worth. The last few weeks I've been thinking a lot about what it must have been like for you, growing up not knowing your real father, uncertain who you are. No matter how good and kind the people were who brought you up, I can't help feeling it's left you at some kind of spiritual disadvantage.'

Gratified that he had given her such thought, Tessa

chose not to examine why she failed to correct his assumption that she had always known she was adopted.

'Seem wrong to you, a man like me talking about spirituality?'

'No, of course not!'

'Prisons are surprisingly spiritual places, you know. People inside are on a journey, whether they want to acknowledge it or not. Though many do. And naturally,' Roy spread his hands and gave an ironic shrug, 'we have plenty of time for reflection. That's pretty rare on the outside.'

'True.'

'So now you've found me, maybe I can make good any gaps left by your adoption. I'd like to think that fate has brought us together for a purpose, to help you be everything you want to be.'

Tessa felt suddenly shy, unsure how to deal with his regard, how to value his belief in her.

'I'd like to get you a birthday present,' he declared. 'What would you like?'

'I don't know. I'll have to think.'

'What about something to wear?'

'Maybe a scarf?'

'Or some jewellery?'

'That's too much!'

'Why? Am I not allowed to spoil you?'

'Well, I wear a lot of earrings. Always nice to have a different pair.'

'You have such delicate wrists. How about a bracelet?'

'I've never really worn bracelets.'

'Which do you prefer, silver or gold?'

'You can't start buying me expensive jewellery!'

'I'd like to.'

'But . . .'

He sat back, laughing. 'It's my freedom they took away, not my money. I still own a house, and the rent just piles up.'

'All the same . . .'

'A gold bracelet then. I'll have it sent to you.'

'Thank you. That's really kind.'

'Wear it next time you come.'

'I will.' She glowed with pleasure. 'Shall I fetch some tea?' she offered, embarrassed that she could do so little in return. 'Cake with cherries?'

'Why not? Thanks.'

'I could get you a few extra pieces, if you like. To eat later?'

His expression changed, became resigned and guarded. 'I'm not allowed.' He hesitated, and then leant forward. 'See the door over there? Once we're on the other side, we're strip-searched. Given a full body search.'

Tessa felt his scrutiny, felt he was testing her reaction. She tried to be as matter-of-fact as possible. 'For drugs?'

'And weapons.' He sat back, more relaxed. 'But I'd love a slice now, thank you.'

As Tessa waited at the counter for the nice WRVS lady to pour the tea, she felt that Roy's acceptance of her offer of cake had somehow been intended as a reward for her tact. She somewhat resented the feeling: why was it her problem if he was in prison? Reminding herself that she shouldn't let herself get too carried away, she returned to their numbered table with the tea tray.

It was as though, while he waited for her, he'd read her mind. 'My turn to tell you a bit more about myself,' he said. 'Can you bear to hear about the tragedy that brought me here?'

'Of course.' Tessa sat down, passing over his tea and pre-packaged slab of cake. She had been ravenously hungry after the last visit so had bought herself some chocolate, but it felt somehow inappropriate to busy herself with it when he was about to discuss such a weighty matter.

Taking a moment to compose himself, Roy lined up the cake in the centre of the plate, and began: 'Angie and I had been together more than ten years. Her family never accepted me, never liked the fact that Angie lived a different sort of life with me. They were decent people, don't get me wrong, but narrow, fearful of anything unconventional. Not surprising that she suffered from depression. I blame myself for what happened. We'd had money problems after I quit a job that was stifling me, and she moved back home for a bit while I sorted things out. But then she slid downhill, got worse and worse. Maybe it went deeper than depression, I don't know. I tried to help, to get her back to her old self. Told her I'd found a new job, got a nice flat ready for us, with a garden, just like she wanted. But . . .' Roy broke off, shaking his head, lost in memory.

'Your tea's getting cold,' Tessa prompted him gently.

Roy took a sip, and got as far as unwrapping his slice of cake and folding up the cellophane neatly before he continued. 'The worse thing is, I can't remember what happened,' he said. 'I've been told that's quite common, to do with post-traumatic shock. I've never raised a hand in anger to anyone in my life, especially not to Angie. She was the love of my life. I wouldn't have hurt a hair on her head. But that day, she got upset and just lost it. It was in the doctor's report that I had scratches on my face where she tried to claw at me, though I don't remember that happening. You have to realise how ill she was. It would never have ended the way it did otherwise. That wasn't the real Angie. It wasn't her fault.'

Tessa sat motionless, with no idea what to say. She had expected a tale of hatred, jealousy or anger, not this declaration of love and regret.

'So sad,' he went on at last. 'A waste of two lives, that's what my barrister said. No one could believe the police charged me with murder rather than manslaughter, but there you go.'

'Thank you for telling me.' Tessa wanted to know exactly how Angie had died, but didn't know how to ask.

'I'm sorry to burden you with it,' he said.

'Don't be.'

'Nothing will bring Angie back, and I have to live with that. But I'd like you to try and understand.'

Tessa dared to sip at her tea. 'I'll try.' Again she tried to formulate some pattern of words to ask what he had not yet told her. 'So you were defending yourself?' she asked. 'When it happened?'

He sat back, regarding her thoughtfully. 'You deserve better.'

'Nonsense.'

'No one wants a father who once made a fatal mistake.' He paused to make a minute adjustment to the position of his mug in relation to his plate. 'I lost control. That was the end of Angie's life. The cause was strangulation.' He looked directly at her, a hint of challenge in his eyes. 'That's what you wanted to know, wasn't it?'

Tessa took a sharp breath. 'Yes. It helps to understand. Not to imagine–'

'To imagine something worse?'

She nodded miserably, and he reached out to touch her hand. When she looked up his expression was entirely sympathetic. 'What stopped me giving up,' he said, 'was how it was Angie's despair that had led to all this. If she'd only been stronger, or her parents had woken up sooner to how ill she'd become . . .' He broke off with a sigh. 'But who knows?' He smiled wryly. 'Maybe some good will finally come of it. Maybe you and I can help one another.'

Tessa nodded, unaware that she had appealed to him for help.

'I can't tell you the difference it makes finding I have a daughter, someone to live for.'

Tessa watched as Roy finally broke off a piece of his

cake and held it up. 'The celebratory feast!' he said. 'Cherries will always be lucky for me from now on.'

'Good, I'm glad.' Her heart went out to him, admiring his courage in volunteering the truth.

Roy watched her as he ate. 'Don't worry,' he said. 'I realise I can't ever be a big part of your life. That's as it should be. But I want you to know that on my side, my feelings aren't because I'm stuck in here with nothing else to think about. They're far more than that, I promise. But I don't expect you to feel the same.'

'I'm still getting my head around it,' Tessa explained, not wanting to hurt him. 'Part of me does feel like this is huge. Of course it is, finding my father. But I haven't managed to make much sense of it yet.'

'Not quite the father you'd been dreaming of all these years!'

Again, Tessa failed to point out that she'd never been given any reason to dream of an absent father, avoided telling him how recent her discovery was, and avoided questioning her own reluctance to confide in him. She looked up and found Roy observing her in amusement. He burst out laughing.

'You're so like me! I can tell exactly what you're thinking. No one's going to pull the wool over your eyes, that's for sure. Bravo for making up your own mind!'

Tessa blushed in embarrassment that he had sensed her caution.

'I'm not laughing at you,' he assured her. 'I'm glad you

think for yourself. Much better that you take your time about trusting me. I prefer it, frankly.'

Tessa laughed in relief.

'I've seen women come in here,' he went on more seriously. 'They write to the men, talk about love, some even get married. But it's all a game, and when the men come up for release, out come the divorce papers.'

'That's so mean.'

'Yes, cruel. So if you'd kicked off by being all lovey-dovey over a convicted killer you'd only just met, believe me, I'd've been high-tailing it out that door over there.'

Tessa was touched by Roy's implicit acknowledgement of his vulnerability. 'Even so, I was aware of our connection straight away,' she assured him. 'Weren't you? Even though we *had* never met.'

He nodded in turn. 'But we'll still take our time and get to know one another. Deal?'

He held out his hand, and she took it gladly.

'Deal.' As she started to withdraw her hand, he clasped it tighter.

'People won't like us being friends. You must realise that?'

'So what? It's between us.'

'Am I a secret?'

'No.' She hesitated, all too aware of the grip of his fingers. 'Private.' Out of the corner of her eye, Tessa saw the red-haired officer start forward, as if about to order them apart.

Roy caught the movement too.

'Don't worry,' he said. 'She's just jealous.' He strengthened his grasp on Tessa's hand. 'So no secrets between us?'

'No.'

'Good.' Satisfied, he let go of her, then turned and looked levelly at the female officer who, Tessa saw with surprise, quickly twisted her head away as if rebuked.

TWENTY-SIX

The row of multicoloured beach huts stood in the lee of the sea wall like jars in an old-fashioned sweetshop. Pamela unlocked the candyfloss-pink door and stood back to allow Hugo to carry in the five-litre bottle of water. It was Tessa's birthday and although Mitch and Lauren no longer saw a picnic tea as a special treat, Pamela had decided to revive a tradition from when they were little and ask her old friends if they would once again let her use their hut for the afternoon.

It was half-term and most of the huts were in use. Their occupants sat on the narrow porches surveying the activities on the beach below with a king-of-the-castle air of superiority. As Hugo set out the pair of painted Lloyd Loom chairs, Pamela took her home-made chocolate cake out of its tin and carefully inserted half a dozen pink-and-white striped candles, a random number but sufficient for the blowing out to be fun. She checked the little bottled gas burner and then went to the open doorway. It was a beautiful day and she was both excited and apprehensive.

This would be the first time she could celebrate Tessa's birthday spontaneously, without any fear of being caught out by tricky questions that might threaten to pull down their house of cards.

Hugo came to stand beside her. His look of surprise as she linked her arm in his saddened her: she knew how seldom she initiated such gestures of affection, and even now long-ingrained habit prevented her from speaking. So many of her conversations with her husband had gone on privately inside her head. *Do you remember*, she silently asked him now, *when we first laid eyes on Tessa?* Erin had not wanted any of her family with her in the delivery room, but the midwife had brought out the little bundle wrapped in a hospital shawl and told them the baby was a girl. She and Hugo had looked into those serious, intently staring eyes and then at one another, too happy to speak. And that, Pamela silently reminded him, was always the moment they'd describe to Tessa when she'd asked, as all young children do, about her birth. It was not a lie, but what could never be said was their acute awareness of Erin, little more than a child herself, lying weeping and exhausted a few yards away. Pamela had gone in to her sister, confused about whether or not to hide her joy, wanting to thank her, uncertain what to say, the beginning of a lifetime of not being able to speak.

But now, she thought, briefly touching her head to Hugo's shoulder, they could all begin to talk. Now she might be able to tell Tessa how much she loved her and had wanted her, how sorry she was that those things could not be said before. Today, for the very first time, Erin's role could be acknowledged as part of the birthday celebrations.

'Let's get the kettle on,' she said to Hugo. 'It always takes so long to boil.' Pamela disengaged her arm and went inside, leaving him standing there alone.

A moment later she heard voices as Hugo attempted to sing a welcoming 'Happy Birthday' and Tessa laughingly tried to shush him. Pamela went to the door and waited to greet her daughter, the glittering sea hard against her eyes. Hugo had unfolded an extra picnic chair, and once the women had hugged one another in their customary undemonstrative way they sat in a row, with Tessa in the middle.

Pamela was pleased that when Tessa unwrapped the gift box she seemed to like the agate earrings she'd chosen for her.

'Your main present is in the car,' said Hugo gruffly. His eyes had welled up when he'd first explained the idea behind it to Pamela. 'It's a magnolia, a white tulip tree,' he told Tessa. 'You always said you'd love to have one in the back garden.'

'I would. That's wonderful, thanks!' Tessa leant over to kiss each of them in turn. 'Great idea!'

Hugo cleared his throat. 'We thought maybe planting a tree together could mark a new beginning.' He glanced across at Pamela. 'Something positive.'

'Thanks,' repeated Tessa, a little more stiffly.

'I brought a spade so we can do later. The kids can help.'

'That'll be nice.'

'They can be in charge of watering until it gets its roots down.'

Tessa nodded. Pamela thought she looked sad, and wondered how much she minded about Sam not being part of things any more, but didn't like to ask.

'I've dug out a few more photos for you, of when you were little,' she said instead, reaching into her bag and handing over the snapshots she had collected. It had made her so happy when Tessa had first asked for pictures of Erin, and she was keen to encourage Tessa's interest and affection. 'I always had copies made to send to Erin.'

Tessa took the envelope. 'Thanks.' She turned to stow them away, but Hugo reached out his hand.

'Let's have a look.' He took the prints out of the envelope and shuffled through them. 'Oh, I remember this!' he said, holding one out for the two women to see. 'This was the year we went to Brittany.'

Pamela looked: there were several colour photos of Tessa aged about five, wearing a striped swimsuit and licking an ice cream cone, standing slightly knock-kneed against a backdrop of rock pools. As with every memory of Tessa's childhood, Pamela felt the piercing arrow of guilt that she had been occupying Erin's rightful place. In consequence, her younger self was always a shadowy figure at the edge of the frame, trying not to be in the picture at all.

'Remember?' Hugo asked Tessa. 'They had blackcurrant flavour and you loved it.' Not waiting for a response, he held out another picture. 'What was this?' he asked Pamela.

'A fancy-dress party,' she told him, turning to Tessa. 'For one of your friends at primary school. You'd be about seven or eight.'

The image showed Tessa in the small back garden of their old house. An attempt had been made to curl her hair and she wore a short red dress with white collar, cuffs and belt.

'Little Orphan Annie,' said Tessa with a grimace.

Hugo laughed heartily. 'Oh well, no more of that!' he said, replacing the snapshots in the envelope and handing it back to Tessa.

Pamela caught sight of Mitch and Lauren making their way along the beach towards them. Lauren cut a rather poignant figure in her unsuitable clothes: half plump child, half presumably some vain attempt to emulate an admired celebrity. But she smiled and waved when she noticed Pamela watching her. Mitch seemed to have acquired a new air of quiet self-possession; always a dreamy boy, Pamela hoped he was happy in his private thoughts.

After the greetings and birthday salutations, Pamela heard the kettle whistling and went inside. She considered risking a nip from the bottle of diluted juice she always carried in her handbag, but then saw that Hugo had followed her. 'Want a hand?'

'If you pour the tea, I'll light the candles on the cake.'

He obeyed silently and went back out with a tray. Pamela decided she could do without, and carefully carried the illuminated chocolate cake out into the sunshine.

As Tessa cut the cake and made her wish, sharp-eyed Lauren spotted the thin gold bracelet on her wrist. Pamela had noticed it earlier and had entertained the wild hope that Erin might have sent it.

'Who gave you that?' asked Lauren.

'A friend.'

'Who?'

'Who wants the first slice?' asked Tessa, not looking at Lauren.

'Me!' Lauren reached for her plate, and Tessa concentrated on cutting the next slice.

'Is it from a boyfriend?' Lauren persisted.

'No!' Tessa was shocked. 'Of course not.'

'So where did you get it?'

Seeing Tessa's cheeks redden, Pamela hoped that perhaps there *was* a new man on the scene, someone to take her mind off Sam. In an attempt to divert Lauren's enquiries, she said tentatively, 'I wondered if you'd thought of giving Erin a ring later?'

'She sent me a card,' was Tessa's reply.

'That's good! You must've been pleased.'

'With some photos of her dogs.'

'Might be nice for you to have a bit of a chat as well?'

'She can call me,' responded Tessa briskly.

Pamela fell silent, ignoring Hugo's reproachful look. He got to his feet. 'I'll put the kettle back on,' he said, and disappeared into the hut.

Lauren moved to take his empty chair, allowing Mitch, sitting on the top step, to stretch out his legs.

'Can I have more?' she said, reaching out her empty plate.

'When I've finished mine,' Tessa replied.

Lauren reached across to the precarious little folding table and picked up the cake knife.

'Just wait!' ordered Tessa.

Lauren subsided for a moment. 'I want to know who gave you the bracelet. You're always hiding things when I come into the office,' she complained.

'Lauren, if I had a boyfriend I'd tell you. I promise.' Tessa's voice betrayed how cross she was.

Lauren's lips curled. Tessa reached out to take her hand, but she snatched it away. 'I don't believe you!'

'Sweetheart, it's true. If you saw me put things away, then it's to do with my adoption.'

'Your mum's allowed to keep some things private if she wants,' Pamela told Lauren gently.

'Everyone's got secrets except me. You all think I'm stupid.'

'No, we don't. But you must try not to blow things out of proportion.'

'You see! No one trusts me,' cried Lauren. She leaned forward and hacked at the cake, splitting off a clumsy chunk that she tipped onto her plate.

'That's too much!' cried Tessa, but Lauren, hunching up in her chair, the plate right under her chin, started to cram cake into her mouth. Pamela saw Mitch shake his head and look away.

Helpless, Tessa put her own plate of half-finished cake back on the table and sat with slumped shoulders, her eyes narrowed against the brightness of the glittering sea, fingering the gold band on her wrist.

Pamela looked past her, along the gulley of tightly packed verandas that faced the beach. The crammed vista – it was impossible to see an end – seemed to mirror the inescapable tensions of family life. She felt for Tessa, remembering the wrenching responsibility, guilt and resentment over an unhappy child, the impossible struggle between elemental love and impotent fury at always being the one to blame. It wasn't fair, she thought, how a mother could never be above the fray. Which was when the other realisation had inevitably followed: she was not a mother.

She had so wished for this birthday to be different, to be light and carefree and silly. She realised now that the disclosure of the secret had not disempowered it; for that to be accomplished would require work, and despite their best attempts might never be achieved.

Hugo appeared in the doorway with the teapot in his hands. 'Who's for another cuppa?' He looked around, taking in the disaffection. 'Or maybe French cricket?' he suggested, another family tradition. 'I bet the old racquet's still in here somewhere.'

Mitch got to his feet. 'Good idea. You coming, Lauren?' He held out his hand and, after some mulish consideration, his sister consented to go with him. Hugo followed with the ancient wooden tennis racquet that now hung as an ornament on the wall inside. 'Tessie? You coming?'

Tessa shook her head. 'In a moment.'

Hugo made his way down to the beach, leaving Pamela both comforted and frustrated by his customary diplomacy. She got up. 'I'll just put the cake out of the sun.' Alone in the hut's dim interior, she reached into her handbag for the plastic bottle. As she raised it to her lips she became aware of Tessa watching from the doorway. Startled, the liquid spilled and she had to wipe her chin.

'Nula, if you please,' began Tessa angrily, 'thinks Lauren is comfort-eating. That I should keep an eye on it.'

'Well, she does seem a little unhappy.'

'It's not my fault. Nothing's any different at home. It's Sam who's changed.'

'I know how hard it must be for you, my darling. But you won't force Mitch and Lauren to choose sides, will you?'

'I'm not! It's Nula who's upsetting them. It's far too soon for Sam to expect them to make themselves at home in her place!'

Pamela recognised the bitterness of the usurped, certain it was what Erin, too, had felt. 'We've all had to fit in around one another,' she began, wanting so desperately to suck the poison out of the wound. 'Sam too. It'll be a while before everyone recovers from all that's happened, but we're still a family. Even Sam. He's still the children's father.'

Tessa looked at her strangely, her mouth set in an obstinate line that reminded Pamela of Lauren. 'I've met my father,' she announced.

Pamela gasped at the collapse of her prayer-like hope that Tessa had dropped all notions of pursuing Roy Weaver. 'You've been to the prison?'

'Twice now.'

'Where? Which one?

'Wayleigh Heath.'

It meant nothing to Pamela. 'You're absolutely certain it's him?'

'We have the same hands.' Tessa raised hers. 'The same eyebrows. And he remembers Erin.'

'What does he remember? What did he say?'

'He asked me specially to tell Erin that he remembers her fondly.'

'Fondly?' For a moment Pamela's heart soared. 'He said that?'

'Yes.'

'And really meant it?'

'Yes!'

'And you believe him, trust him?'

'He may've made a mistake, but he's not a monster.'

Hearing the latent resentment in Tessa's voice, Pamela clasped Tessa to her. 'Of course not!'

'He even said that we should take our time getting to know one another, that I was right not to rush in. He only wants the best for me.'

'Really? Oh darling, I'm so relieved.' Pamela drew back so she could look into her daughter's eyes. 'So everything's going to be all right?' She sank back against the worktop and, in need of its sedative effect, raised the bottle again and took a little sip.

Tessa's anxious look had softened, but now she seemed to sense something suspicious, and her gaze fixed on the plastic bottle. 'What's that?' she asked.

'Nothing!' Pamela said automatically, and immediately regretted the lie. She pushed the bottle away from her on the worktop. 'It's just juice. Such a hot day.'

Tessa frowned, unconvinced.

'Do the children know?' Pamela continued.

Tessa shook her head.

'Will you tell them?'

'Soon. Can we talk about this another time?'

'Yes, darling. Of course. But I can tell Erin, can't I? That you're glad you've met him?'

'Yeah, fine.'

Tessa seemed disappointed, dejected, and Pamela watched helplessly as she retreated into the sunshine. She did not feel able to follow: it was just too difficult. She longed to go after her daughter, drag her into her arms, tell her she loved her, that all she wanted was for her to be happy. But she knew she'd only get it wrong, that she'd failed at motherhood yet again.

TWENTY-SEVEN

Mitch lay in bed with Tamsin. He could scarcely believe it possible to be so happy. His happiness spread out from the bed to fill the room, then radiated through the house, out across Felixham, the world, the universe. It felt childishly ridiculous and simultaneously the most grown-up emotion he had ever experienced.

They had just made love for the third time. Each time had been different. Somehow, he had not expected that. All the expectations that he and his friends had entertained about sex had focused on losing their virginity, and he had never looked beyond. No one had told him that each time you got closer and the sensations felt more familiar, and yet that very closeness and familiarity only increased the desire to be even more at one with each other. Already he was looking forward to what he might discover about Tamsin – and himself – the next time, and the time after that.

It had been Tamsin who initiated their first encounter. Even though she was sixteen now he would never have pressed her to have sex with him, although he'd longed for it. He suspected he knew why she had, and still felt the tiniest twinge of guilt. It was because her father had been so rude and dismissive to him. It had been unnecessary, over nothing, and Mitch hadn't even cared; he knew it was the way Charlie was. But Tamsin had been mortified, and would have felt her atonement rebuffed if he had tried to talk her out of her apologetic seduction. And once they were naked together under her sweet-smelling white cotton sheets, their ecstatic discoveries had been too intense for him to address his scruples.

It was the very ordinariness of the intensity that made him so happy. He could imagine nothing better than the thought that soon they would get up, get dressed, and take Blanco for a walk. What more could he want than to stand with his arms around her, breathing in the scent of her hair and looking out across the marshes to the sharp brightness of the sea beyond? Yesterday the beauty of a pink and dusky grey sunset against the blue sky seemed to wrap itself around them, as if they were at one with the whole of creation. He felt like the luckiest person in the world. They had walked home hand-in-hand, smiling at other dog-walkers, knowing they invisibly carried their joyfulness between them. There was nothing that Charlie Crawford could say or do to mar such a bond.

They were a few days into half-term. It was only a week's holiday, but Mitch had no more exams, no more revision, nothing else to worry about, and the relief of pressure made the days stretch out luxuriously like holidays used to when he was younger. Tamsin had also had exams because at her school they took a couple of GCSEs a year early, but she didn't seem unduly bothered about them. She took it for granted that she'd get good grades and he liked her blithe confidence, so different from his parents' assumption that it would only be by sheer luck if he did well. The way Charlie had talked when Mitch's future was mentioned had been amazing too, as though his ignorance of anything other than success guaranteed it absolutely. It was a good way to think.

After the last three days with Tamsin, Mitch felt there was nothing he couldn't do if he set his mind to it. Before she came home for half-term, sex had been a furtive matter of spunk and used tissues, but now he understood what it was all about. Making love with her, he felt like a dragonfly nymph shedding its ungainly skin and basking in the sun as its warmth dried his silvery wings. Two days ago he and Tamsin had stood on a little wooden bridge watching the dragonflies dart back and forth, the kingfisher blue of their bodies iridescent against the reflective surface of the water. Mitch told her how Grandpa Hugo used to bring him here as a kid and they'd lie down, their faces right at the edge of the water, so they could spot the beetle-like nymphs emerging from the water. 'Nymph' had seemed like the wrong name for these awkward, wingless creatures, he explained to her, until Hugo had encouraged him to watch and wait and he had witnessed the transformation for himself. And now it had happened to him.

Mitch loved how he could tell Tamsin about the dragonflies without her mocking him or thinking he was 'dreamy', which was how one of his teachers had described him to Tessa at the last parents' evening. Just because he wasn't tempted to get a fake ID and go clubbing in Ipswich, then throw up on the station platform coming home, didn't make him a late developer. Even his oldest friend Chris, with whom he used to make dens and stuff when they were kids, and who'd been just as fascinated by insects and birds and shellfish, made out he thought it was lame to still enjoy the countryside. So for the last year or two, the only person he could share all that with had been Hugo. Mitch was sure Hugo and Tamsin would like each other.

He looked at her now, dozing beside him, the untanned white skin under where she'd worn her bikini on her Caribbean holiday, both laughable and awesomely private and precious. He felt no guilt about being here with her like this. In fact he was willing to bet that if Hugo could see them, or even knew what they had just done, in some deep, important way he would actually approve. Hugo understood what really mattered and what didn't. The thought made Mitch feel grown-up and responsible, his dragonfly wings strengthening in the warmth of the sun.

Tamsin opened her eyes and looked sleepily into his, snuggling closer and kissing his shoulder. 'Shall we get up?' she asked.

Mitch turned to kiss her, wanting to make love to her all over again, yet part of him also wanted to savour the ordinariness that was nearly as exciting as the act itself.

The experience of simply standing beside her as she opened the giant fridge door, of taking the juice carton from her hands to pour her a glass, while his skin tingled and her eyes still had that surprised, dilated look, was wonderful.

'Hungry?' she asked.

Realising he was, Mitch twisted to look at the clock beside her bed. 'Yes,' he said. 'Lunch time.'

He got out of bed and picked his discarded T-shirt up off the floor. As he straightened up, he heard a click and a giggle from Tamsin. She was kneeling in the middle of the bed, holding out her iPhone so she could photograph him. He shrugged into his jeans as she took more pictures, then lunged at her, mock-fighting for possession of the device. Straddling her, he took a couple of photos of her naked on the crumpled sheet below him.

'You'd better not stick any of these on Instagram.'

'You'll have to be extra nice to me, then.' she teased.

'No way!'

Laughing, he took her hand to pull her off the bed, stroking her warm back before she pulled lingeringly away. As he put on his shoes he watched her as she dressed, admiring the elegance of her pointed feet as she stepped into her knickers, her swan-like shoulder blades as she slipped a T-shirt over her head. Barefoot, she headed for the door. Mitch looked back at the bed. 'Shouldn't we tidy up a bit?'

'Oh, Sonia will do that when she comes to turn down.' She saw his incredulous look and laughed. 'Daddy likes to believe he's permanently in a hotel.'

Although Mitch shook his head over Charlie's self-indulgence, uncomfortable images came to mind, and he hoped Charlie never saw his mum, like Sonia, turning down the guest beds. Hoped too that Tessa never laid eyes on Tamsin's huge wooden sleigh bed, emperor-sized cashmere throw or claw-foot bathtub with the towelling-covered armchair beside it, and realised how meagre in comparison was her idea of luxury that she offered so proudly.

'But won't Sonia tell your dad?' he warned. 'If she guesses how the bed got so messed up?'

'Oh, I see.' Tamsin giggled. 'I don't think she would, but maybe we'd better hide the evidence.' She went back and dragged up the covers to hide the rumpled sheets. Mitch straightened the other side, hating himself for seeing her carelessness as somehow more classy than his concern.

They found Charlie, wearing a pristine grey tracksuit with a white towel round his neck, sitting at the enormous oak kitchen table reading something on his iPad while eating scrambled eggs and smoked salmon. Quinn sat close beside him, looking over his arm at the little screen. Seeing them enter she shifted demurely, hooking her bare feet up beneath her on the chair, but not before Mitch had noticed that she'd been playing footsie under the table with her employer.

Charlie nodded to Tamsin and returned his attention to the iPad, flicking rapidly as he scanned the information. Mitch glanced at Tamsin, but inured to her father's lack of interest, she thankfully did not appear to find anything amiss between him and the nanny. Mitch despised Charlie for jeopardising his daughter's peace of mind. And wasn't it also his job to keep watch over what she got up to with boys? Yet Charlie never asked where they disappeared off to for hours on end and, amazingly, didn't seem to notice how glowingly different she was these days.

'That looks good,' said Tamsin, nodding at her father's plate. 'Shall we have the same?'

'Sure,' Mitch answered.

'I'll call Sonia to make you some,' offered Quinn, starting to get up.

'We can do it,' said Mitch quickly, instinctively shielding Tamsin from being contaminated by whatever Quinn was getting up to with Captain Gorgeous. Catching Tamsin's look of surprise, he laughed. 'Don't tell me you can't even scramble an egg?'

'No, I can,' she protested. 'I just . . .' She looked bashful. 'Show me?'

'If you have any cream, I could do them the way my dad does. If you add the cream at the end, it stops the eggs cooking too fast.'

Passing behind Charlie, Mitch noticed that his hair was wet. 'Have you been in the sea?' he asked without thinking. 'It's great, isn't it? Bet it was cold!'

Charlie looked at him with a vague frown, and let Quinn answer for him. 'There's a pool downstairs.'

'Downstairs?'

'In the basement,' explained Quinn. 'Next to the gym.'

'How big is the basement?' asked Mitch incredulously.

Quinn looked as if she didn't understand the question, and Tamsin answered for her.

'Not like a lap pool. An endless pool, so Dad can work out.'

Not wanting to show his ignorance, Mitch didn't seek an explanation. 'How many eggs?' he asked instead.

Tamsin handed him things from the fridge and put bread in the toaster, while Mitch arranged the salmon and then spooned judicious helpings of perfectly textured egg beside neat triangles of toast. Laying the plates on the table with a subtle flourish, he looked to see if Charlie was impressed, only to realise with chagrin that in Charlie's life, food was always served like this.

'Really good!' said Tamsin, taking a second mouthful. 'Mmm, yummy!' She looked at her dad. 'Mitch's father opens his restaurant tonight.'

'Where?' asked Charlie.

'Here in Felixham. In the High Street.'

'Oh. So not London.' Charlie didn't bother to disguise his immediately waning interest.

'Mitch showed me round the other day. You know the place Mum loves in Santa Barbara? It's kind of like that.'

Mitch brimmed with pride for his dad, but also saw Quinn tense up at the mention of Charlie's wife, a reaction that disappointingly confirmed his suspicions.

'Mitch and I are going,' continued Tamsin happily. 'You should come.'

'Yeah, maybe.'

'I should check with my dad first,' said Mitch. 'It's going to be rammed. There may not be space.' If Charlie couldn't behave well, Mitch didn't see why he had to be polite, not even for Tamsin's sake.

'Oh, Daddy can always get a table anywhere, can't you?' teased Tamsin.

'Yeah, I'll come,' Charlie announced. 'See what it's like.'

Mitch knew he was being as childish as Charlie to resent this arrogant abuse of power, but was also aware how the presence of Captain Gorgeous at the opening would be a big deal and give a boost to all Sam's hard work. Unable to decide whether he was being craven or pragmatic, Mitch assured Tamsin's father he'd be very welcome.

TWENTY-EIGHT

Tessa tried on three different outfits, each change accompanied by a mixture of increasing despair and absurdity. Throwing aside the rather expensive dress she'd liked so much in the shop, she decided there ought to be an etiquette manual that decreed what a spurned wife should wear to the first public meeting with her replacement! She did not want to look desperate, as if she were trying too hard, but neither did she want Nula to think her frumpy and frigid. In the end she settled on the little black dress. Everyone else at Sam's opening would be in pastels or bright summer colours, but black was always smart and she could not deny that she felt a widow's grief.

The light June evening was warm and cloudless, and she crossed the road to walk beside the sea wall. Now that she had to arrive alone, she regretted refusing Hugo's suggestion that they call for her. Entering under the nautical signage, she threaded her way through the crowd gathering in the cobbled courtyard and went into the packed main dining room. She immediately spotted Mitch and Lauren, who were being paid tonight to work alongside the regular waiters. Both wore black trousers and aprons and new white T-shirts printed with 'Sam's Place' in a stylish red script that she recognised as Nula's work, and were carrying trays of food – mini-versions of all the regular items on the menu. She had seen Lauren's excitement about the evening, and how delighted Mitch was that his dad's months of hard work were about to pay off, and was certain that the event – and the brasserie's future – would be a success. But she ached to participate in an achievement that was no longer hers to share.

Accepting a glass of wine from an unfamiliar young Polish waiter, Tessa took a good look around. It felt strange that this should be her first chance to see inside the finished interior, and she couldn't help admiring the chrome-and-silver mirrors set against navy and white. She spotted Sam by the bar, looking rather glassy-eyed and rabbit-in-headlights, while next to him Nula wrote something on a card and handed it to the woman she was talking to, nodding enthusiastically and pointing out something in a menu, clearly already winning new business. Sam caught her eye and raised his head in greeting, but Tessa pretended not to see.

She toyed with her gold bracelet. Sam had sent her a card but, for the first time, no birthday present. Roy's card, which had accompanied the bracelet, had been an ordinary greetings card but chosen because the photograph showed a rustic table spread with a blue-and-white gingham cloth on which stood a pretty bowl heaped with cherries; inside, he'd written that he hoped she'd always have cherries in her cake, and would think of him as she blew out her candles and made her wish. She had no idea how he'd been able to find such an apt image, but treasured the gesture all the more for the effort he must have put into it.

She regretted that she hadn't told Pamela about her meetings with Roy in a more measured way. She assumed Pamela had told Hugo, and was apprehensive about what they might say to her tonight. Yet if Roy was going to occupy his rightful place in her life, then her visits to the prison would soon have to stop being secret, even from the kids. And after all, if Nula had to be accepted as part of the family, then so did Roy.

Tessa was just beginning to feel conspicuous all by herself when she saw Lauren beckoning to her while clasping the heavy tray to herself with her other hand. Tessa went gladly, reaching for a kiss, but Lauren turned in a different direction. 'Mum,' she said, her eyes shining, 'this is Tamsin Crawford and her dad!'

Tessa greeted a slim, straight-haired girl who smiled in reply while beside her a man in a rather incongruous baseball cap held out his hand. 'Charlie Crawford,' he said with the same perfect smile as his daughter. It lit up his face and made Tessa like him immediately. 'You must be Tessa Parker, right?'

'Right. How do you do?'

'Good, thanks,' he said. 'And this is Quinn.'

Quinn – whom Tessa remembered hearing was the nanny – gave a meek nod.

'D'you like it, Mum?' Lauren indicated the restaurant with a twirling gesture of her head. 'It's so great, isn't it?'

Tessa agreed that it was. Lauren's excitement made her notice how Charlie Crawford at the centre of their small circle attracted heightened attention from different parts of the room. She rather liked the sensation of being included in their gaze. Charlie himself seemed unconsciously to absorb this and rise to meet it, as if the perception of his glamour increased its potency. Proximity to such unassailable confidence increased her own, and she felt her apprehension begin to dissolve.

'These are yummy,' said Lauren, holding out her tray. 'Try one.'

Tessa inspected the chic little portions of fish pie, each served with its own small plastic fork. They reminded her of the treat-sized tubs of ice cream on sale at cinemas, but there were too many butterflies in her stomach to contemplate eating. 'Maybe later,' she told Lauren.

Mitch materialised beside Charlie Crawford, holding a tray covered with little pots of sausage and celeriac mash. Charlie gave it a fleeting glance and, without looking at Mitch, pushed his discarded dish onto it. 'Bring me another of those hamburgers, would you?'

'Daddy!' Tamsin looked appalled and giggled nervously. 'It's Mitch.'

Tessa watched as Charlie glanced up, recognised the face above the waiter's outfit, and nodded. 'Oh, yeah. Hi. Sorry. Such fabulous food, I can't get enough of it.'

'Really delicious,' seconded Quinn. 'And so cute, the way it's served!'

Charlie turned to Quinn. 'We must come here for dinner.'

Tessa saw Mitch glance at Tamsin in alarm, drawing a fraction closer to her before quickly veiling his reaction. Tessa studied the girl more closely. She stood tall and slender in comparison to Lauren, her hair falling sleekly across her shoulder, but her poise was natural and unconscious. If anything, her earnest demeanour seemed to beg you to like her. Tessa caught Mitch's eye, and her son's look of bashful pride revealed the unmistakable intimacy between them: they were in love.

The reasonable part of Tessa registered a poignant amusement, but something more primitive spewed out a dark sense of loss that her curly-haired baby, her boy, was transferring his affections away from her, in truth was already gone. Added to her existing feeling of alienation in her present surroundings, this made her feel old and superfluous.

'They're like so busy in the kitchen,' said Lauren. 'See you later, Mum.'

Following Lauren's progress across the room, Tessa couldn't avoid the sight of Nula at Sam's side, her hand resting on his chest as he bent to speak into her ear. As Nula nodded, smiling up into his face, Tessa reflected that the opening seemed almost equally a celebration of them as a couple. She became aware that Charlie was speaking to her.

'Mitch here seems to have inherited his father's genius for cooking,' he observed. 'He rustled up some pretty mean-looking eggs the other day!'

Tessa was surprised: Mitch had never mentioned being inside the Crawford house, let alone making himself so at home there.

'But Mitch wants to be a lawyer, don't you?' Tamsin turned to Tessa. 'Dad's been explaining what media lawyers do. Mitch thinks it's really cool.'

As Tamsin smiled up at him, Tessa was comforted by the pride that mingled with her sorrow at the inexorable parting from her son.

Charlie Crawford nodded, turning to Mitch. 'You can do anything with a law degree. Have you decided which university?'

'Not yet,' Mitch replied.

Tessa touched his arm. 'We must go to some open days, now the exams are over.'

'Trinity's a good college for law,' said Charlie. 'I knew a lot of lawyers there.'

'But that's Cambridge, isn't it?' asked Tessa, then saw too late from Mitch's expression that her lack of faith would not be lightly forgiven.

'My history teacher said Downing was good too.' Mitch drew himself up, addressing Charlie, not her.

'But not as pretty!' Tamsin said with a laugh.

'I need to have a look around,' Mitch agreed, raising his chin in open challenge to Tessa. 'See if I like it.'

She felt immediate remorse for her meagre vision of her son's potential. 'I'll come with you,' she assured him. 'Whenever you want.'

Mitch shrugged and hefted his tray. 'Better get back to work.' After affectionately nudging Tamsin's arm with his elbow he disappeared into the throng, leaving Tessa with her glamorous new acquaintances.

'Mitch tells me your family's been in Felixham for generations,' said Charlie, and Tessa was grateful for the safe harbour offered by his charm. 'That's rare these days,' he went on. 'Must be good to have strong roots in a place?'

'Yes,' she agreed. 'My grandmother's parents came here when they were first married. And on my father's side, we've been in Suffolk for centuries.' She coloured: only after she'd said it did she remember that Hugo's history was nothing to do with her, that half her family came from the north, from a landscape she had never visited. She felt keenly how different her life – and her expectations for herself and her children – might have been if Roy had been part of it from the beginning.

A little while later Tessa found Hugo and Pamela chatting to some of Hugo's former colleagues from the brewery.

'Tessie,' Hugo greeted her with an anxious smile and a hand on her arm. 'How are you?'

From the concern etched in his weary face, she guessed that Pamela had indeed told him about Roy. Too acutely aware of the hypocrisy of calling them 'Mum' and 'Dad' while so much of her energy was invested in finding out how it felt *not* to be their child, she merely nodded in response.

Pamela leaned in close. 'This must be hard for you, darling,' she said in too loud a whisper.

'It's just a party,' Tessa responded. 'I'm fine.'

Accepting the rebuke, Pamela polished off her glass of wine and reached out for a second. Seeing Pamela's eyes glaze over, a trickle of similar occasions when Pamela had had an extra drink, been tired and gone to bed early, or handed over her car keys and asked Tessa to drive, started to pool into a pattern. The dejection in Hugo's face confirmed her insight, but she rejected pity or sympathy for either of them: she had enough on her plate.

'I think I'm done here,' she said. 'I'm going home. Don't want to keep Carol on duty longer than I need to.'

Part of her cried out for Hugo to detain her, to claim her as his own, to insist on accompanying her, but he nodded in submission. 'You must do what's best,' he agreed.

On her way to the door she saw Charlie and Quinn ahead of her, Charlie guiding Quinn with a caressing hand on her back. She watched as he stopped to shake Sam's hand, clapping him on the arm as if they were old friends, and, over Charlie's shoulder, saw Sam spy her, unanchored and exposed.

At that moment Lauren passed nearby with a tray full of empty ramekins, and Tessa stepped into her path.

'You're coming home tonight, aren't you? It'll be late before it finishes, and Dad will have a lot of clearing up to do.'

'Nula said I could stay and help. It's not like I have school tomorrow.'

'But he'll be tired in the morning. Come home, and leave him in peace.'

'He likes having me stay!'

'That's not what I meant! You and Mitch should come home.'

'Tessa,' Sam greeted her with a kiss on the cheek. 'I'm glad you came. What do you think?'

Her face tight from the exchange with Lauren, Tessa forced a smile. 'I think it's going to be a huge success. Well done.'

He grinned and let out a long, dramatic breath of relief. 'Can't believe it's all gone so well. So far.' He held up his crossed fingers. 'Thanks to the brilliant extra help!' He reached out and ruffled Lauren's hair. She glowed with pleasure.

'Dad, I can stay tonight, can't I?' she asked. 'I'm supposed to be helping. Nula said I could.'

'Couldn't manage without you!' laughed Sam.

'Hello.'

Tessa swung round to face Nula, trying to gather her wits enough to say something suitable.

'Thank you for coming.' Nula reached out and very lightly touched her arm. Tessa jerked as if she'd been given an electric shock. Looking around in panic, she found Mitch beside her and felt instantly calmed and comforted.

'You've done a great job,' Tessa told Nula. 'I really like

the chrome against the wood and brick. Very smart. And of course the food's delicious.'

'Of course!' echoed Nula with a friendly smile. Tessa knew that the brief look of love Nula gave Sam was not intended to be proprietorial, but the warmth of his answering glance slashed through any remaining illusions to which she might have clung.

Sam turned back to her. 'You don't mind if I get the kids cracking again, do you? Though you must stay and try some of the desserts. There's lemon meringue about to come out of the oven.'

'And banoffee pie!' declared Lauren.

'Come on, kids!' Without further farewell Sam moved away, shepherding Nula and Lauren before him. Mitch hovered, uncertain, his gaze following Sam. Tessa grabbed his arm. 'Wait a moment!'

'I don't want to leave Tamsin by herself,' he apologised. 'Her dad said it was fine for her to stay and help out so long as I take her home afterwards.'

Tessa let him go. At the entrance to the kitchen, he turned and gave her a wave before he disappeared.

Alone, Tessa left the heat and noise of the brasserie and encountered the cool breeze from the sea. Felixham was quiet, and the tap of her high-heeled shoes on the pavement echoed off the dark shopfronts. She hoped that maybe, when she got home, one of the guests might need a hot drink or an extra pillow, something simple she could offer someone which would be gladly received.

TWENTY-NINE

Ten days later Tessa sat with Mitch and Hugo on the train to Cambridge. Pamela had originally said she'd come with them, but Hugo was by himself when he'd met up with them at the station. She questioned what his tactful excuse that Pamela was 'a bit under the weather' truly signified. Watching the green East Anglian countryside sweep past the windows of the train, she wondered how far Pamela's habitual reserve over the years had disguised a problem with alcohol, or whether drinking provided an excuse not to face the difficulty of engaging with family life. Either explanation helped make sense of Pamela's absence on similarly important occasions, like choosing Tessa's wedding dress (a sensitive endeavour, since her pregnancy was already showing) or driving to college for her first term away from home. Tessa had always assumed that Pamela had cried off because she hadn't cared enough to put herself out, but now she began to view the past differently.

She couldn't yet decide whether Pamela's fear that her motherhood was merely a masquerade exonerated or further condemned her withdrawals. Surely her repeated failures to share in significant events such as this – Mitch deciding his future – were reason enough to bring the adoption out in the open, so they could all have led normal lives? Either way it felt healthy to Tessa now to admit that she was angry with Pamela for not accompanying them today. Hugo, too, must be tired of covering up for her. She wondered what Pamela's absences must've been like for him. Looking across at him, she thought how careworn he was, the result, she supposed, of years of watchfulness – and possibly loneliness too. He caught her eye and smiled back.

While Mitch explained the reasons why certain colleges were better than others for studying law, Tessa tried to puzzle it out. It would have made more sense if Hugo had been the one to enforce the secret of her adoption: he, after all, had the most to gain from it. But they'd told her that it had been Pamela's decision to obey Averil and say nothing. Why? It couldn't have been that Pamela shared Averil's fear of scandal, especially when an acknowledgement of Erin's motherhood would have absolved her guilt and set her free to love her adopted child in her own way. So why else had Pamela been so scared of the truth coming out?

If Tessa had been on her own in the train with Hugo she might have asked him, but she didn't want to involve Mitch. And besides, the poor man looked miserable enough. Tessa knew how badly she would have wounded him by not telling him herself about her visits to Roy.

Pamela must have told him, but Tessa had not yet had the courage to raise the subject. And if she didn't, she knew he'd be too considerate to bring it up himself.

Once off the train, Tessa wished she'd worn more comfortable shoes, admitting to herself that she'd dressed more smartly than she might otherwise because she found the idea of Cambridge a little intimidating. Reaching the centre of town, they discovered that most of the colleges were closed to the public, with people in elaborate gowns stationed outside the great wooden entrance doors to turn tourists away. Those that were open were expensive to enter, but Mitch insisted they all pay to go into Trinity because it was the college Tamsin favoured.

Despite the flawless green of the lawns, into which were stuck discreet signs forbidding visitors to walk, the heat came in pounding waves off the stone buildings enclosing the Great Court. Amidst such grandeur, Tessa knew it wasn't only the heat that was beating down on her but also the sense of privilege and exclusion. She wasn't sure she could imagine her son here, or picture Mitch's name painted in old-fashioned black and white lettering on the wall alongside those listed at the entrance to each of the dim stairwells where she assumed the students lived during term-time.

But Tessa could imagine Mitch here. With a sinking heart, she knew she couldn't picture *herself* as the parent of a Cambridge undergraduate. The featureless classrooms where she'd learned about hotel management couldn't have been more different from these ancient surroundings. No one in her family, or Sam's, had ever been to university, and Hugo, although fascinated by history and old buildings, was no more than a tourist enjoying the sights. Except, she corrected herself with a jolt, that of course Mitch's grandfather had studied architecture and then become a university lecturer. Maybe, she realised joyfully, Mitch had every right to expand his horizons, just as Roy encouraged her to do.

In her mind, she listened to Roy's voice assuring her that she could be good at anything she set her sights on. So why did she fear to believe that for her children too? What heights might Mitch reach if he succeeded in gaining a place here? Maybe he would become one of those barristers in a wig and gown, inhabiting imposing courts of justice like those she saw on the news. Rather than be intimidated by such a future, she should embrace it.

'There's not much shade around here, is there?' Hugo's question interrupted her thoughts.

'There are one or two other colleges I'd like to look at,' said Mitch, consulting the map he'd bought. 'But we could get a cup of tea first, if you want.'

'Maybe your mum and I can find a bench somewhere,' Hugo suggested. 'And you can explore on your own for a bit.'

Tessa saw the gratitude in Mitch's smile, though he tried to disguise it. 'Be cheaper, too, than all of us paying to go in,' she pointed out, encouraging Mitch to feel free and independent.

'Well, if you don't mind.' He looked at his map again. 'You could sit by the river,' he suggested. 'That might be nice.'

Letting Mitch make his escape, Tessa and Hugo found an unoccupied bench under a willow tree with a view across to a pub that must once have been a mill. They'd bought bottles of water, and were sharing a bag of crisps – a guilty pleasure that took them back to Tessa's childhood when Hugo had always made the pretence of holding out for cheese and onion before capitulating and buying salt and vinegar.

'Whether or not he comes here, it makes no difference to how proud I am of Mitch. He knows that, doesn't he?' he asked.

Tessa watched him fold the empty crisp packet, then store it away to dispose of later: it was typical of his sense of responsibility, his kindness towards the world, and she felt a pang of regret at how little he had gained from all this upheaval in his life. She squeezed his arm. 'Nothing could shake your place in his life,' she told him.

Hugo stared at the ground in front of him. 'I know it's not the same for you,' he said, with an unaccustomed meekness that cut into her heart. She started to reply, but he spoke over her. 'I want to say something. And I don't want you to interrupt because I want to make sure I say it right.'

'Pamela told you?'

'Yes.' His face was suddenly grey and old. 'So it's important you don't think I'm speaking out of jealousy, though

I admit to that – I'm terrified of losing you. But that's not what this is about.'

Tessa could already feel a mild resentment stirring: she would not allow Hugo to speak ill of Roy. Why could no one see how difficult it was to have two mothers and two fathers and have to work out who she was in relation to them all, or understand the impact of discovering a stranger who had such faith in her? How could she listen to them when she was still in the process of becoming her new self?

'This may sound strange to you,' Hugo began, 'but over the years I've felt a relationship with your real father – a kinship. I felt guilty, as Pamela does over Erin, that his loss was my gain. And I'd speculate about what he was like: was he an ordinary bloke like me or someone clever, with special talents, like you?' Hugo reached out and patted her arm. 'And how bitter was he, missing out on this beautiful child, this miracle I got to call my daughter?'

Tessa felt somehow trapped by such kindness, unable to rebel against it, but did as he asked and remained quiet.

Hugo sighed. 'Even when you told us that Roy Weaver was in prison, I made up my mind that if you wanted me to, I'd accept him. Whatever he'd done, I'd shake his hand.' When he spoke again his voice was stronger, more like himself. 'But I also decided that I'd be failing in my duty as your father if I didn't find out everything I could about him, so that, if needed, I could protect you.'

'But I do know about him,' Tessa burst out. 'He wants to play a part in my life.' Watching her verbal blade cut into him, she felt a mixture of horror and voyeuristic fascination; while one part of her screamed at herself to stop, another thrust deeper. 'He cares for me.'

Hugo nodded to himself several times, then spoke at last. 'Of course he does. Anybody would.'

'He's not "anybody",' she protested, appalled now at her cruelty.

'I didn't mean that. I meant that you're worth caring for, Tessa. I don't care whose DNA you've got. You're my child and I love you.'

It was wonderful to hear him say those words, and she longed to believe they carried real power, yet somehow they were not enough; somehow she was beyond their reach.

'And that's why I want to be sure that you understand exactly who and what you're dealing with.'

'I'm not stupid, Dad! Of course I understand. I asked, and he's told me everything.'

'Tell me, then.' Hugo turned to look at her, and she quailed under his calm and level gaze.

'She was his girlfriend,' she answered. 'They'd been together for years. But she was mentally ill. When he tried to help, she attacked him. It was a terrible, tragic accident.'

'That's manslaughter,' said Hugo. 'Roy Weaver was convicted of murder.'

'It was self-defence. He lost control, and she was strangled.'

'He strangled her,' corrected Hugo. 'And got a life sentence.'

'Oh, what's the point of you asking, if you've already made up your mind against him?'

'If he's got nothing to hide, then he won't object to you asking as many questions as you need to.'

'I have! He's told me!'

'Then what made it murder and not manslaughter?'

'You'll just have to trust my judgement,' she said. 'I believe him – that's good enough for me.'

'How long's he been in prison?'

She remembered what Declan had told her about an average life sentence. 'He must be coming up for release soon.'

Hugo flinched. 'How often do you see him?'

'I go when I can. And we write to each other.'

He nodded slowly. 'Will you ask him? Ask him why it wasn't manslaughter.'

'He said his barrister couldn't understand it either.'

'Will you ask him why he was convicted of murder, not manslaughter?'

'No.' Tessa took a stand.

'Why not? Is it that you can't?'

'I can't because it would be rude and insensitive. If it comes up, fine, otherwise I'm not doing it.'

'Then would it be possible for me to come with you one day?'

Tessa tried to imagine Hugo and Roy shaking hands, but good, kind, decent Hugo seemed somehow pale and insubstantial in comparison to her vivid recognition of Roy's shared and inherited traits. She was once again sorry

Roy did not have other children: how wonderful it would have been to discover siblings so robustly like herself.

'I'd like to meet him,' Hugo persisted.

'Meet who?' Mitch had materialised beside them. The shocked expressions with which they both turned to him crushed his excitement about all he had to tell them.

Hugo jerked and his face trembled as if he were palsied. He deferred to Tessa, who, unprepared to take on this further responsibility, got to her feet, brushing at some fallen crumbs.

'Are you seeing someone?' Mitch asked. 'A boyfriend?'

'We're talking about Tessa's biological father,' said Hugo quietly.

'Really? Why? Have you found him?'

Feeling under attack, Tessa avoided her son's candid gaze.

'Tessa has, yes.' Hugo answered for her. 'His name is Roy Weaver.'

He paused, offering Tessa the option to speak, but Mitch was impatient. 'So who is he? What's he like? Can I meet him?'

Tessa remained silent, so Hugo spoke. 'It's not easy, I'm afraid, Mitch. He's in prison.'

'Prison? What for?'

'He killed a woman,' Hugo told him.

Tessa knew she should be the one to explain to her son, but, suddenly afraid of her own reluctance, reassured herself she shouldn't have to be the only one to account for a situation that was not of her making.

'He's a murderer?'

Tessa heard the shock in Mitch's voice and faced him squarely. He was pale, his eyes wide, and she thought how brave he was. 'It was a long time ago,' she assured him. 'She was his girlfriend, and it's his only offence. I'm sorry it's such a shock, Mitch, I really am.'

'You've been to see him?'

'Yes. A couple of times.'

'When?'

'When you were at school.' She curled inwards, away from his expression of disgust.

Mitch pointed at the gold bracelet. 'He gave you that, didn't he?'

'Yes,' she admitted.

'And?'

'And he's my father.' She reached for him, wanting to console him. 'Your grandfather.'

'I've got a grandfather!' Mitch moved to stand beside Hugo, who shook his head in sorrow then awkwardly laid a hand on the boy's shoulder, making Tessa aware of what she had not noticed before – that Mitch was now almost the same height.

'He's a member of your family too, Mitch. You should keep an open mind.'

'So when can I meet him?' he asked.

'I think it's time we all went,' said Hugo. 'Lauren too. She may be young, but let's not have any more secrets. How about it, Tessie? You can make the introductions.'

This was what she'd thought she wanted, but now it felt like an attempt to encroach upon something delicate and private. 'I'd have to ask Roy,' she hedged.

'Why?' Mitch's indignation was unexpectedly fierce.

'Because he has to agree,' she admitted, dismissing the skulking notion that Roy might refuse.

'But he's a criminal. In prison.'

'He still has to send a Visiting Order, or you won't be able to get in.'

'Ok, so when's he getting out?'

Tessa couldn't help but meet Hugo's eyes. 'I'm not sure.'

'So, like, is he going to be part of our life once he gets out?'

'Maybe,' said Tessa. 'But hey, you might be living here by then, a Cambridge law student!'

Mitch fell silent, and Tessa was grateful to Hugo for following her lead in trying to change the subject. Mitch submitted to their questions about his speedy tour of the various colleges, offering only a subdued account of what he had seen. On the journey back to Felixham, it was clear that his preoccupation with this unwelcome information dominated all their thoughts.

As they came off the train into the station car park, Hugo went to open Tessa's car door for her. 'Are you any happier, Tessa?' he asked softly. 'Now that you know him?'

She looked for some stabbing irony behind his words, but there was none. The gentleness of his concern made her feel shabby, as did Mitch's perplexed silence on the short drive home.

THIRTY

Tessa turned off her computer and stood a moment, running through her mental checklist before leaving the house. Her heart sank when she heard a key in the lock and dropped even lower when she heard the front door open and before it even shut again Lauren already calling, 'Mum?'

Tessa went into the hallway. 'What are you doing home from school?' Seeing her daughter's hot and tear-stained face, she went to place a hand on her forehead. 'Are you not well, sweetheart?'

'Miss Hughes wouldn't let me swim!'

'Is it your period?'

'No. She said I need a new swimsuit.'

'Why? We only bought it at the start of last term.'

Lauren hung her head, mumbling: 'It doesn't fit any more.'

'You can't have grown out of it already!'

'It's not my fault!' cried Lauren, her cheeks reddening.

Tessa looked at her watch, in no mood for mercy. 'How

tight is it?' she asked. 'If you could just slim down a little, maybe you could make it last the summer at least? Cut out some of the chocolate and crisps?'

Lauren glared at her, starting to well up again. 'You're the one who gives them to me!'

'Ok, Ok. But you could say no. Take an apple instead.'

Lauren pushed past her and thumped upstairs. Tessa was furious. She knew Lauren was right: every morning she caved in to her daughter's demands to put both crisps *and* a chocolate bar in her packed lunch because it was easier than starting every day with a scene. But if she didn't leave now, she'd forfeit her place in the queue for visits, and, despite the arduous journey to Wayleigh Heath, end up seeing Roy for only an hour. She regretted her sharp words, yet was it honestly too much to ask for a single afternoon when she could do something for herself?

She made her way reluctantly up to Lauren's bedroom. Her daughter was curled up on the bed, still sniffling. Tessa sat beside her, placing a consoling hand on her hip. 'Come on, sweetheart. It's not so bad as all that.'

'You think I'm fat.'

Tessa tried some humour. 'Well . . .' She gave Lauren's hip a playful squeeze, but Lauren whipped around, sitting up and tucking her knees under her chin, staring at her with a mixture of grief and accusation that Tessa wished she could dispel with a wave of a magic wand. If only she could still evoke the simple faith of the toddler and kiss it better. 'It's just puppy fat,' she said. 'You'll soon grow out of it. But maybe we should plan so you eat more healthily. What do you say?'

'No one likes me. I'll never get a boyfriend.'

'Yes, you will, sweetheart.'

'People think I'm sad. I have to eat lunch on my own.'

'Are things Ok at Dad's? You know you can always talk to me. Is this about Nula?' Tessa spoke gently, while wishing fervently that it would all come tumbling out – how much her children hated Nula and had been miserable since Sam had taken up with her.

'No. She's great. She said I was brilliant at the opening party, and they'd pay me if I want to help out there over the holidays.'

Tessa rose from the bed and busied herself folding a pair of discarded pyjama bottoms. 'We'll have to see about that.'

Lauren shot her a look of pure hatred. 'You think I'm useless!'

Shocked, Tessa tried to backtrack. 'Of course I don't, sweetheart. I just think Nula should ask me before promising you things.' She looked at her watch again. 'What about your afternoon lessons? You should go back, shouldn't you?'

'It's the swimming gala. Can't I stay with you? Just once. You can give me a note. We can plan my new diet!'

'I can't today, sweetheart. I have to be somewhere.'

'Where? Can I come with you?'

'It wouldn't work out.' Since Mitch had found about Roy he had maintained a meticulous detachment that Tessa found intimidating; it made her resist being bounced into telling Lauren.

'Then I'll go over to Dad's. Maybe I can help Nula.' Lauren's look of triumph made Tessa's heart sink. She only wanted the best for her kids, but they seemed determined to thwart and upset her. She longed for the security of the visits room, to be cocooned at a table alone with Roy.

'Go, then,' she told Lauren, rising to her feet. 'I'll see you later.'

The traffic on the long drive was slow, with caravans heading for the coast and tourists, unsure which turning to take, jamming on their brakes at every junction. At a roundabout Tessa leaned on her horn when the elderly couple she'd been stuck behind for miles missed chance after chance to pull out into the heavy traffic. Her impatience backfired, as the flustered driver dithered even longer. She knew she shouldn't let herself get so worked up, but she was anxious in case Roy should be offended by her lateness and assume she didn't care enough to be on time. She had phoned, but doubted the officer to whom she'd spoken would pass on her frantic apology.

She was an hour late when she finally pulled into the car park beside the prison, grabbed her bag and ran across to the Visitors' Centre. She dreaded the way Roy's powerlessness would be exposed by her delay and wondered what she could do or say to restore his dignity. She felt outraged at Lauren on his behalf. It must be terrible for all the men in there to be at the mercy of an outside world over which they had no control, to be so cut off and alone with their wounded feelings. It still unnerved her how little she knew of Roy's life beyond the guarded door through which the inmates in their drab tracksuits came and went, how helpless she was to reach after him and make amends.

She was in the very last group to be called across, relieved to escape the Visitors' Centre at last. She'd sat opposite a young mother with a rowdy little boy. When she gave him a hard shake to make him behave, his sister had shot their mother a reproachful look, and in retaliation the mother had hissed in the girl's ear while the child stared back at her with dull rancour. The family group stood before Tessa now, waiting for the electronic door to the transparent holding pen to swoosh open, and both children leaned in against their mother as if for shelter. Tessa supposed Lauren must feel a similar mixture of love and rancour towards her.

Released into the open space of the visits room, the two kids ran straight to the play area, obviously at home with both the rules and the geography of the place, while their mother, her tongue straight in his mouth and her hand on his crotch, greeted a muscular young black guy who was unlikely to have fathered either child. The red-haired officer, whom Tessa recognised from her last visit, called out to them, telling the inmate to sit down, and for them to keep their hands on the table, in view of the cameras.

Tessa, grimly amused, took her seat opposite Roy at the table. She realised he'd been observing her because he indicated the couple and said: 'He's a drug dealer. I bet she only bothers because she reckons he's got cash stashed away.' He nodded towards the play area. 'Doesn't say much for her that she drags them along to a place like this. It's always the kids who suffer, like that little boy.'

He sounded flat and pessimistic, almost bored, and she wondered if it were a mask for despondency. 'I am so sorry I was late,' she told him.

'If you don't want to come any more, Tessa, then just say so.'

'I couldn't help it. Lauren came home unexpectedly. She was upset. And I had to deal with her.' She heard herself gabbling. 'In the end I sent her to her father's. Let him take responsibility for once!'

Roy sat back, unbending slightly. 'I thought perhaps you weren't coming at all, was afraid you'd had an accident or something.'

'Oh, no, I'm sorry. It was just traffic. And thank you so much for this!' She held out her wrist to show off her bracelet, hoping to distract him. 'I love it! And my birthday card. I thought of you as I blew out my candles.' She was relieved when finally he relented and gave her a tiny smile.

'I wish I'd been there,' he said gravely.

'However did you manage to find such a perfect card?' she enthused. 'Is there a shop or something here?'

'No. I found it online, then asked an officer to get it for me.'

'And he did? That was kind.'

'That's her. Janice.' He nodded towards the raised platform where the only female officer was the red-headed woman. Tessa's eyes met hers and Tessa gave a friendly smile, but the woman looked away with what Tessa took to be professional disinterest.

'I handed in a few more photos,' Tessa said. 'Of my childhood.'

He nodded. 'The ones you left last time – I never got them.'

'What?'

'That's what this place is like, I'm afraid. You could put in an official complaint, but it'll be a waste of time.' He sounded bored again, making her panicky, though she wasn't quite sure why. 'The bureaucracy here constantly fucks up,' he went on, 'but it's useless expecting them to admit to any kind of mistake.'

'Roy, I really am sorry I was late. I was so looking forward to seeing you!' He said nothing, so she reached out to touch his hand. 'Are you Ok?'

'While I was waiting, I couldn't stop thinking that there are things a father wants to say to his beautiful daughter.' He sighed. 'Things he should be saying as they stroll along a beach together or snatch a coffee at a street cafe in Rome. Not in a place like this.'

The bravery with which he spoke was enough to break her heart, and she felt guilty that she didn't mind being here the way he did, that she liked being so far away from the rest of her life.

'You need to put yourself first more,' he said. 'Sounds like you're too soft on your kids.'

'Sometimes,' she admitted, pushing from her the certainty of Lauren's unhappiness.

'Your family have to respect your needs too. You mustn't let them hold you back.'

'They don't,' she protested. 'Not really. Things haven't been easy. I've had a lot to think about recently.'

'I hope I'm not adding to your problems?' asked Roy.

'No, of course not.'

Recalling Hugo's suggestion that they should all meet, Tessa tried and failed to imagine introducing the two men, or having Mitch and Lauren sit here with her at this table. A single glance around the room conveyed how little prospect there was of harmonising the two divided aspects of herself.

'So what stops Sam stepping up as a dad?' asked Roy. 'What's his problem?'

Bewildered by the sudden turn, Tessa blurted out her answer without thinking. 'He's hopeless. Always has been.'

'Then you're better off without him. Aren't you?'

As Tessa reeled at the novel thought, Roy sat back, regarding her shrewdly.

'I'm going to make you a promise, Tessa,' he said. 'I will always tell you the truth. You may not like it, but I reckon you can take it. You're strong, like me. Not afraid to accept who you really are.'

Tessa sat very still, rapt by his attention.

'You'll never be the fabulous woman you ought to be if you settle for half-truths, for the kind of pap your adoptive parents have fed you all your life. You mustn't be afraid.'

'I'm not!'

'Honestly?' Roy ran his gaze around the room. 'Look,' he ordered. 'Fear's real. These men know that. I know it. Don't pretend it's not.'

Tessa nodded. 'I'm beginning to understand.'

'If there's no fear, there's no true love. The two belong together, don't you think?'

'I don't know.'

'Were you ever in love with Sam?'

She gasped, looked up to meet Roy's teasing gaze, and found herself unable to answer.

He laughed. 'I'll take that as a "no".' He stretched across to pat her hand before his expression became serious again. 'I don't believe you were,' he continued. 'Not if he's the man you've described in your letters. You could never truly love a weak man.'

Tessa tried to remember what she had written, whether she might have unwittingly revealed Sam's failings. 'He's gentle rather than weak,' she objected. 'Easy-going. I did love him. We were happy together for a long time.'

'Maybe you've not experienced real love yet.'

Tessa opened her mouth to protest, but then found the idea too intriguing to quash until she had explored it further.

'Think about it,' instructed Roy. 'You may surprise yourself.'

'Ok, I will,' she promised. 'Thank you. But now I feel

terrible, turning up late, then dumping all my troubles on you. And I haven't even offered to fetch a cup of tea!'

'Don't talk like that,' he said. 'You're no trouble to me. Stop putting yourself down.'

Tessa blushed. 'Ok. But would you like some tea?'

Roy glanced up at the clock. 'Not enough time,' he said. 'Have you ever been to Rome?'

The second swift change of topic was so unexpected that Tessa laughed, suddenly lighter than she had felt for ages. 'No, never.'

'The city of architects. I hope to take you there one day.'

'I'd like that very much.'

'There's an architectural prize to study in Rome. I should've won it when I was a student. We'll sit in pavement cafes and drink espresso together. No one need even know we're father and daughter – they'll think we're lovers. It'll be wonderful! I'll show you everything. You don't know what you've missed!'

Tessa was pleased, not only at his delight in this harmless escapism but also at the exciting notion that, with him, she would find so much still to unravel, so much more to explore and understand about herself. Although she would hardly have chosen a convicted murderer as her guide, the enticing prospect of discovering what sort of hidden capabilities she might possess, what other possibilities lay in store, was liberating. She wanted to explain herself to him, to make him understand the vital role he already played in her life. 'Since I found out about you,' she began, forgetting that she had let him assume she had always known she was adopted, 'it's like I see my whole childhood in a new light, as if, even though I could never know what was missing, I'd always been lonely for my own kin.'

Roy smiled to himself, nodding sagely.

Tessa glanced up at the clock: only ten minutes to go. 'Please tell me more about your family.'

'Not much of the past I want to hang on to, I'm afraid.' He spent a moment lining up the edges of the table. 'My father died when I was eleven. Left us with my mother, who was an alcoholic. She died of liver failure years ago.'

'You told me you didn't go to her funeral.'

He shook his head. 'I've an older sister, Shirley. She turned her back on me when all this happened.'

'No! That's dreadful!'

'I don't blame her.'

'Why not? How could she just abandon you?'

'We both had a hard time as kids. Shirley learnt to be totally merciless.' He sat back and Tessa tried to imagine the reality behind his words. 'Even though Mum took it out more on me than her,' he went on. 'Mum hated men. I don't know if you've ever had much to do with addicts, but they're not exactly easy to live with. Ends up with everyone for themselves, just to survive. Shirley managed the best way she could.'

Tessa's heart was thumping at the temptation to ask him about Pamela's drinking: surely it wouldn't be disloyal to benefit from his sympathetic insight? But there was so little time left before the bell rang, and she wanted to hear more about his childhood.

'Is it possible your sister might regret things now?' she asked, envisaging a healing role for herself. 'Might even be glad to hear from you again?'

Roy looked at her, his expression as opaque as a rough winter sea, and gave a twisted smile. 'You don't know what she's like.'

'But maybe my existence could open the way? I am her niece, after all.'

'Don't bother!' Roy laughed in contempt. 'I don't like saying it, but she's a cold-hearted bitch. Wouldn't want to know.'

Tessa shook her head in sadness. 'Why are families always so difficult?'

'See that guy over there?' Roy indicated with a nod of his head an angelic-looking young man with a mop of curly blonde hair sitting at a nearby table with an older woman. 'Last time he was up for parole he was knocked back because his girlfriend, mother of his kids, told him to get lost. So he's serving another two years. Having a stable home cuts a lot of ice with the parole board.'

'Is that not his mother?' asked Tessa, eyeing the comfortable-looking woman toying with a biscuit wrapper on the table.

'Yes. But his stepfather refuses point-blank to have him in the house. That's family for you.'

Tessa looked at the young man, earnestly discussing something with his mother, and couldn't help pitying them both. Then the realisation dawned that maybe Roy was tactfully approaching the question of how she might eventually feel about welcoming him into her home.

She looked at him as steadily as she could and took a deep breath. 'I hope you'll be part of my family one day. It's too soon yet for me to promise that you can stay with me when you get out, but–'

Roy burst out laughing and leaned across to clasp both her hands and lift them to his lips to bestow a gallant kiss. 'My darling girl, is that what you thought? No, I have somewhere to go. I told you, I own a house. That's not what I meant at all! Besides,' he added with a mischievous smile, 'if I had, I would have asked straight out. I don't like insinuation.'

At that moment the bell rang to mark the end of visits. But afterwards, as Tessa waited for the succession of gates and doors to be opened, soothed by the electronic *whooshing*, she retraced the trail of their conversation and couldn't see why else he would have remarked upon the importance of having a home to go out to. Roy had never before alluded to either parole or his release. It gave her such a pang of sympathy: she and her father were so alike. Whatever he said about straight-talking, they shared the same weakness, that neither could bear to ask for help.

As she stepped out of the transparent holding pen with a group of other visitors she remembered the missing holiday snaps. It was the red-haired officer, Janice, who was accompanying them, and Tessa turned to her. 'Excuse me, but apparently some photographs I handed in on my last visit were never received.' She felt the awkwardness of not knowing how to refer to Roy (inmate? prisoner? her father?) and wondered how much the woman already knew.

'They may turn up if you wait,' Janice told her, not unkindly. 'Sometimes the system can be a bit slow.' Tessa thought she seemed embarrassed. 'If not, then you can write to the Number Two Governor.'

'Ok, thanks.'

The officer nodded and walked away.

Retrieving her handbag from the locker in the Visitors' Centre, Tessa recognised the woman beside her as the mother of the angelic young man. 'I hope your son gets his parole,' Tessa said impulsively. Seeing the woman's anger, she instantly regretted her words, afraid she'd crossed some hidden line, that maybe visitors weren't supposed to intrude on one another. 'My father told me he's up for parole,' she explained quickly, trying to placate her.

'Fuck him!' said the woman, slamming the metal door of the locker with such force that it bounced open again. 'Roy Weaver playing his nasty little mind games. He knows fucking well my boy's got a whole-life tariff.' The woman slammed the locker door shut. 'And fuck you, too!' She walked off.

In the car driving back to Felixham, it occurred to Tessa that she must have got muddled and been mistaken that the woman beside her at the lockers was the young man's mother.

THIRTY-ONE

Mitch's journey from the station to the gates of Tamsin's school was not as straightforward as the directions she'd texted had led him to believe. So far, he'd had to stop and ask three times – once in a pub, once from someone at a bus stop and once from a woman walking a dog. She had looked at him rather suspiciously, and he hoped she wasn't a teacher. Tamsin had told him to come at five o'clock when it was easier for her to skip games or other activities, but she'd have to be back in time for supper. It had taken him hours to get here, and he was worried about being late because they'd have so little time together as it was. He hadn't seen her since half-term, and although they had used every available means to communicate, the imminence of her physical presence now seemed unreal, as if their earlier magical few days together had been a dream.

Finding his way here was simpler than attempting to meet in London at a weekend when Charlie's unpredictability made planning impossible – even though Charlie was indirectly responsible for his journey. Tamsin had phoned him in tears the previous weekend after she'd walked in on her dad kissing Quinn. Although Charlie had insisted that Tamsin had misunderstood, that it was just a friendly peck on the cheek, a thank-you for an extra task Quinn had taken on, Tamsin had convinced herself that the reason her mum was staying in California for the summer was not because principal photography on the film she was attached to had been brought forward, but because her parents were getting divorced. Which meant she'd have to spend the rest of her life playing gooseberry to her dad and Quinn. Lacerated by Tamsin's misery, Mitch had felt useless. It was weeks before the end of term, and even then Charlie might choose to stay in London. Mitch had longed to be old enough to say he'd get in a car and be right there, but he couldn't. Nor could he even begin to explore the depths of his contempt for Charlie.

He knew he was taking a risk skiving off school, and hoped he wouldn't get caught; so long as he could blag his way out of it, and the school didn't contact his parents, it shouldn't matter too much. All the same, he didn't like the giddy sensation that came from everyone believing him to be in some other place, when in fact no one except Tamsin knew where he was. Living by the sea, he was used to a constant horizon, but here inland he was very aware of the vast vault of sky. He felt very tiny beneath it, and it gave him a sense of being weirdly untethered, of belonging nowhere.

Here at last, beside a discreet royal-blue board with gold lettering, were the school gates. They opened onto a driveway leading between playing fields and shrubberies up to a grand Victorian building flanked by modern extensions. Tamsin's text instructed him to find the public footpath signposted a few hundred yards further on; it led over farmland that bordered the school grounds, and she would be able to wait for him beside a stile, out of sight of the main school buildings. Now he was nervous for, despite the luxury of Tamsin's home in Felixham, the present reality of her elite school gave him a pang of doubt. At home they'd been in their own bubble, but now he recognised how little he belonged in this world. What if he didn't get on with her friends – or even want to? What if they viewed him as some bit of rough from a rural comprehensive, the kind of person the high fence bordering these immaculate grounds was designed to keep out? He knew Tamsin wasn't like that, but *everything* in her life was as perfect as this. All any of the girls at a school like this had to do was ask and they could have it now, and have it delivered. He felt as ignorant of her life as she was of the plumbing, catering and endless laundry of the B&B.

'Mitch!'

He looked up and there she was, sitting on the wooden stile in a pair of frayed denim shorts, a vest and flip-flops, her hair and skin the exact shade of honey that he remembered against the crisp white sheets in her bedroom. She jumped down and came to meet him. All his doubts disappeared and he cupped her soft face in his hands and kissed and kissed her. He wanted to make love to her right there and then, but pulled back, holding her by the waist and laughing. She smiled, and everything in the world was safe again: all the days of missing her, all his fears and anxieties about both their families vanished, and the ground beneath his feet felt steady and firm once more.

'I'm so glad to see you,' said Tamsin.

'And me you. Are you Ok?'

She nodded, her eyes filling with tears. 'I thought my Spanish lesson would never end.'

'I was afraid I'd get lost.'

'But you're here now.'

'I'm here.' Mitch kissed her again, savouring the familiarity of her lips, the way their tongues combined, the shape of her hips beneath his hands. Each kiss was never simply itself, but the memory of every other kiss, of every other physical encounter.

'We should get away from here in case we're spotted.' She took his hand. 'I know a place.'

She led the way up towards a stand of trees. Even while he watched her move ahead of him, light and lithe, he resented how they had to skulk and hide. He had to suppress the rage he increasingly felt against these so-called adults whose self-centredness caused so much trouble.

They had reached the top of the path, and Tamsin led him over the brow of the hill to where there was a scoop of earth missing, as if a tree had fallen and the root rotted away to leave this natural bivouac. From the half-buried cigarette butts and an empty vodka bottle, he imagined it was a frequent haunt of girls from her school. The ground was dry, and they sat together with their backs against the rising ground, out of sight of anyone coming from behind them and with a clear view down into the woods and fields below. He put an arm around her and pulled her close.

'You Ok?' he repeated.

'Not really.' She laid her head on his shoulder and let herself cry while he stroked her hair and spoke soothing words. He understood that her wretchedness was real, a grief at how easily her world could be broken and trampled on without her consent. She was helpless and alone, and he was glad he was here.

'Mum did sound pleased about the job,' Tamsin managed to say at last. 'It's the kind of work she's always wanted. She said she hoped I was old enough not to begrudge her. And I don't. Of course I don't. But . . .'

Mitch knew it was no good searching his pockets; he didn't possess either tissues or a handkerchief. Instead he offered her the corner of his unbuttoned shirt, and was rewarded by her watery smile.

'I know how much you miss your mum,' he said. 'But I'd've been unbelievably miserable if you'd spent the summer in America.'

She snuggled her head into his shoulder. 'Me too. I just want Mum to come home.'

'She will.'

'I hate Quinn.'

Mitch worked out how best to phrase his newly acquired wisdom. 'She's not worth it. You have to think about yourself. Your life will be much easier if you don't hate her.'

'But if I don't hate Quinn, then I'd have to hate my dad.'

Mitch nodded. 'Yeah, I see that.' He didn't know what to say, other than some platitude, but that still seemed better than nothing. 'It'll blow over.'

'So you do think there's something going on?'

Mitch cursed himself. 'I think Quinn's got a crush on him. He is Captain Gorgeous, after all.'

Tamsin made a gurgling sound that was half laugh, half sob, but Mitch could feel the tension seep out of her body.

'It'll be all right. You've got me.'

'And you've got me.'

They sat silently for a while, contemplating the view. The first shadows were just beginning to lengthen, and there was a slight rustle of beech leaves above them. Mitch wanted to tell her about the man in prison. It felt selfish to burden her when she had her own woes, but he had to tell someone.

'My mum's tracked down her biological father,' he said at last. 'My grandfather.'

'Have you met him?'

He did not answer and, as she turned to him, struggled not to blurt out the rest.

'What is it, Mitch?'

'He's in prison for murder.'

'Wow! That's pretty hardcore.' Tamsin stroked his fingers. 'Sorry,' she said simply.

'Bad blood.'

'Why? He's not, like, some famous serial killer or something?'

'No. But he did actually kill someone.'

Her laugh was consoling. 'I don't think being a murderer is genetic.' She had unerringly voiced Mitch's worst fear, and he looked at her, trying to gauge her true opinion, to see if she would now turn away from him in disgust.

'He's nothing to do with you,' she assured him.

'My mum visits him. I worry about her.'

'Can't you go with her?'

'Apparently not. And I can't go on my own till I'm eighteen.' Mitch had found this out for himself.

'Does he have any other family?'

'I don't know.'

'So find out,' said Tamsin. 'See what they make of him. Get yourself some cousins.'

He nodded, comforted by the common sense of her reaction. Maybe, despite watching the calamitous self-control with which Hugo had contained his distress by the willow-fringed river in Cambridge, a parent's agonised love for his grown-up child, it was just a matter of keeping things in proportion.

Despite the sunlight, the sharp crescent of a pale setting moon perched low in the sky, and Mitch could just begin to make out a single star high above it. Tamsin snuggled up to him again, kissing his cheek, whispering that everything would be all right.

Mitch knew he'd have to go soon, but right here and now, with his arm around her, he was content. Suddenly he sensed a movement in the bushes ahead of them and a young fox, its brush held aloft, emerged from among the tree trunks. Silhouetted against the skyline, it looked directly at him, its ears pricked and one front paw suspended in mid-air. It paused just long enough to give Mitch the chance to note the neat line of black around its jaw and its inquisitive yellow eyes before it turned away and stepped delicately down the hill and out of sight.

Tamsin's grip tightened on his: she had seen it too. She sighed, as if she had been holding her breath, and he saw how her enchantment matched his.

'Who's that?' demanded a sharp voice behind them. They sprang apart and looked around. 'Tamsin Crawford. You're out of bounds. I wouldn't have expected this of you.'

Tamsin scrambled to her feet, brushing off the mulch of dirt and dead leaves. 'Mrs Sanderson!'

'And who are you?' demanded the teacher.

'Mitch Parker. I'm a friend of Tamsin's.'

'From where?'

'From home. From Felixham.'

'You've come a long way.' She looked him up and down before turning back to Tamsin. 'Does your house mistress know you're here?'

'No.'

Her gaze returned to Mitch. 'And do you have written permission from Tamsin's parents to visit her?'

'No.'

'Then you've no right to be here.' She turned back to Tamsin, taking in her skimpy vest and shorts. 'Your parents will have to be informed.'

Mrs Sanderson cast her eyes around the litter of earth and leaves and her gaze came to rest on the empty vodka bottle. 'Just what have you been up to?' she demanded.

It infuriated Mitch that this woman expected them to tolerate her rudeness merely because of their relative age and position. He wanted to fight for Tamsin in some way, but feared to make matters worse.

'Come with me,' Mrs Sanderson ordered Tamsin.

Powerless, Mitch felt both desperate and ridiculous. Tamsin pressed his hand and, before she scrambled up the slope and walked away, turned to give him a brave smile that broke his heart.

THIRTY-TWO

Hearing Mitch come in, Tessa called out to him. He put his head around the door of the guests' sitting room where she sat with Declan.

'You're late.' She saw how beat he looked. 'Everything Ok?'

Mitch nodded and then roused himself to greet Declan, maintaining the same polite distance that he'd kept up so carefully over the past couple of weeks.

'There's cold chicken in the fridge, if you're hungry,' she told him.

'Thanks. Maybe later.' He disappeared. She listened to his footsteps drag upstairs and wondered if maybe she should go after him. But Declan cut in, continuing their interrupted conversation.

'So,' he said. 'You're getting to know your daddy quite well?'

She gathered her thoughts – she would check on Mitch later. 'Actually,' she answered happily, 'it's been mainly about me. He's been like a real dad. He listens and encourages and gives me a fresh perspective. Look.' She held out her arm. 'He sent me this for my birthday.'

Declan spun the gold band around her wrist, his fingers brushing her skin. 'It's pretty,' he agreed. 'How did he manage it?'

'I think one of the officers must've helped him. I didn't recognise the handwriting on the package.'

'Really? Can they do that? Sounds like someone took a bit of a risk.'

Tessa smiled. 'Roy wouldn't want to get anyone into trouble.'

'He's still not keen on going into too much detail about himself then?'

'He's told me what happened,' she replied. 'Said he hadn't wanted to burden me with it.'

'And?'

'It's private, you know? It was sad and difficult for him to talk about. He regrets it very much.'

Declan looked doubtful. 'And you trust him on that?'

'Yes. Why would he lie?'

'Lots of reasons.'

'He's in prison. What would he gain by lying now?'

'You.'

Tessa laughed and waved the remark aside. 'What have I got to offer, other than being his daughter? And if I don't trust his sincerity towards me, then what is there to trust?'

'If your daddy takes after you, so to speak, then I'm sure he's a good man.'

Tessa was pleased. Mitch and Hugo's stricken faces in

Cambridge had made her wretched, and she yearned for them, like Declan, to be willing to understand her and to accept her evaluation of events. She sipped her wine, trying to recapture the intense concentration of the prison visits room, of how even a single hour there had to stand in for everything else that was excluded and prohibited, how *real* those hours felt. She would like to explain that to Declan too. 'Things have been pretty fraught here,' she told him. 'It's been nice to have someone who cares about me.'

Declan leant forward and lightly touched her thigh. 'I'm sure you know what you're doing.'

Tessa guessed his touch was meant as a gesture of reassurance, but it was also what she desired. She had known that afternoon, before Declan arrived, that if he still showed interest then she would accept. She had even made some excuse to move him from his usual room into one that did not lie below either of her children's bedrooms. She had made up her mind – or rather, it seemed to Tessa, her mind had made itself up – on those nights when she felt most alone. The first time had been after Sam's opening party. Feeling superfluous and abandoned, she'd panicked and, searching for comfort, let herself imagine how it would be to have Declan in bed with her. She'd been surprised at how swiftly and vividly her little fantasy had taken hold, and more than once since then had escaped into a mild eroticism.

Declan moved his hand away to reach instead for the bottle to refill their glasses. 'And I suppose you're used to sizing people up,' he went on. 'You do it every night, lying upstairs in your beds with a constant stream of perfect strangers asleep below.'

'The guests?' She laughed. 'This house has always been full of people. And I'm very careful,' she continued, almost glad of a neutral topic: she did not want to make a fool of herself with him, after all. 'I always confirm the contact details I'm given.'

'But it must come down to instinct in the end?' he pressed.

'Yes, though if someone's here, and they've paid their deposit, and their phone number or email checks out, I can't very well throw them out on the street just because I think they look a bit shifty.'

'You'd rather let a stranger loose in your house?'

'There's a sturdy lock on the door to our flat.'

'So would you lock the attic door if your daddy was in the house?' he asked.

Tessa felt ambushed. 'He's not going to hurt me! I don't fear him. Quite the opposite.'

'Tell me why not.' He sat back, making himself more comfortable against the cushions. 'Honestly, I'd like you to tell me what it's like there in the prison with those guys.'

Tessa composed her thoughts. 'We're all human,' she said finally. 'They're not monsters or animals, the men in there. The line dividing us isn't so solid. But they've acted out their emotions, their rage, their hurt, their greed. So in a way, they're more honest than us.'

'That's holy smoke, if ever I heard it!'

'It's not! Besides,' she couldn't help laughing, 'you can't hear smoke.'

'True. Which is what makes it so deadly.'

'You think I'm kidding myself.' Tessa was hurt by his scepticism. 'But isn't this kidding ourselves?' She jumped up to switch on one of the table lamps: it was not long after the June solstice, yet although the evening was still light she preferred the cosy glow. 'Making ourselves feel safe? If there's no fear, there's no true emotion, don't you think?'

'It's human nature to huddle around the campfire,' agreed Declan. 'Keep our backs to the dark.'

'But that doesn't make it go away,' she insisted. 'We're just pretending.'

He shrugged. 'Fine by me.'

'I can't pretend,' said Tessa. 'Roy's my father. I am biologically his child. Who knows what that means – how much is inherited, whether your DNA gives you a sense of humour or makes you jealous; but I know I'm his child. And he killed someone. It's not tidy, it's not convenient, it's not nice, but it's true. I can't pick and choose which bits of him to accept. I have to embrace it all.'

Declan considered this and then gave way. 'Well, your attitude is admirable, I'll say that.' He caught her doubtful glance. 'No, seriously, it is. Hell, I work for a supermarket. There has to be more to life than what baked beans you eat or what car you drive.' He leant forward and rested his hand on her thigh. 'There has to be a bit of raw sensation somewhere, right?'

Tessa took a deep breath then covered his hand with her own. 'Yes,' she said, daring to look straight at him. He must have received the signal he wanted, for he smiled and came to sit beside her.

Taking her hand in his, he turned it over and touched her, palm to palm.

'I took a quick peek as I drove past Sam's new place.' He spoke with careful deliberation. 'It looked busy.'

'Yes.' Tessa was aware of Declan watching her, and even more uncomfortably aware of tears pricking the backs of her eyelids. She blinked to dispel them before meeting his gaze. 'I think it's doing very well.'

'Tessa.' Declan squeezed her hand in warning. 'Don't pretend.'

The relief was agonising. 'I don't even have a stake in it any more,' she admitted. 'I've lost everything to do with him.'

'You still love him?'

She thought of what Roy had said to her, the intriguing possibility that she didn't. 'That's the terrible thing. I don't know.'

Declan stayed quiet, waiting for her to explain.

'I got pregnant with Mitch when we were still at college,' she admitted. 'Then it all happened so fast. I don't remember ever deciding that I was in love, that I couldn't live without Sam, that he was the man I wanted to spend the rest of my life with. It just happened.'

'You never considered not having the baby?' he asked gently.

Tessa shook her head. 'No. And of course I can see now that everyone who was in on the secret of my birth was determined that I should get it right this time.'

'You were railroaded.'

'Maybe. I don't know.' Had the older generations made it all so easy for her and Sam, she wondered, because of their determination not to repeat past mistakes? And had that effortlessness become so ingrained in her marriage that neither she nor Sam had ever needed to ask what they really wanted?

'Wherever I look, things turn out to be not what I thought. I don't know what to think. I even . . .' she stopped short.

'Go on.'

'I even got paranoid recently that Sam had been lying to me. That maybe he'd already started something with Nula before he ever went to London.' Tessa hung her head. 'I called the friend who got Sam the job there. I must've sounded completely crazy. He said of course Sam hadn't been having an affair.'

'Guys have been known to cover up for one another,' Declan observed.

Tessa shrugged. 'Like I say, I don't know what to think any more, who to believe.'

'Yourself?' he suggested.

'Me least of all,' she admitted in a small voice.

'Come here, woman,' he said, pulling her closer. 'I'll show you how to recognise your own feelings.' Holding her chin, he turned her face up to his for a kiss. 'If you want me to?'

Tessa closed her eyes and offered her lips. After a while he started to reach under her clothes, and she stopped him. 'Not here,' she said. 'Let's go to your room.'

THIRTY-THREE

The night was hot and Mitch flung off his duvet. When he got home he'd been relieved that his mother was occupied with the supermarket guy, so he hadn't had to lie about his day. But now he was afraid that Tamsin might be in trouble at school because of him. They'd texted one another, but he hadn't wanted to risk further problems by calling her after lights out. He worried, too, whether that vindictive teacher would tell Charlie Crawford stuff that might make him forbid Tamsin to see Mitch again. That would be a disaster when she'd need him most if things really were serious between Quinn and Charlie. He felt nothing but contempt for a father who failed to care as much as he did about so precious a creature.

Mitch knew he wouldn't get back to sleep, and, unable to get comfortable, swung his legs over the side of his bed and sat staring into the half-light of the midsummer night. He realised he hadn't eaten, and remembered Tessa mentioning there was some cold chicken downstairs. He pulled on some jeans and a T-shirt in case he bumped into anyone and eased open his bedroom door.

The hallway lights were off and there was no light showing under Tessa's door. He was sure Lauren must be asleep by now too. The door to the flat was still on the latch, so Tessa must have forgotten to lock it. He slipped down the dark stairs, crossed the landing on the guests' floor and was about to start down the next flight when a bedroom door opened at the far end of the corridor. Out of habit, he melted back into the shadows, against the wall, and waited. All the guest rooms had en suite bathrooms, so Mitch had no idea where the wandering guest would go, and in any case had long ago ceased to take any interest in what they got up to.

The figure flitted in his direction and turned at the end of the hallway to go *up* the stairs. It was Tessa, carrying her shoes and a little bundle of what looked like underwear. He felt sick, and, struggling not to make any noise, flattened himself still further against the wall. At the top of the stairs she too took pains to open the door noiselessly and close it softly behind her. He heard the latch slip, but knew he could let himself back in with the spare key they hid in a jug on the windowsill.

He stumbled down to the kitchen with as much caution as he could manage. Wanting to avoid the glare of the overhead light, he sat at the big table in the dark, rested his head on his arms and, utterly exhausted, let himself cry. The sound seemed to echo back at him from the hard, neat surfaces, making him feel smaller and more alone.

He thought of the blank faces opposite him in the train home, commuters practised in avoiding all human contact; they'd left him even more alone with his anxiety. He knew he should get a grip on himself, recognised that he was hungry and should eat, or at least get back to bed and go to sleep, but the sobs kept coming.

He was tempted to go and wake Lauren, to try talking to her, but he knew he couldn't tell her what he'd just witnessed: she was only fourteen and didn't understand anything about love or sex. She would just make everything worse, and then he'd be responsible for her too. He could call Tamsin at school, but his phone was upstairs and besides, there was no way he was going to stress her out with his problems at this time of night, not when she had enough worries of her own.

At least Tessa hadn't seen him. He thanked his lucky stars for all his years of creeping around the place. But what was she up to? Was she Ok? What if some guest – that Declan guy she'd been having a drink with – had hurt her, assaulted her? But he knew that couldn't be true. Even in the half-darkness from the landing window he had glimpsed the look on her face, had recognised from his own reflection in the mirror in Tamsin's bedroom that absence of tension, that satiated relaxation of all the tiny facial muscles. He had seen her face, and she was happy.

But what did it mean? She'd appealed to him not to leave her alone at Sam's opening. She'd been so upset since she found out about Sam and Nula. But if she was still in love with Sam, what was she doing with Declan tonight? She *might* be in love with one man and enjoy casual sex with another, though he didn't believe his mum was like that. But what did he know? Maybe she had sex with guests all the time, but he'd never caught her out before. He'd had no idea she'd been off visiting this Roy Weaver character in prison while he was at school either. Maybe she had all kinds of affairs and assignations no one knew about. Maybe that was why Sam had left.

He thought miserably that it would've been easier if Tessa had seen him because then at least she would have had to tell him what was going on and it wouldn't be yet another secret he had to keep. He was sick of secrets. It seemed like every single adult in his life had some dangerous piece of knowledge that they kept tight hold of, like keeping the pin on a hand grenade so it wouldn't explode in someone's face. The thought of facing Tessa in the morning – and every morning after that – knowing all this stuff about her made him want to throw up. But his stomach was empty, and he had no more tears. He hated this helpless state he found himself in. He hated Declan, hated Charlie, hated Roy Weaver, hated Sam, hated his mother.

THIRTY-FOUR

Carol, often first in the kitchen of a morning, stood guard over some eggs poaching on the Aga. 'Morning,' she greeted Mitch. 'Your mum's upstairs. I've room for one more in here, if you'd like,' she offered, indicating the pan.

'No, thanks. I'm fine with toast.' Mitch had just made a rather furtive check to confirm that it was Declan's room his mother had come out of last night, and as he sat down he tried not to think of her up in the breakfast room bending over Declan, asking if he'd like cream in his coffee or preferred honey to marmalade.

Lauren was spooning cereal into her mouth, half hidden behind her defensive wall of packaging, which had grown higher since some new row she'd had with Tessa. 'Where were you yesterday?' she asked.

Mitch shot a warning glance at Carol. 'Nowhere. Checking out some uni stuff.' He'd tried calling Tamsin twice this morning, but her phone was off.

'So where did you go?' Lauren appeared not to notice Mitch glaring at her with a meaningful nod towards Carol who, though she had her back to them, would nevertheless be listening

'Tell you later,' he told her sternly, and was relieved when Lauren shrugged and gave up, accustomed to her brother's stonewalling.

Tessa swept into the kitchen carrying a tray of dirty crockery. She put it down on the worktop beside the dishwasher then came to stand behind Mitch's chair. 'How are you this morning?'

He jerked his head away as she ruffled his hair, but she just laughed. 'You never ate the chicken last night. Why don't you have some nice crispy bacon to go with your toast?'

'I'm fine, thanks,' he told her. She sounded happy, and he tried to think well of her. Maybe she really liked this guy and whatever they were doing was a bit more than casual. Maybe being with him would take away all her hurt over Nula, or distract her from this guy in prison. Maybe it was a good thing and he should be pleased for her.

Tessa opened the bottom oven and took out the dish left there to keep warm. 'I can easily make more if they want it upstairs.' She reached over to take his plate. He snatched at it, but too late, she was already piling on the rashers of bacon.

'Mum, really, I don't want any.'

She put his plate back in front of him. 'Go on, good for you.'

Mitch pushed it away without bothering to argue.

'I'll have it,' Lauren declared, helping herself.

'You can't eat all that!' protested Tessa, making as if to take it away.

'Why not, if Mitch can?' Lauren's tone skirted on the edge of a whine and she curved a protective arm around the food.

'We talked about this, sweetheart.'

'I can have *one*!'

'You're supposed to be watching what you eat.'

Lauren picked up a rasher with her fingers, and Mitch could see that his mum wasn't going to push it. Lauren bit into it, then dropped it again. 'Ugh, it's cold. It's horrible when it's cold.' She held the plate out to her mother, who hesitated but then took it from her. Mitch watched Tessa avoid Carol's raised eyebrows as she slid the food back onto the metal dish and popped it into the top oven.

Mitch was suddenly tired of it all. He couldn't be bothered to watch Lauren wheedle and cadge and think she'd scored some great victory just because she got her own way. 'Why don't you just say no to her?' he asked Tessa. He regretted it instantly when he saw a gleam of greedy excitement light up his sister's face that she'd managed after all to get what she wanted – attention.

'She's only had cereal, haven't you, sweetheart?' said Tessa.

Carol put the last of the poached eggs onto plates and escaped with them out of the door.

'If you can have bacon, why can't I?' demanded Lauren.

Mitch looked at her, looked at the craven plea on Tessa's

face, and just no longer had the heart to play the game. Just for once he wanted to tell the truth about something to someone. 'Because you're getting fat. Because you eat too much.'

Lauren's face went red.

'Mitch!' cried Tessa. 'Say you're sorry.'

'Why? I'm not saying it just to be mean,' he appealed to Lauren. 'You don't like being overweight. I'm trying to help. It's no good pretending it's Ok for you to stuff your face.'

'That's horrible!'

'It's simple. If you want to be skinny, don't eat.'

'It's not my fault, is it, Mum?' Lauren's eyes welled up. 'It's puppy fat.'

Mitch could see she was hurt, and was sorry, but he willed Tessa not to back down, to take the opportunity to be straight with Lauren and deal with this.

'Sweetheart.' Tessa opened her arms to offer Lauren a hug. As Lauren clung to her, Tessa spoke to Mitch over the teenager's shoulder. 'That wasn't very nice. Look how upset she is. You should apologise.'

Mitch considered capitulating; what was the point in upsetting people? Lauren turned her head and gave him a calculating sneer. 'Mitch never went to school yesterday,' she said in a vicious singsong. 'He won't say where he went.'

'Fuck you!' Mitch told her. He stood up, pushing back his chair with more force than he intended, so it fell backwards onto the floor. Ignoring it, he headed for the door.

'You come right back here!' ordered his mother.

'Tell her for once! Why can't you tell her?'

'Keep your voice down.'

Mitch shut the door quietly, the injunction never to disturb the guests too deeply ingrained, and turned back to face her.

'Lauren was fine this morning,' Tessa went on. 'I was really happy for once, then you come down like a bear with a sore head and spoil it for everyone.'

Mitch stared at her in frustration and despair. Behind Tessa, Lauren grinned in triumph.

'You've been moody for weeks, and I've had enough of it,' said Tessa. 'All I did was offer you some nice bacon, and you bite our heads off.'

Mitch thought of his girlfriend's tear-stained face the previous day and couldn't imagine how he was going to get though the day. He wanted to crawl back under his duvet and stay there.

'I don't understand why you're like this,' Tessa persisted.

For one moment, Mitch did seriously consider just telling her, describing his sight of her on the stairs in the dark last night, carrying her shoes and underwear and creeping out of some man's room. It was only because of Lauren that he stopped himself. Lauren was useless, and if he got her involved it would all just blow up in his face. 'Sorry,' he said. 'Can I go now?'

Twenty minutes later, he came downstairs and attempted to glide unseen out of the front door. Declan Mills was paying his bill, and Tessa was laughing, the row in the kitchen apparently forgotten. She ignored Mitch, but

Declan nodded pleasantly as he came past. As Declan took back his credit card from Tessa, Mitch caught the gleam of his wedding band. 'Tosser,' he thought, and then looked at his mother's gleaming eyes. 'Stupid cow.'

By the time Mitch reached his classroom at school he had regretted both his words to Lauren and his bitter thoughts about Tessa. When he got home that afternoon he sought her out, finding her on a stepladder changing a light bulb in one of the guest bedrooms.

'Sorry, Mum.'

She looked down at him and though he saw her try to remain severe, she softened and smiled, shaking her head at him: 'I'm busy enough without you two kicking off.'

'Let me do that,' he offered, as she struggled to reach the shade suspended from the high ceiling.

'No, I'm fine.'

'I'm taller than you.'

She looked at him in surprise, and laughed. 'So you are.'

She climbed back down and handed him the bulb, which he adroitly replaced.

Folding up the stepladder, he kept his eyes away from hers. 'Can we talk about your father?' he asked. 'Roy Weaver – that's his name, right?'

'Yes.'

'What's he like?'

'Kind, thoughtful, supportive. Sorry for what he's done.'

Mitch did not want to oppose her, but found it hard to blind himself to the unreality of such a claim.

'So does he have a family?' he asked. 'Do you have brothers or sisters? I guess they'd all be younger than you.'

'No. He doesn't have kids. Just an older sister, Shirley.'

'Have you met her?'

'No, they don't get on.'

'But you might. You might like her.'

'One thing at a time, Mitch.' She smiled a little wearily. 'I'm still getting to know him. Can you pop that back downstairs for me?'

'Sure.' He waited for Tessa to hold the door for him to carry out the lightweight metal ladder. He waited in the hallway as she turned to check that everything in the room was orderly and then closed the door. 'I thought you wanted to know your family, didn't you?' he asked.

Tessa reached out to stroke his arm. 'Thanks for caring. That's really nice. But it's complicated.'

'How?'

'Well, it was really difficult for Roy and Shirley growing up because their mother was an alcoholic. Died of liver disease years ago, and then Shirley simply turned her back on him when he was convicted.'

'You're still related,' he insisted. 'She's your aunt.' Mitch found he rather liked the idea of involving this wider family: it made the facts of Roy Weaver's crime and incarceration less intense, more manageable. He couldn't understand why his mum wouldn't want that normality too.

'Grannie Pamela says Erin's coming back. For a proper visit this time.'

Mitch refused to be sidetracked. 'Will she go and visit him?'

'I've no idea.'

'So what about his sister? You could speak to her at least. Meet her and see what she's like. You don't have to see her again if you don't want to.'

But Tessa shook her head. 'It would be disloyal to befriend a woman who could reject Roy when he was at rock bottom like that.' She looked at her watch. 'Look, sweetheart, I really must get on. That couple from Nuneaton will be here any second.'

Mitch stowed away the ladder then went up to his attic room, an obstinate rebellion forming itself like a physical sensation in his chest. Why should Tessa just expect him to fall into line like that? This was his family too.

THIRTY-FIVE

The luxury of being able to smooth the sheets on the spare bed, knowing that Erin would sleep in them tonight, of taking a fresh batch of shortbread out of the oven, already looking forward to offering Erin some with her coffee, gave Pamela immense pleasure – the kind of domestic pleasure that brought to mind Averil's doll's house. It was as though all the grief and regret that had been sealed up for so long inside that toy mausoleum could finally be dispelled, the little padlocks undone, the whole front of the house opened wide, and life breathed back into the fixed attitudes of the inhabitants. Except, remembered Pamela, there were no inhabitants in this intricate and unchanging world. Averil had removed the dolls when Erin went away. Pamela had found them when she'd been packing up Averil's things after her death, three miniature dolls wrapped up in yellowing tissue paper in an old biscuit tin. She had put them aside, totems of her childhood, and had them still, tucked safely away.

She found the tin at the back of a bureau drawer. The paper had softened with age and she took care not to tear it. Shrouded by the wrapping were three tiny but differently sized dolls, each light as a feather and all wearing faded dresses. Funny how she had forgotten that the doll made to represent her father had disappeared when he died. The remaining three, in descending order, were Averil, herself and Erin. Pamela thought about how she was always in the middle, stuck between stronger opposing forces, never sure enough of what she wanted to stand her ground and fight for it.

She shook herself: Erin was coming! She had rung and invited herself, said she *wanted* to come, and Hugo was already on his way back from meeting her at Heathrow. Things would be different now, they really would. Pamela started to rewrap the dolls and place them back inside the tin. She would give them to Erin. Erin could put them back where they belonged. It would break the spell, lift the curse, start to make things right again.

For too long Pamela had not only believed that she didn't deserve children of her own but also concluded that it was a punishment for taking Tessa away from Erin. That was why she had never defied or even confronted Averil. She knew how much Hugo blamed himself for their infertility – all the medical tests had said the problem lay with him – and that was why he believed that what he wanted didn't count either. But she had made a terrible mistake in allowing him to defer to her, and so let Averil have her way. Hugo was right to condemn her for that. He'd never say it, he was too kind, but she knew he did.

For too long she had drowned her guilt and cowardice in gin. But first thing in the morning after Erin had called to say she was coming, Pamela had rung her doctor and booked an appointment. That had been last week, and although the GP had told her she'd have to wait a few weeks before she could start talking to an addiction counsellor, she'd congratulated Pamela on taking the first step, and Pamela had already succeeded in cutting down a little bit. It wasn't much, but it was a step in the right direction. Maybe with Erin here she'd do even better.

She'd told Erin on the phone that Tessa was seeing Roy Weaver, but that it was fine – he was respectful, caring, had even sent that message about how fondly he remembered her. It was when she'd assured Erin that she really thought everything was going to turn out Ok that Erin had asked if she could come and stay for a couple of weeks. Pamela had been overjoyed: it was as if all the clouds that had hung over her family for so long had blown away, leaving nothing but blue sky.

THIRTY-SIX

Mitch stopped beside a busy roundabout to consult the *A to Z* he had bought at Liverpool Street Station. It was lunchtime, and the streets were a maelstrom of movement and traffic noise. He could not imagine how there were enough pockets of calm for anyone to live or work in such a place. Even the air felt dirty, and if you dared stop to gather your bearings, you were likely to be mown down by a bus, bicycle or rushing pedestrian. Catching flashes of brightly coloured socks or stockings amongst the crowd, a passing swipe of scarlet lipstick and sharp, unusual angles of haircuts, shoes and sunglasses, he felt lost amid a foreign tribe.

Thanks to Sam giving his distracted permission for Mitch to filch his credit card, Mitch had been able to check out premium online records, and was pretty certain he'd located the right Shirley Weaver. Tessa had said she was older than Roy, and this Shirley Weaver was younger, but she was definitely related. She was a designer and film-maker with her own small company in Shoreditch, and

Mitch had found plenty of links to her work: awards she'd won, her photo and her work address. He'd done a pretty intensive search on Roy too, but it had thrown up no new background information, probably because he was already banged up by the time the web really got going. But that didn't matter now that he could ask Roy's sister about him.

Mitch had also fibbed to Sam to borrow enough money for the train fare, and had threatened Lauren not to blab about him taking a bus to the station instead of going to school. This was the second time he'd bunked off, and he hoped his parents wouldn't get to hear of it. Charlie Crawford had been informed of Mitch's unauthorised visit to Tamsin's school, and Tamsin had been gated for the weekend in punishment, though she promised Mitch she didn't care – seeing him had been worth it. But apparently Charlie had ordered Tamsin not to see Mitch again. Despite her insistence that her dad never stuck to threats he made, and her certainty that by the beginning of the holidays he wouldn't even remember the incident, Mitch remained miserable and apprehensive about the future.

At least Tessa had broken it to Lauren a couple of days ago that she was visiting Roy Weaver in prison. Lauren had listened with a kind of wide-eyed excitement, as if some scary horror movie were about to begin, and kept asking whether Tessa was making all it up. Although Mitch was glad it was no longer a secret, Lauren's attitude had upset him more than he let on: if she was going to view their biological grandfather as some kind of Voldemort character, then what did that make him?

Mitch turned left down a narrow street lined with a mixture of solid red-brick Victorian offices and warehouses, dissenting chapels and modern plate-glass bars and shops, and stopped outside a big wooden door. He now regretted his decision not to email Shirley first to request a meeting, but then told himself that if she'd refused it would have made it even more impossible just to turn up on her doorstep.

He pressed the buzzer and the door clicked open. He entered straight into a high open space with whitewashed brick walls, filled with desks and state-of-the-art technology. A very thin young man wearing a headset looked up from behind a white desk by the entrance.

'Who are you here to see?' he asked.

'Shirley Weaver.' Mitch was acutely aware of how obvious it was that he did not belong here.

But the thin young man smiled patiently. 'Work experience?' he asked.

'No,' said Mitch. 'She's my aunt. My great-aunt.'

'Oh, right.' The thin young man pressed a button on his keyboard and spoke into his headset. 'Shirley, your nephew's here.'

Shirley must have registered surprise, for the young man glanced suspiciously at him. This was the moment Mitch had dreaded but anticipated, so he forced himself to stand still and smile calmly. 'We've never met,' he said. 'I'm here to introduce myself.'

The young man relayed his words, and a moment later Mitch looked across the room and encountered the steady gaze of a woman with strikingly cut short hair with a straight fringe, all dyed a smart plum colour. He recognised Shirley from the photos on her website. She wore muted colours, and even though he knew she was in her late fifties, her pitch-perfect fashion sense made her appear much younger. She watched Mitch for a little longer then wove her way over and held out her hand.

'I can certainly see a family resemblance,' she said. 'Come with me. We can talk in the meeting room. Coffee?' This last was directed to the young man behind the desk, who nodded and went off to fetch it.

The meeting room turned out to be a partitioned cubicle at the back of the space with a long table, chairs and a board covering one wall to which was pinned a host of coloured Post-it notes connected by coloured threads wound around pins and linking photographs and what looked like pages cut out of magazines. Shirley smiled. 'Work in progress. The client's coming in later so I won't have long, I'm afraid. Please,' she gestured. 'Sit down.'

Mitch sat down opposite Shirley, who rested her hands on the table and waited. He had rehearsed his opening speech. 'My mother discovered recently that she's adopted, and that Roy Weaver is her father. My grandfather.'

Shirley nodded, not taking her eyes off his face.

'I'm sorry to turn up out of the blue like this, but I'd like to know more about him.'

'I'd like to help you,' she replied pleasantly, 'but I've not been in touch with him for years.'

The door opened and, with a curious glance at Mitch,

the young man laid down a tray with everything they might need. Shirley turned to him. 'Nick, can you bring me my iPad? Thanks.'

'But you know where he is now?' Mitch hated himself for asking the question.

Shirley was pouring the coffee and did not look up. 'Yes.'

'Can you tell me exactly what he did?' asked Mitch; there seemed little point is not being direct.

'Don't you know?'

'Only that he killed his girlfriend.'

'That's right,' she said. Mitch felt enormous relief: at least what Tessa had said – and had been told – was true, and Roy wasn't some pervert who jumped out of bushes and abducted strangers.

Mitch could see that despite her friendly manner, Shirley was trying to disguise a wariness for which he could hardly blame her: she was right to be cautious. 'I realise it must pretty awkward to be questioned by a complete stranger about your brother like this,' he said, 'but I'd like to know whatever you can tell me.'

'You don't look at all like a stranger.' Shirley regarded him with quiet composure. Mitch decided she was pretty smart and that he liked her. 'I can't tell you much,' she went on. 'I know his victim was someone he'd lived with for quite a while, but I'm not sure I ever met her. Roy had walked away from us long before his conviction.'

'So he's not, like, a psychopath? Sorry,' added Mitch, aware that he was blushing.

But Shirley looked amused. 'Who knows?' she said. 'But he had been in trouble before.'

'What for?'

'Again, I don't know for certain. But he had to give up his teaching job. Some kind of inappropriate behaviour with a female student.'

Mitch was aware of her looking at him, scanning his features, his hands, his proportions.

'He was lecturing in a university, so she must've been over eighteen. He'd lost touch by that point, but I don't think he ever went back to teaching. And I suspect maybe it wasn't the first time,' she added gently.

'He told my mum that you don't get on because your mother was an alcoholic,' Mitch told her bluntly.

'What?' she exclaimed. 'That's nonsense. Typical Roy bullshit!'

Mitch couldn't believe that such an unguarded reaction was anything but truthful.

'He said you were older than him too.'

'Yeah, poor little Roy!'

Mitch wanted to ask her what she meant, but Nick tapped at the door, handed Shirley an iPad and disappeared.

'Oddly enough,' she said, 'I've just been digitising some family photos.' She touched and swiped the screen to find what she wanted, then turned the device around to him. 'That's Mum.' She pointed to a pretty woman smiling shyly at the camera, flanked by two teenagers. 'If she had a glass of sherry at Christmas, she thought she was living the high life. She most certainly was not an alcoholic. That's me,' she added, 'and that's Roy.'

Mitch felt ill again: the clothes and hairstyle were old-fashioned, but the face of the teenage boy was his own.

Shirley flicked at the screen so it displayed a second photograph. 'Roy's graduation.'

Roy wore an academic gown and hood and held an official scroll tied with red ribbon, standing in the traditional pose with a three-quarter turn to the lens and a fixed smile; once more Mitch saw his own face beneath the mortar board.

'I'll print these off for you, if you like.'

Mitch swallowed, unsure that he wanted them.

'I've not seen my brother in twenty-five years,' she told him. 'Maybe more. And he chose not to come to Mum's funeral. So seeing you standing there in reception just now, so like him – well, it was very strange indeed.'

Mitch looked at her miserably. 'I want to know what kind of man my mum's dealing with. None of us have met him.'

Shirley nodded and sat back, taking a sip of her coffee. 'I don't honestly know for sure. But Roy was always . . . I don't know, self-centred, manipulative, used his charm as a strategy to get what he wanted. And wasn't very nice if he didn't get his own way. I guess that's why he stopped bothering with us. But as for actual criminal behaviour, I have no idea how far it went.'

'But he murdered a girlfriend.'

'Yes.' She turned her coffee cup around in the saucer so the handle was in line with the edge of the table. 'I was told that before he killed her, she had obtained a restraining order against him.'

'What's that?'

'It meant he could be arrested if he went anywhere near her.'

'My mum goes to visit him,' said Mitch, willing himself not to start crying like a little kid.

'Well, she can't be in any great danger in a prison.'

Mitch wasn't too sure about that. A couple of times he'd seen Tessa come home with a sort of feverish sparkle that didn't look right, and now he was certain they were the days she'd visited Roy Weaver. 'What if he gets out?' he asked.

'Is that likely?'

'I don't know.'

'I'm afraid I was glad not to get involved,' Shirley admitted. 'You can imagine how his conviction devastated my poor mum. Thank goodness Dad didn't live to see it. All the same, Mum and I decided we had to be there, in case he wanted anything from us. I mean, imagine starting a life sentence. We kept on writing every couple of months for the first two years. He never replied.'

'He told Mum you turned your back on him.'

'He's always told lies. Pointless lies. Except they're not, once you start to see the pattern. Some of it's mind games – putting the other person at a disadvantage, clever him getting one up on you. Gives him a thrill. And the rest is about how it's never his fault. Big bad sister who dumped him. Alcoholic mother who abused him. He always was a

. . .' Shirley rose abruptly to her feet. 'Forgive me, but I'm going to stop here. This isn't easy.'

Mitch rose too. He could see how angry and upset she was, and hoped she didn't blame him. 'I'm sorry for bothering you,' he said humbly. 'I didn't know what else to do.'

'No, you were right to come.' She held out her hand with a warm smile. 'I hope we can stay in touch. I don't have kids, and my mother died last year, so I'd like to have some family around me, to get to know you. If you want a great-aunt, you know where I am.' Shirley laughed, her tone light and natural for the first time, and Mitch was glad that she seemed to like him.

He was already back out on the street when Shirley called to him. 'Mitch? Tell your mother – warn her – if he's fixed his attention on her, then he won't let go. Tell her to take care.' She slipped back inside, closing the big wooden door, leaving Mitch to find his way back to the station alone.

On the return journey, he was too exhausted to think about the visit in any detail. Apart from Tamsin, he wasn't sure who else he ought to tell. Not his sister, for sure: although Lauren promised not to tell her friends at school, Mitch didn't think she'd manage to keep quiet very long. Nor did he want to admit to Sam why he'd not sought his advice and had acted alone (and fibbed about it), which made it difficult now to confide in Hugo without being disloyal to his dad. Given how reluctant Tessa had been to raise the subject again once Lauren had been told, it wasn't going to be easy to tell her where he'd been today. Except he ought to deliver Shirley's warning, explain about Roy's pointless lies and discover in what other ways the evil bastard was getting a kick out of outsmarting his own daughter.

As the train neared Felixham and passed through more familiar places, Mitch tried instead to focus on imagining a future in which he had a great-aunt with a successful design business in Shoreditch, a future in which he might be at home among the girls in their art-student clothes beside hipsters in narrow jeans and plaid shirts, and remembered the awareness he'd had in Cambridge, exploring those narrow, high-walled streets all by himself, that he could be whoever he wanted to be. But as quickly as he invented alternative futures for himself, those visions were tainted by the superimposition of Roy Weaver's uncannily familiar face, by his crimes, his mind games; it made him angry, and his anger made him feel unsafe.

THIRTY-SEVEN

When Tessa opened her front door, even though this time she was expecting to find Erin waiting on the step, she recalled the morning three months earlier when she'd turned up unannounced. This morning, looking agitated in pale slacks and a tailored blue-and-white striped shirt, Erin's brightness seemed false and contrived. She'd rung the previous day to suggest they have 'a good chat', and although it was difficult for Tessa to spare the time with the B&B fully booked throughout the summer season, she could hardly refuse. At least the kids were still busy with the final few days of term and she didn't have them to think about too.

'Can we sit in here?' Erin asked at the door to the unoccupied guests' sitting room. 'Would you mind?'

'No, of course not.'

As Erin sat down and rummaged in her big handbag Tessa inspected the room, which had been freshly cleaned and aired this morning, the curtains nicely draped, the cushions plumped. She hadn't actually sat in here since her evening with Declan: the memory was pleasant. He'd called her a couple of times since, and though he'd kept things light, his attention gave her confidence. She smiled to herself, aware that she had every intention of indulging herself again on his next visit.

Erin drew out what looked like an old biscuit tin and leaned across to press it into Tessa's hands. 'Pamela gave me this.'

Tessa settled herself on the couch and prised open the tin: nestled in tissue paper she found three little dolls she had never seen before.

'Pamela wants me to put them back.' Erin nodded towards the doll's house. 'She said my mother took them out when I went away.'

Tessa looked more closely at the faded little figures, but their significance burdened her so she put them aside. 'Maybe we should get rid of that thing? Forget the past. Start from where we are now.'

Erin opened her mouth to respond, but then looked down, inspecting her immaculately varnished nails for a few moments. 'I hear you've been meeting up with Roy Weaver,' she said. Tessa could imagine her opening a business meeting with that same upbeat tone.

'Yes.' Tessa had struggled with what she'd been forced to admit was jealousy at the thought of Erin seeing Roy again, yet supposed it was inevitable that the two of them would wish to meet. She was weary of endlessly having to negotiate, explain, mitigate her own relationship with Roy, while she always seemed to remain an invisible part of the equation. Sometimes, she thought fiercely, it was as if Roy were the only person who actually saw *her.* 'I haven't told him yet that you were coming. I wasn't sure how you'd want to play it.'

'Pamela said he'd sent me a message?'

'Yes, that he remembered you fondly.'

'Anything else?'

'He said you'd failed a music exam or something.'

Erin nodded. 'That's why I said yes when he asked me to go off for a walk with him. Averil was cross with me, said I hadn't done enough practice, so I wanted to get back at her.' She paused, her expression unreadable. 'He must have a pretty good memory to hang on to a detail like that!'

Tessa picked up on the bitterness in Erin's laugh, and wondered if maybe she still carried a torch for her first lover, still suffered from the old hurt that he'd left Felixham without a thought for her. 'He liked the photographs I showed him of you when you were young,' she offered, trying both to be generous and to bring the conversation back to the present. 'He wrote that he'd been half in love with you.'

Erin seemed to wince, but refreshed her smile so fast that Tessa could not be sure.

'What do you make of him?' Erin stared at her daughter. 'Do you like him?'

Caught off guard, Tessa laughed. 'Yes.' She could feel herself blushing. 'Of course.'

Erin nodded and began to twist one of her big fashion

rings around her finger. 'I liked him too. Thought he could charm the birds out of the trees.'

'Do you want to come to the prison, to meet him again?'

'No.'

Tessa was taken aback by Erin's vehemence, and it seemed as if her question had resolved something for Erin, for she stopped playing with her ring and raised her chin.

'There's something I never told anyone except my mother,' she began. 'I'm not sure how much of it Pamela ever really knew or overheard. In any case, it doesn't matter – Averil never believed me. And maybe she was right not to.' She paused again, her determination appearing to ebb away.

Tessa was gripped. Erin was the only other person who'd met Roy, who had her own intimate connection with him. 'Will you tell me?' she asked.

'Yes.' Erin drew in a deep breath. 'It's why I came back. It's funny that you're the only one I can talk to about him. Roy didn't want to meet my friends, or Pamela, so I had no one else's opinion to go by. And now I'm not sure any more what I've remembered or imagined or made up.'

'Pamela must know?'

Erin shook her head. 'I'm not going to discuss this with her. It's best we keep this between you and me.'

Tessa was appeased: during Erin's earlier visit she had felt marginalised by the intensity of the sisters' reunion, but now she was to be central to whatever this mystery was about. She watched Erin glance around the room as if taking herself back in time, repositioning herself as the teenager she'd once been. Tessa reminded herself that she – a mere seed in the womb – had also been present: it had been the simple fact of her existence that set such vast upheavals and displacements in motion.

'It was Roy's last day in Felixham,' Erin began. 'He was here for a week, and we kept bumping into each other. I was learning how to flirt. He was older, but didn't look it somehow, he wasn't tall or big, so I didn't question why he was interested in a schoolgirl. All the same, I'd been told not to go off with boys I didn't know. If Averil hadn't been so cross with me for failing that exam . . .' Erin fanned her hands out across her pale slacks, examining her scarlet nails. 'He took me out along the edge of the marsh, where the ground rises, where there are sheltered places in among the gorse. He didn't threaten or hit me, he just didn't let me say no.'

Tessa was too shocked to speak.

'Averil said it must have been my fault, because if I was telling the truth then my clothes would've been torn, I'd've had cuts and bruises.'

'You're not saying . . .' Tessa didn't dare utter the word in case saying it made it true.

'I don't know. It hurt, but then it was my first time. Maybe he just took advantage. What man wouldn't? I probably led him on – that's what Averil said. But I don't remember wanting him to.'

'You were fifteen.'

'She said I should never have gone off with him like that.'

'What happened afterwards?'

'He walked me home. You see?' Erin looked hopefully at Tessa. 'He'd never have walked me home if . . . So maybe I *was* just ignorant and silly and he did nothing wrong? It's all so long ago now, I can't be sure of anything.'

Tessa found she was clasping her gold bracelet, and let it go as if it were red-hot.

'But you've met him,' Erin went on. 'You know him. You know what's he's done, why he's in prison. What do you think?'

'No, no, I can't believe he'd ever do anything like that.' But deep in Tessa's mind reverberated the impact of a metal locker door being slammed and a woman's aggressive voice: *Fuck him! Roy Weaver playing his nasty little mind games.* She had a moment's panic: what if she were wrong?

'The woman he killed,' asked Erin, 'it wasn't . . . like that?'

'No,' Tessa confirmed, relieved to scramble back to surer ground. 'She was his girlfriend. They'd been together a long time. He loved her. It was virtually self-defence.'

Erin sighed and sagged back a little against the soft cushions. 'I'm so glad. I wasn't sure whether or not I should tell you,' she said, 'but when Pamela rang to say you were visiting him, that he might get out and come here . . . I thought it'd be so wrong not to let you decide for yourself. I had to come and put you in the picture.'

'Thank you, but I promise, he's . . .' Tessa strove to put into words the scrupulousness of Roy's behaviour. 'He's very proper, exact, almost old-fashioned. Courteous. I can't imagine him threatening anyone like that. I really can't.'

'And it's so long ago. People change. I've changed!' Erin got to her feet and held out her hands to her daughter. 'I didn't mean to cause yet more trouble, spilling out all this ancient history. I'm so glad you think it's all right.'

'He's my father,' Tessa assured her. 'He wants to be my father. He cares about me.'

'That's good to hear.' Erin gathered up her handbag, not looking at Tessa. 'I just couldn't forget the poor woman he killed, kept worrying that maybe if I'd spoken up . . .' She shook herself and forced a smile. 'I spend too many hours in hotel rooms with nothing better to occupy me!'

'It's fine,' said Tessa. 'Honestly.'

'I shan't say anything to Pamela,' said Erin, leaning in to kiss Tessa's cheek. 'Let's never mention this again, what do you reckon?'

Tessa nodded, inhaling the smell of her mother's face powder. She was exhausted now and wanted her to leave. In the doorway, Erin turned. 'I never meant to lie. Averil said it must've been my fault and I'm sure it was. And then there was you! The future to consider. I was simply too young to understand what he'd done. That's what you think, isn't it? You do believe me?'

Tessa tried to think how she would react if Lauren came to her with some overheated tale of seduction by an attractive summer visitor, and couldn't help but acknowledge an ambiguous sympathy for Averil.

'I do believe you,' she assured her mother. 'Roy's a good man.'

THIRTY-EIGHT

Even though Blanco was pleased to see him, skittering and sliding around the wide solid oak planks of the kitchen floor, Mitch was hesitant about entering Charlie Crawford's house. But Tamsin assured him that her dad was too busy with the arrangements for a big party he was throwing the following weekend to care about something that had happened weeks ago at her school. And sure enough, as she led Mitch into the kitchen, Charlie merely glanced up and said 'Hi' before returning his attention to his iPad. Mitch was almost disappointed – he liked the idea of defying Charlie for Tamsin's sake. But after lunch Charlie's indifference allowed Tamsin to take his hand, lead him up to her bedroom and draw him down beside her under her cool white sheets.

Heading home along the seafront later that afternoon, Mitch felt as if he were walking on air: it seemed certain now that Tamsin would probably remain in Felixham for the entire summer holidays, which meant that they could be together for a whole six weeks. Plus, when he'd remarked on how cordial she seemed to be towards Quinn, she'd said she hoped maybe the affair was already blowing over. He was happy that she wouldn't be made miserable, or be anxious about how much to say to her mum. It meant, too, that he could tell her about Tessa and that Declan guy. He still hadn't made up his mind how much he minded, and Tamsin didn't seem to think it was a big deal, but it was good not to carry the secret any more.

For once he enjoyed being a part of the summer throng. He'd never understood before why anyone other than small kids armed with buckets and spades and makeshift cricket bats on the beach would want to spend a holiday here, but now he realised that, for the adults, it was about sex. If what Felixham offered adult holidaymakers was an opportunity for the same kind of blissful island of time he'd just relished in Tamsin's bed, then the place was an absolute fairy kingdom.

But it wasn't only about going to bed with Tamsin. He'd also been able to share his concerns about Roy Weaver. He'd already told her on the phone about his visit to Shirley, about how he'd instinctively liked and trusted her, that she seemed really smart and clever and not at all like a woman with a grudge against her brother. Now he'd been able to confide in Tamsin how he still hadn't found the right moment to communicate Shirley's warning to his mother. Tessa still wore the gold bracelet she said Roy had given her, which must mean she wanted to feel close to him, close to a man Shirley had described as self-centred and manipulative, a liar and a killer. At this point Mitch had shown Tamsin the print-out Shirley had given him of the photograph with his own face looking out from Roy Weaver's graduation gown and hood. Tamsin had hugged him: he was nothing like Roy Weaver, and certainly wasn't going to start turning into a werewolf at full moon! It was good to be teased and be able to laugh about something that had made him so uneasy, though he didn't think he could explain even to Tamsin how contaminated he felt, knowing he carried the genetic imprint of a violent man who'd harassed and maybe molested women. Maybe if he'd been allowed to meet the guy it would be different, but meanwhile the idea of his mum cosying up to this criminal was disgusting.

As he neared the B&B he noticed Sam's car parked outside with the hatchback door open. Sam was leaning inside, arranging carrier bags and a cardboard box that seemed to be full of shoes. His father straightened up when he saw him. 'Lauren's coming to stay with us for a while,' he explained. 'I think your mum needs a bit of space.'

'Ok.'

'Tell Lauren I'll wait out here.' Sam shrugged awkwardly. 'Probably best.'

Mitch let himself in and stood for a second, listening to the sounds of the house. He could hear sobbing and shouting upstairs, and felt a sneaking disloyalty that he was glad Lauren was going; the rows with Tessa seemed endless and she'd be much happier with Sam and Nula, who'd find jobs for her in the brasserie that would let her feel grown-up and important. Not wanting to burst his own bubble of contentment, he decided he'd try to deliver Sam's message, slip up to his room to grab a sweater, then escape. Tessa would expect him to side with her, and right now he wasn't sure he could.

But what he found was worse than he expected. On the first-floor landing he found Lauren, tear-stained and wild-eyed, an overstuffed carrier bag in each hand.

'It's not my fault!' she cried as soon as she spied him. 'I didn't mean to, I just forgot, and I've said I'm sorry.'

'What the hell's going on?' Mitch followed Lauren's terrified nod towards the door to the nearest guest bedroom through which he could see a curtain of water cascading down across the open doorway to the bathroom beyond. Inside Tessa was on her hands and knees trying to haul a pile of sopping white towelling off the floor and into the bath. The tiled floor was covered with water.

'What did you do?' Mitch turned to Lauren.

'I was rinsing off my swimming things in the sink upstairs, then Evie rang and we were talking and I forgot to turn off the tap.'

'Jesus, Lauren!'

'I said I was sorry! She won't listen.'

'Mitch? Is that you?' Tessa called from the bathroom.

'Dad's waiting for you by the car. Go,' he told Lauren firmly. 'I'll call you later.' She obeyed gratefully, and Mitch went in to face Tessa.

'Look at my brand new bathrobes!' she exclaimed.

'They'll wash, won't they?' said Mitch.

'How could she be so stupid! The water must've been running for half an hour at least. She's caused hundreds of pounds-worth of damage.'

'Won't the insurance cover it?'

'Yes, but there'll be the excess to pay, and then the premium will go sky-high.'

'It was an accident, Mum. Lauren's said she's sorry.' He held Tessa's gaze as steadily as he dared. He could see she'd had a fright, and had reason to be angry, but he willed her now to stop lashing out at everything around her. But although she dropped her eyes as if accepting his rebuke, she opened another line of attack.

'Where were you?' she demanded.

'Tamsin just got home for the holidays,' he said, his unconquerable happiness at the simple fact returning despite the chaos around him.

Tessa shook her head. 'What do I say to tonight's guests? All my hard work, destroyed!'

Mitch had already heard the front door bang behind Lauren, but now he heard heavier footsteps on the stairs. He hoped Sam had decided after all to come and help sort things out. Mitch went to meet him, found Hugo instead and immediately felt better. 'Grandpa!'

'What's the damage?' Hugo smiled and jokingly reached up to ruffle Mitch's hair as he'd always done when Mitch was little.

In the guest bedroom Mitch could see the cascade was already draining away to a trickle, and hoped perhaps the worst was now over.

'There's a mop and bucket downstairs, isn't there?' Hugo asked. Mitch nodded in relief and went off to fetch it.

As he moved items around in the basement storeroom to make space to wrestle the bucket and mop out of its corner he tried to feel more sympathetic towards his mum. He knew how much it mattered to her that the guests were impressed and went away full of compliments, and Lauren had been careless and too easily distracted, but she'd said she was sorry. If Tessa could forgive a murderer, then surely she could manage to be a bit kinder to Lauren? His sister was obviously genuinely upset about what she'd done. He thought of the box of shoes in the back of Sam's car and realised they signified a longer stay than just a few days. Maybe she'd spend the whole summer with Sam and Nula, in which case Mitch was glad – she'd be properly looked after and he would no longer have to feel responsible for her.

When he came back upstairs he could hear their voices – Tessa more high-pitched and staccato than usual against Hugo's deep murmur – before he could make out the words.

'I just want to be left alone,' she was complaining. 'I'm tired of having to look after everyone else. I just want some peace and quiet, for other people to respect my needs for once. Is that too much to ask?'

Mitch drew back a little, hoping not to attract their notice. He knew it was his duty to deliver Shirley's warning, yet also recognised a kind of survival instinct that made him reluctant to intervene. If Tessa just wanted to be left alone, and thought her precious father was Ok, then fine, let her get on with it. Even if he told her she'd been taken in by an abusive creep who told lies about his own mother and got sacked for fiddling around with a student, she'd probably find a way to blame the messenger. He couldn't be bothered. All he wanted to think about was Tamsin.

He looked around the door, wondering what to do, as Hugo crossed the open doorway to the bathroom, reaching out to her. 'Hey, Tessie, come on now,' Mitch heard him say. 'This isn't like you.'

'How do you know what I'm like?' his mother hissed back.

Mitch placed the bucket and mop cautiously inside the door of the bedroom, tiptoed upstairs for a sweater and then back down, flattening himself against the wall as he would if wanting to remain invisible to guests. Gaining the ground floor he escaped into the sunshine, closing the front door carefully behind him.

THIRTY-NINE

It was with conscious irritation that Tessa inserted the key into the tiny padlocks at the side of the doll's house. She'd promised Erin, who'd promised Pamela, that she'd put back the dolls, even though she herself thought it was stupid. People weren't dolls, and removing these symbols of humanity all those years ago had not succeeded in rendering Averil's make-believe world powerless or safe. Her grandmother's attempts to neaten and tidy away the tumultuous realities of life, to miniaturise the huge emotions within her family down to the bearable scale of this toy house, had been both foolish and cruel. No wonder she'd always felt so ambivalent towards this shrine to Averil's need to control her family.

Tessa pushed back the door, which stretched the width of the house, and took the three dolls out of the tin in which Pamela had safeguarded them for nearly forty years. The obvious way to arrange them was around the Formica kitchen table, but if these toys were supposed to replicate life, then, to her mind, they did not belong together. Since

Erin's reappearance, Tessa felt as if her whole family had dissolved in front of her. Defiant, she stuck each little figure in a separate room, hooked the door shut and fastened the padlocks.

She was upset, had been upset for days, but no one seemed to notice. Pamela was taken up with Erin, who showed no sign of wanting to return home. She barely seemed to exist for Sam. Mitch diligently did everything asked of him, but only so that he could disappear off at the earliest possible moment to be with Tamsin Crawford.

Tessa missed Lauren most of all. The house seemed horribly empty without her. She knew she shouldn't have lost her temper over the flooded bathrooms and cracked ceiling, and had rung her daughter a couple of times to apologise and suggest she come home. But Lauren had answered with polite monosyllables then cut her off, leaving Tessa hurt and frustrated and also guiltily relieved that, for once, Sam could take charge. Tessa felt daunted by Lauren's ability to arouse in her such a helpless and complicated fury, when all she wanted was to drag her daughter into her arms and tell her she loved her and wanted her to be happy. What was wrong with the child that she couldn't be happy? Where did she get the power to resist so ruthlessly?

Tessa went to stand in the bay window, seeking the calming view of the sea. It had been raining all morning, so although the summer season was well under way the beach was virtually deserted. She looked out towards the horizon, silver-grey against silver-white, losing herself in the vast movement and emptiness of sea and sky.

Sometimes she wanted to be a child again herself, and flee to her own parents, let them sort everything out. That was their job. But they'd messed up, and expecting comfort from Pamela and Hugo was impossible. She no longer belonged with them. Pamela was intent on making out that everything was now rosy, cloudless and bright, and refused to notice the permanent sadness that hung over Hugo. He, as always, continued to smooth things over and make everything work, but his reasonable tone dismayed and infuriated Tessa: could he not see that things had never been right, that patching them up wasn't going to do the job any more? It was scarier than anything to discover that even Hugo, on whom she had always depended to make her feel safe, was fallible and mistaken.

Underlying all her hurt and irritation was suppressed panic at what Erin had really meant by her story. Was she the child of rape? Even if 'only' date rape? The thought was terrifying. Too terrifying to be true. It could not be true. Averil had not believed it, and even Erin herself was uncertain. Erin had left her to decide. Tessa knew Roy, knew what he was like, what he might be capable of, and she refused to believe it. He must have been convinced that afternoon he was doing what Erin wanted, had failed to comprehend her inexperience, and, yes, maybe got a bit carried away. He was a young man, maybe not that experienced himself, but that did not make him a rapist. She could find nothing in what he had ever said or done during their meetings or in his letters that lent any weight to a counter-argument. She was not stupid: she'd discussed her impressions candidly with Declan, an open-minded, sensible man, and he'd not flagged up any alarms. She wished Erin had not spoken!

And besides, whichever way Tessa worked her way around the ambiguities of the past, she came up against one absolute certainty: it was incomprehensible that a man who'd gone to such trouble to find a birthday card with cherries on it had simultaneously carried in his mind the knowledge that he was sending it to the offspring of a callous and deliberately brutal encounter. The two facts simply did not fit together. He was a loving father, not a predator.

Tessa comforted herself that she already had another visit booked with Roy. It was important to see him again before the fears aroused by Erin's doubts became nightmares. In fact, she found the idea of returning to the prison empowering. As Roy had told her, there was no love without fear, and facing up to difficult realities could only make her stronger. How else was it ever possible to maintain authentic relationships? Her childhood, deprived of essential truths, had proved that. A contemptuous glance at the doll's house convinced her how her relationship with Roy had enabled her to open a window in a stuffy room and allow herself to breathe freely again.

Carol put her head around the door. 'I've finished the stairs,' she said. 'Thought I might have a cup of tea before we start on the beds. Would you like one?'

'Oh, yes, thanks.'

Tessa followed Carol down to the kitchen and placed the kettle on the Aga's hotplate. 'Sit yourself down,' she told her. 'I'll make it.'

'It's the big party on Saturday,' Carol observed.

'Party?'

'At the Crawfords'. Thought Mitch would've mentioned it.'

'You know what boys are like. Never tell you anything.'

'You not invited?'

'Me?' asked Tessa. 'No!'

'I heard from Sonia Beeston there's to be fireworks and all sorts.'

'That'll be fun.'

'Mr Crawford's here for the whole summer, apparently.'

Tessa busied herself putting tea bags into mugs. 'I hope the rain clears up before the weekend.'

'So Mitch is still seeing Tamsin Crawford?'

'Yes, I think so.'

Carol nodded. 'Sonia says he spends a lot of time over there.'

'I think they take the dog for walks.'

'They grow up so fast these days, don't they?' Carol gave Tessa a shrewd look.

'They're just kids,' smiled Tessa, not wanting to encourage Carol's speculation. She willed the kettle to boil faster.

'Sonia cleans Tamsin's bedroom,' Carol persisted. 'She thinks Mr Crawford ought to keep a closer eye on what the kids get up to.'

'That's the nanny's job, isn't it?'

'If that's what she is,' Carol remarked darkly.

Tessa had just finished making the tea when the letterbox upstairs rattled. She saw that Carol, too, had heard the muffled thud of post hitting the floor, and quickly handed her a mug, picking up her own. 'I might take my tea upstairs, if you don't mind. There's a mound of paperwork to get on with.'

'I can manage the beds on my own,' sniffed Carol. 'I don't have to disturb you.'

Tessa realised she'd offended her, but there was no way she wanted to condone Sonia Beeston's gossip. 'Give me a call once you've had your tea,' she said. 'No rush.'

Scooping up the damp mail, she smiled at the sight of Roy's handwriting on one of the envelopes. Even though she'd be seeing him next week, and even though the number of letters he could send was limited, he had chosen to write anyway. Nevertheless, she still felt a certain trepidation opening the envelope, as if somehow he could know that there had been a shift in her perception, sense that she might read his words less innocently, testing them for hidden evidence. Her doubts felt like a betrayal of trust.

My dearest Tessa, he wrote in his elegant italic. *I have a proposition to put to you, and wanted to offer an opportunity to consider it before we meet. My hunch is that you will refuse, and I'd like you not to.* Tessa's throat tightened with apprehension. *You know how important family is to me, even though I've been deprived of it. I've read in the papers the expense these days of university tuition. I told you I'm not short of money, so I would like to help Mitch with his university fees. And Lauren, too, in due course. I hope you will allow me this small indulgence: they are my grandchildren, after all.* Under Roy's signature was a PS: *I assume Hugo will be doing the same. I don't want to tread on anyone's toes. I'll give whatever's appropriate.* The way in which the letter's contents were laid out on the sheet of paper suggested that the PS was not an afterthought but an integral part of the design. Familiar now with Roy's love of exactitude, Tessa decided the lack of spontaneity was not strategic but evidence of his reluctance to make demands, of his fear that she might view his generosity as an imposition.

The shameful dread that had gripped her since Erin's muddled account of the summer tryst amongst the gorse bushes lifted and was replaced by remorse at how she would have to disguise the hostile reality that Mitch was unlikely to accept Roy's offer. Her own fear that she might have been wrong about Roy made her yet more impatient with her family: why couldn't they credit her with enough sense to have thought through their objections for herself, and be willing to accept her judgement? For how much longer did her father have to go on being so misunderstood? Why couldn't any of them focus on how hard this all was for her?

FORTY

Quinn and Sonia had been busy since first thing in the morning supervising the various florists, caterers and stylists arriving from London to prepare the house for Charlie's party. Tamsin had a couple of school friends staying, Emily and Phoebe, and Mitch could see how much the three of them were enjoying the flurry of activity and the rapid transformation of the downstairs rooms and enclosed garden, where colourful paper lanterns were being hoisted and a tree adorned with fairy lights. He felt a little guilty at lending a hand here when he should have been at home helping his mum, especially given that some of Charlie's party guests were probably booked to stay overnight at the Seafront B&B. He compared the misplaced pride Tessa took in her imagined heights of sophistication to the money-no-object magic they would witness here, and immediately condemned his own disloyalty. It was only money, yet it created such a gulf between his worlds.

Over the course of the afternoon a small army invaded every corner of the house, and by eight o'clock the house and garden were already filling with people. Tamsin had changed into a shift dress that she told Mitch had cost over a thousand pounds, even though it looked to him like no more than two panels of golden fabric sewn together at the side and shoulder seams. She said Charlie had bought it for her in London on a weekend exeat from school. She wore nothing else except golden flip-flops, and, with her long gold hair, looked amazing.

At dusk Mitch suggested that they take Blanco for a quick walk before he was shut away for the night. He was glad to have a moment alone with Tamsin. He'd been apprehensive about meeting her friends, though they turned out to be not so different from Lauren, just chatting about clothes and hair and giggling over what celebrities were coming. They found every parking space taken up by expensive cars; two even had uniformed drivers, eating sandwiches and watching TV on their dashboard screens to pass the hours before gliding their clients back to London in the wee small hours. The air was warm and muggy after the rain of the past few days, and as they waited for Blanco to sniff around the base of one of the Napoleonic canons on the Green, Mitch could hear the strength of the swash and backswash of the waves against the shingle. A few windows in the houses clustered around the Green were lit up, the curtains not yet drawn. In one a man sat reading the newspaper, in another a woman in yellow gloves was washing up. He thought of *The Great Gatsby*, the book he'd studied for his exam, and the green light at the end of Daisy Buchanan's dock. Despite the unreality of Charlie's party preparations, Mitch felt that Tamsin was the only solid, real, dependable thing in his life. He moved closer, close enough to smell her hair and feel her warmth. She turned her head and, smiling, kissed the tip of his nose.

Back indoors, he was glad that she kept tight hold of him, and hoped it was because she was proud to be seen beside him. He saw that he blended in unremarkably with the other men, and understood why she'd told him to wear black jeans and his least faded black T-shirt. In fact, Tamsin whispered, giggling, she'd seen at least one casting agent take a second look, just in case she'd missed the new hot acting talent Charlie had discovered. She seemed to know most of her father's guests and was punctilious about introducing Mitch and her friends to everyone who stopped to greet her.

Mitch spotted Charlie beckoning to them. 'Your dad wants you.'

Charlie held out his arm, drawing Tamsin against him. 'You remember my daughter?' he asked the hawk-eyed woman in designer glasses beside him. 'You should get her to come and intern for you. She's learning the saxophone at school. She's very musical.'

'One lesson, Daddy.'

'But you play drums too, right?'

Tamsin agreed politely. 'Nice to meet you,' she told the woman, taking Mitch firmly by the hand to lead him away. 'She's a sound designer,' she explained to Mitch. 'Dad tells the DoP that I take terrific photographs and the production designer that I'm an incredible artist.'

'Do you want to do any of those things?'

'No. Though I might like to do costumes, like my mum.'

'Maybe I should tell them I'm related to a serial killer,' he joked.

'Yeah, cool!' She saw him roll his eyes. 'No, seriously. They'd love that!'

Emily caught what they were saying and stared at Mitch with fresh interest. 'You're not, are you?' she asked.

Despising himself, but unsure how else to repudiate the girl's frisson, Mitch played along. 'Yeah, actually. My grandfather's serving a life sentence for murder,' he told her.

'Wicked! What's he like?'

'Hannibal Lecter?' suggested Mitch.

Emily's eye's widened. 'Really?'

'No. I've not even met him.'

Tamsin threaded her arm through his. 'Let's get out of here.'

The four of them made their way out to the fairground garden, picking up glasses of champagne as they went. Mitch noticed Quinn, a couple of jackets over her arm, checking that people had drinks. She had clearly been relegated to 'staff' for the evening, and was making a bad job of hiding her humiliation, glancing repeatedly towards Charlie, who remained oblivious to her. Although Mitch managed some pity for her – young and far from home, she'd been all too vulnerable to seduction by Captain

Gorgeous – he was pleased: faithful only to Tamsin, he had hardened his heart against anyone who did not share his devotion.

Mitch found himself listening to a humourless thirty-something who seemed to assume that he knew every detail of Charlie's business, and was glad to be rescued by Tamsin, who'd been giggling in a conspiratorial huddle with her friends. 'Come with me,' she said, laughing and pulling faces at Emily and Phoebe, who remained in the garden.

'Where are we going,' asked Mitch as he followed her upstairs. Instead of entering her own room she opened the door to Charlie's bedroom. Mitch hovered in the doorway, unwilling to trespass, and watched Tamsin flit over to a modern bureau, open a slim drawer and remove something from it. She glided back to him, whatever she had taken concealed in her hand. She grinned at him. 'Phoebe wants it for later,' she said, tucking whatever it was down the front of her dress.

As they rejoined the party, Mitch felt his phone vibrate in his pocket and discovered it was Lauren. He moved aside to answer it, but could barely hear in the crush. A glass-panelled door led from the kitchen to an inner hall off which were a pantry and laundry room. He opened it and slipped through, though he could still hear music, loud voices and laughter.

'Hey, Lauren. How are you?'

'Dad and Nula are working. Will you come and see me?'

'Not right now.'

'Where are you? At the party?'

Not wanting to increase Lauren's envy, he opened the door to the laundry room, assuming it would be quieter in there. Enough light came from the small window to reveal a man leaning back against the row of machines, his mouth open, his fingers rhythmically kneading the hair of the woman who knelt in front of him, her face in his crotch. As Charlie stared right at him, Mitch realised the kneeling figure was Quinn.

He backed out quickly, closing the door. 'Have to speak later,' he told Lauren, ending the call.

Ten minutes later Quinn, clearly oblivious to the identity of the intruder – if, indeed, she had been aware of any interruption at all – came to ask if he and Tamsin wanted some of the hot food now being laid out in the kitchen. Unable to avoid Charlie's gaze over Quinn's shoulder, he knew his intrusion would not be forgiven.

'I'm tired,' Mitch told Tamsin. 'How about a bit of time out?'

'I have the very thing to perk us all up,' she assured him. She beckoned to her friends, and Mitch had to make the best of it. At least she was heading upstairs, away from Charlie.

In her bedroom, she closed the door, rummaged in a make-up bag, brought out a small mirror and then produced a slip of paper which she handed to Phoebe. Mitch watched apprehensively as Phoebe unfolded it and tipped a tiny heap of white powder onto the mirror.

'Is that cocaine?' he asked, trying not to sound too shocked.

'What else?' said Phoebe sarcastically. 'I need a credit card,' she told Tamsin.

Tamsin went to fetch her bag. Phoebe took the card and proceeded to chop the powder into four thin lines. Tamsin rolled a bank note into a straw ready to hand to her. Emily, like Mitch, hung back, watching.

'Have you done this before?' he asked.

'No, but Daddy and his friends do it all the time,' said Tamsin. 'It's fine.'

'What your dad gets up to isn't much of a recommendation.'

'What d'you mean?'

'Nothing,' he said, regretting his slip. 'Doesn't matter.'

'Tell me.'

'It's nothing,' Mitch assured her.

Too late Mitch saw Phoebe listening, and didn't like the avaricious look in her eyes. Tamsin's vulnerability was heart-rending, and he panicked. Her world was too much for him. He watched in horrified fascination as Tamsin tossed back her golden hair and bent down to inhale the line of coke. 'Who's going to care anyway, except me?' he thought bitterly. She raised her head, looking at him with strange, glittering eyes, and offered him the rolled-up note. Aware of Phoebe's supercilious gaze, he took it. 'Show me how you do this stuff,' he said.

FORTY-ONE

As Tessa made the short walk across from the Visitors' Centre, she thought how odd it was that a maximum-security prison should so swiftly have become a place where she felt at home. Yet it was true: she no longer minded the searches, the appraising stares of the officers, the waiting and unlocking, because she so looked forward to the intimacy of the visits room – a confessional with its own ritual constraints. And, as usual, Roy was neatly dressed, his grey hair cut short, his fingernails trimmed: he could perfectly well have been a psychotherapist or a priest. She smiled to herself as she threaded her way though the tables but then, seeing him waiting beside his chair, unable to stroll over to greet her, hands kept in sight of the cameras, she remembered with a pang how very different his experience of the prison was from hers: he was forced to stay while she was free to go.

All the way here she'd been unable to stop her mind tumbling over itself, various thoughts and ideas revolving like familiar garments coming into view inside the drum of a washing machine. One moment she was remembering Declan's body rolling over hers in bed, the guest room alien in the pale light from the open window; the next she was thinking about Erin and the impossibility of understanding what she had really meant; then, again, always, her devastation that nearly a week had passed since Lauren had packed up and gone and she still showed not the slightest intention of coming home. The deadliest hurt came from her daughter's ease with the situation: it was neither defiance nor a sulk. Lauren neither wanted nor needed her. Lauren was happier with Nula.

Greeting Roy with a kiss on the cheek and taking her seat opposite him, Tessa forced the clamouring tumble to a halt: she must not allow her troubles with her family to muscle in on her treasured oasis here. But Roy was studying her face carefully. 'You're upset,' he said. 'What is it?'

'Oh, just domestic stuff,' she said, afraid she might burst into tears.

'You need a holiday. If only I could whisk you away!'

She smiled, grateful that he had the tact not to press her for details. 'That would be heaven,' she told him. 'I haven't had a proper holiday in years. I can only really go away in the winter, and then, with Christmas and school holidays, it never works out.'

'Once the kids have left school. Then you and I can travel.'

She accepted the comforting fiction gladly. 'That sounds good!'

Roy sat back, tugging at his cuffs, positioning each button at the edge of his wrists. 'Did you receive my letter?'

'Yes. And I don't know what to say! I'm really touched, but it's honestly not necessary.'

He looked steadily back at her, his expression serious, although there was something behind his eyes that she couldn't decipher.

'Every penny was earned by honest means. I'm not a bank robber or drug dealer, if that's what you're worried about.'

'Of course not! It would never cross my mind.' However many times she'd tried rehearsing her answer, she still hadn't worked out how to confess without insulting him that she hadn't even mentioned his proposal to her family because of their hostility to Roy's very existence.

'Is Hugo the problem?'

'He wouldn't stand in Mitch's way. But we haven't got as far as talking about fees and things.'

Roy nodded, satisfied. 'Well, when you do.'

'Thank you. It's extremely generous.'

'If you want to thank me, then I have one very simple favour to ask in return.'

'Of course!'

'Don't forget to bring me photos of Mitch and Lauren. I want to see every minute of my two grandchildren growing up.'

Tessa had not forgotten Roy's earlier request, and felt undermined by her reluctance to comply with his wishes. Of course she wanted to show off her children to their grandfather, to laugh over the similarity of physical traits, to recount their childhood exploits, but how would Mitch and Lauren feel about her doing that? Seizing at a straw, she asked if the missing photos she'd brought in of herself had yet been found.

'No,' Roy answered. 'They'll turn up eventually.'

'Should I write to the Governor?

'I wouldn't bother. The cogs of this malevolent old machine grind very slowly.'

'I can imagine.'

'So how are Mitch and Lauren? Behaving themselves?'

'Mitch is never at home. He has a girlfriend.'

'Ah! So what's she like?'

'Very sweet. Her parents are in the film business, rather glamorous.'

'Sex, drugs and rock 'n' roll?'

'I don't think so!' Tessa laughed, but was uncomfortably reminded of Carol's latest warning.

'Do you suppose they're having sex?'

Tessa was taken aback by such a blatant question, but Roy's face showed concern. 'He is my grandson,' he said. 'I'm allowed to ask. There can be consequences, as we know,' he added with a fond smile.

She tried to make light of it. 'Well, not in my house, they're not.'

'What about drugs?'

'No, not Mitch!'

'Would you know if he was?'

'I think so. I hope so.'

'I know about addiction, how easy it is to be in denial.'

'They're just kids.'

Roy turned his head and deliberately swept his gaze around the big room. 'A lot of these guys were just kids,' he said. 'Zero tolerance. That's the only way.'

Tessa was surprised. 'I'd've thought there'd be more understanding, here of all places, about why people do drugs.' As she, too, looked around the dozens of men in their fluorescent tabards, she noticed the angelic young man from her previous visit. He was sitting with his mother, and Tessa noted with dismay that it *was* the same woman who had cursed her beside the lockers.

'If you turn a blind eye to your kids taking drugs,' Roy was saying, 'then you might as well hand them a syringe and be done with it.'

'It must have damaged your childhood, your mother's drinking?' Tessa asked gently.

Roy shook his head in contempt. 'I knew what she was.' He leant forward across the table. 'It's you I worry about, Tessa. If you do find that Mitch is using, then you can't help. You must walk away. Addicts have no respect for anyone. He'll lie and cheat and steal. Him and his little slag of a girlfriend. You have to look after yourself.'

Tessa was shocked. 'They're nice kids. I know you had a hard time, but—'

'Hand on your heart,' Roy continued, 'would you know if someone in your family was an addict? Sometimes the secrecy is a big part of it.' He must have seen Tessa's flare of alarm, for the tight, angry muscles of his face and neck unclenched. 'I'd like to be there for you. Teach you, help you. More than just these visits. I'd like to be able to phone you.'

'I didn't know you were allowed to?'

'Phone cards are a major currency in here!' He sat back, waiting for her response.

Under pressure, Tessa struggled to assert the realities of her life. 'It's not always easy to speak privately, with guests in the house morning and night.'

'Don't worry. I can't phone you if you don't give your permission.'

'I hardly get a moment to myself, that's all,' she apologised.

'When the prison contacts you, all you have to do is say no.' He gave a brief, stiff smile. 'I already have your number, from your printed letterhead.'

It's so hard to say 'no' to you! Tessa thought. And yet, she reminded herself quickly, his demands were not really demands but only further proof of how much he cared about her, how much he wanted to be involved in her life. How could she deny him when he had so little? The thought reminded her guiltily that she had yet to tell him that Erin was back in Felixham. Would he want to see her again?

'Is it possible for me to call you?' she asked instead. 'Then I could ring when things are quiet.'

'It doesn't work that way,' he said. 'And I can't promise to ring you at certain times either. There's always such a queue for the phones.'

'You might get Carol, my housekeeper, picking up.' She

felt impatient at having to keep making excuses, as if she were being unfairly tested.

'Look, forget it,' said Roy. 'Forget I ever asked. I know so little about your daily life, and I've no right to expect you to make room in it for me. Or not yet, anyway.' He reached across and laid his hand on hers. 'I've made you feel bad, and that's the last thing I'd ever want to do, my darling girl.'

'If it was just me . . .' she began, but he gripped her hand to command her silence.

'Three more months and I can apply for parole.' The red-haired officer, Janice, patrolling between the tables, passed close behind him, but he ignored her, holding tighter to Tessa's hand. 'Then none of this will matter.'

Tessa searched for some consolation she could offer to make up for her intransigence. 'What you said about addiction and secrecy,' she said. 'I think maybe Pamela has a drink problem.'

'That would explain a lot.'

'I don't know how serious it is. I'd not even noticed until recently. But I think she keeps a bottle in her handbag. Pretends there's just juice in it.'

'So many secrets,' he sighed. 'You've been nourished on them, haven't you?'

Tessa nodded, and Roy pressed her hand. 'Don't blame yourself. You mustn't.'

'I don't!' she responded. 'And I don't really blame them so much now either. They had their own stuff to deal with.'

'So what?' said Roy. 'I've learnt the hard way how easy it is to make excuses for people, especially people you care about. Leave them. We'll go to Rome, leave them behind, make up for lost time together.'

'An adventure!' Tessa laughed, glad of the distraction. 'Once Lauren's left school, that would be a treat.'

'Why wait? She can live with Sam. We can go as soon as I get parole. Rent an apartment.'

'I have a business to run!'

'So what?' repeated Roy. I have enough money for both of us. Come on, Tessa! You're not just some small-town girl. You're different. You're my daughter.'

Tessa pulled her hand free. 'Roy, it's a lovely idea, but I can't go off and live somewhere else.'

But Roy just laughed. 'We belong together. You belong with me.'

Tessa reluctantly admitted the acute discomfort that had been gathering for some minutes. Had this wilfulness always been here, and she'd failed to see it? It was like one of those trick drawings where you see either a wine glass or an old crone. Sometimes it's impossible to make out both images, but once you have, their dual existence can't be denied. Dread began to creep into her veins: had his refusal to hear 'no' enabled him to lead Erin in among the gorse bushes and persuade himself it was what she wanted and expected him to do? Had Angie's 'illness' been her attempt to say what he didn't wanted to hear?

'Why wasn't it manslaughter?' she blurted out.

Roy's lips thinned with displeasure, but he regarded her

steadily. 'The jury chose to believe Angie's family,' he said simply, gesturing with his hands that she could take it or leave it. 'They couldn't face up to the fact that they'd failed her, that she needed me, not them.'

But he killed her, Tessa told herself. What woman needs a man who strangles her?

'I don't blame her parents,' Roy went on, oblivious to her thoughts. 'They'd lost their daughter. The guilt must have been terrible.'

'Let me get you some cake.' Tessa rose abruptly to her feet. 'Before they close.' Without waiting for permission, she made her way over to the counter, relieved that he was not allowed to follow her.

Her hands shook as she handed over the tokens. Taking deep breaths, she glanced at the clock to work out how soon the bell would ring to signify the end of visits. She dragged out the transaction, changing her mind about which biscuits to buy, and promising herself that she would, after all, ask Declan if his colleague could get hold of the transcripts of Roy's trial. She hoped she was wrong, but she was not the naive teenager her mother had been, and she must not continue this relationship without finding out exactly to what and to whom she was consenting.

FORTY-TWO

As Tessa prepared to leave the prison the red-haired officer, Janice, approached her to say that she'd been unable to locate the missing photographs Tessa had previously asked about. Preoccupied, Tessa thanked her and moved on, eager to escape and reach the uncontaminated safety of home. But impulsively she turned back and asked Janice if it would be possible to have a private word. Although the officer did not seem particularly surprised by the request, she spent a long moment considering before quietly remarking that her shift finished in half an hour and she could meet Tessa at the pub in the nearest village.

Now, sitting with a fruit juice at a corner table in the dingy bar, Tessa wondered what on earth she'd been thinking: how could talking to a prison officer possibly help? And what unintended negative repercussions might there be for Roy? If she wanted to learn more about her father, why hadn't she taken Mitch's sensible advice and got in touch with Shirley Weaver? She tried to persuade herself that today's unease had more to do with how tired and overwrought she'd been recently, that it would be better to slip away before Janice arrived. It was her growing sense that Roy was manipulating her for some purpose he had yet to reveal that kept her there, even while she debated with herself what harm a man safely locked up in prison could possibly do anyone.

Janice entered the bar, looked around, located Tessa with a nod and came to join her. Out of uniform she was a plain woman, her red hair her only noticeable feature.

'I wasn't sure you'd come,' said Tessa. 'Whether you'd be allowed.'

'I'm finished there anyway,' she answered with odd emphasis.

'Can I get you a drink?'

'Pete knows me. He'll bring one over.' Janice waved to the barman. 'Roy lost it with you today, didn't he?'

Tessa was a little shocked by her directness. 'What do you mean?'

'I saw it. There's always a point when he can't keep it together any more.'

'You know I'm his daughter?' Tessa asked, thinking perhaps Janice wasn't aware of their relationship.

'Yes, I know.' Janice reached out across the greasy table and touched Tessa's gold bracelet. 'How do you think he managed to send you that?'

Tessa withdrew her arm. 'He told me you bought the card for me as well. That was kind. Thank you.'

Janice laughed, a short bark. There was something terrier-like about her, thought Tessa, in her covetous eyes and fierce stance. 'Though he let me think you were his new girlfriend,' she said.

'Why?' Tessa wondered if the woman was a little mad. But the barman brought over a glass of what looked like vodka and a small tonic, and Tessa noted that he did not greet Janice as if she might be barmy. He asked Tessa if she'd like another, but she hadn't yet finished her juice: she'd considered a stiff drink to steady her nerves when she'd arrived, and was glad now she'd kept her wits about her.

'He likes to wind people up,' explained Janice, watching Tessa shrewdly. 'So what was his spiel today? The two of you against the world?'

'He did get a bit carried away with dreams for the future,' Tessa admitted. 'I imagine they all do.'

'Looked to me like he gave you a bit of a fright.' Janice knocked back half her drink. 'So what is it you want to know?'

Tessa's heart skipped a beat. This was likely to be the unvarnished truth, and suddenly she wasn't sure she could face it.

'What did he tell you he's in for?' asked Janice. 'The tragic accident story?'

'Are you allowed to talk about an inmate like this?'

'No,' Janice answered. 'But it doesn't matter. This is my last day.'

'You're leaving?' asked Tessa, vainly postponing the real conversation.

'I reckoned if I quit first, they won't bother prosecuting me.'

Tessa was alarmed. 'For talking to me?'

'For all the things I've done for him.'

'I don't understand.'

'You asked about your photographs,' said Janice. 'They didn't get lost.'

'So where are they?'

Janice downed the rest of her drink. 'They were of you as a kid, right?'

'Yes,' said Tessa. 'He asked for pictures of my children too. That's Ok, isn't it?'

'Is one of them a boy?'

'Yes.' Tessa was puzzled. 'Roy wants to see them both growing up. They're his grandchildren,' she explained needlessly.

Janice nodded. 'He wouldn't have been allowed them otherwise. But you're still not getting it, are you?' She laughed again. 'You've seen that young guy with curly hair in the visits room?' she asked. 'Paul. Looks like an angel, doesn't he?'

'His mother said he has a whole-life tariff,' Tessa remembered with sudden terror.

Janice nodded. 'Only his mother ever comes to visit him. Roy got your photos Ok, thank you very much. Then he sold them. But Paul said he'll pay even more for pictures of boys. Paul likes boys. Loves them to death. Younger the better.'

Tessa cupped her hand over her mouth, afraid she was going to throw up.

'There are quite a few prisoners who pay well for certain

kinds of material. Even of just a kid in a swimsuit. These perverts will take whatever's on offer. So we keep a pretty close eye on kiddie photos.'

'I don't believe you,' cried Tessa, though she knew this wasn't true.

Janice shrugged. 'Unless Roy gets an extension on his sentence tariff, he'll be out soon. He's clever enough to fool the parole board.'

'You think he's dangerous? That he'd hurt my kids?'

'You rather than your kids, I'd reckon. I've read his official file,' Janice went on. 'I bet it's not the same yarn he spun you.'

'Stop,' begged Tessa.

'You asked to talk to me.'

'I can't take it all in.'

'Roy was on bail when he cut his girlfriend's throat,' Janice went on remorselessly.

'He said she was strangled!'

'He was also charged with two counts of rape and assault. Those charges were left to lie on file.'

'But she was ill,' Tessa protested. 'Paranoid. Her parents turned her against him.'

'If she *was* ill it was because he'd terrorised her for months. She'd left him because he wouldn't let her out on her own. Took away her shoes, her phone, her computer. He had double-glazing installed with locks on all the windows.' Janice paused. 'She was a bright woman, a solicitor. Yet she didn't manage to stop him.'

Tessa felt faint. Why had she never asked, positively

avoided wanting to know? How idiotic and unkind she'd been not to recognise Hugo's love and concern when he had questioned her. Under the table, she pulled the gold bracelet off her wrist and dropped it into her bag. When she looked up she found Janice watching her with a mixture of triumph and sympathy.

'He had two previous arrests for unlawful imprisonment,' Janice continued. 'Even a suspicion of arson, but no one could make it stick.'

'I think he raped my mother,' Tessa said, 'but no one believed her.'

To her surprise, Janice nodded, her face losing its fierceness. 'I was like you when it started,' she said. 'He made me feel special. Beautiful, desirable. I actually looked forward to going to work. When you started visiting and I saw the way he held your hand, kissed it, looked into your eyes, I wanted to die. I'd have done anything for him.' She paused to signal to the barman for another vodka. 'He loves that control. Really loves it. But that's all he loves.'

'But you're an officer! You're in charge.'

'I didn't want to lose him.'

'Why are you telling me this?'

'He's up for parole in three months, and I'm scared.'

'He's not that bad,' pleaded Tessa. 'He can't be.'

'The word of a disgraced prison officer won't count for much with the parole board. But his daughter . . .' Janice waited for the barman to put down her second drink and walk away. 'You can write to the parole board, tell them about the photographs. He's a lifer. They don't ever have to let him out if they don't think it's safe to do so. And this would be more than enough to turn him down. I'll back you up,' she continued eagerly. 'He doesn't know yet that I've quit, so he won't have got rid of them.'

'I don't know,' said Tessa. 'He's not actually done anything to hurt me.'

'I'm not making it up. It's all on record. I can move away and change my name if I have to. Not so easy for you, I imagine.'

Tessa cast around for some hope to cling to, desperate for none of this to be true. 'He offered to pay for my son to go to university.' But as she uttered the words she heard Roy ask his favour in return: don't forget to bring more photos.

'You want him turning up on your doorstep?' asked Janice.

'No, but I'm his daughter.' Tessa knew she was clutching at straws. 'He says I belong to him. Surely he wouldn't . . .'

Janice gave an ugly laugh. 'That's what he said to me.' She downed her second vodka. Her hand shook as she lowered the empty glass. 'And he really means it. Believe me.'

FORTY-THREE

The full horror of her self-delusion hit Tessa on the road home. She pulled into the nearest lay-by and sat shaking as cars, lorries and coaches thundered past. She hardly dared look at the rear-view mirror in case she caught a glimpse of her blind, ridiculous, stupid face. She hated herself. She could never go home and face up to what she had done. How was she ever going to admit to her family that she had been taken in by this abusive, controlling man; worse, that she had been only too willing to *let* herself be taken in? And what could she say to Erin?

Roy had repeatedly assured her that it was all about her, about enabling her to be her best, her real self, and she had swallowed it, drunk down his words, told herself he was the only one who understood or cared for her, that her family's concern was mere jealous interference. She pulled the driving mirror around and made herself look into it. Who was she? In whose eyes did she exist? She shrivelled at the thought of how she'd quoted Roy's trite phrases back at Hugo and Mitch. This man had raped her mother, and she had rushed to his defence. Her behaviour was even more culpable than his.

Why had she believed in him and not in the people who loved her? Tessa was afraid of the answers: selfishness, stupidity and vanity. No wonder Sam and Lauren and Mitch were all better off without her. How could any of her family ever love her now?

She drove the rest of the way home trying to imagine how she could ever begin to put things right. As she let herself in, Charlie Crawford came out of the guests' sitting room.

'Your housekeeper said you'd be back an hour ago.' His statement was an accusation.

'Sorry, I was held up. Hello.' Tessa tried a smile, but it was not returned.

'I have to talk to you at once,' he said. 'I need to get back to London.' He disappeared into her sitting room.

Tessa did not follow him but instead went downstairs to get a drink of water and let Carol know she was back.

'I gave Mr Crawford some coffee,' Carol told her. 'I wasn't sure whether you were expecting him or not.' She pointed up at the board where the names of the night's guests were written. 'The first two dropped their bags and have gone out. The others aren't due till late, but I can stay on if you need me.'

'Thanks, Carol. But you can get off now.'

Carol's tactful silence as she fetched her bag and cardigan seemed ominous, so Tessa drank her water standing at the sink, looking out at the small back lawn beyond the area wall. The ground around the magnolia that Hugo had planted for her birthday hadn't yet settled, and the young tree looked somehow both makeshift and defenceless. It was an effort to bring to mind what Charlie Crawford could possibly want, and she felt blank, unprepared to cope with whatever he had to say. Rinsing her glass, she went upstairs to find out.

Charlie was standing in the middle of the room. He held out his hand, and for a moment she thought he meant to shake hers; then she saw that he was brandishing a mobile phone. 'Look at this,' he ordered.

Tessa took the phone and sat down, curling into herself to guard against his peremptory manner. She looked at the little screen and saw a photograph of a young girl, naked, on a bed. Shocked that Charlie should show her this, and still reeling from the obscenity of Roy's betrayal, she handed the phone straight back to him. 'No, I won't.'

He refused to accept it. 'Scroll through,' he ordered again. 'Look at the others.'

Her head full of what a convicted paedophile had paid to do with holiday snaps of her by a rock pool in Brittany, she covered the screen with her hand. 'No, I won't look. They're private.'

'Your son took them.'

Now Tessa looked, and realised the young girl was Charlie's daughter, Tamsin.

'There's more,' he said. 'Of him too.'

'That's not Mitch's phone,' Tessa managed to say.

'No. It's Tamsin's. She left it in my car.'

'Then you have no right to look.'

'She's barely sixteen.'

'You still have no right. I don't want to see them.'

'I'd like to know how long this has been going on,' Charlie insisted.

'Have you asked her?'

'You know Mitch turned up at her school? In Kent.'

Tessa did not know. She realised with a jolt that for months she had seldom known where Mitch was or what he was doing; had not cared, if she were honest, so long as he made no demands on her.

'The teacher who found them said there was an empty vodka bottle nearby.'

'No!' cried Tessa in disbelief.

'Where is he?' demanded Charlie.

'I've been out all afternoon. I . . .'

Charlie went out into the hall. 'Is he here?' he called out.

Tessa went after him. 'Please. Come back in here.' She had a sudden recollection of Charlie's magnetic effect on the crowd at the opening of Sam's brasserie, but saw now the petulance and self-indulgence that lay beneath his air of command. 'Tell me what Tamsin has said,' she insisted.

'Tamsin's leaving. She's going to spend the summer with her mother in Los Angeles.' Abruptly Charlie softened, looked a little chastened, and consented to return to the sitting room. Tessa closed the door behind them.

'I've sacked her nanny,' he said. 'And spoken to Sonia, our housekeeper.'

Tessa froze: she could guess the flavour of Sonia's gossip and didn't want to hear it from this man. 'Let me fetch Mitch,' she told him. 'He's probably upstairs.'

Tessa climbed the stairs unwillingly. She felt unqualified to negotiate her way through whatever was about to unfold, feared that she would get it wrong, and prayed with every step for someone else to appear and to wave a wand to make everything all right. After what she'd learned from Janice, she had no way of judging what humanity might be capable of, what depravities she might fail to consider. She felt shaky, incompetent, a danger to others.

As she reached the attic flat Mitch came out of their living room, a book in his hand, and smiled warily at her. She knew she deserved it: he'd tried to talk to her about Roy and she'd cut him short, not trusting his good intentions. She reached out now to give him a hug. He submitted, but barely returned it.

'Charlie Crawford's here,' she said. 'Did you know?'

'No. What does he want?'

'You'd better come down.'

'Wait, Mum. What does he want?'

'It's about you and Tamsin.'

Seeing how he flushed a deep red, Tessa felt completely overwhelmed. 'You'd better come down,' she told him, turning away.

'Mum!'

'Mitch, I've had a very long day. You have to sort this out for yourself.'

'Where've you been?' he asked. 'To the prison again?'

The accusation she heard in his voice was too much. She felt panicky and hysterical, knew it would be better not to speak. 'What have you been up to?' she demanded. 'Do you know what he's just made me look at? I shouldn't have to deal with this!'

'Mum, wait! What are you talking about?'

'Have you and Tamsin been having sex?'

Mitch hung his head, and Tessa thought he was about to cry.

'What's wrong with you?' she shouted at him. His face crumpled the way it used to as a kid when punished unfairly, and her anger fell away. 'Mitch, I'm sorry.' She reached out for him again but he dodged aside, out of her grasp, and headed downstairs. It took every ounce of her strength to follow.

Charlie had drawn himself up just enough to be able to look down at Mitch, who, though clearly apprehensive, greeted him courteously. 'Is Tamsin Ok?' he asked.

'She's on a plane to LA,' Charlie replied.

Mitch swallowed hard. 'For how long?'

'We'll have to see. I don't want her back here if you're going to harass her, keep turning up at her school.'

'Once! And she asked me to go!'

'I don't want this sort of thing to continue.' Charlie held up Tamsin's iPhone. Mitch looked puzzled. 'If I'd known about this when the school rang me, I would've called the police. Maybe I should do it now.'

Mitch, frowning and incredulous, turned to Tessa, who could see that he had not yet understood what Charlie meant about the phone.

Tessa was afraid. She knew nothing of what Mitch had been up to, but he must have taken these photographs of the two of them naked together. What if Charlie did call the police, and they found out that Roy was Mitch's grandfather? What if Charlie were right, and Mitch had been hassling Tamsin at school, stalking and controlling Tamsin the same way Roy had any woman he thought belonged to him? Terrified, she looked into her son's unblemished face and suddenly saw only his physical resemblance to Roy.

Mitch looked back at her and must have seen her momentary dread, for he paled and backed away.

'I love Tamsin,' he cried to both of them. 'I went to see her because she was upset.'

'Upset about what?' demanded Charlie.

Mitch gave Charlie such a look of contempt that even Tessa could see Mitch had hit a nerve. 'Tamsin was upset about you and Quinn,' Mitch said. 'Ask her.'

'If you're going to start inventing ridiculous stories–'

'Ask her!'

'I'm not listening to this garbage,' said Charlie.

'I saw you with Quinn. You know I did.'

'You stay away from my daughter, do you hear? I should've known better than to let her mix with you.'

'When is she coming back?'

'Never, so far as you're concerned.'

'You know we go up to her bedroom,' Mitch cried. 'But you never cared because it suited you. You're useless!'

'How dare you say that to me! Who do you think you are?'

'You never even noticed that she took cocaine out of your room, never made sure she was Ok.'

Tessa whirled around to face him. 'You've taken cocaine?' A terrible image of Mitch at a table in a fluorescent tabard flashed into her mind. 'Have you?'

'It was his.' Mitch pointed at Charlie. 'Tamsin says he does it all the time.' He turned on Charlie. 'You didn't even notice it was missing.'

Charlie gave a sneering laugh. 'This is fantasy!'

'Ask her friends,' insisted Mitch. 'Why aren't you talking to their parents?'

'What's the matter with you?' cried Tessa. 'Do you want to end up in prison? Locked away like Roy?'

Too late, Tessa registered Mitch's anguish. He barged out of the room, and moments later the front door banged.

Left looking at one another, Tessa finally saw Charlie betray a flicker of unease. She seized her advantage and held open the sitting-room door with a trembling hand. 'You'd better go.'

'I won't contact the police this time,' he told her, shamefaced. 'But make sure he stays away from my daughter.'

Tessa left him to walk down the hall and let himself out. Close to collapse, she went into her office and dialled Sam's number.

FORTY-FOUR

Mitch sat on the beach, chucking pebbles into the water. Around him, families were packing up for the day, hunting for missing shoes and shaking sand out of clothes and towels. Tired children whined with the effects of too much sun while their parents, contented after a good day out, chivvied them back to the car. The tide had begun to turn, and he watched as the low creamy waves crept further up the beach.

In the distant haze he followed the dot of an aeroplane as it made its way across the sky, and was stabbed by an actual physical pain at the thought of Tamsin sitting in her seat, headphones on, watching a film as the packed jumbo flew onwards, further and further, thousands of miles away from him. He took his phone out of his pocket and stared at it: even if she wasn't on a plane he couldn't call her, because Charlie had her phone. The thought of Charlie looking at the images of him and Tamsin was intolerable. Almost reflexively, Mitch bent his arm and flung his own phone into the sea. It was a good throw, following the same arc as all the pebbles, and only as the device hit the water did the thought strike him that, without it, Tamsin wouldn't be able to call him. He leapt up and ran to the water's edge. He already knew, from all the times as a kid that he'd searched in vain for lost treasures, that it was gone, but kicked off his trainers and waded out. He parted the moving waters with his hands, trying to see down to the shifting sands beneath, but it was futile.

Cursing himself, his jeans soaked up to his thighs, he threw himself back down on the sand. If he'd been alone he would have wept unrestrainedly, sobbed his heart out like the exhausted toddler being dragged past him by a mother whose arms were too laden with beach gear to pick the child up. He couldn't bear it. Tamsin was gone. Charlie had ordered him never to see her again. His one hope was to be believed, yet even his mother had looked at him as if he were the Devil. And maybe he was.

The very worst pain, the one that ate into him, corroding every good thing that had ever happened to him, was the thought of Charlie making cheap assumptions about photographs taken so light-heartedly when he and Tamsin had believed themselves to be so happy and free. The idea of Charlie casting his jaded, grubby eyes over the best and purest moments of Mitch's life made him mad with despair. He recalled the sight of Quinn kneeling on the laundry-room floor, her face buried in Charlie's crotch, Charlie's animal mouth snarling in the darkness. It was horrible that such a man should interfere with anything to do with Mitch's love for Tamsin.

But then he thought of the savage, self-centred emotions he'd experienced when he'd snorted Charlie's cocaine. He'd understood why people became addicted not to the physical effects but to the escape from self-imposed restriction, had recognised it in many of the people around them at the party. The sense of wild power it bestowed was dangerously seductive; whatever he did or thought, he was absolved by it being not him but the drug, and he'd reckoned that he might as well make the most of it while the effects lasted. If, under the influence, Tamsin had found a bigger stash in her father's bureau, he knew he would have snorted the lot. But he did not like the kind of person be became. He would hate for Hugo, for instance, to have witnessed how callously he and Tamsin had pushed through the throng to grab the best view of the fireworks, how they had acted and spoken to other people as if no one else mattered, or what they'd done with one another later that night. In the morning, sharing the breakfast table with her two friends, he felt he'd tarnished something irreplaceable and despised himself for his weakness. Deep down he feared that this was why Tamsin had agreed to fly away without saying goodbye.

Everything was wrong and confused. He didn't know what to think about anyone or anything. How own mother had just looked at him as if he were a stalker and a pervert; she'd not believed him when Charlie accused him of harassing Tamsin. And maybe she was right. He'd been a coward not to have told her straight away about his visit to Shirley. She'd never believe him now, and it would be his fault if that murderer hurt her in any way.

Mitch lay on his back, staring up at the sky. His wet jeans were clammy against his skin, but the sand had not yet lost its warmth and the faint breeze felt summery. The beach was almost empty now, and although it wouldn't be dark for another hour or so yet, a pale moon was already rising. He would have to make a move soon, before the incoming tide reached him, but it no longer mattered to him what he did. He might never see Tamsin again. Life was pointless. He supposed he should go home. Tessa would yell at him, but he didn't care. He deserved it. Everything was ruined, and he felt like a criminal.

FORTY-FIVE

Sam arrived along with the last two guests and went to sit in the kitchen while Tessa showed the couple to their room. Sam's assurance that he was in no hurry – the brasserie was now running smoothly enough for Jozef to be left in charge for an hour – reminded her how distant and unreachable such mundane concerns had suddenly become.

Ten minutes later she found Sam at the kitchen table. He'd made spritzers from an open bottle of wine in the fridge and pushed hers towards her as she sat down. She told him first about Charlie Crawford, trying to justify how she'd handled things with Mitch. But Sam wasn't inclined to regard Charlie's threats as serious, though he hoped Mitch wouldn't be hit too hard by Tamsin's abrupt departure. 'It'll be a shame though,' he said, 'if Mitch spends his summer holiday nursing a broken heart.' Tessa wasn't sure whether to be irritated or consoled by how lightly he judged the matter.

Then, haltingly, she tried to explain some of what Janice had said in the dingy pub. She realised how difficult it was going to be to make anyone understand the intensity of the visits room, the impetus of the hope and expectation that had carried her there, and the horror of having that hope betrayed. She had decided she could never tell anyone about the photographs. Possessing that knowledge herself was bad enough, and she feared its contaminating power. If she told no one, then maybe eventually she could even erase it from her own memory.

Hearing herself tell Sam the truth about Roy's criminal past, and believing in her very gut that these were not mere words but actual vicious deeds, Tessa hung her head in shame: Sam, Hugo, Mitch, Pamela, Erin – they had all tried to protect her from herself, and in return she had scorned them.

And so she was unspeakably grateful when Sam nodded and spoke kindly. 'So where do you go from here?' he asked. 'Do you still think he deserves any kind of place in your life?'

'No!'

'Good.'

'But I've let him in, haven't I? We're his family. I *am* his child, Mitch and Lauren *are* his grandchildren. We have to deal somehow with what he's done, with what that makes us. Oh, I can't forgive myself for what I said to Mitch!'

'That was pretty unfortunate,' Sam agreed. He reached over and took hold of one of her hands. 'But there's nothing wrong with you, Tessa.'

Tessa had wanted for so long to hear him say such words that she hardly dared look up and meet his eyes. She felt as though Sam was offering the only known antidote to a patient who had been lethally poisoned.

When she did not trust herself to reply, Sam spoke again. 'Don't worry too much about Mitch. He's young enough to bounce back. It'll blow over.'

'But can you understand why I panicked?' she appealed to him. 'Especially about the drugs. It was only a moment. A split second. And there *is* addiction in the family; Pamela drinks on the sly, did you know that?'

Sam shrugged. 'Sure.'

'Is it only me who fails to see these things?' she asked.

'It's easier when you're not so close to people.'

'Mitch looks so like Roy sometimes. Then it's hard not to think of the terrible things Roy has done.'

'Even if Mitch *is* like him being a criminal isn't genetic,' said Sam. 'Roy didn't bring you up, and he's never so much as laid eyes on Mitch. He hasn't influenced your identities in any way.'

'You don't think there's some awful inheritance?'

'No.' Sam gave her hand a bracing squeeze. 'Mitch is being a typical teenager, and, by the sound of it, Charlie Crawford is an arrogant prick who likes throwing his weight about.'

Tessa allowed herself to laugh, though she was very close to tears. 'Are you sure?' she begged him. 'Are you sure Mitch is really Ok?'

'He's a great kid,' declared Sam. 'A credit to us both.'

Tessa nodded. She wanted to blow her nose and drink her wine, but most of all she wanted Sam to keep holding her hand. 'I know a lot of it's been entirely my own fault, but it's all been a bit much recently,' she said.

'I know. And we need to talk about that.' Sam let go of her hand as he picked up his glass. He got up and wandered over to the window. Tessa remembered how he always used to do this when he had something he wished to avoid saying.

'It's partly my fault too,' he confessed to the panes of glass. 'I'd already guessed Mitch and Tamsin were sleeping together, but ignored it because it made me so angry.'

'Angry?' asked Tessa, surprised: not that Sam should appear prudish, but that she couldn't remember when he had ever admitted to being angry. 'Why?'

'I was so terrified he'd repeat our mistakes,' he said at last.

Tessa shivered. '*Were* we a mistake?' she asked in a small voice. 'Did you ever love me, Sam?'

'I didn't say *you* were a mistake,' he exclaimed in exasperation. 'Why do you always do that? Turn it against yourself, so I can never explain what I mean. You getting pregnant was the mistake. Never having a chance to find out what we really wanted was the mistake.' He came and sat beside her, cupping her cheek. 'I was never allowed to think things through. Of course I love you, and the kids, but so long as Averil was alive, I was never allowed to decide anything for myself. I couldn't breathe!'

She looked into his eyes. 'And now you can?'

'Yes. I never meant to break us all up, to make the kids have to shuttle between us. But I had no choice.'

As Sam sat back, Tessa felt a great calm descend upon her. He had finally explained himself, had finally spoken and told her why he'd left. 'So it wasn't me?' she asked. 'You don't hate me?'

'No! No, Tessa. But I felt so awful about leaving that for a long time afterwards I couldn't even bear to look at you. I'm sorry.'

'It's all right. I didn't know who I was either. And I've made an even worse mess of working it out!'

'We'll manage better now, won't we?'

'We can try!' They clinked glasses and drank to it. As more of her tension melted away with the wine, Tessa voiced her other shame. 'What about Lauren?' she asked. 'Does she hate me?'

Sam smiled. 'Of course not. Don't worry about her. She's doing fine. We've been paying her the minimum wage to help out in the brasserie kitchen, and she loves it. Amazing what a bit of responsibility can do.'

'Really?' Swallowing her resentment that Nula had been able to help her child when she had failed, Tessa ordered herself to be glad for Lauren's sake.

'I'll bring her over tomorrow,' promised Sam. 'You both just needed a bit of space, that's all. She's a kid. Forget it.'

'How did we manage to get ourselves in such a state?' asked Tessa, going to fetch more ice. 'I can't tell you how miserable I've been, Sam.'

He joined her as she refilled the ice tray at the sink. 'I'm sorry,' he repeated. 'There's a lot I should've handled better.'

Tessa turned to face him. 'I'm sorry too.' She took a deep breath, letting go of years of hurt. 'It's so *horrible* being jealous!'

Sam laughed and, out of long habit, put his hands around her waist to pull her to him in a comfortable hug. 'What a pair, eh?' he said into her ear.

Tessa returned his hug, laughing too with the wonderful relief of it all. 'Oh, Sam! Let's be friends again.'

FORTY-SIX

On the beach, Mitch got to his feet, brushing off the sticky sand. He looked out to sea, sighing over his utter stupidity in jettisoning his phone: one more thing for his parents to shout at him about. The horizon seemed to expand forever, and he felt very small, a mere dot, just like the aeroplane in which Tamsin was now travelling. He rubbed away the tears that prickled at his eyes at the thought of her, relaxed and oblivious to him, in her flying metal tube. It couldn't be! The idea of having to survive the remainder of the summer without her was impossible.

He climbed up to the promenade and crossed the road to the Seafront B&B. Aware of his mucky jeans, he let himself in quietly and slipped upstairs, hoping to avoid any guests. As he went up the last flight to the flat he heard his mother gasping. Gripped with guilt that she was weeping over his sins, he knocked once on her bedroom door and went in. She lay on the covered bed, her skirt around her waist, her blouse pushed up, one breast exposed. A man lay on top of her, naked from the waist down, thrusting between her legs. Tessa's face turned, her eyes focused on Mitch, and she grabbed a fistful of duvet to try and cover them both. 'Sam!' she cried, attempting to wriggle herself free and draw down her skirt. 'Sam, stop!'

Mitch fled.

By the time he reached the marshes, his chest hurt from the effort of dragging in enough air to keep running. It didn't help that he was crying, and, with a blocked nose, could only breathe through his mouth. At last he had to stop to bend over, panting, waiting to take in enough air so that he could stand upright without feeling dizzy. He must have run almost two miles, and could look back towards the twinkling lights of South Felixham and, beyond, the distant glow of North Felixham where he'd left his parents in bed together. It wasn't yet dark, but the moon stood out more brightly than the setting sun. Knowing he'd never return, he'd had the sense to stop on his way out of the house to grab his waterproof jacket from the hall and, with fumbling fingers, steal two twenty-pound notes from Tessa's handbag in her office. So she'd call him a thief on top of everything else, but it didn't matter what she thought of him now. The instant she'd recognised him standing in her doorway he'd known she would hate him for seeing her nakedness and Sam would hate him for witnessing his betrayal of Nula. He could never go home again.

He carried on, slowing now to a walk, not caring which path he took, where he went, just so long as Felixham lay behind him. He wished for a moment that he had Blanco to whistle to, but the pain caused by the thought of never seeing Tamsin again felt dangerously sharp, and he banished the notion. He was on his own, and might as well get used to it.

His head felt full of whistling static, as if he'd been slapped and smacked until his ears rang. He could not believe the layers and layers of lies that adults told just so they could get what they wanted yet still go on pretending they merited respect. He was used to it from teachers, but he'd *trusted* his parents. They were supposed to set an example of special goodness, to do everything within their power to keep the family safe. But the fortress he'd stupidly thought was his family had collapsed. There were no ramparts. The walls were flimsy, unreal, a lie. He longed for the sense of abandonment and escape the cocaine had given him, wished for some drug to take away his pain.

Mitch stumbled, and realised it was getting too dark to see his way. The moon was not quite full and there were hazy clouds from the day's summer heat; he knew they would gradually clear, and hoped the brightness would be enough to light his way. But he had not considered the extreme contrast of the shadows that sliced across his path, obliterating hazardous detail and slowing his pace. He stopped to take his bearings, and became aware of all the night noises. The faint rush of the sea, invisible except for its slight phosphorescence, came to him like the sound of a shell held to his ear. He couldn't remember being able to hear it at this distance during the day. Nearer at hand, marsh water lapped irregularly against mud, driven by the breeze that rustled between the reeds. Far off – he couldn't make out the precise direction – he picked up the rasping cough of a bullock in a field. He realised he had expected to hear traffic, some sound of human activity, but there was nothing, and the nearest lights seemed very far away.

But he had made his decision, and he had nowhere else to go – he couldn't turn up at a friend's house at this hour. Hugo was the only person he could turn to, but what if he, too, believed what Charlie had said and despised him? That was too calamitous even to consider. Besides, how could Mitch explain why he'd run away? Would he even be believed? He didn't want to think about the consequences of what he'd seen. If his parents *had* got back together – though he didn't reckon that was what had happened – then it was too late for him to be glad about it. Although it had been terrible when they first split up, it was far better now for Sam to stay with Nula, better for Lauren too. So if he kept away,, then maybe no one need ever find out what they'd done, and no harm would follow.

As for his mother, he couldn't think straight about her, he felt so betrayed. Tessa no longer seemed to care what she said or did to anyone. She'd excluded him from this whole Roy Weaver thing, crept about at night so that she could sleep with Declan, and had chosen to believe Charlie rather than him. It was bad enough that Tessa thought *he* was a liar and a pervert, but now she'd turned Sam into a liar and a cheat as well.

Mitch trudged on, raising his collar and pushing his hands into his pockets for warmth. He realised he couldn't keep moving all night, but for now it seemed the best thing to do. He was afraid that if he had nothing to distract his thoughts, he'd have to think about how he was going to survive if he never heard from Tamsin again. He couldn't believe he'd been so stupid as to destroy his phone, and prayed Tamsin wouldn't conclude that he didn't want to speak to her. *If* she ever tried to call him. What if she agreed with Charlie and never wanted to speak to him again? He might as well stay out here alone on the marsh forever.

A mist was rolling in, blanketing both the faint glow of the sea and the denser blackness of higher land against the sky and obscuring any identifying landmarks along the higher ground. The reeds rustling around Mitch soon merged with the outer darkness, and he could no longer even make out the path. He began to be afraid. It would be all too easy in the dark to slide into cold mud and deep water and be unable to gain a firm enough foothold to pull himself out. He knew very well how dangerous the marsh waters could be. He stopped and squatted down on his heels, fearing the chill of lying or sitting on the damp ground. Hugging his knees to conserve body heat, he began to shiver, less from cold than from the perishing wound of hurt and grief and self-pity. Suddenly, in his mind's eye, a fox stepped delicately out of the trees in front of him, gave him a look and went on its way. Mitch's physical panic subsided, but the tearing pain of blame and loneliness increased. He was cold, hungry, thirsty and lost, and it was hours until sunrise.

FORTY-SEVEN

When Tessa woke it took her a moment or two to locate the source of her unease: how on earth was she to face Mitch? It was early, but she got out of bed and opened the curtains to a pale moonstone sky. It would be hot again today, and if this week's fine weather continued it would draw hordes of day-trippers to Felixham over the weekend. Tessa felt too embattled to struggle through dawdling, ice cream-licking crowds or even to face her own cheerful guests.

Sam had departed almost immediately after Mitch had found them together. If only their son had not walked in on them, then she and Sam might have laughed in embarrassment, straightened their clothes and parted amicably with something between them settled. After so much misunderstanding and estrangement the sex had been no more than a gesture of comfort and familiarity, the undoing of a painfully tight knot. And it was wonderful to discover that she was not, as she had feared for so long, unlovable. But how could they ever explain that to a romantic seventeen-year-old? It would be impossible to convince Mitch that what he had seen was not the start of a shameful affair but an affectionate farewell to their marriage.

Tessa had tried to stay awake until she heard him come in, but had been too exhausted from the tumultuous day. Beyond her immediate concern for Mitch lay the obscenity of Roy's actions, and the knowledge of her own complicity. No high solid walls, razor wire, gates, locks or security cameras could keep her safe if she herself was negligent. And she had been; she had very nearly agreed to hand over images of Mitch and Lauren as toddlers and pre-teens. How could she ever have faced her children again if she had actually done so? What kind of mother was she?

Going for her shower, Tessa saw that Mitch's bedroom door was closed as usual, and couldn't help hoping that today he would sleep late. She dressed quickly and went downstairs, glad to focus on the regular tasks of the day. She found Carol in the kitchen – another person whose loyalty she had rewarded with ingratitude. Maybe yesterday had been the final wake-up call she needed to get her life back on track. She would banish Roy from her life, apologise to her family, and hope they could all have a fresh start. Maybe she could even go round later and straighten everything out with Charlie Crawford too.

For the next hour or two Tessa worked alongside Carol, preparing, serving and clearing the guests' breakfasts. In a spare moment, she took Mitch up a late breakfast. She wanted to apologise for what she'd said to him, and maybe have a quiet chat about her and Sam. It would be wrong to ask him to keep quiet if he didn't want to, and she cowered from the idea that, even tacitly, she would have to ask him to lie for her, but perhaps, if he let her explain, he might see for himself that it would be kinder to protect Nula from the truth.

She knocked on his door and, getting no answer, looked in. Mitch was not in his room. Thinking perhaps he'd slipped out while she and Carol were busy, she rang his mobile, but the message told her that his phone was either switched off or out of range. Disheartened, she accepted that he had every right to block her excuses until he was ready to talk.

Downstairs, she answered queries about local walks and attractions and did her best to make small talk with departing guests as they settled their bills. Once the public rooms had been straightened, she set off to the farm shop and only on her return did she ring Mitch's mobile again. As she listened to the same message, it occurred to her that, when she'd opened his bedroom door earlier on, she'd only half registered how the room contained the stillness of unmoved air. The conviction took hold that he had not been there overnight.

She went back up his room, forcing herself to think rationally. Mitch was good about tidying his bed in the mornings, so she couldn't be certain whether it had been slept in last night or not. Trying to remember if this was how his bed had been left the day before, whether she'd come in here yesterday, she felt the first prickling of fear.

If he hadn't been there overnight it wasn't simply because he'd gone off somewhere: her actions had driven him away. The angles of the sloped ceiling seemed suddenly sharper and more precarious, the roof of her house neither solid nor sheltering.

She shook herself. She couldn't pretend that Mitch wouldn't be upset, but surely he was too sensible to do anything stupid? She doubted he would have gone to Sam's, but he might have spent the night at a friend's house or with his grandparents. If he had gone there, maybe it would be better if it didn't look as if she were checking up on him. She went to sit on the window seat and looked out at a perfectly ordinary day. Below her was a typical English scene, with families spread out across the sand and elderly couples filling up the benches on the promenade. Among the crowd on the beach, Tessa watched a mother suddenly leap up and dash to the water's edge, snatching her unsteady toddler away from the incoming waves.

By the end of the afternoon, Mitch had not appeared, Carol said she hadn't seen him since the previous day, and his phone was still turned off. Affecting a casual tone, Tessa called the homes of three of his school friends. There was no reply from his best friend Chris, another hadn't seen him for days, and the mother of the third was pretty sure Mitch wasn't hanging out with her son today. Tessa recalled the plummeting, weightless drop into fear she'd felt when Evie's mother had called to say that Evie and Lauren had not come off their train from Norwich after a shopping trip, yet that had turned out to be merely a lost phone and a teenage failure to communicate. Why should this be any different?

But Tessa knew why: this was her fault for failing to heed that earlier warning. The world was not a safe place, and what safety her son had, she had destroyed.

She wondered if she should alert Sam, and with a leaping heart was certain that Lauren would know where he was. She pressed her number without further thought, and heard laughter and street noises in the background as Lauren said hello. 'Where are you?' Tessa asked anxiously.

'Shopping with Evie. It's her birthday and she's having a big sleepover at her house tonight. Gotta go. Bye, Mum.'

Tessa called Sam's number, and only when she heard his wary 'hello' did the leaden swing of their culpability knock her sideways.

'Hi, Sam,' she said as naturally as she could, though her voice quavered. 'Is Mitch with you?'

'No. Why?' Sam was instantly sharp.

'He's not come home.' Tessa didn't need to spell it out.

'You've not seen him since?'

'No. Have you?'

Sam was silent. Tessa waited.

'He's not with Pamela and Hugo?'

'I don't know. His phone's off. And I haven't called them yet.'

'Want me to?

'Ok. But, Sam, wait!'

'What?'

Tessa swallowed. 'What will you tell them?' She could almost feel Sam's shame wash down the phone at her. 'We could say Mitch was upset because of Charlie Crawford,' she suggested, when he said nothing. 'At least for the time being.'

'Ok. Bye.'

Tessa waited for Sam to ring back, which he soon did.

'They've not seen him,' he said. 'Hugo will let us know right away if they do.'

'What shall we do?'

Sam did not answer immediately. 'If he's not back by supper-time,' he said at last, 'perhaps we should call the police. What do you think?'

Tessa had not prepared herself for this. She started to shiver. 'What can they do?'

'I don't know. But are you going to wait a second night for him not to come home?'

'No.' She had a vision of how time could expand into vast, unknown realms without them ever knowing where Mitch was, and tied herself back to the present. 'I'd like you to be here,' she added. 'But I guess that's not such a great idea.'

'No,' Sam said gently. 'Speak later.'

At six o'clock Pamela and Hugo let themselves in, claiming they'd come to help with arriving guests. Tessa had never been so glad to see them, and hugged each of them with a fierce new tenderness. Pamela offered to make supper, but watching the kitchen clock tick on, Tessa knew she wouldn't be able to eat. At seven Sam arrived.

He'd spoken to Hugo and agreed that, with Mitch's phone turned off, they should at least inform the police of their concern. He'd spoken to some central switchboard operator, who told him not to worry and they'd send someone over, just to get the details.

Sergeant Fowler arrived just after eight o'clock and Hugo brought him down to the kitchen where Tessa waited with Sam and Pamela. A serious young man, he reassured them as best he could and listened as Sam and Tessa gave as truthful an account of the events of the previous night as they dared: Mitch had been upset about his girlfriend, then run off. Answering the police officer's preliminary questions, Tessa wanted either to laugh at such a ridiculous waste of his time or to cry out in fear and lament.

Learning that Mitch's girlfriend had unexpectedly left for Los Angeles the day before, the sergeant asked for Mitch's passport. While Tessa went to look for it, Hugo accompanied him on a search of the house. Watching from the hallway as they went upstairs, Tessa thought it was as if they were playing some absurd game of hide-and-seek with Mitch waiting to leap out and go 'Boo!' Her hands were cold and she felt sick, but it was impossible yet to believe that this could turn out to be real.

Tessa doubted that Mitch would have remembered where the key to the document safe was hidden, and, as she expected, found his passport beside her own and Lauren's. But she was unprepared for her intense disappointment, the strength of her hope that Mitch had run off in pursuit of Tamsin on some crazy adventure they could all laugh about another day. She realised that she wouldn't mind not knowing precisely where he was, just so long as she knew his purpose. At what point, she wondered as she shut the safe, would she have to accept that she was one of those parents to whom the very worst had happened? Ought she to prepare herself for such acceptance, and, if so, just how exactly did one steel oneself for what one could not begin to imagine?

Hugo appeared, white-faced, to ask for the key to the padlocks on Averil's doll's house for the police sergeant. It hung on a labelled hook beside all the room keys. 'I'll take it to him,' she said. 'You go downstairs.'

She found Sergeant Fowler sitting on his heels peering in through the miniature windows. As he got to his feet, he brushed back his hair, embarrassed.

'I found Mitch's passport,' Tessa told him, handing him the padlock key.

'Right. We'll circulate his details on the Police National Computer,' he said. 'Juveniles are automatically assessed as Medium Risk, and all cases reviewed after forty-eight hours. The vast majority are quickly resolved.'

She found his reliance on official phrases more frightening than his earlier optimism. The officer undid the padlocks and opened up the doll's house – more for form's sake, Tessa was sure, than because he expected to find anything significant.

'It belonged to my grandmother,' she told him, as he gave her back the key. 'She tried her best to pretend that life could be kept tidy and in order like that. But it can't, can it?'

'I'm sure he'll be home soon,' said the officer.

She shook her head. 'If something terrible has happened, then it's my fault.'

'Is there anything you'd like to tell me, Mrs Parker, while there's no one else present? Anything that might help?'

'Whatever's happened, I'm the only one to blame.'

'Why? Do you know of anyone who might have harmed your son?'

Tessa nodded. 'Me. I'm responsible,' she said. 'I'm his mother, and I failed him. Now he's gone, and it's too late. I don't know how to bring him back.'

Sergeant Fowler regarded her carefully. 'In what way are you responsible?' he asked.

She sank down onto the couch. 'I didn't believe him.'

'About what?'

Tessa had no idea where to start, how to explain. 'His girlfriend's father was upset about some photos they'd taken of each other on her phone. He accused Mitch of harassing her.'

'What's her name?'

'Tamsin Crawford. Her father has the big house on the Green.'

'The one that's been done up recently?'

Tessa nodded.

'We'd better have a word with him.'

Tessa hung her head. 'Mitch explained, but I didn't believe him.'

'Do you have a recent photo of your son?' asked Sergeant Fowler.

The request made Tessa think of Roy. if she *had* given him photographs of her children, she would now be tearing the prison apart to retrieve them.

'Mrs Parker?' prompted the officer.

'Yes,' she said. 'I'll find you one. But what will happen to it? You won't give it to the newspapers?'

'It's unlikely we'll get to that point,' he said carefully. 'And it wouldn't happen without your permission.' He took a notebook from his breast pocket. 'Can you remember what he was wearing?'

'Jeans and a T-shirt. Green, I think. And his jacket's gone. Black waterproof. One of those outdoor brands. What happens now?'

'We'll do the obvious checks,' he told her. 'Hospitals, any traffic or other incidents. The coastguard's been alerted.' He closed his notebook.

'Where do you think Mitch is?' she asked in desperation.

'It's most likely that he's run away. In which case, statistically, he's also likely to come home of his own accord in the next few days.'

'If not, where would he go?'

'London? A lot of kids think they'll find work, that it'll be easy.'

'He doesn't know London. He's not streetwise. He wouldn't manage in London.'

'Then he's less likely to put himself in danger, or get

mixed up with unsavoury characters. Was he under any other stress? Other problems? Exam results coming up, for instance?'

'Yes, but it's not that. This is my fault.'

'Was he depressed? On any medication?'

'No.'

'Into drugs at all? You need to tell us, Mrs Parker. He won't be in any trouble if he is.'

'There was cocaine at Charlie Crawford's house, but it's not that either.' She looked up at the young officer. She was certain he would never understand, but she had to say it – someone had to hear what she had done. 'Mitch's grandfather is a murderer and a rapist,' she said. 'He's serving a life sentence in Wayleigh Heath, and I've been visiting him. I told Mitch he's just the same, that he'd end up in prison like his grandfather. That's why he's run away. That's what he's running from. Me.'

FORTY-EIGHT

As Pamela lay in Lauren's single bed, she could hear the familiar sound of Hugo's muffled snores through the wall. She was glad he was asleep, and hoped Tessa too would manage to get some rest. She thought about Erin who had insisted on remaining at home, at least until it became clear how seriously they should take Mitch's disappearance. For a split second Pamela had half thought that Erin couldn't comprehend the urgency of their concern because she'd never had children of her own. She'd corrected herself immediately, but her shame still burned. Yet somehow, she reflected, having Erin here for a proper stay, going on a couple of outings and doing ordinary domestic things together, had made Pamela see herself as a mother in a way it was clear that Erin was not. While this did not lessen her regret about the past, she realised she was beginning to feel more confident, more authentic.

It was well after midnight, and she had left the curtains open to let in air from the open window. She watched the full moon riding high across wispy clouds and wondered where Mitch was now, praying, as much for Tessa's sake as for Mitch himself, that he was safe. She hadn't really understood Tessa's garbled story about the row with Tamsin's father, nor quite what she and Sam appeared so penitent about, but Mitch was a sensible boy and the mystery was sure to be resolved soon.

Once the young policeman, and then Sam, had left, Tessa had said she wanted to apologise to them both. The gist of it seemed to be that this man Roy Weaver was not who she'd hoped he'd be, that she'd allowed herself to be taken in by him, but that it was over now, and there'd be no further contact. If Pamela hadn't known that Erin had had several talks with Tessa she might have pressed her for more details. But if Erin was fine, and Tessa wasn't going to see this man again, then what did it matter? Best to leave the past alone now: it had done enough damage.

In any case, as the long evening wore on, all any of them could think about was Mitch. None of them really wanted to go to bed, but in the end Hugo had insisted. It was strange being back in her old home. She hadn't spent a night here since the babysitting years had ended. She thought further back to when this room had been hers. Averil had not created the attic flat until the B&B began to be successful, by which time Pamela was already in her teens. But she had slept in this room the night before her wedding. Hugo always reminded her a little of her father, whom she had loved very much, and she had never regretted marrying him, had only ever regretted that she had failed to make him as happy as he deserved.

Suddenly the phone rang in the sitting room across the hall and Pamela sat up in bed, her heart pounding. Almost instantly she heard Tessa's door open and it seemed only seconds later that she picked up and the ringing stopped. Was it Mitch, to say he was safe? Or was it the police, about to break some kind of dreadful news?

Pamela crept to open her bedroom door so that she could listen and be ready. 'Where are you?' she heard Tessa ask, and her heart leapt, though simultaneously she could tell from the tone of Tessa's voice that she was not speaking to Mitch. 'Don't worry,' she heard Tessa say next. 'I'll tell him as soon as I see him.'

At least it did not seem to be anything serious, though Pamela had no idea why anyone would ring so late. She waited for Tessa to come out of the living room. 'Any news?'

Tessa shook her head. 'It was his girlfriend, Tamsin Crawford, calling from America.'

'Has she heard from Mitch?'

'No. And I didn't tell her anything was wrong. Not yet. But she says she can't get hold of him either.'

Pamela didn't like the sound of that; she knew that kids these days had to talk constantly to one another.

'She wanted to leave her mother's number in LA so he could call her.' Tessa voice cracked and she began to cry. Pamela went to hold her tight.

'Hush, my darling,' she said. 'Hush, Tessie. I'm here, I've got you.' Tessa sobbed, and Pamela led her back into her bedroom, folded back the covers and seated her on the bed, stroking her back just as she used to do when she was little.

'I'm so scared.' Tessa shivered, though the air was not cold.

'There, there.' Pamela got up to find a box of tissues, handing them out one by one until the crying stopped.

'He wouldn't do anything terrible to himself, would he? No matter how upset he was, you don't think he'd ever–?'

'Hush now. No, of course not.'

'Two nights and no word! What if he's had an accident, and he's lying out there bleeding or with a broken leg or something?'

'He would've been found by now.'

'He wouldn't hitch a lift or get in a car with anyone, would he?'

'Mitch will be Ok,' Pamela said firmly. 'Things always seem worse in the middle of the night. He'll probably be on the doorstep in the morning, but wherever he is, he'll be fine. However long we have to wait for him to come back, we have to go on believing that he will.'

'Oh Mum. It's all my fault.'

'Maybe it is,' Pamela told her briskly, 'but thinking that is a luxury. It won't help.'

Tessa looked at her in surprise.

'I indulged in that for years, and look where it got us,' said Pamela. 'Don't waste your time or your energy. That's what Erin's been telling me, and she's right. Now get into bed. Try to sleep.'

Tessa lay down obediently and let Pamela tuck her in and give her a kiss. 'Get some sleep, my darling. That's the most useful thing any of us can do right now.'

As Pamela closed Tessa's door, an automatic reflex focused her mind on the kitchen cupboard downstairs where she knew Tessa kept a bottle of gin. But she drew herself up, realising proudly that she actually didn't want a drink, and that it wasn't even a struggle to push the impulse aside. As she crossed the hallway to Lauren's bedroom, she suddenly wondered, though, what she *did* want, and hesitated on the threshold. She almost rejected the idea that came to her because it made her shy, reluctant, embarrassed, but once more she straightened her shoulders and moved softly towards Mitch's room where Hugo was sleeping. She opened the door quietly and looked in. The phone had not disturbed him and he was still snoring, the sound almost like the purr of a cat. The moonlight was enough for her to find her way across to the narrow bed and slip in close beside him.

FORTY-NINE

Once again Tessa woke at first light, unable to remember falling asleep but aware that she'd forgotten something vitally important. The moment it all came back, she threw herself out of bed and went straight to Mitch's room. For a moment, seeing a sleeping shape under the duvet, she believed it was him, safe and sound, the confusion of yesterday a nightmare. But then Pamela raised her head from the pillow. 'Any news?' she asked, struggling to sit up.

'No, nothing. It's not even gone six yet.'

Pamela immediately fell back to sleep. Tessa quickly showered and dressed before going down to the kitchen. There she found Hugo already up, listening to the news on the radio. Tessa switched it off: other people's wars, famines and disasters had crept too close to be mere background noise any more. Glad of Hugo's comforting silence, she stood beside the Aga trying to gather in its warmth, but her skin felt paper-thin, her body bloodless, her bones too dry to absorb any heat.

She made coffee, more for something to do than because she wanted any, and put a mug in front of Hugo.

'I used to fantasise about clearing off,' he said. He seemed almost to be speaking to himself. 'When trying to deal with Averil got too much, when Pamela wouldn't listen. I'd get so angry sometimes that I didn't know what else to do with myself. I just wanted to disappear.'

'Did you ever go?' Tessa was curious; Hugo so seldom talked about himself.

'No. But perhaps Mitch had to. For a little while at least.'

She sat down beside him, longing to unburden herself. But during the sleepless hours before Tamsin's phone call she had realised that while some secrets were dangerous, not only in their substance but also in the power that accrued around them, some needed to be kept. Until Mitch was found, she and Sam would say nothing about what he had seen, why he had run off, nothing that would hurt Nula. Once Mitch was safe, they must let him decide what to reveal and to whom. Nor could it help anyone to know the truth of her violent conception, or about Roy's grotesque abuse of her trust. Those were secrets she must keep.

'I think you're right,' she told Hugo. 'Mitch has had too much to deal with. I'm to blame. I should have listened better.'

'We've all been to blame, Tessie,' he said. 'No one can be their best self if they haven't been told who they are.'

She shook her head. 'But I do know who I am, only I didn't think it was enough.' She looked into his tired, beloved face. 'I'm so sorry for hurting you.'

'You're my girl.' He squeezed her hand. 'You've never been anything else.'

'What can I do, Dad? How do I bring Mitch home?'

'We'll find him,' he promised.

When Carol arrived, Pamela and Hugo insisted on helping her to serve breakfast and deal with the guests. Watching them bustle around, making tea and coffee, carrying trays and stacking the dishwasher, Tessa realised how insane it was to carry on the business of caring for strangers when her child was missing. Without consulting the others, she sent off a series of emails cancelling the week's bookings. Among them was Declan's monthly visit, and for a second she hesitated: part of her would welcome his pragmatic affection. She thought about telling him what had happened, but knew he'd call to ask if she was all right, and she wasn't sure she could cope with that. She sent him the same email as the others, then rang Bobbi and other proprietors to on enlist their help, before going into the breakfast room to explain to the four couples eating bacon and eggs and toast and marmalade that she would refund their payments and offer them a complimentary weekend another time, but that regretfully they all had to leave after breakfast.

When they had all gone and the house was empty, Tessa experienced a wonderful sense of liberation. Apart from Christmas or when trade was slack, this was the first time she could remember feeling that the house belonged to her. If Hugo and Pamela stayed here again tonight – and maybe Erin could join them – then they could use more comfortable rooms. And she vowed to herself that when Mitch came back, he would return to a home and not to the Seafront B&B. She had things the wrong way around: the business should serve her family, not they the business.

An hour later Sergeant Fowler came to report that there had been no sightings, but he could confirm that Mitch had not been the victim of any known accident or assault. They had spoken to Mr Crawford, who had been helpful but could shed no further light on where he might have gone. Sergeant Fowler also explained that he'd discussed with his senior officers the possibility of a full local search, using dogs and even a helicopter with thermal imaging, but with so many miles of coastline on a busy August weekend, and with no certainty anyway that Mitch had gone anywhere near the sea, they had decided to concentrate on other lines of enquiry.

Tessa told him about Tamsin's phone call, but Sergeant Fowler said Mr Crawford had already supplied her number, and he planned to speak to her himself in case she knew of any people Mitch might go to or places he might be. Meanwhile, with Sam and Tessa's permission, he wanted to take away Mitch's computer, to check his email and social networks for any leads.

All this had taken place in the guests' sitting room with Hugo and Pamela present. Tessa escorted the police sergeant to the front door and followed him out, needing to voice the private fear that had been growing all morning. 'It's about Roy Weaver,' she began. She had earlier told him about what Janice had said about the photographs, about Roy's lies and abuse.

Sergeant Fowler nodded. 'We've passed on your intelligence to the prison governor, so they're aware of the situation. They'll be monitoring Roy Weaver's letters and calls for any mention of Mitch.'

'So you think it's possible?' Tessa tried to keep the panic out of her voice. 'You think he might have got someone to hurt Mitch?'

'But you said he'd never met your son? Why would he want to hurt him?'

'To get at me? Because he breaks the rules, he manipulates people?' Tessa was aware how irrational and far-fetched her fears must sound: only a few months ago she would not have believed a word of what Janice had told her in the pub. 'What if he got someone outside, maybe someone recently released, to do something?'

'I think that's highly unlikely,' said the officer. 'Unless there's something you've not yet told me?'

She shook her head. 'I let Roy Weaver into our lives. If he hurts Mitch I'll never forgive myself.'

'Please try not to worry so much, Mrs Parker. Most runaways act on impulse and return within a few days. I see no reason to think this case is any different.'

'But you will check, won't you? You will make sure it can't be anything to do with Roy?'

'We will look into every possibility,' he assured her. 'We won't give up until he's found.'

Tessa let him go, standing for a moment on the step to

look out to sea. Below her the beach was thronged with holidaymakers. She scanned the crowds: surely Mitch was among them, only just missed out of the corner of her eye? But the miserable truth was that he had been invisible to her for weeks.

She went back indoors and began the task of persuading Hugo and Pamela to go home for an hour or two, insisting she needed some time to herself. Promising to ring if she changed her mind, she finally closed the door behind them and went slowly upstairs, letting the air of the empty house settle around her. She went into Mitch's room and sat on the window seat, pulling her knees up under her chin as she had often seen him do. She stroked the pane of glass with one finger, as if absorbing any traces his presence might have left. She could feel her fear sinking into her organs, muscles and ligaments, becoming an organic part of her that would remain even if he were to walk in right now. She thought about how she'd heard parents on the news whose kids had been abducted and murdered say how they'd sensed that their child was dead even before a body was found. Thankfully, she had no such second sight: Mitch was not dead, he was missing, only missing, that was all, and she must use all her strength to resist darker thoughts.

It had been a relief to speak to Sergeant Fowler again about Roy. She'd received no letters from him since her last visit, but expected one from him soon. She could hand it over to the police to deal with. She thought instead about the letter she would write to the parole board, the letter that would keep Roy in gaol. As she was wording it in her head, the doorbell rang and she rushed down the stairs. The front door opened, and Lauren flung herself into Tessa's arms, wrapping herself tightly around her. 'Mum!'

Tessa hugged her, inhaling her smell, reacquainting herself with the feel of her child's skin. 'Sweetheart!' She couldn't bear to let her go.

Over Lauren's shoulder Tessa saw first Sam and then Nula.

'No news? Sam asked, though he already knew the answer.

'Not yet.' Tessa spoke brightly, aware of Lauren listening with huge anxious eyes. 'Come in.'

'Thanks, but I won't stay,' said Nula.

'We've only just picked Lauren up from Evie's,' Sam explained.

'We brought you some food.' Nula held up a heavy picnic bag. 'So you don't have to think about it.'

'That's kind, thank you.'

Lauren clung to her mother's arm as Sam took the bag and placed it on the floor.

'Thought we might give Lauren some jobs to do today, if you're happy with that?'

'Is that Ok, Mum?' asked Lauren. 'Do you mind?'

'No, it's a good idea. Much better for you to keep busy.' Tessa looked into her daughter's face. She seemed taller, brighter, more grown-up.

Nula held out a hand to Lauren. 'Come on then.'

Tessa made a huge effort and smiled at Nula. 'Thank you,' she said again. Nula nodded in return, her face full only of kindness and concern. Lauren gave Tessa another hug. 'See you later, Mum. Love you.'

Sam paused in the doorway. 'Do you want me to stay?'

'What if Mitch goes to your place and you're not there?'

He looked relieved. 'That's what I was thinking. Better get back then.'

'Ok.' They both smiled gratefully but were careful not to touch one another. As Tessa closed the door behind him, she realised how easy it was to let him go.

FIFTY

Two more days passed without a word. After the fourth night not knowing where Mitch was, Tessa woke again at dawn, but this morning she opened her eyes convinced of what she must do to bring him back. She didn't care how foolish it was to manufacture her own magic; she had to try everything she could to protect her family. More than anything else, she feared the moment when there would be no more to do.

She had not once left the house, convinced Mitch would only come home if she were there to welcome him, but today she asked Hugo and Pamela to keep vigil at home, and asked Erin for her help in accomplishing a particular task.

Neither of them spoke as they made their way to the heart of the marshes, and Erin occasionally fell behind on the narrow path. Tessa drew to a halt at the edge of a deep pool. The amber-coloured water lay eerily still, the only movement the dragonflies' zigzag darts. The surrounding reeds barely stirred. Though the sky rose high above them, an unbroken blue, the bleached yellow fronds stood at shoulder height, foreshortening the view almost claustrophobically. Tessa felt in her pocket for the bracelet that had lain in the bottom of her handbag since she'd eased it off her wrist in the dingy pub. She held it out in the palm of her hand while Erin watched silently, asking no explanation. Willing the smooth gold to carry with it everything she wanted to be rid of, Tessa raised her arm and cast it as far as she could out into the centre of the pool. It disappeared with barely a splash, though the dragonflies shot away and a small bird rose from among the sedge, piping its alarm call.

'There!' She turned to Erin. 'He's gone. Out of both our lives.' She took a deep breath of sea-laden air and released it in a long sigh.

'I'm sorry I told you what he did to me,' said Erin. 'Even more sorry that it was true.'

'It must have been awful when Averil didn't believe you,' said Tessa.

'Well, I've been thinking about that, thinking maybe she did.'

Tessa remembered how difficult it was ever to know what her grandmother was thinking, to be sure that she was really as hard and unemotional as she made out. 'But if she believed you, how could she bring herself to send you away?'

'Don't you see?' asked Erin. 'It was because she *did* believe me. She sent me as far away as she possibly could in order to protect me. And you.'

Tessa watched the insects hover over the water. 'Because I was the child of rape?'

'Yes.' Erin linked her arm in Tessa's. 'I believe she meant to protect both of us from having to live with that.'

Tessa was not convinced: such foresight did not fit with her view of Averil.

'When Mum said she didn't believe me,' Erin went on, 'I hoped she *was* right. I wanted her to be right, and that, if I went away, it need never be true.'

'Until I brought it all back,' said Tessa, 'by bringing Roy Weaver into your life again.'

Erin shrugged. 'I did nothing to warn you. I said it was a summer romance.'

'What else could you have done?'

Erin inspected the manicured nails of her free hand. 'Before you were born,' she said, 'I was so scared that I wouldn't be able to love you.'

'Because of Roy Weaver?'

'Yes. And I think Averil saw that. I *wanted* Pamela to have you.'

'A lot of people rearranged their lives to care for me, didn't they?' Tessa squeezed Erin's arm. 'Thank you.'

'I didn't think I'd ever get over leaving you.' Erin touched her head to her daughter's for a single moment. 'But you see, people *do* come back,' she said. 'And Mitch is going to come home too. I know he is.'

Together they turned away from the water and began the walk back towards Felixham. Even though Tessa had her mobile with her, she couldn't help quickening her pace as the first houses came into view. The streets around the beach were lively, and she concentrated on threading their way between the holidaymakers, watching out for cars cruising distractedly in search of parking spaces. The markings of a distant police car made her heart stop, and she was aware of Erin grasping her arm, but the car turned a corner, away from them. She heard a shout behind her – 'Blanco!' – and a Dalmatian dog lolloped past, trailing its lead.

'Blanco!' Tessa turned and recognised Sonia Beeston, red-faced and puffing her way up the promenade. 'That blasted dog,' she exclaimed, recognising Tessa in turn. 'He's too strong for me.'

Sonia hurried on in pursuit, and Tessa's gaze automatically followed. The dog ran up to a car – some modern American retro model – parked outside the Seafront B&B and stopped. Coming out of a daze, Tessa realised that Blanco was enthusiastically wagging his tail in greeting in front of a lithe young figure clambering out of the passenger seat.

'Mitch!' Tessa screamed. She ran towards him, not caring how roughly she pushed people out of her way.

A woman with short hair that was almost the same aubergine colour as her car appeared from the driver's side, a big smile on her face.

Tessa almost tripped over the dog, which was jumping up at Mitch, trying to lick his face. Mitch was grinning in delight and fondling the Dalmatian's ears. Tessa had to be content with reaching out to touch her son's shoulder.

'Hi, Mum,' he said shyly, pushing back the hair that flopped over downcast eyes.

The woman came up behind him as he grabbed Blanco's lead. 'You must be Tessa,' she asked, holding out her hand. Bewildered, Tessa shook it.

'This is Shirley,' said Mitch. 'She brought me home.' Noticing that Erin hung back at the edge of the group, Mitch acknowledged her politely.

'From where?' asked Tessa, still hardly able to believe that Mitch was here, right before her, apparently unscathed. He occupied himself with making Blanco sit before handing the lead to Sonia, who, all agog, seemed reluctant to continue her walk.

'He stayed with me in London last night,' Shirley explained. 'Turned up at my office looking a bit dishevelled. Said he'd been sleeping on a park bench.'

Mitch looked at Tessa apologetically. She held out her arms to him. 'Come here!' Mitch submitted to her hug, while she whispered in his ear: 'I'm so sorry. Please forgive me.'

Mitch met her eyes, nodding. He seemed to find what he needed in hers, for he gave her a friendly smile. 'Sorry if I scared you,' he said.

'Oh, you—!' Tessa laughed. 'But where have you been? I don't understand.'

Mitch looked at Shirley, who once again spoke for him. 'Mitch came to introduce himself a few weeks ago,' she said. 'I'm Shirley Weaver. Your aunt.'

Before Tessa could quite take this in, Hugo appeared beside her. 'Well, there's a sight for sore eyes!'

'Hi, Grandpa,' Mitch said. He dipped his head, inviting Hugo to ruffle his hair.

Tessa found herself crying, and Hugo, laughing, put his arm around her shoulders and pulled her close. 'All's well that ends well.'

'Where's Pamela?' asked Erin. 'We should go and tell her.'

'We must call Sam and Lauren too,' said Hugo.

Tessa turned to Shirley. 'Will you come in? Please?' she added, seeing Shirley hesitate.

'I'd love to, thanks.'

Hugo shepherded everyone indoors. In the hallway, Mitch turned to Tessa. 'I lost my phone. Has Tamsin called?'

'Yes. She left her number.'

Mitch's face went pink. 'Can I call her now? Do you mind?'

'Call your dad first.'

'Ok.'

'I wrote Tamsin's number in my day book. It's on the desk.'

Mitch went into the office and closed the door. Erin, already calling out to Pamela, disappeared downstairs with Hugo. Tessa turned to Shirley. 'Is Mitch Ok?' she asked quietly.

Shirley nodded. 'I think so. I didn't ask questions, just fed him and washed his clothes.'

'I can never thank you enough.'

'I happened to be nearby, that's all. And he's a nice kid. You should be proud.'

'You'd better come and meet the rest of the family.' And Tessa led the way to the kitchen where Hugo and both her mothers were waiting.

ACKNOWLEDGEMENTS

My thanks first to Tony Moores not only for reading but also for showing such compassion towards my characters. This story began in my head a long time ago, so some people may have forgotten the help they provided. For my experience of prison visiting, my thanks to everyone at the New Bridge. I would also like to thank Claire Baker, Hanna Bottomley, Elizabeth Buchan, Lisa Cohen, Geoffrey Munn, Angela Neustatter, Merle Nygate, Elaine Randell, Geoff Weston, my wonderful agent Sheila Crowley and the team at Curtis Brown and my equally wonderful editor Jane Wood and all the gang at Quercus. All errors are my own.